Insomniac
Micah & Peyton

AN ENEMIES TO LOVERS, WORKPLACE
ROMANCE DUET

USA TODAY BESTSELLING AUTHOR
PERSEPHONE
AUTUMN

BETWEEN WORDS PUBLISHING LLC

Books by Persephone Autumn

Lake Lavender Series

Depths Awakened

One Night Forsaken

Every Thought Taken

Devotion Series

Distorted Devotion

Undying Devotion

Beloved Devotion

Darkest Devotion

Sweetest Devotion

Bay Area Duet Series

Click Duet

Through the Lens

Time Exposure

Inked Duet

Fine Line

Love Buzz

Insomniac Duet

Restless Night

A Love So Bright

<u>Artist Duet</u>

Blank Canvas

Abstract Passion

<u>Novellas</u>

Reese

Penny

<u>Stone Bay Series</u>

Broken Sky—Prequel

Shattered Sun

Fractured Night

<u>Standalone Romance Novels</u>

Sweet Tooth

Transcendental

<u>Poetry Collections</u>

Ink Veins

Broken Metronome

Slipping From Existence

Poisonous Heart

Beneath Wildflowers

PUBLISHED UNDER P. AUTUMN

<u>Standalone Non-Romance Novels</u>

By Dawn

contents

RESTLESS NIGHT

Prologue	5
Chapter 1	11
Chapter 2	19
Chapter 3	30
Chapter 4	38
Chapter 5	47
Chapter 6	65
Chapter 7	73
Chapter 8	81
Chapter 9	89
Chapter 10	96
Chapter 11	106
Chapter 12	115
Chapter 13	130
Chapter 14	137
Chapter 15	148
Chapter 16	160
Chapter 17	169
Chapter 18	182
Chapter 19	199
Chapter 20	210
Chapter 21	220
Chapter 22	228
Chapter 23	238
Chapter 24	247

A LOVE SO BRIGHT

Chapter 1	257
Chapter 2	265
Chapter 3	282

Chapter 4   290
Chapter 5   299
Chapter 6   308
Chapter 7   323
Chapter 8   337
Chapter 9   343
Chapter 10   350
Chapter 11   365
Chapter 12   373
Chapter 13   382
Chapter 14   392
Chapter 15   398
Chapter 16   409
Chapter 17   415
Chapter 18   421
Chapter 19   430
Chapter 20   437
Chapter 21   447
Chapter 22   455
Chapter 23   464
Epilogue   469
Thank You   479
More by Persephone Autumn   481
Insomniac Duet Playlist   483
Acknowledgments   485

Connect with Persephone   487
About the Author   489

Restless Night

BOOK ONE

For all the people who picked on me when I was younger
because I was weird.
I'm still weird, but at least I kick ass.

Past...

Another day, another round of bullshit. High school... it goes one of two ways.

You are either popular—the queen bee with a swarm of followers. Every girl wants to be you. Wants your boyfriend. Dresses and talks like you. Is at your beck and call without question. And you are artificial as fuck.

Or two—my current life status—you walk around with a "kick me" sign stuck to your back. Girls point and laugh and say fucked-up shit. They write your name on bathroom stall walls with the word "trash" or "loser" or "slut" beneath it. They gather their posse and gang up on you. Start rumors and throw shit in your direction. Toss out every possible degrading word with your name to boost their own esteem and make others laugh and point.

How I landed in category two is beyond me. But here we are, another day in hell.

I exit the bus and spot them as I step off. As if they waited for me to arrive in the big tangerine beast. Just to antagonize me. To start their day with a fresh load of assholism.

Do mean bitches have nothing better to do with their lives?

"Mandy, did you hear the school slut banged the baseball team last night?"

That would be Mercedes, Queen Bitch.

"Ew." And that would be Mandy, the girl parked so far up Mercedes's ass, she no longer sees light. "But what else do sluts do?"

They laugh and start following me as I pass them without so much as a glance. As pretentious and mighty as they believe they are, one would think they have more in life to do than follow "trash" like me around campus. But whatever.

I walk through campus and head for my locker. They continue their not-so quiet artifice. And I continue to ignore them as best I can. After dealing with their bullshit for the last four months, I learned to tune them out. On occasion, anyway.

I spin the dial on my locker as they prattle on. Voices loud as they encourage others to join in on their hate fest. Only one other does. Meredith. Now my day is complete. Triple M is here and in their full glory.

While I swap my books and folders in my locker, I laugh at my own wayward thoughts. *Triple M. Damn, those are big tits. Slut tits. Who's the slut now?*

"What's so funny, loser?"

Shit. Did I laugh out loud? Oh well. No backpedaling now.

I spin around to face the blonde trio. Hair, makeup and clothes pristine and wrinkle free. Unlike me. My blonde locks currently wear a thick layer of black dye. My makeup equally dark and thick around my eyes. And my ensemble... you guessed it. Black. Let's just say the current phase of life revolves around the saying *black is life*.

Courage bubbles in my chest as my nails dig crescents into my palms. Sick and tired of these bitches, I am ready to blow my top. Go full-on banshee and punch the smiles off their cakey faces. But not now. Maybe just a dose to appease my dark heart.

Just a dose.

"You," I say with a laugh. "You're what's funny." Confidence builds and I run with it. "If you're not careful, someone might think you're in love with me. Obsessed. I mean, god, you seek me out. Follow me like a lost pet. Talk about me all day. Like you have nothing else you'd rather be doing." God, this feels good. Talking shit to her face. Calling her out in front of others. Should I kick it up a notch? Add to her embarrassment? *Do it!* "Hey, everyone," I shout and several eyes glance our way. "Mercedes is in love with me."

Her face turns stop sign red. If possible, steam would shoot from her ears. Her arms stiffen, hands fist at her sides and she literally stomps a foot. I bite my cheek to resist laughing at her charade, as it will definitely worsen the situation.

She shoves a finger in my face, centimeters from my glasses. "You'll pay for that. When you least expect it." She spins on her heel and storms down the hall with her followers up her ass.

At least she is gone for the time being. Shouldn't see her or the other two until sixth period. Thank fuck.

Classes start and end as the day ticks by uneventful. And soon, the bell rings and a sea of bodies ambles toward the cafeteria. I hoist my messenger bag up my shoulder and follow the masses.

A strange square chunk of mystery casserole, a banana and water bottle on my tray, I weave through the tables in search of an available seat. Parked in the corner, I poke at the food and remind myself—again—that I need to bring food tomorrow.

The buzz in the room quiets an octave when a group enters the cafeteria. Micah Reed and half the district-winning track team. They saunter past several tables, all eyes on them, and sit at their usual spot. Chatter resumes and people pick at their mystery lunch.

But I keep an eye on Micah through my raven locks.

The first time I paid any attention to Micah Reed was a week into the school year. Parked under a tree, I read *Wuthering Heights* for English Honors. Micah and several others on the track team jogged out of the gym in tank tops and short shorts in the school colors, with bright running shoes on their feet. I followed them as they went toward the paved oval track surrounding the school football field. Watched as they stretched and bounced on their toes before they took off running.

I dog-eared my page and observed Micah with fascination. His long, lithe frame glided over the pavement like the gazelles on nature documentaries. Blond hair a bird's nest from the breeze. Cheeks red as he huffed and circled the track.

He never saw me under that tree. No one did. No one ever sees me. And I am okay with not being seen. Okay with being the odd girl that makes others gawk. The loner who sits in the corner and keeps to herself. The quiet girl who admires a guy from a distance.

The next time I peek up, Mercedes stands beside Micah in the cafeteria. She smiles and laughs and flips her hair, all but begging for attention.

"Fake bitch," I mutter to myself.

As if she hears the words leave my lips, her eyes scan the room and land on me. She notices the one time my eyes dart between her and Micah, and I hate the action immediately. Because a slow, wicked grin plumps her cheeks.

Fuck.

She combs her fingers through Micah's short locks. He peers up at her with a *what the hell are you doing* look on his face. But what she says next wipes the look off his face.

"I had a good time the other night," she says to Micah loud enough for half the cafeteria to hear. Especially me. "Sorry I'm not as easy as the school slut, though." Her lips protrude in a fake pout, but her eyes scream pure evil.

Not that I have expressed my baby crush on Micah, but she saw it the second I let my eyes drift to him. And I royally fucked myself.

Micah shakes his head and doesn't feed into her comment. This pisses Mercedes off.

"Didn't you hear?" she asks, as if her lies are common knowledge.

"Hear what?" he says with boredom in his voice. And he doesn't meet her gaze.

"Little Miss Slut" —she points her polished dagger directly at me— "had an orgy with the baseball team."

My face lights on fire as every set of eyes in the cafeteria turns my way. *I fucking hate her. Hate. Her.*

But the way Micah looks at me flips my stomach upside down. Has the mystery casserole ready to reappear.

The first time Micah Reed notices me, really sees me, and he stares me down as if I am an easy lay. A conquest to mark on his bedpost and brag over with his jock buddies. His eyes narrow as he rises from the table. For a split second, I think he may walk off and ignore the bullshit Mercedes dishes out.

But I am dead wrong.

"Hey, pretty slut." Eyes searing my skin, Micah fists his dick through the denim and licks his lips. "The track team is always game."

The silence of moments ago vanishes as the entire cafeteria bursts into laughter. Fingers point my direction as eyes spill tears from laughing so hard.

Whooshing floods my ears as the laughter fades and the room swallows me whole. Pressure compresses my rib cage and squashes the tiny, erratic beating organ in the center. The small bites of casserole in my stomach threaten to make an appearance.

God, I want to stab something. Or someone.

And just like that, I am done.

Can't. Do. This. Anymore.

I shoot up from the table, scream at the top of my lungs and throw my tray toward Mercedes. And before I act on my irrational thoughts, I scoop up my messenger bag and run. Run from the cafeteria. Run from every person in this piece of shit school. Run from a life I didn't ask for and don't deserve.

Fuck this place. Fuck Mercedes. And fuck Micah Reed.

one

MICAH

Present...

Music blares in my ears and vibrates my bones as I walk through Roar.

Hot, sweaty bodies rub against each other in time with the music. Hands grope and lips tease and hips grind. Alcohol drains from glasses faster than refills can keep up. And clothes get looser. As do inhibitions.

I weave through the crowd, brush arms with several women, and toss out my flirtatious smile. Some smile in return. Others reach out and graze an arm or my chest. And I let them. It comes with the territory when you manage a night club. Can't work in a place like Roar without being groped or hit on at least once a night.

I love and hate the attention in equal measure.

Love it because I have easy access to women. Love it because most of the women that come to Roar are hot as fuck. I have a different woman between the sheets each week. None complain when we go separate ways. And none beg for another round. They know the hookup is a one-time deal. No names, no numbers exchanged. Just sex.

Which is part of the reason I hate it. Hate my official manwhore status. A badge I wear often because of my cheating ex, Rochelle.

I hate that I let her tear me down. That she still holds power over my thoughts and life. That her actions still sway my decisions.

After walking in on her, I should be free. Free of her and the bullshit. Small things I didn't notice until after she was caught in the act. I had been her pawn. A middleman in her game to get an even younger guy. Cougar isn't an appropriate term for Rochelle. More like super cougar. Jaguar. Maybe she likes it when he calls her mommy.

A shiver rolls up my spine and I shake away all thoughts of Rochelle. I may be down to try new shit in the bedroom, but that isn't one of them.

"Hey, man," I shout as I approach Dan, one of the bouncers. "All good?"

Dan, a man twice my muscle mass, gives a thumbs-up. "Yeah, boss. Busy tonight." He scans the crowd with a straight, serious face. All business once he punches his time card, Dan is one of our best bouncers.

Outside of work, Dan is all smiles and laughter. But I appreciate his professionalism inside the Roar walls. Never know what someone will do after too much alcohol.

I pat his shoulder. "Let me know if you need anything." He nods and I move on.

Several times a night, I weave through the club. Check on each staff member. Make sure everything is on the up-and-up. And I always end each round at the bar. Where Peyton pours drinks like a bartender from *Cocktail*.

Peyton Alexander. The bane of my existence. Pure, undiluted, sexy-as-sin torture.

She glides around her end of the bar. Flirts with males and females alike. Bats her lashes and pushes up her breasts to enhance her cleavage. Licks her lips and leans in close.

I fucking hate her. Hate that she flirts with every goddamn person who sets foot in Roar. Every person but me.

Most of all, I hate that this eats at my psyche. Keeps me up at night while I fist my cock between the sheets.

I step behind the bar—where I hang when not doing rounds on the floor or managerial tasks in the office—and unleash my undesirable jealousy.

"Peyton," I shout. And I know she hears me because her spine straightens. Her fingers coil, then flatten out.

She glares past Adam, another bartender, and curls her lip a beat. "Yeah, boss," she shouts back, voice saccharine.

"Quit fucking flirting and pour drinks," I bark out. Adam cringes beside me as he pours a beer from the tap.

Peyton lifts her middle finger to her forehead and mock salutes me. "You got it, *Micky*."

"Bitch," I mutter.

She turns her back to me and goes back to flirting. *Goddamnit.*

Like every other night I work with Peyton, I regret the day I hired her. But one of the owners interviewed and loved her before I had a say in the matter. So now, I grit my teeth, make her life miserable, and trudge forward.

Peyton actually tends the bar better than the other employees. People gravitate toward her each night. Loiter at her end of the bar and wait patiently. Buy more drinks when she tosses them a bright smile and flirts without care. And her tips are proof the crowd loves her. She earns double, if not triple, what the others do in tips.

Her only downfall… she seems to hate me to the pits of hell. The *I want to gouge out your eyes* kind of hate. And I have no idea why.

Unable to witness her endless flirting any longer, I exit the bar and distract myself with another round. Engage in idle chitchat with the staff and patrons.

On the dance floor, I pass a curvaceous blonde. Her golden locks remind me of a certain feisty bartender across the room. So, I step closer and do a little flirting of my own. One song fades into another as she grinds her ass against my dick and wraps her hands around the back of my head to keep me close.

I'm not going anywhere.

Ani and Sean, the club owners, don't mind if the staff join the scene. In fact, they encourage it so long as the partying doesn't interfere with business. Drinks are acceptable, but we don't go past tipsy. Grinding patrons on the dance floor is fair game, but we don't make anyone uncomfortable or assume it will go further. If it does go further, it happens outside these walls.

So, I dance with the woman who grabs and rubs me like she would fuck me in the middle of the room. I kiss down her neck and fist her hips. When the song transitions into the next, I step back. She spins and pouts and it is adorable as fuck.

I bring my lips to her ear. "Gotta work, sorry. Stick around till close?" She nods. "Wait for me. We can have fun after." I back away and she smiles.

The next few hours go by as per usual. Alcohol flows freely, intoxicating the patrons as much as the music. Every now and again, I look down at the other end of the bar and watch Peyton. Inconspicuously stare at her as her eyes glitter under the lights. As she bites her lower lip and half smiles. As she throws her arms in the air and dances behind the bar and several people wolf whistle.

During those hours, my dick strains against my zipper. Aches for an ounce of her attention. To have those glittery eyes shift their focus my way. Her plump lips around my cock. Her curves bouncing above me in a dark room on cool sheets.

But that will never happen.

The blonde from the dance floor wiggles her way between people at the bar. After serving a drink, I saunter her way and she smiles at my approach. I catch Peyton in my periphery and note her not-so-subtle staring at our interaction.

Good.

"Should be done soon. Still good with waiting?"

She licks her lips and I hear Peyton groan. "Yeah. Got nowhere else to be."

And just to irritate Peyton further, I pinch the blonde's chin between my thumb and finger, then crush my lips to hers. The kiss quick and angry and meaningless and all for show. I give two fucks about this woman. Actually, only one fuck.

"Hey, *Micky*," Peyton shouts. Her nickname for me makes my blood pressure rise. She says it just to piss me off. And I let it, but don't flaunt that fact.

"Yeah, bar wench," I throw back with a cocked brow.

She bristles and my insides sing. "Shouldn't you be, I don't know, managing something." Her words meant to be a stab. To throw my own words in my face when I tell her to quit flirting.

But unlike her, I take her bait and roll with it.

I point to the blonde. "That's what I'm doing." Peyton

furrows her brows. "Managing my hookup." Her eyes go wide at my bluntness. The fact that I own my manwhore status shocks her. "Should try it sometime."

She glances at the blonde, then back at me. Bass rattles the air around us while I wait for her comeback. Our banter turns me on and fuels the hungry beast inside.

"Nah," she shrugs and taps her chest. "Not one-night stand material." She turns her eyes on the blonde. "I have standards when it comes to who lies in my bed." Her eyes shift back to mine. "Sluts aren't my thing."

Internally, I laugh. But I mask it and come to the blonde's defense—kind of—who shoots daggers at Peyton.

"But sluts are so much fun," I tease. The blonde turns her attention to me. Her jaw drops, but closes when I suck my lower lip in my mouth. "Don't like fun, wench?"

God, I'm hard as fuck right now.

"Oh, I love fun." Peyton saunters closer, but keeps a good five feet between us. "Never been a fan of venereal diseases, though."

I don't hold back my laughter this time. In fact, I double over and release the sexual tension between us. She may not recognize it as such, but what the hell else would it be?

The blonde mutters, "Bitch."

Peyton faces the blonde, leans on the bar and cocks a brow. She shakes her head with light laughter. "I'm the bitch?" Peyton pushes off the bar and takes a step back. "Maybe I am." She shrugs. "But I'd rather be a bitch than spread my legs for every guy who gives me attention."

Heat crawls up the blonde's neck and blooms on her cheeks. I should be worried, but this whole situation amuses me too much to care.

The blonde shifts her attention from Peyton to me. "I'll wait at a table." She points in a general direction behind her.

"Be done soon." I pinch her chin again and crush her lips. "Don't worry about her."

The blonde melts in my hand. "She's just jealous." Then she turns and wanders to an empty table.

Peyton and I return to our typical uncomfortable, disgruntled silence. I pour a few more drinks before last call gets announced. The crowd thins and the first set of overhead lights kicks on. I grab and clean drained glasses. Then wipe down the empty sections of bar top.

When the next set of lights flicker on, ninety percent of the club is vacant.

I toss my towel in the bleach mix. Closing out the registers, I take the tills and tip jars to the office. Once the tills are reset and the cash balances, I stash the cash in the safe and lock up the office.

In the club, the blonde scrolls over her phone screen while Peyton throws her a murderous glare. Peyton has yet to see me walk out, so I hang back a moment and observe. How she washes glasses with aggression. How she wipes down the bar like she needs to remove the varnish.

Interesting. Is she actually jealous? Her actions indicate a flare of jealousy.

So, I use this to my advantage.

I step out from the hall and pass the end of the bar. Peyton locks on to me as I stroll over to the blonde. Her eyes burn my skin —not with hatred, though. They burn with bitterness and maybe a hint of lust. The fire trails over my skin and I stow it away.

I will need it in an hour.

"Ready?" I ask, approaching the blonde.

She peers up from her phone and smiles. In the light, she still flaunts pretty features. Not *take my breath away* gorgeous, but pretty enough to look at while I fuck her brains out. And when I flip her on her hands and knees, I will picture a different blonde.

"Yeah." She locks her phone and stows it in her back pocket. Her eyes shoot over my shoulder and narrow before coming back. "Let's get out of here." She slides off the stool. "Mine or yours?"

"Yours," I say as I wrap an arm around her shoulders.

No one comes back to my house. Ever.

"Perfect."

We head for the exit, but I halt us a moment and glance over my shoulder. "Peyton," I bark out and she glances up from the bar with a bored expression. "Bar better not look like shit in the morning."

Her jaw muscles tighten and shift. Scarlet pricks her cheeks. "Has it ever?" she bites.

I don't answer her question and opt to bark another order. "Don't leave until everything's spotless."

The blonde and I head for the door, but I don't miss Peyton's grumbled *asshole* as we walk out. The ammunition I needed to get through the next couple of hours.

two

PEYTON

"Morning, sunshine." Reese kisses my hair as he stumbles past the breakfast bar to the Keurig.

"Morning, bum." He swats me away over his shoulder and I laugh. "Late night?"

He sets his cup under the drip, inserts a pod and presses the button. Then he twists to face me. "Surprised you didn't hear." I widen my eyes as a chuckle spills from his lips. Not that Reese's shenanigans are anything new. "You either sleep like the dead or you came in much later than me."

"Probably the latter." I lift my own mug to my lips and sip the creamy brew. "Manager Asshole was in rare form the other night."

Reese adds sugar and hazelnut creamer to the mug, then gulps his morning elixir and sighs. He stands opposite me, hip leaning on the kitchen island, brow cocked in question.

"Sounds juicy. Tell me more while I make breakfast."

Before I get in a word of protest, Reese turns his back to me and grabs pans from the cabinet. I love when he makes breakfast. Everything he cooks tastes ten times better. Even scrambled eggs. Plus, it gives me more time to sip my coffee.

"He just raked my nerves more than usual."

Reese peeks over his shoulder with a devious smile. "Most people call that flirting, sunshine. You should fuck him already."

I shudder and he laughs. "Well, I sure as shit am not flirting with Micah Reed." The idea of purposely flirting with Micah makes my skin crawl. "Nor do I want to fuck him." I ignore the shiver that rolls up my spine. "He's just as much an asshole now as he was back in high school."

Reese grabs eggs, milk and cheese from the fridge. Then a bag of hash browns and sausage patties from the freezer. He cracks half the carton of eggs, adds milk and whips them longer than I ever do. Probably the secret behind why his scrambled eggs are so damn fluffy. I just don't have the patience.

He pours the mix into the pan and adds two handfuls of cheese. In two other pans, he starts the hash browns and sausage. I stare after him in fascination. Not that I can't cook. I just prefer to make simpler foods that only take one pan. Or the microwave. Less dishes equals less cleanup.

"Still think he doesn't know who you are?" Reese sips his coffee, then tends to the pans.

Does Micah know *who* I am? All signs and interaction with him lead me to believe he has no clue.

One—the first time he laid eyes on me, I was in my all-things-black, loner-girl phase. Black hair, black clothes, black makeup. If it was black, I probably owned it.

Don't get me wrong, I still love black. But the dark shade no longer rules my life. Sometime in the last decade, yellow took precedence. I don't plaster it everywhere like I did black as a teen, but I have splashes of it here and there.

Two—Micah looks at me differently now. In high school,

he jumped on the Triple M hate train without learning a thing about me. Back then, he looked at me like gum stuck to his shoe. He said shitty things because he was a popular jock and it was funny to pick on the loner girl.

But now… his eyes hold intrigue when they look my direction.

He must think I don't notice his traveling eyes or the frequency of his stares. But I don't miss a single glance. Don't miss the spark of lust in lapis-blue eyes. Or how they drag over my curves when I face away from him.

I have always noticed Micah Reed.

His angular jaw and lean frame. His slight reservation unless he wants to impress someone. Or the truth his eyes tell, but lips can't manage. I once believed Micah was a good guy. Someone who would stand up for others when they need it most. But that rule seems to only apply to family, close friends and impressionable people.

Here is my opinion. Micah Reed can suck my dick. If I had one.

"He has no idea," I answer confidently.

Reese dishes scrambled eggs on to three plates, then adds a hefty portion of hash browns and sausage. He sets the mountainous plate on the bar, then hands me a fork. "His loss, sunshine. Think he'll figure it out?"

I shrug. "If he does, it'll be too late."

He picks up the two other plates and levels me with his gaze. "You say that now, but…"

"But nothing," I say around a forkful of food.

"Alright." He starts for his bedroom. "Just prepare yourself for the day he puts two and two together. May not be anytime soon, but it'll happen."

I point my fork at him. "Go feed whoever's in your room

and leave me be."

He strolls down the hall, chuckling. "Love you, sunshine."

"Yeah, yeah. Love you, too."

~

"Is this right?"

Ms. Jenkins peers down at the yarn and hooks in my hand. Scrutinizes my crochet skills with crinkles at the corners of her eyes and lips.

She pats my hand. "Such a fast learner, dear. You'll make a hat or scarf in no time."

"Let's not get carried away. Plus, when would I wear a scarf? The one day a year it gets cold?"

She laughs, then lifts a hand to her mouth as it transitions to a strangled cough. Decades of smoking evident in the harsh, nonstop hack. If the doctor allowed it, she would still smoke today. But being attached to an oxygen tank and smoking doesn't mix well. So, she quit. Now, she almost always has a toothpick in her mouth.

"No, dear. You take a trip when it's cold up north and use it then. Thought you were smart enough to figure as much out."

Ms. Jenkins was once a world traveler. On my days at the assisted living facility, she takes me on journeys with her stories. Adventures I dream about taking one day. My bucket list grew miles longer when I learned of all the places she'd visited.

Hiking mountains and valleys and sand dunes. Camping under the stars in the middle of nowhere without a care in the world. Witnessing the aurora borealis. Seeing the pyramids in Egypt. Visiting the Inca citadel in Machu Picchu. Wandering the hanami—aka the cherry blossom festival—in Japan.

I envy her younger, fearless years. Packing a bag and exploring the globe on a whim. One day, I want to travel the way she did. Just get up and go. When? No telling, but I made it a goal.

"Never seen snow," I admit.

"What?" She stares at me in mock horror.

I laugh and raise my right hand. "Swear." She shakes her head. "Where would you recommend? For a first timer."

"You kids." We both laugh. In her eyes, I am still a kid. Not like we bring up age, but I haven't technically been a "kid" for fourteen years. "Where's your sense of adventure?"

My sense of adventure is on the back burner. Who has time or money to travel? Most people my age work more than one job just to live. Me included. I work at Roar four nights a week. And although I earn enough from Roar to pay the bills, I still work two days a week at Gulfside Assisted Living.

The small paycheck from the ALF helps pad my savings and save for rainy days. But adding to my savings isn't the sole reason I work here.

Before Gulfside, I spent several days a week with my grandma. We chatted mostly, but other memories were also made. Baking bread and cookies and pies. Tending to her small garden in the backyard. Sipping tea and coffee on her back porch while bird-watching. Organizing old photographs and adding them to albums. Short walks in the park.

Time with Grandma Isabel warmed my heart. She was a selfless woman. Did whatever she could, within her means, to help others. Always had a shoulder to lean on and offered sound advice freely. I remember her gentle spirit, and that she didn't take shit from anyone.

When she contracted pneumonia, we all thought she would pull through. Her fighter spirit had survived much worse. But her older immune system couldn't fight off the pneumonia. Not after all the years she smoked. Her lungs gave up the fight before her spirit.

I promised her I would give back in her memory. Help others, even if that meant contributing my time or learning to crochet baby hats. Plus, it lessens the void of her loss when I visit the residents of Gulfside. When I sit with Ms. Jenkins and talk about living life to its fullest.

"It's there, I promise. Just have some other obligations to tend to first."

She sets her hooks down and narrows her eyes. "I hope those obligations don't involve a man."

This makes me laugh harder than it should. "No, ma'am."

"Good. Women don't need a man to stand tall." She looks me square in the eye. "If my Stephen was still here, he'd tell you just as much too. We loved fiercely. But he never smothered my light. He helped me shine brighter." She lays her hand on mine. "That's what a real partner does. Helps make you a better version of yourself."

One day, I pray to have a love as fierce as the one she shared with her late husband.

"Enough of that," she says. "Let's finish. Then, you can wheel me to the dining room for lunch."

Over the next hour, I crochet two rows of a baby hat. After I wheel Ms. Jenkins to the dining hall, I hug her goodbye and promise to see her tomorrow.

Exiting Gulfside, I text Aunt Leanne to tell her I am on

my way. Every Monday, we meet for a late lunch after I finish my shift at Gulfside.

I have always had a close relationship with Aunt Leanne. She feels more like a second mom than an aunt. When Dad passed ten years ago, I made a point to spend more time with family. To never take time or the future for granted. You never know what will happen from one day to the next.

On Monday, I spend time with Aunt Leanne.

Two songs and a radio commercial later, I park in front of our usual café. We hop out, exchange hugs, and wander inside. After we order, we chitchat and catch up on what we have missed in the past week.

She asks about Ms. Jenkins and how my crocheting is coming along. Asks if Mom and Harold are well—although she checks in with Mom every other week. And then she broaches the subject of Roar. She always skirts around the Micah topic, but she doesn't fool me. I see her secret need to ask intrusive questions and know all the dirty details.

Aunt Leanne, bless her soul, is a gossip queen. The unflattering trait has evolved over the years, but she still knows everyone's business. After our conversations, she forms her own opinions on why Micah is an asshole. I choose to ignore those opinions.

"So…" She drags the two-letter word out to ten. "How's nightlife going? Meet anyone interesting?" I also tend to believe Aunt Leanne lives vicariously through me. She states life wasn't as interesting in her late twenties to early thirties. I beg to differ.

"Good. And yes, I meet interesting people every night I work."

I play coy. Every time she asks, I dance circles around the

answer. The way her eyes narrow as I tease her makes me laugh. She never lets me off the hook, though.

She tosses her best death glare across the table, but gets disrupted when our server delivers our food. She stabs at her salad with faux aggression, then points at me with her full fork.

"Why are you avoiding the answer? Did something happen? You better tell me."

I bite into the sandwich and chew slowly to give myself more time before answering. The slower I chew, the thinner her eyes get. When the bite is soup in my mouth, I swallow and mentally prep for the onslaught of questions. Questions I don't want to answer.

"Nothing new happened. Not really." *Shit.* Why the hell did I add the last part? Might as well have handed her the gas canister while I held the match.

"Elaborate," she commands, her fork pointed my way again.

"Put that thing down. You'll take an eye out."

"Quit avoiding."

I sigh. Aunt Leanne knows bits and pieces about Micah. She remembers people bullied me in high school but doesn't know Micah was among them. All she knows of him now are the tidbits I share from time at work. His asshole tendencies, but also the way I spot him checking me out.

She has her own hypotheses on all things Micah Reed. And after today, no doubt she will add even more.

I rehash the events from two nights ago. Reiterate his order barking. Bring up the blonde and how he acted around her with me nearby. Like his goal was to make me jealous. How we went tit for tat. I give the whole rundown. And when I finish, her shit-eating grin irks my nerves.

After a moment of pause, she asks, "You want honesty?"

Yes. No. We never lie to each other, but occasionally keep opinions to ourselves. I want honesty, but don't want another person to say Micah is flirting. I have been on the receiving end of flirting many times. What Micah and I do is not flirting. Our back-and-forth exchanges are more about getting under each other's skin. And it doesn't take much effort.

I know my motivation. But what prompts Micah?

"Always." Even if I don't want to hear it.

"He likes you." She sips her drink. "More than likes you."

I shake my head. "How? This isn't elementary school. Adults don't pretend to hate someone because they have a crush on them."

"Says who?"

"Society."

She rolls her eyes and shakes her head. "So, because society says something, it makes it true. Really, Peyton?"

I hate when she gets semi-philosophical. I also hate when she makes a valid point when I thought otherwise. Ugh.

"Okay, fine. Say he acts like an asshole—"

"Peyton," she scolds me like a juvenile.

"Say he acts like a *jerk* because he likes me. Should I really pursue a relationship with someone with such childish behavior? Why not just come out and ask me on a date?" I pause to sip my water. "Not that I'd say yes."

"Oh, my dear sweet Peyton." She reaches across the table and pats my hand similar to how Ms. Jenkins does. "Because men don't always know how to use their voice. It's easier for them to act the fool than express how they feel."

I tip my head back, stare at the ceiling tiles, and let my vision blur. "Argh. This is so annoying."

"Yet another reason why I stay single. I prefer friendships. Less drama and scrutinization."

With this, she leaves the topic alone and we finish our lunch. Our conversation shifts to something that doesn't spike my blood pressure. She tells me about a new candle shipment they received at work. Practically sells me each scent. But she loves the small, independently owned shop. They sell a variety of knickknacks and stay busy near the beach.

Finished with lunch, we pay the bill, slide out of the booth and head toward our cars. We stop at the back of mine, exchange hugs and promise to see each other the same time next week. I unlock the car and toss my purse onto the passenger seat.

"Peyton?"

I spin back to face her. "Yeah?"

"Not everything is black and white. Be sure to look for the hints of gray and occasional splashes of color."

Skirting around her thoughts, Aunt Leanne just told me to consider the possibility that Micah may have feelings for me. Not the I-hate-everything-about-you feelings he so boldly displays. But perhaps the exact opposite.

Even if he does, I don't see the point. Micah may not remember me from fourteen plus years ago, but I sure as hell remember him. Remember the hurt he put me through and the web of lies he spun. The harsh words on his lips and how he painted me the fool among our peers.

Micah Reed is an asshole and a manwhore. No point seeing him as anything except that. He treats me like trash whenever possible. And dips his dick in anyone with a hole. No thanks, I will pass.

But I appease my aunt for the time being. Toss out a smile and tell her what she wants to hear. "Will do. Love you."

"Love you, too. See you next week."

Next week… Hopefully, I won't have anything new to share about Micah Reed. Not him ogling me behind the bar. Not him flaunting his promiscuity in my face. Not him barking at me to crawl under my skin. Nothing. Only him leaving me the hell alone.

three

MICAH

I love days like this. Days when I kick back with my best friend and enjoy the outdoors. Hanging with Gavin equals time at the beach. The sun heats our skin while the sand sticks to it. Coconut and brine float in the air. And bodies fill every possible open space between the seagrasses and surf.

Just like old times. When life was less complicated and stressful.

I need more days like today.

Gavin said we should hit the beach. And wherever Gavin goes, so does Cora. Who called and invited Shelly—which is no big shake. Definitely like old times.

When Gavin flew back to the Bay Area last year for work, I knew shit would go down with him and Cora. With how they left things when his parents moved him to California, I expected shit to blow up. But sometimes, life works out when two people are meant to be together.

Maybe I will get lucky one day and find *the one*.

Gavin and Cora just click. They did from the very beginning. The ease of their relationship annoyed me. Hell, it still annoys me. Because I never found a parallel bond with a woman. Never shared a connection so deep, I felt lost without my other half.

My envy knows no bounds. And now that they are married, envy is too small a term for what I feel regarding their relationship. It isn't fair to begrudge my friend for finding love and happiness.

At one point, I thought Rochelle was *the one*. The woman I would ring shop for and get her name branded over my heart. The woman to make me say *I do*, invite friends over for game nights, and grow old and gray with in rockers on the porch.

Unfortunately, I saw Rochelle with blinders on.

Rochelle sought me out. Approached me. Brought up the conversation of a more serious relationship first. And I fell for each crumb she tossed at my feet. I never suspected a woman of her maturity level would treat me with such juvenile tendencies. Would stoop to such low-level actions. In my bed, no less.

All thanks to Rochelle, I now have an issue seeing women as anything other than a means to an end. Sexual gratification. A temporary fix to what ails me. A warm place to stick my dick when the loneliness peaks.

And I fucking hate it.

I don't want to see women as objects. I don't want people to look at my sister like she is good for one act and disposable otherwise. But after trusting a woman with my heart, I fear putting it out there so freely again. Fear the vulnerability of fully exposing myself. Fear another woman crushing my heart when she tires of me and moves on.

I glance at Gavin, my best friend of nearly twenty years, and notice how he eyes Cora. His observation isn't territorial.

He has her heart, and she has his. No, his fixed gaze is more a fear of what he will miss if he looks away.

That is the type of love I want. Where you don't take your eyes off one another because you can't bear to miss a moment.

While Cora and Shelly swim, I opt to ask the questions I don't want the girls to razz me over.

"So," I say, and Gavin breaks contact with Cora to face me. "How's married life? Tired of each other yet?"

Gavin tips his head back and chuckles. "I will never tire of her, bro. Never." He pauses to look at his wife briefly. "But things are different than before."

Hmm, color me intrigued. "How so?"

He purses his lips and takes a deep breath. "Guess the best way to describe it is we're the same as before, but also new."

Now, I laugh. "Yeah, that explains nothing, my cryptic friend."

"Sorry." He shrugs. "When Cora and I first met, we lived in a fantasy world. Yes, we were madly in love. Although teenage love is intense and all-consuming, you're blind to what happens after high school. College, moving out, the weird phase of wanting to experience life on your own." He pauses and shakes his head. "We skipped all that. And tons of relationships don't survive those years post high school."

"So, you think you and Cora would've split after high school?"

He stares out at the water and watches Cora as she laughs with Shelly before returning his gaze. "No, I don't think so. But we wouldn't appreciate each other the way we do now. Thirteen years apart really fucked with both of us. We never forgot each other. But we remembered each other differently. I missed her, but the years of resentment I held for my parents painted the memories differently. Cora had no one to hate but me. And even then, she only hated me on the surface."

Yeah, I definitely envy my best friend. None of the girls from school were "forever" material. They all thought their shit didn't stink. They were either too consumed with themselves or had ugly personalities.

"How did that translate into how things are now?"

"Neither of us wanted a serious relationship with anyone but each other. Sure, our reunion wasn't pretty. But we had a lot of pain to hash out. And I deserved to feel every ounce of her pain. I fucked up, man. I left her when I said I never would. Instead of finding a solution, I took the easy way out." He presses his hand to her name tattooed on his chest. "Her pain is my pain, bro. Plain and simple. And I'll never intentionally cause her pain again."

God, I want to talk to Gavin about my own shitty love life. Or lack thereof. Neither of us is an expert. No one is an expert when it comes to love. But maybe he can steer me in the right direction with advice.

Great as it is to experience life and all it has to offer; variety isn't always what it is cracked up to be.

Part of me longs for the comfort that comes with being in a monogamous relationship. Getting to know someone on a deeper level. Seeing the world through their eyes. Evolving with the same person. I don't envision children or gray hair at this stage—I am not that far ahead.

But I do see the same person at my side, day after day. Waking up with the same woman in my arms. Wrapping my arms around her and hugging her close. Kissing her ear, her neck, her shoulder. Loving her—not just physically, but in all aspects of life.

At thirty-two, though, I feel like time doesn't weigh in my favor. And I have no clue how to remedy the situation.

"Can I ask you something?"

Gavin pushes his glasses down the bridge of his nose and gives an inquisitive stare. I see the line of questions form, but he won't ask them. "Always, man. What's up?"

"If you and Cora hadn't reconnected, do you think you would've made a life with someone else?"

Without hesitation, he answers, "No. I tried relationships in California. Never stuck. I compared every woman to Cora. Which only made me want her more." He looks out at the water. "She's all I've ever wanted. Everyone else just filled time and provided a temporary distraction."

I nod. "There's someone…"

Without looking, I know his eyes are on me. "The blonde behind the bar?"

My eyes snap to him. "How?" It's the only word my lips form. Because how the hell does he know I meant Peyton? Have I mentioned her to him?

As of recent, my head has been a fucking mess. Whatever.

"The sexual tension between you two can be felt miles away. The bickering and constant eye contact. I only caught a glimpse, but sure as shit felt it. What's her story?"

Fuck, I wish I knew her story. The not knowing is half the problem. Peyton is elusive. An unsolved crime with a six-inch-thick file folder of stats. Only they are written in a foreign language.

"Wish I knew, bro." I shake my head. "For whatever reason, she's hated me since day one. And I did nothing to offend her."

Gavin laughs at this. Laughs so hard he bends at the waist as tears stream down his cheeks. *Dickhead.* I give him his moment to laugh at my expense. Let him get it out of his system.

"Gonna tell me what's so fucking funny?" I prompt.

"Mr. Hot Shit can't get a girl." He laughs again, but it doesn't linger as long. "You have always been a *lady's man*. You always got the girl with your smile and a one-liner. Insert new girl, one you actually *want*, and she won't give you the time of day. She actually throws shit back in your face." He winces. "Hate to say it, brother. Sounds like karma is working her mojo on you."

Ugh. Why the hell did I ask? Should have known Gavin would give me shit.

But I hate to admit… he has a point.

Over the last sixteen-plus years, I have been an asshole. Not just with women, but in general. I always saw myself higher and mightier than the guy next to me. Is this my punishment? To look, to want, to dream about, but not to touch. To never have the chance to show I can be a good guy.

I have no clue how to come back from that. How to make up for all the shit in my past. For all the one-night stands. For picturing one woman while I stared down at another. For wanting to belt out another woman's name when I orgasm.

Yeah, I am a goddamn prick. Is redemption even possible at this point? Or should I just give up and leave things how they are? Would be easier.

"Quit thinking so fucking hard over there." I peer over at Gavin, who drills holes in my temple. "You like her, man?"

"Yeah, but I don't know if it's because she fights me at every turn, or if it's actual attraction."

"Forbidden fruit always tastes better," he admits.

"Truth."

"But there's something to be said about having a favorite

fruit. The one that never lets you down. Always tastes the same and makes you happy."

I chuckle. "This fruit analogy is getting dirty, bro."

He smacks my chest. "Shut up and listen a minute." I swat his hand away and feign pain. "You need to sit down and really think about this. Think about her. Whip out pen and paper. Write down what you're attracted to, the parts that make you want more. Then make a list of all the things that make you insane."

I stare at him, incredulous. "Gavin. Brother. Are you seriously telling me to make a pro/con list of this woman?"

He shrugs as if it is that simple. "More or less. You got any better solutions?"

If I had a better solution, would I be asking for help? After Rochelle, women are a haze of mixed signals and lost translations. The more time passed, the less I tried figuring it all out.

Keeping things short and sweet makes life a hell of a lot easier. It also keeps me from getting my heart broken again.

"No, obviously I don't."

I stare out at the horizon and let my focus relax. Can I do this? Write a pros and cons list on Peyton? The idea of writing down what I love and loathe about this woman makes me itchy. But what other option is there?

Any time Peyton is near, I gravitate toward her. Something about her is so familiar and bewitching. But I can't figure out how to scratch the surface. Get past the anger she harbors. Anger I don't quite understand. Anger she unleashed when Ani and Sean left the room and we were alone for the first time.

That rage stems from somewhere deep. A niggling voice in the back of my head tells me I am the root cause of it all. But how?

I met Peyton only a year ago. Right? I search my memory bank; search the long list of women I have been with over the years. But no hits pop up on my radar. Peyton is definitely someone I would remember.

But the boulder beneath my diaphragm begs to differ. And I have no clue where to go from here.

four

PEYTON

I park in the employee lot behind Roar and survey the other parked cars. Most everyone is already here. Including Micah.

Great.

I really should talk to Ani about switching some of my days. Micah and Gina, the other manager, draft the staff schedule, but I would love at least one shift without Micah in the picture. A reprieve from his constant stares and assholism. If I talk to Ani, though, she will blather until my ears bleed and probe me harder than an alien abduction.

So, that is a no go.

Guess I just suck it up like a good cookie. Doesn't mean I should make his life easy, though.

Walking through the back door, I stash my purse in the employee lounge, clock in, then head to the bar. No sign of Micah yet. Good. If I'm lucky, he is in the storage room or doing paperwork in the office.

Without the worry of bumping into Micah, I get to work on my prep. I cut citrus and fill the bar condiment boxes. Stash the extras in the fridge beneath the counter. Next, I replenish the napkin stacks, drink umbrellas, and straws.

Finally, I double-check the glassware is clean, wipe the counters down again, and scan the liquor bottles and keg levels.

Recently, Wednesday and Thursday nights have grown in popularity. After work gatherings hosted by local businesses or special events with larger parties keep the drinks flowing and the music booming. Fewer bodies and chatter, but still a busy night. My favorite weekday perk; the bar also closes hours earlier. And the tips are still great. Different populous, different mindset, different tipping standards. Of course, Friday and Saturday always bring in the masses and flood the tip jar. But I love the weekday vibe.

Tonight—and any other Wednesday without scheduled events—is Woman Crush Wednesday. Cliché, I know. Basically, it's ladies' night with an updated name. On ladies' night, we serve fruity drinks at half price.

Half price drinks equals lots of ladies soothing their workday with colorful, alcoholic beverages. Lots of ladies drinking and de-stressing equals hefty tips. Works in my favor.

The overhead lights flip off and the colorful lights come on. Music pumps out of the speakers. Not the same music we play on the weekend, but still upbeat and catchy. Moments later, Micah appears from the back and unlocks the front door.

He seems different today.

I shake off the thought as a flock of women storm the bar. Time to whip up some magic.

Five thousand nine hundred and a bazillion fruity drinks later and I am officially beat. One more hour until the door locks. Hallelujah. Then, I can clean up, drive home, and sleep until noon.

Micah joins me and Adam behind the bar. He fills drink orders, cleans glasses and restocks the napkins and fruit. He moves behind the bar as if this is his job, not managing the rest of us. Oddly, he doesn't look my way. Not once. Considering we never go one shift without snapping at each other, I question what parallel universe we landed in. Because silent-and-closed-off Micah is just… weird.

Maybe something happened with his family or a close friend. I peek down the bar, give him a brief once-over, and hope he doesn't notice.

He doesn't look sad or angry. No downturned lips or eyes. No slumped shoulders and hunched back. He just looks… blah. Meh. Like his emotions took a hiatus.

Does it make me a dick if I want to stir the pot? Provoke him a little for my own pleasure. Probably. But work isn't the same if Micah and I aren't going at it like alley cats. And his boring side makes the night drag out.

"Hey, *Micky*," I shout over the music. His spine stiffens and I know I hit the mark. Sweet relief.

He rolls his eyes and turns to face me. "What is it?"

His words have no punch to them. Although I hear the annoyance in his tone, the usual sting is missing. Part of me wants to drop it. Give up and call it a wash. But the feisty side of me says *hell no*. I like feisty me more.

"Your cat die or something? You get your period today? Take a break, I got this handled."

The muscles in his jaw tighten as he grinds his teeth. Inch by inch, his face stains red. His nostrils flare. But he takes slow, measured breaths and lets his frustration or anger with me pass.

Challenge accepted.

"Best watch what you say to me. Seeing as I'm your boss."

Ooh, he wants to play the boss card now. Game on. "Actually, you aren't technically my boss. Ani and Sean are my bosses. You just do everyone else's job plus paperwork and count money."

This pisses him off. The red resurfaces, and he turns his back to me briefly.

What's the matter? Does little Micah not know how to keep his feelings in check? Poor little baby.

He faces me again and steps forward until we are a foot apart. This close, I see the heat from his cheeks has trailed down his neck and onto his upper chest. Smell the woodsy amber scent of his cologne. Hear how hard he grinds his molars and resists speaking, the words dangling on the tip of his tongue.

But I want to coax every word from his lips. Want to hear the hatred and anger. The desire and lust.

I am no idiot. Micah Reed may hide parts of himself from others, but I have known him a long time. Longer than he has known me. For years, I watched Micah from a distance. Saw who he was when everyone was looking. But I also saw who he was when he thought no one was nearby.

Micah is an asshole and a manwhore. Nothing changes that truth. History cannot be erased. It is what it is.

But he is also a big brother and protector. A loner, when his posse isn't around. Although he humiliated me in high school, I still crushed on him. Still followed him when no one paid attention. Still got a glimpse of the guy behind the facade.

My stalker ways faded when Micah graduated and I still had a year left. Senior year was the best year of high school. No more Triple M and no more Micah Reed. The lack of harassment was a nice reprieve. But I hated that I missed seeing Micah every day. I hated that I wondered what he was doing out in the world.

"Maybe you should read the employee handbook again, *wench.*" There he is, even if his tone still feels squishier than normal.

"Is this the Micah Rules Roar handbook? Because Ani never gave me a manual to do my job. She knows me better than that."

The few women left at the bar side-eye each other and throw smirks at our back-and-forth. *That will be ten dollars for your evening entertainment, ladies.*

If steam could waft from his scalp, it would be now.

"What is your problem?" he blurts out. He throws a cleaning towel in the sink and steps closer. So close his breath tickles my cheek. The sensation triggers a tingle at the base of my spine. "Why is it your mission to piss me off?" His hissed words only loud enough for me to hear.

Beside us, the women at the bar ooh and ahh. But I don't focus on them. I can't. Not with Micah close enough to press his lips to my skin. To my lips or my neck.

A light sheen of sweat slicks my skin. I resist the urge to step back. To let him win. I got this. Micah Reed doesn't hold power over me. Not anymore.

"I love how easy it is," I tell him. "And because I need to."

He cocks a brow at this. "You need to?"

Too close. He is still way too close. I need to step back. Need clean, cool air. Need to see something other than his supple round lips and beard stubble. Stubble that probably feels so good between—

Shut. Up. Peyton. Do not go there. Do not think of Micah Reed and sex simultaneously. Just. No.

"Someone needs to put you in your place," I croak out. Great. Nothing like sounding less confident when I need to come across bolder.

"And where exactly is my place, Peyton?"

He called me Peyton. Not bar wench or wench. Peyton. That doesn't happen often. It never happens when we stand this close to each other. Hell, we never stand this close. Ever.

"You don't know?" I tease.

His head shakes subtly. "Enlighten me."

The angry part of me wants to yell, "In the pits of hell." But I don't need to scare off the small number of people that visit on Wednesday nights.

I don't want to lie to him, but throwing down my whole hand makes me vulnerable. Micah Reed doesn't own those rights. He doesn't get to choose when I open myself up. Only I get to decide. Me.

So, I take the easy way out. Toss out a statement that still applies, but doesn't reach the heart of the matter. That he hurt me. He may not remember, but one day he will. And he needs to feel what I felt when it all hits him.

"With all the other assholes and manwhores." I step back and smirk. "No doubt there's a special place in hell for all of you. Don't you think?" I take another step back and twirl the length of my hair.

He winces. I expect him to lash out. To step back into my space and give as good as I deliver. But he doesn't.

Instead, he takes a step back. Then another. And without another word, he retreats and heads for the office.

The women at the bar watch his retreat, then snicker among themselves. I cash them out and they leave me a heftier than normal tip. Does bickering with Micah in front of customers equal better tips? If so, I need to turn that shit all the way up.

Once all the customers leave, I start my nightly cleaning routine. Micah has yet to return from wherever he went. He may not help clean up, but he needs to run sales numbers and take the tills to the office. Which means avoiding me until we leave is impossible.

The tables have been cleared of glasses and wiped down. The condiment boxes refilled and stowed in the fridge. Glasses cleaned and napkins restocked. When I start cleaning the floor, Micah reappears.

Not irritated. Not angry. But maybe a little defeated.

Did I cross the line? Was I too harsh? Banter and frustration are nothing new with Micah. But tonight feels different. Micah *seems* different. And I have no idea why.

Do I cave and apologize? No. Nope. Not happening. If I apologize, he wins. Not that the constant tension and barking at each other is a game. For me, it is all too real.

I have been on the receiving end of his shit and the people he associates—associated—with. I know what it is like to go home and cry until I pass out. Know what it is like to just want friends, not even a boyfriend, and have that squashed like a bug.

Micah Reed may not be the sole reason for my pain, but he holds a significant piece of the pie.

"Why?" I startle at his voice. His proximity. When did he step so close?

I swallow down the sudden lump in my throat. "Why what?" I choke out.

"Why do you hate me so much? Give me a real answer. Not some bullshit reason."

He wants the truth? How convenient. How fortunate.

Well guess what, Micah Reed? You need to work for the truth.

I face him head-on and shake my head. My gaze locks with his and all the words on my tongue swirl like alphabet soup.

Have I seen his eyes this close before? Seen how they shimmer under the brighter light. Earlier, I thought his eyes were lapis blue; a rich, dark blue. Now, with his proximity, I really see the resemblance. And the hints of gold. Like stars in the night sky.

Focus, Peyton. Now is not the time to get lost. Especially in his addictive irises.

"Always want things the easy way, huh?"

His brows pinch at the middle. His eyes dart between mine and try to read all the words left unsaid. But I don't wear my emotions on my sleeve. Not anymore. Now, I cover them in armor.

"I don't know what that means."

Of course, he doesn't. Why would he? Instead of sitting down and thinking, he just wants the answer handed to him. Sorry, Micah. No such luck.

"It means, if you want the answer, you'll have to work for it. Dig deep. Real deep. The answers are there. You're just looking in the wrong places."

Before he asks me another question, I back away and head for the storage room. I fetch the dustpan, but don't leave immediately. Instead, I grab hold of the shelf, bend at the waist, and heave for air.

Did I really do that? Did I tell Micah to go hunt for the truth? To search his past—our past—to find answers?

Damnit.

This isn't how it is supposed to go. I should keep up the back-and-forth quips. Not hand over the key to everything.

What if he unlocks the door? What if he remembers me from years ago? Remembers who I am, what he did and the cruel words he said. Will he look at me with fresh hate? Pity me, perhaps? Stir the pot and try to shove me down? Again.

No. Hell no.

You know… I hope he unlocks our history. Hope he remembers who I am and all the shitty things he did. Maybe, if I'm lucky, he will man up and apologize. Grovel. Beg for my forgiveness.

That would be a sight.

But I see the flip side of the coin. If it all comes crashing back, I picture him playing it off or acting ignorant to save face. Because that is who he is. Micah Reed. Asshole extraordinaire.

five

MICAH

Holy. Fucking. Hell.

Hot water sprays down my spine, but the temperature isn't what heats my skin. The scalding spray is the excuse my mind created so I could bury the guilt. The guilt that ensues as I grip my thick, angry cock in my palm and tug with too much aggression. Stroke and squeeze with eyes pinched tightly as I slap my free hand on the tile.

No matter how long I stroke myself, no matter how firm or soft my technique, satisfaction never comes.

My cock doesn't want my hand. What it needs is a feisty blonde who I can silence with my dick.

Fuck.

I finish jacking off, feeling no relief in the end, then wash up double time.

Peyton wants me to think. She wants me to dig deep to find the answers. Well, I did plenty of that last night while I had lain awake in bed, staring at a cobweb on the ceiling for hours. I scavenged the corners of my mind and came up blank. Not a goddamn explanation. Hell, a hint would be helpful at this point.

The way she spoke… as if I *know* her. Or I did, once upon a time.

But I would remember Peyton. Her sexy as hell curves. Champagne locks and addictive eyes. Her unparalleled spunk and vicious banter. No chance I would forget any of those qualities.

Question is, if I *did* know her, was she not who she is now? Quite possible. If so, then yeah, I have no idea who Peyton is—or was—and rewinding time, week by week, is the only way to find answers.

That takes a lot of time and effort. Neither of which I will expend today.

Today, I suit up and prepare for battle. Give Peyton a taste of what she is missing. Give her a taste of what I have to offer.

"Game on, hellcat."

Stepping out of the shower, I towel off. I add product to my hair and comb my fingers through to give it that just-fucked look. The look women seem to ogle and beg to touch. Sliding open the closet, I yank a navy button-down and charcoal slacks off the hangers. After I zip up my pants and latch the last button, I add a splash of cologne, then slip on socks and dress shoes.

One last glance in the mirror—because looks need to kill tonight—and I smile at my reflection.

Before leaving for work, I cook a quick dinner, packaging half of it to eat during break later.

The drive from Clearwater to Tampa isn't clogged this time of day. Driving over the causeway allows me time to clear my head and take in the scenery. Sunny, blue skies with the occasional cotton-puff clouds. Salty breeze off the Bay. The occasional boom of music as I pass beachgoers. And the obvious jubilance of people as they enjoy the weather. The energy here invigorates me.

I park behind Roar forty minutes later. No one else has arrived yet. I don't expect to bump into staff for at least another hour.

In the office, I go through my normal routine before the crew trickles in. Reset the register tills. Count and verify the cash from the previous night. Log the sales numbers. Prepare the bank deposit for Ani or Sean. And do a once-over of the interior while the space is empty.

Ani enters the office just as I seal the deposit bag. "Hey, Micah."

I peer up from the computer and lean back in the chair. "Ani," I say with a nod. "How are you?"

Since tension has been slowly building between Peyton and me, I hesitate on what's safe conversation with Ani. Peyton and Ani have an obvious relationship outside of Roar, but I'm not sure what it entails. Ani hired Peyton without input from Sean, Gina, or me. One thing I have learned working for Ani and Sean, if Ani makes such a snap decision, she has her reasons. Which she keeps to herself.

"Good, good. Sean and I have been drumming up new ideas for the slower nights. If you have suggestions, shoot us an email. Business hasn't been bad, but I'd love it to be better."

Slow nights tend to be Monday through Thursday for Roar. Typical with most bars, clubs, and restaurants. When we changed Wednesday to ladies' night—aka Woman Crush Wednesday, Roar style—our profits doubled the first month. Tonight, Roar does Throw Back Thursday. Hours of '80s and '90s music and half-priced beer on tap. This draws more of a male crowd. Thursday sales... they tripled the first month.

Monday and Tuesday are my days off unless Gina goes on vacation. Monday and Tuesday at Roar are worse than sweaty balls stuck to your thigh. I suspect those are the days Ani wants to improve. Can't say I blame her.

"Sure thing. I'll think on it and shoot you guys an email later tonight or tomorrow."

Ani takes the deposit bag from the desk and stows it in her duffel-sized purse. "How're things otherwise? Any staff issues I need to be aware of?"

A layer of sweat builds in my armpits. Is she searching? Either that or I am reading into her words too much. *Paranoid much, Reed?* Bound to happen when you have a one-track mind.

"Not off the top of my head," I tell her. "We may need to hire more staff if you're plotting new ideas."

She taps a finger to her lip. "Good point. Let's see what we come up with and we'll go from there." Ani starts for the door. *Thank god.* I never sweat in front of my boss, but today is an exception. Just as I breathe again, she spins to face me. "Hope you and Peyton are getting along."

Whiplash. Where did that come from? And why the hell is it important?

Tread lightly, Reed. "We get on fine."

She nods as her eyes look away from me, thoughtful. "So, she's doing well?"

Why does this conversation make my stomach twist? I don't recall past conversations where Ani seemed so invested in my compatibility with Peyton.

"Yeah. The crowd loves her. Hasn't messed up orders. People are genuinely happy to see her." I want to ask Ani why all the questions, but I remain tight lipped. No need to open another door.

"Glad to hear." She turns away from me and twists the doorknob. "Have a great night, Micah." Then Ani disappears, leaving me in a state of nauseated confusion, like I just exited the county fair roller coaster.

What was that all about?

Yes, Ani and Sean vet employees to make sure everyone meets specific criteria. Hardworking, ambitious, friendly, ethical. But they also aim to hire people who will fit in with our little family. Ani asking questions about Peyton is... odd. Especially since she hired her without anyone's input.

So, why the questions?

Who the hell knows. I also don't have time to ponder her reasons. Staff will be here soon and shit needs to get done before the doors open.

I finish reports and place supply orders. After I wrap up calls to businesses interested in hosting at Roar, I exit the office. The main floor smells of lemon bleach and artificial pine. The usually dark or dimly lit room is *shield your eyes* bright as the janitorial staff deep cleans every surface.

"Hey, Ma," I say and smile at the woman older than my mother. "How are you?"

Linda stops cleaning to wrap me in a hug. Hugs from Linda are like toasty blankets while watching windy beach sunsets. All you want to do is hold on and keep her close. No doubt her kids and grandchildren love her hugs too. Roar dubbed Linda and Norm—her husband and co-cleaner —Ma and Pop of our little family. They have worked here since the beginning and always lend an ear or strong opinion.

Linda releases me and holds me at arm's length. "Looking sharp today." I don't miss the twinkle in her eye. "Hot date after work?" She waggles her brows.

I laugh and shake my head. "If I'm a good boy," I tell her and smirk.

A hand slaps my chest. "Need to find you a nice girl. One that'll make ya want more from life."

What if I don't want a *nice* girl? What if I want a fiery, rip-the-clothes-from-my-body girl? One that begs me to spank her and cries when I don't. One that loves when I grip her throat. How about one of those girls?

"If you find her" —I pat Linda's shoulder— "be sure to send her my way."

Linda looks past me and smiles. "Will do, honey." The gleam in her eye doesn't go unnoticed. But she gets back to work before I question it.

When I spin to see what caught Linda's attention, I spot Peyton. Hope it was sheer coincidence she was here when Linda stared this way, all googly eyed.

Behind the bar, Peyton has her back to the main floor and I steal the moment to check her out.

A sleeveless black shirt hugs her like a second skin. Hair up in a high ponytail with soft curls sweeping her upper back. I lick my lips as my eyes trail the sun-kissed skin along her neck and arms. The way she glides from one end of the bar to the other, reaches high and bends low… I adjust myself and take a deep breath.

She spins to prep the front side of the bar, peers up, and rolls her eyes when she catches me looking. Funny enough, my dick gets harder. Like it loves this side of her. The spirited fighter banging their gloves together in the corner of the ring. Always ready to go.

Well, guess what? Me, too, hellcat.

I stroll toward the bar, crank my neck left, then right, and prepare to have a little fun with Peyton. She pretends not to watch, but fails. Time and again, I witnessed her scurry down the bar to someone with their hand up, just in the cusp of her periphery. So, her subtle *I don't see you* bullshit won't work. Not with me.

As I approach, she keeps her eyes downcast on the limes. She cuts them with such slow precision, I picture her screaming inside her own head. The thought makes me want to laugh, but I bite back the urge. Her stubborn determination to ignore me provokes me further.

Peyton and me… there is no love. Maybe shades of like, but definitely no love. The fire between us stirs a tolerate-hate relationship. And I live for the whirling pleasure in my chest each time I antagonize her.

"Cut those limes any smaller and they'll just be peels."

Her hand freezes mid-slice as she lifts her gaze. Eyes narrow as they meet mine; a slight snarl on her lip. "How about you let me do my job and you" —she waves the knife inches from my face— "go do whatever it is you do."

I prop my forearms on the bar and lean in, the knife dangerously close to my eye. But I don't flinch or back down. "This *is* what I do."

"What? Annoy the hell out of people." She lowers the knife and massacres the limes more. "'Cause it's working," she mumbles.

The corner of my lips kick up as I bite the inside of my cheek to not laugh. "No, wench. My job is to make sure you do yours." She rolls her eyes. "Probably why Ani was asking about you today."

That gets her attention.

She sets the knife on the cutting board and peers up at me as curiosity tugs at her brow. "She asked about me?" Her voice squeaks at the end. Wonder why Ani asking about her makes her nervous?

"Mmhm. Standard stuff. How you're doing in your role. If the customers like you. If there's been any issues." I cock a brow. "And if you get along with the staff. Me included."

She swallows and her tension piques my interest.

"What did you tell her?" She tucks fallen strands of hair behind her ears, then shoves her hands in her back pockets.

I want to toy with her. Drag out the silence to inflame her uneasiness. After all the times she gave me shit, after all the times she threw daggers at me, I want her to feel a hint of discomfort before I answer.

This is me and Peyton. We go head-to-head. Give as good as we get. Purposely piss each other off and bask in the other's misery. Dangle bait and tempt the beast. I love and hate the way we bicker like juveniles. Her enthusiasm and irritation—which I'm not certain is real—fuel me on.

Do my snappy retorts give her ammunition too?

Her hands slip from her pockets, ball into fists, and rest on her hips. *Tap, tap, tap.* A foot taps the floor in sync with her head bobs. Lips pursed, eyes narrowed, Peyton is at the end of her lit fuse. And I love the surge of power it delivers.

She opens her mouth to speak, but I hold up a hand and stop her. A huff from her lips makes mine tip up.

"That you're a pain in my ass," I say with my best poker face.

Her jaw drop is priceless. "What the fuck, Micah?" *Micah, not Micky.* She scans the club as if Ani will jump out and berate her.

I let her panic to the count of ten, then put her out of her misery. "Peyton, calm down." Her dilated pupils land on me and suck me into a black hole. "I didn't actually say that to her. I may be a dick, but I would never do that without coaching you first."

Left, then right, her shoulders loosen. Her chest deflates faster than a balloon. And her eyes smooth out at the corners as her lips lose the paleness of tension.

"Why are you such an asshole?"

With a shrug, I say, "Natural talent, I suppose."

"Don't know why I believe a word that comes out of your mouth. Been nothing but bullshit since day one."

Since day one? What the hell is she talking about?

The day Ani introduced Peyton to the staff, I was all smiles. How could I not be? A gorgeous new woman to distract me while I worked. Ani must have thought the world of her to hire her on the spot. On her first night at Roar, as Ani introduced her to everyone, Peyton's eyes lit up, she smiled and said a kind *hello* to everyone. Except me. When Ani introduced me, Peyton remained straight faced and gave a lackluster wave. No verbal greeting. No smile or kindness.

Initially, I thought her disrespectful. But after a year, her behavior seems rooted in something incomprehensible. The worst part... she won't fucking tell me what about me bothers her.

"Since day one?" Peyton throws me a smug half smile. "Funny. The only hostility I recall on that first day was all you. Which I still don't get, but whatever." Before she counters me, I turn on my heel and go back to the office. "Don't need this bullshit," I mumble on the way.

The next hour, I scour mindless ideas online for Ani and Sean for the slower business days. Most of it is a crapshoot. Man Crush Monday would be a lame addition, but I won't veto it until something better pops up. Monday and Tuesday just aren't days most people want to go out. Attracting them won't be easy. But I have confidence that between the four of us—Ani, Sean, me, and Gina—we will find something better.

A knock at the door distracts the numbness of scrolling search engine results. "Come in."

The door swings open and Peyton fills the frame. Earlier, I didn't glimpse her fully behind the bar. But now, I see her crown to heel. The skintight black V-neck flashes her ample cleavage. Pants equally skintight hug her curvy hips and show off her muscular legs. Pulled altogether with heeled boots.

I fight the desire to lick my lips or adjust myself in her presence. That would give her the upper hand. Give her something to wave in my face and tease me with endlessly. Strong women are a turn-on. But the foreplay is so much better.

Clack, clack, clack. Her heels clap the concrete floor as she steps closer to the desk. Inches away, she stops, leans forward and plants her palms close enough to touch.

Don't look at her tits. Don't look at her tits.

I swallow as subtly as possible. "Something I can help you with?"

A slow grin lifts the corners of her mouth. Like she knows I struggle with her proximity. "Mmhm." But she doesn't elaborate. It pisses me off and makes me hard at the same time.

"Well…"

"You don't know?" My brows cinch together. "Guess you aren't all-knowing." *Poker face. Keep your poker face.* "Ted needs you," she says after a minute of silence.

Ted needs me? She came in here, went all temptress on me, for that?

Ted, another bouncer, works Monday to Thursday, so he isn't bored at home. All in all, Ted is a nice guy. But if he *needs to talk* to me about another one of his fishing trips, I may keel over and die a slow, boring death. I get it, the man is lonely. Just because we have the same genitalia, doesn't mean I like and do all the same activities. Sometimes, men want to swim or read, go bowling or play putt-putt. Organized and unorganized, sports aren't my jam.

"Did he say what for?"

Her eyes drift down the column of buttons on my shirt as she shakes her head. When her eyes meet mine, I detect a hint of mischief in their violet hue. "Nope." She pops the P.

The chair stutters back as I stand. And fuck my life as my eyes drop and zero in on her cleavage. *Damnit all to hell.*

I check my watch at note we have ten minutes until open. "Come on." With a hand, I gesture toward the door. "Get back to the bar and I'll go see what Ted needs."

Peyton saunters down the hall in front of me as I lock the office. A rumble rises in my chest as I witness the sway of her hips after getting an eyeful of her cleavage. Mix it with her fierce attitude and I want to fuck someone against the wall, here and now.

As I head toward Ted, Peyton goes behind the bar. When I reach him, he seems bewildered at my showing up.

"Need something, boss?"

At least some of the staff respect my position. "Peyton said you needed me for something."

Ted looks past me at what I assume is Peyton. Eyes back on me, he shakes his head. "No, I'm good. But since you're here…"

For the next nine minutes, Ted talks my ear off about his day. Fishing near the causeway. His buddies that he wants to introduce me to—he swears we will be buds in no time. All the fish they caught today. He offers to bring me some of the smoked fish tomorrow night after he cooks them. I humbly accept his generosity. May not like to bait hooked poles and catch fish, but I do eat them.

When the doors unlock, I walk behind the bar and prepare to help Peyton and Adam. After the initial rush, I sidle up next to her and smile at her sharp intake of breath.

"That was cute."

She side-eyes me. "Don't know what you're talking about." Her game face is strong tonight.

I point toward the main door. "Telling me Ted needed something. Cute."

She gives a one-shoulder shrug. "Thought that's what he said. Maybe he didn't say, 'I need Micah'. Maybe it was, 'I feed us dinner'. As in the fish he caught." Her nonchalance irritates and turns me on.

So, I turn the tables on her.

I step closer to her. Slip into her personal bubble. Invade her space. She shoots me a look of warning, but I ignore it. Instead, I push on. Breathe in her minty coconut scent and step within inches of her.

"You can admit it."

She turns to face me, her nose a breath from grazing mine, eyes narrowed. "I'll play along." A pause. "Admit what?"

My chest expands and contracts as quick as hers. Neither of us steps away. Both of us equally stubborn and unwilling to own it.

I inch impossibly closer. Kissing her would be easy. So fucking easy. "That you wanted me out here. That you wanted my attention."

Eyes locked in a silent battle of wills, now is the first time I spot small gray flecks in her vivid violet irises. Like a dusting of stars in a nebula. The contrast commands my attention. Invites me in like an old witch in the woods with cookies. I don't want to look away. Can't look away.

Then, in my periphery, her tongue darts out and wets her lips. Without second thought, my eyes drop to bear witness. Soon as her tongue disappears, her lips kick up in a wicked curve.

"Hmm…" My eyes meet hers again. "Maybe I did. Maybe not." Her shoulders lift, then drop. "Even if I did, I'd never admit it." Without shame, her eyes drop to the bulge in my pants. Her smile in response makes me sweat. "But you admit it without a word spoken."

Before I bite back, she turns on her heel and goes to the end of the bar. Where customers stand idle and tap the bar top to the beat of the music. *When the hell did the door open?*

Passing Adam, I bolt to the bathroom with a limp in my step. In the privacy of a stall, I undo my pants, whip out my dick, and jerk myself to relieve the ache.

Argh!

Why the hell does this woman rake my nerves so much? *Thrust, pump.* What spurs her on? What did I do to her? *Thrust, pump, pump.* And why can't I stop thinking about her? *Pump, thrust, pump.*

I groan as my load splashes into the bowl. And then the bathroom door swings open. I freeze and don't make a sound. Well, any other sound than my semen splashing in the toilet. At least it sounds like normal bathroom business.

After I clean myself up, I straighten my shirt and pants, then exit the stall. I open my mouth to extend a friendly greeting to whoever came in. But I slam my mouth shut before a single word leaves my lips.

"You alright?"

My arm flies up, my forefinger pointing to the door. "What are you doing in here?" I belt out. "Get out!"

Peyton crosses her arms under her breasts, pushing them up in the process. I hate that I don't want to look away, but force my eyes to hers.

Her face shifts from professional poker player to pouty schoolgirl in point five seconds. And *fuck* if it doesn't wake my body back up.

"Is poor baby Micah okay?" she asks in a mocking baby voice while looking down at my crotch.

Gah! Why is she so frustratingly sexy? I should be irritated with her. The way she taunts and teases me. The way she shamelessly checks me out, yet acts as if I turn her off.

But I see the way her nipples pebble beneath her top. The way she steps closer and her breath comes in quicker bursts. Deny all she wants, but Peyton craves me too. And as bad as I ache to give it to her, I refuse. I refuse to be the one who caves first. Who gives in to the obvious chemistry and tension between us. Nope, my feet will stay firmly planted in place.

"Maybe you should come closer and inspect him yourself?" I cock my brow in challenge.

For a beat, she just stares at me wide eyed. The cogs in her mind spin over and over as she searches for a snappy response. A laugh bubbles up my chest and I bite my cheek to stave off my amusement.

When the pieces click into place in her mind, she grinds her teeth. "A little much, don't you think? Ani might not like hearing management is sexually harassing employees."

Banter with Peyton is similar to walking through a minefield. Always on alert, mindful of where you step and ears focused for any little sound. And now it would appear I stepped on a land mine. Can I defuse the situation?

"You're joking, right?" I shake my head and chuckle.

She slaps her hands to her hips and narrows her eyes. "Do I look like I'm joking?"

Time to test the water. "Go on, call her. I'd love to hear what you tell her." Her knuckles whiten as her shirt stretches at her hips. "*Hey Ani, I lipped off to Micah. Then followed him into the men's room and asked him about his dick. But then he made a sexually suggestive comment to me and my feelings got hurt,*" I whine out in an attempt to mock her. Her face grows redder by the second. "I'll stand next to the phone when you call. That way I can explain the real situation when you're done bitching."

Head tipped back, Peyton screams at the ceiling. Splotchy redness coats her throat and chest. I stand frozen in place, unsure what to do.

"You're such an asshole." She pauses, her eyes sweep down and up my body, then her lip curls. "Never thought I'd be this disgusted by you. Guess things never change, do they?" Then she storms out of the bathroom and leaves me stunned.

What the fuck was that?

Jesus, this woman frustrates the hell out of me. If someone threw hundreds of mixed signals into a blender and pressed liquefy, that might come close to what swirls in my head right now. Maybe.

I wash my hands and do a quick appearance check in the mirror while drying them. If Peyton wants to play hardball… game on. After all the bullshit surrounding my breakup with Rochelle, I refuse to bow or break for another woman. Ever.

Hours of '80s and '90s music drone on. At least the deejay plays enough variety we don't hear the same song until three or four weeks later. I go about the night as per usual. Helping behind the bar. Schmoozing the customers. Sparking conversations with pretty blondes. For the most part, the slower days draw an older crowd. Monday through Thursday has more of the thirty-plus crowd. The weekend is more the twentysomethings. I enjoy both.

Two hours in and I can't stop talking with a woman at the bar. Intelligent, gorgeous, and flirty as hell. From what I learned thus far, she works in corporate accounting and recently broke up with her boyfriend.

"He was too clingy," she says with an eye roll. "I'm forty, for crying out loud. Not fourteen."

My type of woman. "Some men don't understand the need for independence. I get it, though."

We chat and flirt and make plans for when the bar closes. Her maturity turns me on and is a nice change from the childish, younger women. I love a woman who knows what she wants and goes after it. A woman who stands tall and proud and self-sufficient. All qualities I deem sexy.

Down the bar, Peyton does her best to not look my way. She flirts and laughs and talks with several men. And as focused as I am on the woman in front of me, my eyes and ears drift to the other end of the bar every other minute.

Don't let her dominate your thoughts, Reed. No woman owns you.

The crowd thins as the evening comes to a close. I follow my usual routine and start cleaning and closing out the registers. When all but the blonde leave, I speed up the closing process.

"In a hurry for disease transmission," Peyton barks, loud enough for the blonde to hear. I clench my jaw and ignore her. But she doesn't give up. "Baby Micah feeling better? Know he had issues earlier."

Done. So fucking done.

I stomp over to her and immediately step into her space. "What's the matter, hellcat? Jealous?" Note, this is the first time I call her hellcat to her face. Usually, I reserve that nickname for when it's just me, my fist, and my cock.

She scoffs. "Please. Jealous?" A finger jabs her sternum. "Why would I be jealous?" I don't miss the slight crack in her voice.

I take a step back and wave a hand up and down my body. "Because you hate how much you want me. You hate that you love when I piss you off."

"Cut the music," Peyton calls out as she slashes her fingers in front of her throat. The music dies a second later. "You think I *want* you? After all the bullshit you've put me through." Word by word, her voice escalates. "News flash, asshole. The world doesn't revolve around you." Her eyes zero in on the blonde, who looks slightly alarmed. "You're aware he fucks two plus different women a week, right? Might want to save yourself now."

The blonde slaps me with her glare. Before I offer an answer, she shoulders her purse and walks toward the door.

Every cell in my body explodes with rage. She doesn't want me? But she doesn't want me with anyone else either? Did someone pick me up by the ankles, flip me upside down, and shake me? Because I have no clue what the fuck is going on.

Back in her space, I jab my finger in her face. "What's your problem, Peyton?"

"You," she screams. "You are my fucking problem."

My feet stumble back two steps. "Why?" I want to yell, but my traitorous voice is feeble and small.

"Because you ruin everything you touch." She pauses and

shakes her head with glassy eyes. "Because you ruin lives and don't care enough to remember."

I narrow my eyes and *really* look at her. "What... I don't know what you're talking about."

She huffs and shoves past me. Feet pounding against the concrete floor as she heads toward the back. I follow with no clue what is happening. She retrieves her purse from the locker and shoulders it.

Before I ask where she is going, she knocks her shoulder with mine and exits.

"I hate you," she screams.

What the actual fuck just happened?

six

PEYTON

"Asshole," I scream as I slam the car door and bang my fists against the steering wheel. "Why? Why do I let him get to me like this?"

Question of the century. Too bad no one answers it.

I start the car, but don't leave right away. My eyes drift shut and I work to recenter myself. After a few deep breaths, my blood pressure lowers and my body sags with slight relief.

Every now and again, I question my sanity. Question why I keep working at Roar when Micah drives me mad. Question why I put up with his shit four days a week. Then I remind myself of the endgame. The discussion Ani and I had about the future. A future I refuse to let Micah Reed steal from me.

Digging through my purse, I locate my phone and send Ani a quick text.

Heads-up. I left before close.

Anything I should be concerned about?

Oh, ya know. Micah just being Micah.

He said you were getting along. Want me to talk to him?

No and no. But I'll let you know if I change my mind.

Hey! Do me a favor. Think up ideas for Mondays and Tuesdays for the bar and text them to me.

On it. Miss your face.

After my phone connects to the car audio, I crank the music, roll down the windows, and drive home. The loud lyrics, thumping bass, and wind on my cheeks slowly wipe away the anger Micah brought to the surface. And before long, my mood is ten times better as I park next to Reese's car.

Every light in the apartment appears to be on as I unlock the door and walk in. I pray Reese doesn't have a houseguest tonight. Not that I mind the company. My silent plea is answered when the door swings open and I spy Reese on the couch with a platter of tacos.

His eyes land on me as his lips freeze around the taco. "Home early," he mumbles.

Reese is exactly what I need. A soothing presence with the occasional laugh. An ear to listen as I gripe about life and words to give advice as I navigate what to do next.

"Any more of those?" I point to the taco.

He takes a bite and chews a few times. "In the kitchen."

I toss my purse on the floor, dash to the kitchen, and inhale the taco-scented deliciousness. I stuff the tacos full, add refried beans and cheese to the plate, then park myself next to Reese on the couch.

"Whatcha watching?"

"*The Haunting of Bly Manor*. Want me to start it over? Started it just before you walked in."

I shake my head. "Just tell me what I missed."

The next hour passes with the slow demolition of tacos as we can't look away from the screen. When the episode ends, I hope Reese wants to watch the next. But he presses pause and stares at me without a word. The air thickens and I have the sudden urge to cower. To shrink in the corner like a scolded child.

"You gonna tell me? Or do I have to pull it out of you?"

This is what happens when someone has known you as long as we have. Almost twenty years of friendship equals knowing someone better than you know yourself. And Reese reads every emotion I have better than anyone.

"Another day at the office, dear," I joke and he rolls his eyes. "Micah was in rare form tonight. And…" I pause, tip my head back and stare at the imperfections in the ceiling. "And I blew up." I level my head and meet his gaze. "I left work early. Ani knows, so at least I'm covered there."

Reese collects our plates and wanders to the kitchen without a word. Water splashes against plates and pans and utensils. Then the dishwasher kicks on. A moment later, Reese walks back in with two pints of ice cream and spoons. A man after my own heart.

Neither of us speaks as we dig into the creamy confections. Mint chocolate chip for me and cookies 'n cream for Reese. If one thing remains the same, it's our favorite ice cream flavors. Sure, we eat other flavors. But why not just enjoy the one you love?

"Sorry you have to deal with him," Reese says around his spoon.

I nod, swallow my bite, and twist to face him on the couch. "The worst part of it all… he doesn't remember."

Reese goes wide eyed. "Any of it? How is that even possible?"

My shoulders lift to my ears. "Your guess is as good as mine. I get how people forget from early childhood. But teen years are different. You make conscious decisions then. You *choose* to be nice or cruel."

"True. Maybe something happened to his brain." Reese laughs and I can't help but join in.

"No doubt." I sigh, stare down at the ice cream as I scrape the spoon over the surface. "I may not look the exact same, but how does he not know who I am?" The handful of times he's been in my face recently, how does he not *see* me? The goth chick he teased and bullied for three years.

The screen saver on the television flickers off and we continue eating our ice cream. Just as I scoop a heaping spoonful, Reese steals my pint and takes it back to the kitchen. "Hey!" I protest around the melting minty cream.

He returns to the living room, plops down on the couch and grabs hold of my biceps. "I have an idea." His warm, tawny-brown eyes sparkle as his lips kick up in a devilish smile.

"Don't know what you have in mind, but I'm suddenly scared."

The deep chortle I have come to love echoes from Reese's chest. "No need to be scared, sunshine. You'll like it."

"Says you. Bad enough I have to deal with Micah's annoying ass at work. I don't need anyone else adding to the problem or baiting him."

Reese gasps as he slaps a hand to his chest. "When have I

ever made things worse?" He cocks a brow. When I don't answer, he continues. "Exactly, I haven't. Trust me, please."

Do I want to put Micah in his place? Hell yes, I do. But I also don't want to cringe every time I walk inside Roar. I love my actual job. Reese stirring the pot could cause future problems.

"Fine," I say with heavy exaggeration. "What do you have in mind?"

For the next thirty minutes, Reese spills his plan. During the first minutes, I wince. A lot. My forehead sore and tense from pinching. A slight headache forms beneath my brows. And my eyes beg to close for the night. Like a good friend, though, I sit and listen to every word.

"Sound like a plan?"

Actually, his plan does sound fun. Reese was never on the receiving end of Micah's bullshit, but he heard all the gossip. In high school, rumors and artifice pass faster than STDs. Although none of the shit was said about him, it impacted him as if it was his name and "slut" written on the walls. Ironic how the tide shifts.

"Yeah." I lean over and hug him hard. "Thanks for always being here for me. You're the best friend a girl could have."

We rise from the couch and head for our respective rooms. "Don't go getting all soft on me now. Need you in tough-bitch mode tomorrow night."

I salute him. "Yes, sir." His laugh is the last thing I hear before he shoves me in my room and shuts the door. "Good night," I yell into the darkness.

"Go to sleep, sunshine," he says before his door clicks shut.

～

The energy inside Roar buzzes more than usual. But the buzz is nothing compared to the adrenaline in my veins. Not sure if it's the crowd or the fact Reese will be here soon.

The spring break crowds fizzled out over the last two weeks. Now we get a slight lull until late May. The lighter traffic is a nice reprieve. Just means I have to work harder for the extra tips.

For the most part, Micah has distanced himself from me tonight. But it won't last long. When nine o'clock hits, the crowd always triples. Should really talk to Ani about getting an additional bartender for Friday and Saturday, even if just for a few hours.

Beer flows freely from the taps. Colorful fruity drinks get adorned with pierced cherries and citrus on plastic swords. And cash tips fill the jars behind the bar.

Just as I deliver a drink, I spy Reese at the end of the bar. I thank the man who tips me and move down the line to Reese.

I lift the flap at the end of the bar and step out to hug Reese. His arms wrap around me like the summer sun and I sigh, relieved he's here. Since the summer between seventh and eighth grade, Reese has always been my person. The one I could go to with anything and everything. We don't hide the truth from each other. And our shared truths are full spectrum. Nothing left out.

"Glad you made it," I mutter against his chest.

"I'd never let—"

"Peyton," Micah barks and I stiffen. I keep my eyes on Reese and steady my urge to scream. "You planning to work tonight? Or make out with the customers?"

Several sets of eyes home in on me and my face heats. *Fucking asshole.*

"You go," Reese says. "The night is still young." A

sinister smile stretches his lips and tips up the corners of his eyes.

I spin around, step behind the bar, and bark back at Micah. "What? You the only one allowed to get handsy with customers?" I hold my hands up in surrender and push out my lips. "Sorry, *Micky*. Didn't know the rules were lopsided."

"Just get to fucking work," he bites out, then storms to the opposite end of the bar.

Over the next hour, I make and pour countless drinks. A rainbow of colors flash and dance over exposed skin and gyrating bodies. Bass vibrates my bones and treble sings in my bloodstream. I get in my groove, dancing behind the bar as I fill orders. Every fifteen minutes, I chat and fake flirt with Reese. It reminds me of when we turned twenty-one and we would use each other to fend off undesirable hookups.

When a club favorite song comes on, half of the Roar crowd loses it and heads for the dance floor. With the bar quieter a minute, I hang out at the end with Reese.

"You bored yet?" I tease.

He throws his head back and laughs harder than necessary. All part of the game. "Nah, sunshine. Been scoping out the eye candy. Eye fucking a few."

I shake my head and chuckle. "And how will this" —I gesture between the two of us— "work if you leave with someone else?"

Reese leans across the bar and curls a finger at me. I lift up on the bar and meet him in the middle, our lips a breath apart.

Reese and I, we will never be anything other than best friends. We tried more once and it felt wrong. So, we went back to how we have always been. Besties.

But that is not to say we won't kiss on the lips for extenuating circumstances. Circumstances such as this. A kiss between us is just that—a kiss. Nothing sexual, just two sets of lips pressing together. Like acting, and only when necessary.

"He can't keep his eyes off you," he says, only loud enough for me to hear. "And if I want to hook up tonight, I'll just tell whoever that I'm here to help make some dipshit jealous for my friend. Don't worry about me."

Reese closes the space between us and kisses me. He and I both know it is all for show. And I think we put on one hell of a show.

Question is, does Micah fall for the facade? If so, does it piss him off? That's the question I need answered.

Seven

MICAH

Who the fuck is this guy? Who is this motherfucker with his lips on Peyton?

And why does seeing her kiss another guy make my vision red?

I grip the bar, knuckles white as pain shoots up my forearm. A spear lances me in the chest. Spreads fire through my middle. But I take hold of the pain and squeeze it tight in my palm. Shape it into a weapon. Hot and heavy swirls of green in my fist.

Call me a hypocrite, I don't give a fuck. But Peyton won't be sucking face with some prick. Not in front of me, anyway. Yes, I own my whorish ways. Yes, society doesn't degrade manwhores the same as women. Only so much I can do about that. And yes, my inner supreme asshole is about to make an appearance.

Whether it is jealousy or the fact she won't cave to my advances or that I can't figure out why she hates me so much, the charade has gone on long enough. Doesn't matter if I have flirted with the same woman all night. I won't condone Peyton and some fuckboy.

"Peyton," I yell down the bar. She continues to kiss mister tall, dark and possessive, ignoring me. But I am not having it. "Peyton," I yell louder. "Time to quit playing with your fuck toy and do your job."

Several sets of eyes land on me and I bite my inside cheek. Adam sidles up to my right. "Boss, might want to go over and talk to her," he suggests with a quiet hiss. Adam means well and I don't want to dole my skewed emotions out on him.

I shoulder slap him in thanks and nod. "Sorry for the outburst." Kaylynn, working the far end of the bar, forces a smile my way. Scrubbing a hand over my face, I give her a sad smile and mouth *sorry*.

My eyes shoot down to the end where Peyton lingers. Thank god she no longer has her tongue shoved down some guy's throat. Though, every other second, she makes eyes at him. Smiles so big I swear her face may split in two. Has she smiled this much before? Can't think of a time when she glowed like this.

Has she smiled at *me* before? I sift through night after night. Replay shift after shift. Not a single night flashes through my mind where Peyton smiled. Not at me, anyway.

Sure, she smiles and laughs and teases other men in the bar. But never once has she done that with me as the recipient. With me, she spits vitriol and abhorrence and repulsion.

More than once, Peyton has suggested I dig deep for answers. Indicated we share history during some point in our lives. I have yet to peg down when we met or when I knew her. It has me second-guessing her and the possibility she has me confused with someone else.

The spear beneath my ribs thrusts deeper. Tightens as it twists and digs. Burns as I consider the prospect of what I may have done to Peyton in the past. Something wretched enough to warrant her immediate hate.

But how can I apologize for missing moments? How can I redeem myself when I don't know what I have done?

I stop three stools down from Peyton and fill a drink order. Then I swallow my pride. Something I haven't done in years.

"Peyton…" I say, loud enough to be heard, but softer than usual.

Eyes focused on the drink she pours, she ignores my call. But I don't budge. After she serves and thanks the customer, she spins to face me and plants her hands on her hips.

"What, Micah? What is it you need that can't wait?" She waves a hand down the bar. "You have eyes. And I have work to do."

Why can we never have civil conversations? Just now, I planned to apologize. But her bitterness dissolves the apology on my tongue like acid.

"You're right. Wanted to offer an olive branch, but nah." Her eyes widen and I wonder if she regrets not hearing what I had to say. Oh well. "Get back to work. And quit fucking around."

I turn my back to her. "The day you apologize, the day you offer me kindness…" My feet are tree roots anchored to the earth below. I don't look back, but can't move until she finishes speaking. "That day will mark history." Now I peer over my shoulder and furrow my brow. "The day Micah Reed says something nice about me. That's a day I'll never forget."

What am I missing? Wish I fucking knew. Unfortunately, now is not the time to relive the last thirty-two years of my life.

Peyton goes back to work and I exit the bar to do rounds in the club.

I walk the perimeter of Roar. Check in with the servers and bouncers as per usual. Hang out by the door with Ted and catch up on his life. He and his wife recently welcomed their second child. When there is a lull in the line, he takes his phone from his pocket and shows me pictures.

"Here she is," Ted all but squeals with delight. "Baby Rose."

Image after image, he scrolls through with a heart-stopping smile. Pictures of a pink bundle in a bassinet. Pictures of their three-year-old son, Theo, holding his baby sister with pure awe on his face. Ted with baby Rose. His wife cradling her. And so many family photos.

Ted stares down at the screen as if nothing but those three people exist. And part of me wonders what that feeling is like. Aside from Shelly, my parents and extended family are all I know. But familial love doesn't compare to love that smacks you in the chest and doesn't let go. Love so powerful, you lose all sense of morality. You don't know which way is up or down—and it doesn't matter.

Once upon a time, I loved Rochelle. The sentiment never passed either of our lips—thank god—but the emotion settled comfortably in my chest. My thoughts sparsely drifted to the image of wedding bells, but I wanted more with her than a notarized document bonding us. I wanted to experience life and the world beside her. Unfortunate for me, she just wanted a younger fuckboy.

"She's beautiful, Ted." I lay a hand on his shoulder and squeeze. "You did good. Congrats to you and yours."

I continue my leisure rounds and park myself in a corner. One song after another plays as I people watch. When I glance across the club and spot Peyton laughing with the guy again, I groan.

What irritates me most with Peyton is the not knowing. The invisible truth that hangs in the atmosphere between us. That she won't help me find the missing puzzle piece and snap it in place.

People dislike each other all the time. But her anger with me is rooted deep. Stuck in place and unwilling to budge.

I push off the wall and weave through the crowd. Before I make it to the bar, a hand wraps around my arm and stops me. I turn to see a slightly younger, pretty brunette. Her smile lifts some of my weighted thoughts.

"Want to dance?" she shouts as her other hand grabs the opposite arm.

The distraction she could provide has me agreeing without hesitation. Music swims around us as she swings her hips left and right. Ass pressed against my groin, hands over her head. I grab her hips and tug her impossibly closer. Close my eyes. Get lost in the rhythm, her body plastered to mine. Her head tips to the side and I press my lips to the spot beneath her ear.

Fingers comb through the back of my hair and fist the strands. With a slight shift, she lifts her lips to mine. My hands glide across her body, fingers splayed on her belly. A moan rumbles from her mouth and vibrates my chest.

In the middle of the dance floor, I mouth fuck this woman. Taste sweet strawberries on her tongue. Inhale the floral scent on her skin. Graze her heated skin as she spins to face me and I slide a hand up her back until I fist the hair at her nape.

I love and loathe everything about this woman.

No doubt, she is beautiful. I love her bravery and extroversion. How she takes what she wants and doesn't shy away from it. How she owns who she is and flaunts her charm. Her boldness turns me on more than anything.

But... she isn't my type.

It is no secret, I love blondes. Don't get me wrong, there is room for every woman in my world. But the women I find most attractive all look the same. They all look like Peyton.

Fuck my life for realizing this while I kiss another woman.

I break the kiss and hate myself for my wayward thoughts. "I have to work." She tilts her head with narrowed eyes. "Club manager."

She pushes out her lower lip and makes weepy eyes. Damn, she is cute. I resist the urge to lean in and suck her lip.

"We were having so much fun," she says.

Yes, we were. "And we can have more fun later, if you want. But it'll have to wait until after close."

Leaning in, she presses a chaste kiss to my lips. "I'm good with that."

I take a step back and run my hands down her arms until I reach her hands. Another step back. "Catch me later. Either behind the bar or wandering the club."

She winks and I walk off. The brunette may not be my first choice, but I will never turn down a beautiful woman who pursues me.

As I near the bar, I spot Peyton talking with the guy again. All smiles and laughter. It pisses me the hell off. Time to cut the rope. She may know him, but I don't give a fuck.

When Peyton sees me, her spine stiffens and she steps away from the guy. Perfect.

I insert myself between the guy and the customer at the bar beside him. "Hey, man." Slowly, he faces me. "You know Peyton?"

The smug bastard smirks. "Yeah, we go way back." He doesn't elaborate and I grind my molars.

"*Great*," I mumble with a layer of cynicism. "Then I'm sure she's told you how busy this place gets." He cocks a brow, but doesn't respond otherwise. "And that she needs to focus on paying customers."

He lifts a tumbler of Jack to his lips and sips it. "Yep. Last I checked, I paid for this drink. So…"

Who the hell is this guy? My fingers curl into fists at my sides. In and out, I breathe deep and remind myself of where I am and the position I hold. The last thing I need is to lose my shit over a woman who mind-fucks me four days a week. The last thing I need is to lose my job over defending said woman who royally hates me.

"So… as one of the managers, I ask you to not hoard my staff when she has a job to do."

He glances down the bar where Peyton pours and blends drinks faster than Adam and Kaylynn combined. "Seems like she has everything under control, boss man." He sips his drink behind a smug grin.

Don't know who this fucker is, but he grates my last nerve each time his lips part. "Yes, unless she's over here talking with you. So, do me a favor, *friend*. Let her do what she's getting paid to do. Her job."

I push off the bar and turn to walk away. But his words stop me. "Oh, I'll let her do her job. Now… and later tonight." I grind my molars, but don't face him. "Cheers, boss man."

For the next hour, I occupy my mind with paperwork in the office. Yes, coming in here is a pussy move. But if I didn't step away and calm down, things would get ugly. Real quick. If I dive headfirst into a different task, the distraction will help extinguish the fire in my blood.

Calm and collected, I head back out to the club. I make my rounds and settle in behind the bar between Adam and Kaylynn. One song blends into another and the drinks flow easily. Peyton and I keep our distance, but she never leaves my sight. Neither does her *friend* at the end of the bar.

As closing time nears, the crowd thins. The brunette from the dance floor sips a strawberry daiquiri twenty feet from the bar. Adam and Kaylynn start the bar closing cleanup while Peyton preps to leave. Friday and Saturday nights, the three of them rotate who stays past close. And tonight, Peyton leaves early.

Finished with her tasks, she lifts the bar flap and heads down the hall to get her things. Before I walk after her, she reappears and loops her arms with *him*. I stare after them as they head for the exit.

My eyes still on them, everything turns red when *he* peers over his shoulder, meets my gaze and winks with a smug smirk on his lips.

And then, they vanish. A chill blankets me as I question if Peyton actually does know him. Or did she just leave with a strange man? A man who seemed all too eager.

The protector in me wants to run outside and chase after them. To tell Peyton not to leave with some random guy who claims to know her. But I don't. Can't. Instead, I stay put and finish my routine tasks.

When I leave, it is with a brunette on my arm. A woman I don't want to spend time with, but will, in order to distract myself from the woman I want but can't have.

eight

PEYTON

Best night at work. Ever.

Reese and I walk out of Roar in a fit of laughter and clenching our stomachs. Every minute behind the bar with Micah tonight was nothing short of perfection. I bit my tongue so often it went numb. He fired round after round at me, but I restrained more than normal to get a rise out of him.

Each time I seemed unaffected by his words, his jaw flexed and face reddened. His response was quite intriguing.

Micah spends more time barking versus biting. Spends more time whoring himself around the club than caring about me or the staff. Tonight was different. Micah flashed a new side of himself. An anomalistic side.

The possessive, semi-protective side of Micah Reed made an appearance. And it has me seeing him in a new light. A light similar to the early days, before he jumped on the Triple M train and ruined my teen life.

Reese and I reach my car and I unlock it. "Food?" he asks as he unhooks my arm from his.

"Definitely."

We agree to meet at our favorite twenty-four-hour diner

near home. Once I crank the engine, Reese jogs over to his car and gets in. Within minutes, we drive over the bridge, crossing the Bay and wind through Clearwater.

The diner is busy as always. Bright lights shine down on worn booths and paper placemats with crossword puzzles, word searches, and hangman. A coffee mug full of crayons sits next to a napkin dispenser, salt and pepper shakers, sweetener packets, and a half-used bottle of ketchup on the table. Fresh brewed coffee scents the air with a hint of bacon grease and toasted bread. Mumbled chatter, the clinking of cutlery, and the cook calling finished orders echo throughout the dining area. The hostess, an older woman with a messy updo and a pencil behind her ear, hands us laminated menus.

"Andy will be over in a minute." Then she resumes her position near the front door, rolling cutlery in paper napkins.

Don't know why either of us reads over the menu, we always order the same thing. But we read the long list of greasy goodness anyway. When Andy arrives, Reese orders the western omelet with home fries and I get the two pancake breakfast with an egg, crispy bacon and hash browns. Decaf coffee for both of us. Andy takes our menus and waltzes off with exaggerated enthusiasm.

"He has it bad for you," Reese says after the coffee carafe and mugs are left at the table.

I fill my mug and ignore the fact Reese refers to Micah. Grab a packet of raw sugar from the caddy, shake it, tear it open and add it to the coffee. Peel back the lid on two creamer pods and dump them in the mug. Stir with more noise than necessary, all while staring at the decaffeinated beverage and not Reese.

I lift the mug to my lips and blow on the surface. "What

makes you think that?" The coffee sears my tongue but tastes like heaven.

Reese fixes his coffee how he likes, then stares at me as if to say, *"You're joking, right?"* He doesn't, though. "Let's count them off, shall we?"

I roll my eyes so hard it causes ocular muscle pain. With a wave of my hand, I say, "If it makes you happy, enlighten me."

For a moment, he leaves me hanging. Sips his coffee and holds my gaze with a hint of mischief. I white knuckle my mug and this makes him laugh.

"Fine," he huffs out. "One, the man can't keep his eyes off you. Literally. Every time I looked his way, his eyes were on you or us."

"That doesn't mean anything." Micah stares at anything with boobs.

"Maybe not to you, but guys don't look—not like he was —unless there is definite interest." I shake my head and gesture for him to continue. "Two, the way he tries to steer you from men. It's quite telling. Possessive."

"You mean when he barks orders? That's just because he's an asshole."

Reese sets his mug down and shakes with laughter. "No, my dear, sweet best friend. He barks at you, and only you, when you give other men attention. It's his way of making you stop and telling the guy to back off."

Why can't men just be straightforward? Although I would still despise Micah, maybe the intensity of said hatred would be less if he were honest. Honesty says a lot about character. And when it comes to Micah, honesty may tip the scales in his favor. Slightly.

"Whatever you say. Still think it's because he's an asshole."

Reese reaches across the table and lays his hand over mine. "Not denying that. But you should accept the fact he has a thing for you. Even if it makes your skin crawl, it doesn't make it less true."

I open my mouth to argue, but the server interrupts as he sets plates between us. My mouth waters and stomach grumbles. All thoughts of work and Micah and his possible infatuation with me go out the window as I dig in.

I stab the last bit of pancake, swipe it through the last of the yolk and bacon grease, then shove it in my mouth. *So freaking good.* Tonight, I will sleep solid. I swallow down the last of my coffee and we settle the bill.

"See you back home," I tell Reese as we each get in our cars.

The drive home takes less than ten minutes. And some of the conversation with Reese at the diner rolls back in. I don't know how to feel about any of it, so I shove it away for another time.

Reese parks in his space as I hop out of my car. Thankfully, neither of us has to be up early. Late nights/early mornings aren't new to either of us, but Reese aims to be in bed—not sleeping—before midnight. I regularly tease him about his *old man status.*

Inside, we hug and go opposite directions at the end of the hall.

"Night, sunshine."

"Night, Reese. Thanks again for tonight."

He bops me on the nose. "That's what best guy friends are for."

I go about my nighttime routine and soon switch my

bedside lamp off. As the light fades to darkness, my mind flips on and runs ramped up.

Reese's words from the diner repeat in my head. *"The man can't keep his eyes off you. Literally."*

Does Micah look at me *that* often? Not possible. Reese only noticed Micah looking because he was keeping an eye out for such things.

"The way he tries to steer you from men. It's quite telling. Possessive."

Is Micah really trying to keep me away from other men? Does he actually believe he has a claim on me? Ha! Not a fat chance in hell, Micah Reed.

What I don't understand is why Micah would feel possessive. On day one at Roar, I radiated nothing but abhorrence when we were introduced. He felt it, too. Mom always said hate is a strong word. I use the term sparingly and only associate it with a handful of people. Since age fourteen, I have hated Micah Reed. He was cold and callous and hurt others to make himself look good.

Question is… is it time to grow up? Is it time to let go of teenage pain and trauma? Is it time to give someone I have loathed more than a decade a fresh start?

Maybe.

I don't want to live life with hate in my heart. Don't want to be someone who focuses solely on all the negative aspects. If I let go of the past so easily, does it make me weak?

Part of me says yes. By giving in, all the hurtful words, constant teasing and bullying… it feels as if I accept them. That Micah and those bitches all get a free pass. I may be the bigger person by extending forgiveness, but I don't want to be a doormat.

The other part of me says no and states, in order to grow

and evolve into a better version of myself, I must make peace with my past. To make peace, I have to battle my inner demons. The voices of doubt that tell me to build a wall around my heart, to keep people like teenage Micah Reed out. People who know nothing about me, yet hand out opinions like Halloween candy. People who know nothing about my life, yet they mock and judge and lie about me.

I am not that girl anymore. That fragile teenage girl who only wanted to be accepted for who she was. Now, I stand tall. Strong—physically and mentally.

Perhaps it is time to expand my strength to emotionally as well. Perhaps it is time to be the bigger person and give Micah Reed a chance. A chance he probably doesn't deserve, but maybe needs.

Tomorrow, I will offer up his second chance. How he handles it is up to him.

~

"You planning on handing out heart attacks tonight?"

I glance over my shoulder in the body-length mirror at Reese in my doorway. His eyes rake over the length of my body before he whistles. The reaction is exactly what I hoped for, and I laugh.

"One. Maybe." I spin to face him. "Think it'll work?"

In three long strides, Reese stops in front of me and grips my shoulders. "Yes. And if not, someone might need to visit an optometrist." He shakes his head. "Damn, sunshine. You don't play fair. Best have 911 on speed dial."

I step out of his touch and go to my dresser. Add a few spritzes of perfume to my wrists and at the base of my skull. Snap on my favorite leather bracelets. Swipe one last coat of clear gloss on my lips. I have never been the type to wear a lot of makeup, but I do like to accentuate the features I love about myself. So, my eyes and lips always get attention. Even if minimal.

After I fetch my four-inch-heel boots from the closet, I plop on the bed and finish getting ready.

Not sleeping the first three hours I had lain in bed last night, I devised a plan for work tonight. Let's just say I will test Reese's theory about Micah. And in order to do that, I have to be on my best behavior. I have to be the first one to hold up the surrender flag.

But there is no reason to not look like the smoking-hot temptress I am. Mom always said use what life has given you. She probably meant talent and skill, but I reserve the right to believe she silently included beauty too.

I shoulder my purse and head for the front door. Reese follows in my wake. "Never said I played fair. Do you blame me?"

The corners of his mouth droop slightly. "No, of course not. But it wouldn't be right if I didn't give you some shit before you left."

"True." I turn and hug him. "Thanks for everything."

His arms tighten around my middle. "What'd I do?"

I loosen my grip and kiss his cheek. "Nothing. Just being you. And that's exactly what I need. So, thank you. You really are the bestest best friend."

As the words leave my lips, Reese slaps my ass. Hard. "Get out of here, sunshine."

I rub my butt and jab a finger in his chest. "Damn, that stings."

"Good. Now go." He shoos me out the door. "And you better tell me everything in the morning."

Pivoting slightly, I lift a hand to my forehead in mock salute. "Yes, sir. I'll have my report on your desk at oh-three-hundred hours."

He shakes his head. "You're such a weirdo. Love you."

"Love you, too" I blow him a kiss before he shuts the door.

Now, on to the most challenging night at work. Hope my claws don't come out.

nine

MICAH

Have I stepped into another dimension? Either that or I am seeing shit. I rub my eyes and blink a few times.

No fucking clue.

Glass bottles clang against loud music as they get tossed in bins. Sweat mixed with perfume and alcohol floats through the air. Colored lights dance down from the ceiling and bounce over exposed skin and gyrating bodies.

Roar is in full swing, as busy as any other Saturday night, yet I don't see or hear any of it.

Because Peyton fucking Alexander just smiled. At me. Smiled.

Has hell frozen over and I missed the memo?

"Can you hand me that jigger?" Her dainty finger points to the steel measuring device less than six inches from my hand. But I don't move. She waves a hand in front of my spaced-out eyes, a bright as sunshine smile on her face. "Hello? Earth to Micah. The jigger."

I shake my bewilderment away and hand it over. "Sorry."

She doesn't bitch or scowl. Nope. She simply laughs it off. "No worries. Thank you."

For a moment, I scan down the bar and throughout the club. Looking for something else out of place. A camera, maybe. Or people watching us as this whole turn of events takes place. I wait for the shoe to drop. For everyone to burst out laughing at my expense.

But everything looks… normal.

Then a knife stabs me between the shoulder blades as realization hits. A thought I don't *want* taking up residence in my mind, but would make sense, if true. Because, let's face it, Peyton is an attractive woman. An attractive woman who left here with a guy last night. A guy I have never seen at Roar but swears he's known her years.

Is Peyton happy because she hooked up with him?

My stomach churns and I turn my back on the bar. I grab the back counter and take shallow breaths with my eyes closed. Swallow down the bitterness on my tongue, the thick lump in my throat.

No woman, aside from family, has bent me out of shape. Has riled me up or tossed me to the wayside. But for some unknown reason, Peyton does. She spirals in like a tornado, tears my world up, then leaves me dazed in the aftermath.

Her combative side is one I enjoy, though. The unpredictability and sarcasm and tough as nails exterior. Where others may see her as a bitch, I see her as fierce. And damn if that doesn't make me want her more.

But this…

A hand rests on my shoulder and I glance to see the owner. Of course. Peyton.

"You okay?" Her violet irises scan my eyes, my cheeks, my lips with an edge of concern. "You look kind of pale." She hasn't taken her hand off me yet and I don't know if I should enjoy it or freak out.

"I'm fine," I croak out, then clear my throat. "Just need some water. Probably something from dinner." The lie rolls off my tongue with too much ease.

"Go sit in the back a minute. We'll be fine." Then her hand slides down between my shoulder blades and rubs small, gentle circles. I close my eyes and relish the touch until she removes her hand.

When I no longer feel the heat of her body near mine, I turn and exit the bar. I rush to the office, plop down in the chair, plant my elbows on the desk and my head in my hands. I take slow and steady breaths. In through my nose, out through my mouth.

What is going on? And why does this change in Peyton put me on edge?

Since the beginning, she has been nothing short of hostile toward me. Is it weird that her wrath is something I look forward to? After a year of working together, her malevolence is all I know.

Over the next hour, I occupy my mind with the staff schedule. Stare at the empty boxes on the spreadsheet and will them to fill in. Then I remember Ani asked for fresh ideas for the slower days. I switch my focus and zone out as I search the web.

A soft knock, followed by the office door opening, snaps me out of my incessant scrolling. Page after page and I still haven't found worthwhile ideas to spruce up Mondays and Tuesdays.

I look up to see Peyton smiling near the door. As heart stopping as her smile is, seeing it so much in one night has me dizzy.

"Getting a little crazy out there. Might want to do your rounds and help Adam and Kaylynn after."

Any other night, she would bark at me for slacking off. She would have stormed in here without knocking, stepped up to the desk, slammed her hands down, and bitched at me for not doing my job. But not tonight. Tonight, she offers suggestions and uses polite tones.

"Yeah, sure. Thanks for letting me know."

"No problem." And then she leaves and closes the door behind her. Quietly.

I make my way back out into the club and do my rounds. After I touch base with the last staff member on the floor, I weave through the crowded dance floor.

Working anywhere with high capacity, you have to be okay with random people touching, bumping, or engaging with you. It comes with the territory, no matter which role you hold.

But as people dance beside me, rub up against me, reach out for and grope me, my tolerance level vanishes.

The world shrinks and blurs. People appear out of nowhere and steal my air. The music booms louder and thumps harder. Sweat breaks out across my skin and my breath won't come quick enough. My pulse whooshes behind my ears. The room spins and I wobble on my feet. I stumble out of the crowd and stagger sideways until I hit a wall. My stomach churns as I drop to the floor, shirt drenched.

And then she is there. Peyton. In my face. Holding my cheeks and yelling. But I don't hear her. She shakes me gently and yells again. This time, the faint tones of her voice break through the white noise.

"Put your head between your legs, Micah." My brow tugs together at her words. "It'll help you from passing out."

Oh. I nod and do as she says. Head between my knees, I close my eyes and breathe steadily. A chill hits my neck, but I don't move. It feels good. Settles the pang in my chest and stops the constant flow of sweat. Fingers comb through my hair and a wave of comfort washes over me.

I want to lift my head and see if Peyton is still here. If she is the one nursing and consoling me. Providing me with this unfamiliar comfort. Comfort I don't want to end.

"Micah?" Her voice is soft next to my ear. "Slowly sit up straight. You need some water."

I do as she says and she hands me a glass of cold water. One sip at a time, I drink the cool liquid. She watches me like a mother would a sick child. I love and hate that I worried her, but am glad I didn't collapse.

"What did you eat for dinner? Maybe you got food poisoning."

Here comes my inner asshole. Yes, I lied to her earlier. Said maybe it was something from dinner. Which isn't possible. Because I haven't eaten. Not since yesterday.

"Uh, I may have fibbed about dinner earlier." Her brows creep down. "More like I haven't eaten since yesterday."

"Oh, Jesus." She shakes her head, rises from her haunches and offers her hand. "Come on."

"What? Where are you—"

"You need to eat something. Before you actually *do* pass out."

I wince but recover. "I have snacks in the office. Maybe we can grab something to eat after work. Together." The word vomit leaves my mouth before I stop it. No way to retract or turn back now.

Hour-long seconds drag out. Peyton stares at me with a novel of confusion written on her face. Confusion morphs into something akin to struggle. I hate that she has to put so much effort into the decision. And I have half a mind to rescind.

"Sure. How about Teddy's?" she proposes.

Teddy's is a modernized version of homestyle. Open twenty-four hours, they let you order anything from the menu any time of day. Best part, it is less than a mile from Roar.

"Sounds perfect."

She proffers her hand to help me stand and I take it without hesitation. Once upright, I hold steady a moment and get my bearings. Less dizzy, I put one foot in front of the other and inch my way down the hall toward the office.

"Eat something," she hollers down the hall as I open the door.

"On it, boss."

This grants me a smile just before she walks off. I swear I have seen more smiles from Peyton tonight than I have in the last year. Combined with the lack of food in my system, the constant smiles fuck with my head. And body.

On the tattered couch in the office, I lie back and eat one of the emergency packages of peanut butter crackers. When I reach the bottom of the package, the room looks less like a house of distorted mirrors and my hands tremble less. My stomach grumbles, suggesting the crackers better be the appetizer.

I close my eyes and throw an arm over them. The music from the club vibrates the walls and lulls me to sleep. A hand shakes my shoulder and whispers my name. I ignore the dream until it happens again, a little louder.

"Huh?" I lift my arm a bit and spot Peyton's chin and lips.

"Time to wake up, sleepyhead." Slowly, I sit up and she inches back. "If you're too tired, we can skip food."

I shake my head. "No, I'm good. Just give me a minute." Now is when I notice the silence. The lack of music or blended chatter. "What time is it?"

"Almost three."

Well, damn. Definitely needed the sleep, but I didn't mean to sleep the last three and a half hours. With tomorrow off, the additional sleep shouldn't throw my schedule off much.

"You ready to go?" I ask as I stand and stretch.

"Whenever you are." She points to the desk. "Brought the tills in."

"Thanks."

After I stow the money and lock the vault, we leave through the back. We head for our individual cars and I wait for her to put hers in drive before I take off.

In the seven minutes it takes us to drive from Roar to Teddy's, I question every reason why Peyton agreed to eat with me after work. Was it out of sympathy? Did she feel bad because I almost fainted in the club? The Peyton I have known the last year would have left me on the floor and hollered at someone else to call 911 while she stood behind the bar and watched.

But something is different about her. And, for the life of me, I have no clue what.

We step inside Teddy's and are promptly seated at a booth in the corner. Peyton smiles ear to ear as she scans the menu. Meanwhile, I stare at the laminated page and let my eyes lose focus.

I just don't get it. After all this time, why be nice now? What does she stand to gain? Is this a game?

Or has she turned over a new leaf?

My hope leans toward the latter. Because if this is just a game, the end may be severe.

Ten

PEYTON

Why am I here? Why did I agree to come here with him?

Obviously, I am an idiot. That's why.

I have been to Teddy's enough times to know what I want to eat. The best breakfast sandwich this side of the Bay. Egg, sausage, hash brown patty, and cheese slapped between two pancakes.

So. Freaking. Good.

But I dart my eyes over the menu as if I need time to figure it out. Meanwhile, I spot Micah in my periphery. Staring at me like a stoner. He doesn't open his mouth to speak, doesn't flinch or move his eyes to read the menu. He just stares straight ahead as if he's broken.

The wicked part of me wants to reach across the table and slap his cheek to wake him up. Instead, I sit here like a friend would and fake read the menu. I scan the egg breakfast plates so many times I have the entire section memorized. So, I move on to the sides.

Just as I read cheese grits for the fifth time, our server arrives with a pen pressed to her green guest check pad. From across the table, Micah eyes me with a silent request to order first. I bite my cheek to stop myself from laughing.

After I order my sandwich and juice, Micah orders enough food for two and a coffee. Wasn't kidding when he said he hadn't eaten since yesterday.

"So…" It feels awkward just sitting here. But I have no clue what to talk about with him. Not like we have ever been friendly.

"So…" he repeats, but continues. "Sorry about earlier."

About to tell him he doesn't need to apologize, I get interrupted when the server drops off our drinks.

"Just don't do it again."

A corner of his mouth kicks up as he stares down at his mug and dumps several packets of sugar in the brew. "Didn't mean to. Nice to know you were concerned." He picks up his spoon, stirs the overly sweet caffeine and lifts his eyes to mine. "Nice to know you wouldn't leave me to die."

I roll my eyes with a headshake. "Things may not be great between us, but I'd never wish death on anyone. I'm a firm believer in karma."

"Lucky me," he teases.

We both go silent a moment. My hands sit firmly between my butt and the booth while Micah has his clasped in front of him on the table. He fumbles with his lower lip like he wants to ask me something, but doesn't know how. His reluctance and uncertainty douse my blood with a thrill. Funny yet odd, I have never been this excited by someone feeling out of sorts.

He takes a sip of his coffee, then slowly sets the mug on the table, eyes fixed on the steam. "If you don't mind my asking…" His eyes lift to meet mine. The gold hints shimmer in the brighter light and it throws me off balance for a breath. "Why do you hate me so much?"

I stare back at him with pursed lips. It would be so easy to just tell Micah my reasons. To spill my truth and help him remember the past instead of learning the answers on his own. But I won't. After years of having to rebuild my confidence and strength, I vowed to never let anyone walk all over me again. Especially the man sitting across from me.

"The answer to that would take more time than we have tonight. And I'd have to answer that when *I'm* ready. Hope you figure it out before then."

He drops his hands to his sides and leans back into the booth. "See, that's what I don't get." I lift my brows in question. "More than once, you've insinuated we knew each other. Before you worked at Roar."

I lean back and match his position. Stare at him and study every line and twitch of his face. Look for indications of deception in his brow line, eyes, or lips. But all I see is honesty and perplexity.

"You really have no idea, do you?"

He leans forward and wraps his hands back around the mug. "No. So, will you please tell me?"

"Not tonight," I whisper before picking up my juice to drink. "Let's talk about something else. Anything else."

Anger still eats away at me for all the pain and embarrassment Micah and half the high school student body created. Yes, it happened several years ago. Yes, a therapist once told me I would never get past it if I don't let go. But damn, letting go of such cruelty inflicted on me is difficult. If only he remembered. If only he apologized.

Maybe then I could move past the imprisoned emotions. God, it would be nice to free those demons.

"What do you do when you're not at work?"

He wants to know about my life outside the bar. Learn

more personal details. The question is vague enough to leave it open for any response. I doubt he wants to hear about my grocery trips and spring cleaning. He wants dirty details. Like if I have romantic interests with anyone. Especially after seeing me with Reese last night.

But he needs to work harder to earn that information.

"Mondays and Tuesdays, I work at an assisted living facility."

His head jerks back in surprise. "You do?" I tuck my lips and nod. "What do you do there?"

Does he really want to know? Or is this just some jab at polite conversation?

Micah Reed finding anything I do interesting seems far-fetched. But he also doesn't remember who I am. Not the younger me, anyway. Would he still be keen on knowing me if he did remember? A voice in the back of my head screams *no, you dumbass!* A different voice chimes in with *what if he has changed?*

Is it possible he has matured? That he actually cares about what women have to offer, other than what lies between their legs. I suppose all things are possible.

"Mostly crafts and games. I entertain and give them someone to talk to. Many don't have family in the area and they get lonely. Friendships within the ALF help, but it isn't the same."

"Wow." His lapis blue eyes hold mine and sparkle with amazement. "She's beautiful and kindhearted."

I don't know how to respond to his sentiment. The compliment throws me off balance and makes me question what I have thought of him over the years. I may have started out the night with a charade, but it has opened my eyes slightly. It has shown me a side of Micah

Reed I didn't know existed. A softer side with gentle words.

"Well, my family would murder me in my sleep if I weren't. So…" I shrug, drop my gaze to the table and toy with the corner of the napkin.

He laughs. "Mine, too."

This grabs my attention. Makes me want to shake his shoulders and yell, "Well, they obviously don't know everything about you." But making a scene will open up a fat can of drama I don't want, so I keep my thoughts to myself.

Before the air around us shifts to awkward, uncomfortable silence, the server steps up to the table with our food. Soon as my plate hits the table, I reach for my sandwich and chow down. The server drops one large and three small plates in front of Micah. He dives fork first into the biscuits and gravy before the server asks if we want drink refills. We both give a thumbs-up.

Odd to think, but it feels like tonight has been pivotal between me and Micah. Like we have reached the center of our book and the story is shifting. Flowing more smoothly. The tension has eased slightly and made room for something else. What that something is, I have no clue.

Not sure if I want to know.

The server returns with a fresh glass of juice and refills Micah's coffee. After he steps away, Micah spears a sausage link on his plate, then points it at me.

"Don't think just because food arrived we're done talking." Why not? I want to ask, but bite my tongue. "What do you do for fun?"

I would be an idiot to ignore his obvious attraction for me, now that I'm paying closer attention. Can't exactly say Micah is hard on the eyes, either. Before he opened his mouth my freshman year, my black heart swooned over him. Hard. Then he crushed it with his words. Over and over again.

Now, though, he seems different. A bit more mature, if I discount our never-ending banter and his predilection for a new female every night of the week.

Are women what he does for fun? Fucks 'em and leaves 'em? I don't picture him playing basketball with the guys or having a movie night with piles of junk food.

"What I do for fun would probably seem lame or old ladyish to you."

He eats the last of the sausage off his fork. "Humor me."

Micah Reed wants to know what I do for fun. Alright.

"Fun for me is curling up on the couch with a good book or movie. Maybe bingeing on my favorite ice cream and greasy takeout with a friend." I sip my juice. "Working where we do, I don't care about going out to party. What about you?" He tilts his head. "What is it you do for fun?"

Micah cuts into his French toast, dips the chunk in syrup, then brings it to his lips. For some idiotic reason, I follow the entire process with my eyes and salivate when he opens his mouth to eat it. I pray I don't look like all the other women who fawn over him.

Last thing I need is him getting the wrong idea.

But he watches me with obvious interest. Watches as I bring my own food to my lips and distract myself from whatever it is that is happening. Is this some weird version of food porn? People who get off watching other people eat. A sexual fetish. Like *"Hey girl, eat the toast next. Does it have butter? You like it all buttered up, don't you?"*

And now I have that stuck in my head. Fuck my life. Guess my dreams will be bizarre as hell tonight.

"A little bit of this. A little bit of that," he says after a sip of coffee that makes his face scrunch. He grabs two packets of sugar and adds them to the cup.

"Vague much?" I point to the coffee he now stirs. "I like sweet stuff, but I think you have sugar issues."

He waves me off. "Nah." Another sip and his eyes blissfully close. "And maybe I like to be mysterious." His brows waggle.

"Or... you don't want people to see the real you."

Across the table, he pushes scrambled eggs around his plate with a fork as a child would. Finding ways to avoid eye contact. Doing menial things to distract from the conversation at hand. Doing everything and anything to not own the truth.

"I let someone see the *real me*, as you call it."

What? That's it? Finally going to open up, then shut it down just as fast. Why am I not surprised?

"And?"

His brows pinch at the center as he forces out a breath. "And... she fucked a guy ten years my junior while she thought I was working. Except, I left work early that day. Thought it'd be nice to surprise her. When I walked in on them fucking, it was definitely a surprise."

The teenage girl inside me wants to jump up, poke my finger in his chest and yell, *"Ha! That's what you get."* Maturity clears her throat and wags her finger. Damn maturity.

"Sorry that happened to you," I tell him instead. "Can't say I know what that feels like."

"I don't picture guys stepping out on you," he mumbles, but I hear it clear as day.

True. No guy I dated has cheated on me. Two of my three serious relationships ended somewhat tragically. I believe all things happen for a reason, but I wish they could have happened differently. Death should never ever be the reason you lose love.

"So mysterious, Micah. Tell me what you do for fun." I work to pass the somber mood.

"Relentless, aren't you?"

I shrug. "A trait I've gotten good at over the years."

He plucks a grape from his plate and pops it in his mouth. "Hang with buddies, I guess. Friends of mine get together on Sundays and we just bullshit and catch up. When the weather's great, we hang at the beach. And the occasional gathering with the fam."

"Sounds nice. I lost some family and would give anything to spend time with them again."

Just like that, I bring us right back into sad territory. Not that my life is sad. I make the most of what I have. Spend time with Mom, Harold, and Trina—my stepfather and stepsister—when able. I see my aunt Leanne more often, though. She reminds me so much of Dad.

The server steps up to the table and surveys our empty plates. After stacking the plates on his arm, he lays the check facedown on the table. "They'll cash you out up front." Then he walks off.

I go for the check, but Micah beats me to it. "It was my idea to come here. I'll pay."

The notion unsettles me. Only because it makes tonight seem more like a *date* and not two coworkers grabbing a bite to eat after work. And this was not a date.

"That's nice of you, but I don't mind paying for myself."

He scoots to the edge of the booth and rises. "Look, you're independent. I get it. But it's okay to let people buy you a meal every now and then." He starts for the register near the door. "It's the least I can do after my episode earlier."

I don't want to fight with him. Not after we have spent the last hours cordial. "Fine." I cave. "But only if I get to tip the server."

"Deal."

While Micah pays, I toss a stack of bills on the table. I wave to the server and head for the exit, Micah on my heels. Feels like his eyes are on my ass, but I don't check.

He walks me to my car. The air thicker as we approach and I dig the fob from my purse with shaky hands. My throat drier than burned toast as I swallow. My teeth clack together as I press the unlock button.

This isn't a date. And we aren't technically friends. So why the hell am I so fidgety?

Tonight ends with us both getting in our cars and driving away. Alone.

There will be no affectionate exchanges. No kisses or promises to talk later. No "I had a nice time." or "Let's do this again."

None. Of. The. Above.

Yet, this still feels like the end of a date as Micah opens my car door. As he looks into my eyes, equally as confused.

He steps closer, his arm lifting up. Is he going to hug me? No. Nope. Not happening.

I move to get in the car and he drops his arm. "Glad you got some food in you. Don't do that again."

His eyes drop to his feet, then meet mine again. "Yeah, sure," he says as he closes my door and I roll down the window. "Drive safe."

"You, too." The corners of his lips curve up slightly. "Night, Micah."

He steps back. "Night."

I leave Teddy's and make it home in record time. That is the beauty of driving the highway in the middle of the night.

After I brush my teeth and dress in pajamas, I snuggle under the blanket and shut my heavy eyes. My body relaxes one limb at a time. On the verge of sleep, I hear a fire truck siren nearby and it jolts me awake. Once it passes, I wiggle in place and try to settle my alert brain.

But my brain and I are obviously not on the same wavelength. Nope. Now, my brain wants to do a minute-by-minute replay of the whole evening. What it was like to have a cordial evening with my archnemesis. To smile and laugh and share a healthy conversation. To feel something, if only for a moment, other than hate for this man.

Good thing I don't work tomorrow. It's going to be a long night of overanalyzing.

Stupid brain.

eleven

MICAH

I park behind Gavin's Range Rover, two houses down from Jonas and Autumn's place. Our Sunday get-togethers are the best tradition started with our group. Friends, family, and food —three of my favorite F's. My other favorite F wouldn't be appropriate in a group setting. Not my kink.

Feet from the front door, hickory hits my nose as rock music vibrates in my eardrums. I knock and Autumn yells from the other side. "It's open."

I twist the knob and step inside. In the open floor plan, I spy Autumn as she bustles around the kitchen. Takes buns out of packages, dumps cold sides into bowls, grabs condiments and toppings from the fridge. Her pace makes me dizzy.

I set down a bag with beer, tortilla chips, and salsa. "Anything you need help with?" Mom taught me and Shelly to always offer assistance, especially when we are guests. Long as Autumn doesn't need help cooking, I will pitch in.

My cooking skills are a running joke in the Reed family. When we were growing up, Mom wanted to make sure we were all—me, Shelly, and Dad—self-sufficient in the kitchen. That we knew how to make basic meals in case she wasn't able to. Let's just say I flunked from day one when I made gummy pasta with burned tomato sauce. Not my finest hour.

Can I cook now? If following microwave directions counts, then yes. If ordering takeout or dining out counts, then yes again. Basic breakfast foods and I are friends. But it works best for everyone if I stay away from stoves and ovens. Besides, every now and again, Mom stops by because she is "in the area"—she lives a solid twenty minutes from my house—and brings me a casserole dish of my childhood favorites.

Or nights like tonight. Everyone leaves with a container of leftovers. Autumn demands it. No matter what, I never starve or burn down the house.

"Could you dump the snack foods into the big bowls?" She points to a stack of large bowls at the end of the counter.

"On it."

Maybe Shelly told her not to let me near anything that requires heating. If so, I need to thank her later.

As I dump cheese puffs into a bowl, Jonas comes in from the backyard with Clementine on his heels. She is the cutest little girl ever. A spitting image of her mom, but with additional sass and a major bond with Spartan, Jonas's husky.

"Hey, man. Didn't realize you were here." He steps up to me and we backslap hug. "Gavin and Cora are out back with your sister and Erin."

"What? They left Autumn in here to do everything. Shelly is definitely getting a ration of shit."

Autumn shoves a large spoon in the coleslaw and spins to face me. "No, leave them be. I forced them outside."

"But you asked me to help?" I deadpan.

She shrugs. "I like to rotate through my helpers. What can I say?"

A knock at the door has Spartan running to the window and peeking through the blinds. His tail wags just as Jonas opens the door to Penny, Rex, Reznor, Tatyana, and Ashton. Everyone files in and exchanges hugs. The house is abuzz with chatter. Smiles and laughter float around the room easily.

But right now, I feel the odd man out.

Although I'm not the only person without a significant other here, it feels… wrong at my age to be so alone. The moment my thoughts veer down this path, Shelly comes out of nowhere and bumps my shoulder with hers.

"Hey, big brother. What's new?" I wrap my arms around her and lift her from the floor. She squeals and smacks my back. "Put me down, dumbass."

I set her back on her feet and she swats my chest. Hard. "Ow! What was that for?"

"Did you really need to pick me up?"

"Are you my sister?" She rolls her eyes. "Nothing too exciting."

She grabs my hand and leads me out the door to the back-yard. "Too crowded in there." She plops down on the lounger and brings me with her. "Life may not be exciting, but surely there must be something you've done since we last spoke."

Gavin and Cora take a seat across from us. Hickory clouds billow from the smoker, thin out with the mild breeze, and scent the air. A Bluetooth speaker shuffle plays rock music near the house. The late April temperature's mild enough to not make you sweat outside this time of day.

Three sets of eyes on me feel like a packed concert crowd.

"Work is much the same. Maybe less chaotic."

"The blonde?" Gavin pipes up and I want to slap him.

"Yep." I grit my teeth.

"What blonde?" Shelly asks Gavin.

Great. Here goes the attention I do not want or need.

"The bartender he banters with. You remember her from our last outing?" Shelly rests a finger on her lips, deep in thought. Gavin trudges forward and I want to smack him upside the head. "The one getting Micah all hot and bothered."

Shelly taps her lips and looks to the heavens. "Must've been otherwise distracted. Tell me more, big brother. What's her name?"

If I don't open up now, Shelly will be on my ass all night. Annoying the hell out of me.

But what is there to say about Peyton? We work together. She drives me absolutely mad, in the best ways. Her body is stellar, and I bet she isn't all fire and claws. Although, I like those aspects of her.

Hanging out with my sister and friends and talking about a woman I work with seems... wrong. Inappropriate. It feels like hair salon gossip. But if I keep my mouth shut, she will spend the next few hours in my face. Then she will pay a visit to Roar. Ogle my every move as Peyton and I work behind the bar. That is the last thing I need.

"You are a pain in my ass," I say.

She sticks out her tongue. "And you wouldn't want me any other way."

I inhale a deep, methodical breath and speak on the exhale. "Her name is Peyton." Shelly jerks back as her brows pinch together. "What?"

"Peyton?" she asks and I nod. "Has to be a weird coincidence."

"What are you talking about?"

"In high school, there was a girl. Peyton. She was a year ahead of Cora—and me, if we'd gone to the same school.

Anyway, I remember Cora saying she was super nice, but half the school bullied her. I heard all of the horror stories second-hand, but…"

A fist wraps around my stomach, squeezes and twists. Bile rises up, up, up in my throat.

No. No, no, no.

"Do you remember her last name?" I croak out.

Five seconds feels like five hours as Shelly looks to Cora, then back to me, tilts her head and stares. Written all over her face is *you seriously don't remember* and *how did you not recognize her.* I bite the inside of my cheek until tangy iron hits my tongue.

"Alexander," Cora answers.

I bolt up from my seat and dash around the corner of the house to vomit in the yard. But seeing as I haven't eaten in hours, making room for the feast here, I spend more time dry heaving than actually expelling stomach contents.

A gentle hand rests on my shoulder. Soft floral, citrus, and earthy notes hit my nose. Shelly. As only a sister would, she rubs small circles on my back and remains silent. When I stand up, she hands me a napkin and bottled water.

Without a word, she guides us back to where we sat. The moment I return, I expect everyone's eyes on me. But my friends don't embarrass me with daunting stares and endless questions. When I stepped off, and Shelly followed, they sparked new conversations.

Now that I have returned, though…

"So, I assume you don't remember her from school?" Shelly asks for clarification.

I shake my head before taking a sip of the water. The cool liquid soothes the residual burn in my throat. "No. How do I not remember? People don't change *that* dramatically from high school to early thirties. Do they?"

Shelly turns her attention to Gavin. "You said she's blonde?" Gavin nods as he lifts a beer to his lips. Shelly faces me again. "That's it."

Dear, sister. Please elaborate for the rest of us who cannot hear your thoughts. Sincerely, brother. "What's it?"

"Sorry." Shelly smiles, then taps her temple. "Cora, correct me if I'm wrong. In high school, Peyton wasn't blonde. She was a goth chick. Black hair, black clothes, black everything. It's why…"

The way she trails off sends a chill up my spine. I flashback to high school, some of the best and worst years of my youth. Frame by frame, I search old memories. Try to see Peyton with dark hair and clothes. But I didn't pay attention to girls like Peyton. At least not the type of girl she was then. My preferred type has always remained the same.

Looking through four years of memories will take longer than tonight. Maybe Cora and Shelly will do me a solid and jog my memory with more specifics.

"I hate it when you leave me hanging, Shell." She winces. "Just lay it out. I'm a man. It's why what?"

Shelly finds every means to procrastinate. One small sip of water after another. She eyes Cora, who shrugs and flaunts the *might as well* face. Argh! Any second, I am going to lose it if someone doesn't speak up.

"It's why she was bullied," Shelly says. That wasn't so hard now, was it? "By you."

Wait, what? "Come again." I glance around to my closest friends. The ones I spent time with during those years. And they all nod at me.

When the hell did I bully Peyton? Pain scrapes my throat

as I swallow. I chug half the water as I think harder. When the hell did I bully anyone? My hand fists my hair, tugging at the strands until pain shoots down my neck.

"It happened the year before we started high school," Cora chimes in. "Think she was a year behind you. But the rumors ran wild during my freshman year too. Girls wrote on bathroom tiles with Sharpie, *Peyton Alexander is a slut.* Never stayed on the tile long, but was up again within a day or two. Guys whispered, *Micah Reed called her a slut,* and with your popularity status, people believed. From what I heard, you called her names in the cafeteria in front of half the school."

The nightmare of that day rolls in like an evening thunderstorm—angry and violent. My friends and their lighthearted chatter disappear. A second-by-second replay of the day flashes through my memory.

Mercedes and her bitch friends were annoying the hell out of me that day. Coach had been pressing me to push harder on the track. And Mercedes found me at the perfect moment to verbally bash some unknown girl. Peyton.

All Mercedes ever wanted was to be seen and heard. My popularity on the track team attracted her. But there was nothing about her I deemed attractive. She was a bitch. Through and through.

That day, she pranced over to me and I wouldn't give her the time of day. So she riled me up. Told me the girl in the corner had been eye fucking me for days. Then she told me the girl had slept with half the baseball team and was slut-shaming the guys. In my hazing thoughts, I thought *this bitch isn't messing with any jocks at this school.*

So, I shut her down. Or at least that is what I thought I was doing.

Obviously, I had no moral compass. Instead of opening

my mouth, I should have left well enough alone. I should have known Mercedes was a conniving bitch. But I was too wrapped up in myself. Worried some girl would try to ruin what was already toeing the line.

Leaning forward, I rest my elbows on my knees and my face in my hands. "Jesus," I mumble into my palms. "What was I thinking?"

Shelly rubs a hand up and down my back. The motion meant to soothe me. But hatred runs rampant inside me like a viral contagion. "Think of this as a second chance. A way to right your wrong."

"No wonder she hates me. I was so self-absorbed, I gave no fucks about her feelings. Or how my words messed up her life."

"Yes, you screwed up big time." I peek up at my sister and she shrugs. "If Mom and Dad knew, they'd be pissed. All those years of teaching us to put other's thoughts and feelings before our own."

I comb my fingers through my hair and sit up, eyes on Shelly. Her eyes, just as blue and sparkly as mine, stare back at me with deep sympathy.

"How do I fix this, Shell?"

She takes my hands in hers and holds my gaze. "First, you apologize. Apologize like you never have before. And mean it." I nod and she continues. "Second, you beg for her forgiveness. Grovel if necessary. After what you did to her. After how she was treated during those pivotal years, she may not forgive you. That's her call. You can't just ask for forgiveness, either. Show her you want it."

"How do I do that?"

"Be the man I know you to be. The man Mom and Dad

raised. Simple gestures and kind words. They go much further than most expect."

I take mental notes of the sound advice only a sister can provide. "I will."

"And lastly, don't do anything to hurt her. Ever again." I nod and she pokes my chest with a finger. "I mean it, Micah. You already hurt her once. Who knows what would happen if you did again."

When I don't respond, Shelly turns toward Cora and chats about the next bowling or karaoke night. Everyone around me carries on various conversations. Me? I stay in my own head and sort through the onslaught of memories and advice.

Little by little, I devise how I will fix this. Fix what I broke all those years ago. Fix the hatred Peyton harbors.

Because I like her too much to let her hate me any longer.

twelve

PEYTON

After a full crank of the handle, the black-and-white ball rolls down the shoot. I pick it up, twirl it in my fingers, then peer up at the crowd of hopeful eyes.

"B4."

Whack, whack, whack. The slap of bingo markers fills the room, followed with the occasional groan or *yes* with a fist pump.

Ms. Jenkins looks up from her ten-card spread, gives me a thumbs-up and a wink. The woman to her left, Ms. Roberts, darts narrowed eyes to me, then Ms. Jenkins. They exchange words as I crank the handle for the next ball to drop. Ms. Jenkins waves a hand at her, then shakes her head.

"G53," I call the next number, then crank the handle again as the bingo markers create music. "I25."

"Bingo!" Mr. Calhoun croaks from three tables back. He lifts his winning card and waves it above his head. One of the nurses takes the card from him and brings it to me to verify his win. Once I confirm Mr. Calhoun's win, several people ball up their cards and grumble.

Metal chair legs screech against the linoleum in stilted

beats as several players inch back and rise from their seats. Ms. Jenkins lets her reading glasses hang around her neck as she stuffs her lucky bingo markers in the seat of her walker. She wheels to the front table where I clean up the bingo cage and master board.

"Sticking around for lunch?" She tugs her pink cardigan closer to her midline.

"Wouldn't miss it. I'll meet you there."

I stare after Ms. Jenkins as she leaves the game room and notice her gait stutters more. Since I started at Gulfside, I have never not noticed her slow pace. But the hobble is new. Seeing her wear herself out to leave the room pinches my heart.

Once I have the game components boxed and stored, I walk over to one of the nurses still in the room.

"Hey, Jim."

"How are you, Peyton?"

I give him a weak smile. "Same old, same old." I shrug. "Hey, is Ms. Jenkins okay? She seems more frail today."

His eyes divert to the door then back to me, lips slightly downturned. The pinch from a moment ago intensifies and I press my palm heel to my chest.

"Last night, she pressed her panic button. When the nurse got to her room, they found her on the floor. She says it was a slip when she walked from the bathroom to her bed. But the nurse thinks she may have fallen out of the bed."

A hand slaps over my mouth. "Oh no!"

"Although she argued, they took her to X-ray. No broken bones. Just bruises—on her hip, arm, and ego."

Ms. Jenkins is a sweetheart. Willing to help anyone in need. Talk your ear off for hours and listen with equal skill. Teach you how to crochet or knit as if she invented the craft.

Most importantly, she gives the best hugs. So full of warmth that has nothing to do with temperature. She may be up there in age, but she still has so much love to give.

"Just glad she is okay."

Not sure what I would do or how I would feel if I lost Ms. Jenkins. Seeing her smile and being wrapped in her arms each week provides me with so much love and happiness. A solace I once shared with my grandmother, Isabel. A peacefulness that shattered three years ago when she passed away.

I didn't start working at Gulfside to replace what I lost with my grandmother. But being here with Ms. Jenkins each week helps sew the fissures of my heart. The fault lines that opened when Nana passed. The ones that barely started to heal from losing Dad seven years earlier.

I shoot Aunt Leanne a quick text and tell her I'm eating at Gulfside today. She responds and says we will catch up next week.

Down the corridor from the game room, I hook a left and enter the dining hall. The beige painted walls hold several pictures from over the years. Of staff and residents. Special events and holidays and birthdays. Alongside the photographs are paintings and drawings from current and past residents. Plus, framed posters with beautiful scenery and positive sentiments. Long wooden tables are spread throughout the room, with four chairs on the long sides and one on each end. Each table decorated with a centerpiece for the season. Residents can walk to the counter and get food, cafeteria style. Or they can sit at the tables and have the staff bring food to them.

The setup is pleasant and welcoming and provides a level of independence and community.

At eleven fifteen, the lunch crowd has already packed the room. I shuffle to the end of the line and grab a plastic tray.

After I select a sandwich, fruit and water, I pay and find Ms. Jenkins at her usual table.

We catch up for a bit while she enjoys her tomato soup and grilled cheese, and I have my turkey sandwich. She tells me how upset Ms. Roberts was during bingo. Swearing I only called numbers on Ms. Jenkins's cards. Which is laughable.

As lunch fills our bellies, I contemplate how to ask about her fall. Last thing I want to do is upset or embarrass her. But I need to know if she really is okay. Since the day we met, Ms. Jenkins has been nothing but forthcoming and honest with me. It is one of the reasons I love her so much. No beating around the bush.

"So…" She sets her spoon down and grants me her attention. "Jim tells me you had a fall."

Anyone who says eighty-seven-year-old women can't roll their eyes or show indignation needs to meet Ms. Jenkins. Her skills could trample teenagers, which is quite telling.

"He needs to mind his tongue."

I rest a hand on hers. "He only told me because I noticed your limp and I asked about it."

Her other hand pats, then covers mine with a layer of reassurance. "Don't you worry about me. A little fall won't keep me down."

Therein lies the problem. I do worry. If the last decade of my life has taught me anything, it is that time with people you love should never be taken for granted. Losing too many loved ones matured me in many ways. It also inhibited me in others.

People I love? I love them fiercely and let them know often. And I have learned to let smaller fights go when it comes to loved ones.

But losing them also hardened my heart. Made letting new

people in that much harder. I loved hard in a few committed relationships, but life just kept throwing me one curveball after another. So, I threw in the towel. My heart couldn't take the endless cycle of pain anymore.

Now, I don't allow myself to travel down the road to love again. Not saying it will never happen. But when heartache knocks on your door over and over again, you find every possible way to not let it in. Turning my heart to ice has been the only method to work.

I appease Ms. Jenkins, but only because she is stubborn and will shut me down if I keep talking about it. "Alright. But if I hear this happens again, you're not allowed to argue about me caring."

"It won't, so the point is moot."

That's it. End of conversation. When Ms. Jenkins puts her foot down, it is best to just bite your tongue and let it go. Although, I plan to check in with the nurses more frequently and have them reach out if something else happens. I may only work here more as mental support, but I adore Ms. Jenkins—and several other residents at Gulfside. They're like a second family.

We finish our lunch in relative silence. After I take our trays to the bin, I help Ms. Jenkins to her feet and we wander from the dining hall, through the community room and exit the double doors that lead outside. I walk at her pace and never give her the impression she needs to hurry.

Today, Ms. Jenkins selects the wooden bench between two old oak trees. The canopy shades the seat, but allows the occasional sunrays to highlight your skin. Birds chirp from the branches as squirrels run from tree to tree in a game of tag. A gentle breeze tames the too warm spring temperatures—not that either of us mind the heat. Hints of jasmine and rose drift in the wind from the flower garden to our left and I let the perfume fill my lungs.

The facility also has a fruit and vegetable garden. Residents with green thumbs are welcome to tend to the plants but aren't required to keep them maintained. The facility has a groundskeeper that checks the plants weekly and tends to any needing attention.

As per usual, we sit the first few minutes in silence. Both of us soaking up the warmth and breathing easier.

"Peyton." Ms. Jenkins rests a hand on my forearm and brushes her thumb over the skin. Her touch is gentle. Soft. Kind. A reminder of my nana. "You worry about me too much." Her words are tender and quiet. "I have lived a full life. And as you get older, things change. Your perception of life, what matters… it all changes."

Why is she telling me this? Has a new health issue come up that I don't know about? I don't like that she talks about herself as if she doesn't have much time left. It unnerves me. Makes my stomach twist in knots. Robs me of breath.

With a slow twist of her body, she faces me head-on. The crinkles near the corners of her eyes and mouth turn up. "I love that you come to see me. That you want to spend time with a cuckoo old bat. But sweetheart, you need to live life too. You're so young. Have so many years ahead of you. Don't waste them visiting me."

I shake my head, unwilling to absorb her words or give them life. "No. You don't get to say that." The backs of my eyes sting. "Coming to see you matters to me."

"Why, Peyton? Not that I don't enjoy our time together. But why does seeing me matter?"

Because you make me smile. Because I love hearing your stories similar to those my nana told. Love how I experience a simpler happiness with you. And how life doesn't feel as messy and complicated when I get to talk with someone wiser.

"Seeing you makes me happy." My thoughts summarized in that singular line. It doesn't matter why. Spending time with this woman makes me happy. Provides some peace.

She pats my forearm, then leaves her hand to rest there. "Okay, Peyton."

The next half hour ticks by with the sun on our shins. We don't speak again until I walk her inside and leave for the day. She gives me a hug and says she will see me tomorrow. As I drive home, pain radiates beneath my rib cage. Pulsing and pounding and unrelenting.

Why did it feel like Ms. Jenkins was saying goodbye?

Reese laughs as Mom regales us with one of the weddings she catered over the weekend.

"Over the years, I have seen every kind of wedding. Or so I thought. But having livestock in the crowd and pictures… definitely new."

"Cows?" Reese asks and Mom nods. "Pigs and chickens?"

"Yep. The whole shebang. Cows, pigs, chickens, goats, horses. Ducks, too."

"Why?" Reese voices the question we all want answered.

Mom shrugs. "Said she grew up on a farm out west. She moved to Florida two years back to be with her now-husband." My brows lift. "They met through a dating app," she clarifies. "When the couple started planning the wedding, she got the groom's approval for a country theme. But I don't think even he knew how country she meant."

Wow. Just wow.

After being less than cheerful once I left Gulfside, Mom's story definitely lifts my spirits. Not one hundred percent. But some is better than none.

Reese and I attempt to help her make dinner, as we have every other time we visit, and she shoos us away. Suppose that's what you get when your mother cooks and bakes and caters for a living.

Sweet T's isn't a big operation. Mom caters four to five events a week. Most of them office events or weddings with less than a hundred people. She appeals to the masses and is willing to explore all food and baking options with her clients. With two full-time employees working alongside her, they are a booming small business.

I may be biased, but her quiche, almond cake with layered fruit and whipped cream frosting, and macaroons are pure heaven. Being the daughter of a woman who loves the kitchen is never a bad thing. Unless you are concerned about your figure. Which I am not.

"Tracy, you have to take me to the next wedding," Reese tells Mom. "I need these stories firsthand."

She waves a hand at him. "They're not all this outlandish."

"Maybe not, but I love weddings. Don't you, Peyton?" Reese flashes me with sparkling irises.

What the hell is he talking about? Reese and I have never discussed anything wedding related unless chatting with Mom. And never once have I mentioned a love for weddings. Hell, I barely hold on to boyfriends.

"Not so much," I respond with narrowed laser eyes.

Mom adds roasted root vegetables to a serving bowl and the lemon-rosemary chicken to a platter. Without request,

Reese takes them to the large cedar table in the dining room. Mom preps the last of the salad as I add a sliced baguette to a basket.

"You two sit. Be back in a sec."

Mom wanders down the hall and disappears from view. Off to get my stepfather, his daughter, and her girlfriend. Who never seem to participate in family time until absolutely necessary.

Don't get me wrong, Harold is a great guy. He loves my mom fiercely, which she needs and deserves after what happened with Dad. His job is safe and nine-to-five typical in the print shop he owns, Designs of the Times. But he is otherwise aloof. At least when I am here. Mom says Harold is simplistic and introverted. When it's just the two of them, he is more outspoken and affectionate.

As for my stepsister, Trina, she just does her own thing. Five years my senior, Trina Williamson struts around like she knows all. I long since gave up offering support or opinions. Since Mom and Harold first started dating three years ago, we have always been cordial with one another. But it isn't difficult to read her body language and determine she would rather not spend time with me or Mom.

As adult children, yes, it is weird to have our parents find new love. Especially when we both had parents we loved. Harold's first wife, Trina's mother, and he divorced when she was thirty. They had been married thirty-one years. But in the last year of their marriage, the misses went through a late midlife crisis. She wanted freedom and independence. With no way to recoup his marriage, Harold agreed to let the love of his life go.

Three years later, he met Mom.

She had a booth set up at the local Saturday market. So

did Harold. Before the influx of traffic, Harold stopped at her booth and sampled some of her food. They kept in touch after that day. Harold initially said it was for business, but later told Mom he couldn't stop thinking about her.

Their story of finding love again melts my heart. Mom dealt with major depression after losing Dad. It is one thing to grow apart in a relationship. But when the person you love dies in a tragic, fatal accident, there is no easy way to overcome the pain. Harold helped steer Mom from the darkness. For that, I am eternally in debt to him.

"Hey, guys." Speak of the man. "Sorry I didn't come out sooner. Was finishing up with a new client."

If he can print it, Harold does it. Business cards, fliers, bookmarks, car wraps, trinkets, and more. Harold started his business decades ago. Once a one-man operation, Designs of the Times has boomed over the last five years. Partly because Harold had nothing but time when he and his ex-wife separated. But also because Mom encouraged and supported him wholeheartedly.

"No worries. We were just catching up with Mom," I tell him.

Trina and her girlfriend, Sierra, walk in. No *hello* or *how's it going* or even eye contact. None of us dislike each other, but Trina isn't fond of her father remarrying. She and Mom get on fine. But Trina loves her own mother and has admitted as much to her father when she thought no one else was listening. Not that she wasn't especially quiet about it.

So, Trina tolerates me and Mom. Her problem, not mine.

After everyone fills their plates, idle chitchat circulates the table. Harold tells us about the new client he and Trina just acquired. Yes, Trina works with her father. It isn't odd they work together, but it surprises me she doesn't want more distance from her parent.

Reese mentions the influx of people at the restaurant and rec center. Mom blathers on about her upcoming week and the next wedding she will cater. Reese immediately jumps in and asks to attend and Mom shakes her head with a laugh.

Then the table goes silent. Too silent.

I glance up from my fork and knife, ready to bring the bite of chicken to my lips, but stop when I notice all eyes are on me.

"What?"

Mom gives a small smile. "I asked what was new with you. Anyone new in your life?"

Oh, lord. Here we go.

Since Mom and Harold fell in love, she has been adamant about finding someone for me. I love my mother's natural determination and desire for me to have the best in life. But her meddling in my love life is *not* something I want to deal with.

I spear the chicken harder than necessary and shove it between my lips. Chewing the bite until it turns soupy won't take long, but at least it gives me a moment to mentally prepare. Because this conversation won't finish with my answer.

"No, Mom."

She sips her wine, then sticks out her lower lip. "Aw, Peyton." I hate when she does that. Makes it sound like my choice to be alone is horrible. "Sweetheart, I know things ended on a sad note with James, but don't let that darken your heart."

James. My last boyfriend. The first guy I had truly loved since Chad—my first everything. James said he would always be there for me, through thick and thin. But when Nana passed, and I mourned, he didn't know how to be there for me during the darker days. Said he didn't know how to make me smile or love me anymore. He went to two joint therapy sessions with me, but couldn't seem to grasp why I didn't easily snap out of my sadness.

Bless his heart for trying, but we drifted apart after a year and a half together. Deep down, we still had love for each other. We just weren't meant to be more than what we had.

And we were okay with that. Although we broke up two years ago, we still catch up from time to time. His current girlfriend understands our friendship and has zero jealousy when we talk. She is a true woman.

"Mom, James and I are still friends. Nothing about us *darkens* me or my heart."

"I just hate to see you so alone."

Why won't she let this go? I don't want to hurt her feelings, but the continual conversations about relationships make me feel as if she thinks life isn't worthy if you don't have someone at your side.

I take a deep breath and prepare for the calm storm that is Tracy Williamson.

"What if I want to be alone? Have you considered that?"

"Why would you want to be alone?" Her voice shakes slightly.

I stab at the lettuce and cucumber in my bowl. I don't want to fight, not with Mom. But she needs to understand that not every person *needs* another person to have happiness. It is possible to be happy and be single.

"Mom, there's nothing wrong with being single. I come and go as I please. I don't have to worry about upsetting someone if I don't come home immediately from work. I get time to feel comfortable in my own skin, without the pressure of pleasing someone else. The list goes on and on." She goes to speak and I hold up a hand to cut her off. "And before you say something like *what about love…* Mom, I've had love. Twice. One I lost and can never get back. And the other, well, it morphed into a different love. I have come to terms with both of those. But for now, I want time for me. If I get lucky enough to find love again, I will accept it with grace. I won't go hunting for it, though. When it's meant to be…"

"I just feel like you're missing out," Mom mumbles to her plate.

Mom is the second person to indicate as much to me today. Although Ms. Jenkins didn't necessarily mean love, she thought I was missing out on life by hanging out with elderly folks.

Everyone at the table falls silent. Not that Trina or Sierra have said much anyway. I didn't raise my voice at Mom, but this is the first time I have really laid it all out in front of others. Reese knows how I feel. He teases me about dating every once in a while, but he gets that I'm enjoying me time. Mom, on the other hand, doesn't seem to get why I want independence. Maybe because she loved belonging to someone. It made her whole.

But I want the ability to feel whole *without* someone. Once I achieve that, being with another person is a bonus.

The rest of dinner goes by with quieter, blander conversation. After we help Mom clean up, Reese and I exchange hugs with Mom and Harold and say our goodbyes.

Back at home, Reese and I change into comfy clothes and he tells me to grab my Caboodles box of nail polish. The very same Caboodles I have had since high school. Once upon a time, it held only black polish, black mascara, black eyeliner, and shades of black shadow. Now, a rainbow of polish rests inside. Nothing else.

Reese plops down on the sofa with two bottles of beer and chips. After he tears the bag open and pops the top from the beers, he grabs my feet and starts rubbing them.

"Did Mama T upset you tonight?"

I shake my head and moan as he massages the ball of my foot. "No. Just wish she'd let me live life how I want."

"She means well."

"Yeah, I know. Her persistence frustrates me, I guess. It's like she doesn't understand that women don't *have* to be in a relationship to be happy."

"True." Reese switches to my other foot. "But all she knows is her own experiences. It's hard to speak of what you don't know or understand."

"I get that." Grabbing my bottle from the table, I take a sip. "But after countless conversations, you'd think she'd understand *my* stance on the matter. I love that she wants me to be happy. But she doesn't get that romantic relationships don't always equal happiness."

Reese grabs his beer from the table and extends it toward mine to clink necks. "Cheers to that." We both drink, then set our bottles down. "So… you went out with Micah the other night."

"Not now."

When I agreed to eat at Teddy's with Micah, I texted Reese. All I got in return was a slew of emojis and obnoxious GIFs.

"Fine. But we will talk about it. I don't care what does or doesn't come of it, we will discuss Micah Reed."

"Fine," I agree with a huff. "For now, will you just paint my toenails."

"Only if you do mine." Reese drops his feet in my lap and wiggles his toes. "I'm feeling the sky blue." I grab said blue from the Caboodles along with the bottle for my toes. I toss it at Reese and he looks at the color. "Really?"

"Yep."

"You got it."

For the next hour, we decorate each other's toes. Reese's in a bright baby blue. Mine in a rich, bold red. The color I reserve for when I want something. Thing is, I don't exactly know what I want. Mom's and Ms. Jenkins's words continue to ring through my head.

Is it true? Am I missing out?

thirteen

MICAH

Peyton hasn't been the same since last Saturday. Can't pinpoint what is different, but something just seems *off*.

Wednesday and yesterday, we only spoke when absolutely necessary. Every time I peeked in her direction, she appeared lost. Somewhere besides Roar. Eyes staring off in the distance, but without focus. She chatted with patrons in the bar, but her conversations lacked their typical zeal. Her harrowing smiles seemed forced.

Between the early morning hours of Sunday, when we parted ways at Teddy's, and early Wednesday evening, something shifted in Peyton's world.

But my life and perspective had shifted too.

After the conversation at Jonas and Autumn's Sunday night, I didn't sleep for shit. Didn't get much sleep the two days following, either.

What I had done to Peyton all those years ago weighed heavily on my mind and heart. Made me twitchy and restless, night after night. I had lain awake in bed for hours and replayed all the horrible words I'd said to and about her. Each night, I counted the bubbles in the popcorn ceiling to distract myself or fall asleep from boredom. But it neither distracted nor induced boredom. To my amazement and pitifulness, the highest I counted was 412. The only reason I stopped... the wind kicked up outside, swept the tree branch near my window and the dancing shadow caught my attention.

Exhaustion is no comparison to how I feel. My cement-pillar legs drag with each step forward. My lead-beam arms and robotic hands move only because my mind wills them to. Thank goodness my lungs and heart do their job without directive.

Did our conversation Saturday upset her? Dredge up old memories?

I grit my teeth and hang my head, ashamed at the person I was to her years ago. Had my parents known how I behaved back then—especially to a girl—they would have had me booted from the track team and on house arrest for months.

The question now is... how do I fix this? How do I make up for the asshole juvenile I once was? Will she forgive me and my deplorable behavior? Or will she forever harbor hatred for me in her heart?

When a crowd favorite booms through the speakers, the horde of bodies shifts from the bar to the dance floor.

I inch closer to Peyton, her eyes downcast, and focused on the glass she has cleaned three times. I knock her shoulder and she lifts her gaze and blinks.

"Everything alright? Seems like you're somewhere else tonight."

She smiles, but it doesn't reach her eyes. "Yes. No. I don't know."

"Want to talk about it?"

One shoulder shrugs as she sets the glass down. "Not now. Another time, maybe."

Seeing Peyton like this stirs the memories I recalled this past week. Although I was a royal prick to her, I did see her around school. I honestly don't recall any feelings for her—positive or negative. Back then, Peyton was just a random girl. Day after day, week after week, month after month, she remained the same. Decked head to toe in black. Baggy pants and a hoodie with the hood up. A black-and-white, checker-print backpack hooked on both shoulders. A folder, textbook, and mass market-sized book clutched close to her chest. Head up, but eyes on the ground.

Yes, Mercedes and her twat gang of besties got me to call Peyton a slut. But when I caught sight of her during my senior year, I wondered why those girls had it out for her. Were they jealous of her individuality? Did they envy she had male friends without having to put out? Was it her curves that had them calling her names and spreading lies? Or were they just bitches who refused to like people not similar to them?

Not that it matters now, but I think it was all of the above. Plus, Peyton wasn't a follower. Still isn't. She does her own thing, in her own time.

Before she walks off, I wrap a hand around her forearm. Her eyes drop and stare at her arm a beat before she lifts her gaze. "Meet me at Teddy's after work," I say with an added softness in my voice. Hoping she doesn't hear it as a demand.

Her eyes dart between mine. Brows twitch imperceptibly. Glassiness highlights the gray flecks in her vibrant violet irises. She licks, then tucks her lips between her teeth.

Not sure why, but she looks on the verge of tears.

The chambers of my heart contract and expand faster. An ache climbs from beneath my ribs and up my throat, lodging itself at my Adam's apple and swelling. I swallow and it does nothing to taper the sensation. To quell the emotion stuck firmly in place.

The overwhelming urge to hug her weighs my limbs. To haul her into me and press her close to my chest. Wrap my arms around her waist, squeeze tight and slide a hand up her spine to her neck. To feel her breath and heat on my skin.

"I'll think about it," she says hoarsely.

I drop my hand and she drifts to the end of the bar. A smile dons her face, but the gesture is all for show. The feisty and vivacious woman that lights up the bar four nights a week is nowhere to be found. In her place is a woman with a difficult past and wounded heart.

Hopefully tonight, she will let me heal part of her wound.

Neck deep in logging invoices, I press the heels of my palms to my eyes. This is what happens when I lose focus. Shit piles up. Work doesn't get done and mounts up day by day.

Invoices don't necessarily take long to input. But my mind has been elsewhere this week. Focused on a woman I hope joins me later at the diner.

"Only a dozen more to go. Just get it done, Reed."

The stack thins as I key stats into the spreadsheet. Three invoices from the bottom, a knock at the door startles me out of my zone. Then it swings open. I finish keying in the line, then look up to see who entered.

Peyton stands just inside the door, the fingers of one hand picking at the nails on the other.

"What's up?" I swivel in the chair to face her head-on.

"Three things." I lift my brows. "Yes, I'll meet you at Teddy's later." A corner of my mouth kicks up, but falls flat as she winces. "Dan has an issue with someone's ID at the door. And Ted is trying to break up a fight near the bar."

"Shit." I bolt from my chair and race out the door with Peyton on my heels. "Let Dan know I'll be at the door as soon as I'm done with Ted."

"On it."

The moment I round the end of the hall, chaos smacks me in the face. A crowd encircles Ted and two men. A woman hovers behind one of the men and I assume she is the reason the two men are throwing punches.

When I approach, Ted spots me with wide eyes. He has one man pinned in his grip, but the other won't calm down. I step between the two and get in the free man's face.

"Back the fuck up," I yell.

His bloodshot, glassy eyes wobble as he stares me down. He holds his ground; well, rocks a little. "Asshole touched my wife."

I step into him but don't make contact. Yet. "I said, back the fuck up."

The man peers over my shoulder with narrowed eyes. Jaw muscles taut. Shoulders to his ears. He jabs his finger in the direction of the other man. "I ever see your face again, you best run." He meets my gaze, takes a step back and nods. "I mean no disrespect. But no one touches my woman without permission or repercussions."

I lift both my hands to either side of my face. "I get it, man. But take the fight outside. Can't be having that shit in here." I peer over my shoulder at Ted and lift my chin. He escorts the other man to the door and I turn back to face the couple. "You're welcome to stay. But no fights."

He extends a hand and we shake before I walk to the door to resolve issue two. Thankfully, this resolves much faster.

Fake or forged IDs get spotted easily with all the UV lighting. The hardest part is convincing the person we know it is tampered with. The old days of laminated or non-hologram licenses are long gone. Fakes are easier to spot and confiscate.

"Your fakes may work at other bars and clubs, but not this one. Have a good night." I take the ID, grab the scissors we keep at the podium near the door, and cut the ID into jagged pieces. Then walk off as the punk curses me out.

Back in the office, I collapse in the chair behind the desk and run my fingers through my hair. I love my job, but sometimes it sucks.

I love the fast pace and upbeat energy that bleeds from the walls and floats in the air. The thump of the bass and pitch of the treble. The bright lights and dark corners. The smiles and bright eyes and exhilaration. I love it all. Hell, I even love the desk work. Filling orders and spreadsheets. Writing schedules and implementing procedures. Inventory is a beast, but I do it with a smile on my face.

But every once in a while, my job comes with a pile of bullshit.

The occasional bar fight over women or spilled drinks. Fake IDs and dealing with underage people trying to enter. Idiots harassing the staff or touching them inappropriately. Dealing with people who can't settle their tab.

Each instance is never pretty, but most resolve without bloodshed or police.

I focus back on the computer and the last of the invoices. *Almost done.* Just finish the last of the desk work and wrap the night up behind the bar. Get the brunt of the work done, then round out the work night with Peyton nearby.

With a deep breath, I pick up where I left off. Line by line, I input the last of the invoices and save the spreadsheet to the cloud. Once everything is filed away and I straighten up the desk, I roll back the chair and exit the office.

Smile on my face, an extra bounce in my step, I walk down the hall and out to the bar. Peyton glows like the sun. Her bright smile hasn't quite returned, but I hope to make it shine again later.

Peyton agreed to meet me at Teddy's. And tonight, I will man up and apologize for every time I hurt her in our formative years. I pray she accepts and allows me to make it up to her. However she deems worthy.

Peyton saying yes gives me hope. I hold on to that hope with every ounce of strength I own. Because hope is all I have right now.

fourteen

PEYTON

I really wanted to say no to Micah when he asked me to Teddy's after work. But the severity in his eyes wouldn't let the word slip between my lips. When I said I would think about it, I hoped my resolve would strengthen. That the word *no* would fall from my tongue with greater ease.

Alas, it did not.

Which leads to now. Me, parking my SUV and getting out to join Micah inside the bustling diner up the street.

We step inside and the hostess seats us right away. More than half the tables are occupied. Conversation and laughter erupt from all corners and the spaces between. The hostess seats us near a back corner. The two tables near us empty.

"Thanks for agreeing to meet me here again."

I nod and scan the menu. Although I always order the same thing, I feel a change of pace might be nice. Just as the server steps up and deposits water glasses on the table, I decide on the two egg breakfast with crispy bacon, home fries, and a biscuit. Micah orders the same as last time and we both ask for coffee.

The server takes our menus and wanders off to check on another table before going to the kitchen.

"So, why'd you ask me here?"

Micah fiddles with the edge of the paper placemat and avoids my gaze. His reluctance to speak or make eye contact has me curious and a little on edge. Since last weekend, Micah has been... different. Quieter. Hesitant whenever he gets within twenty feet.

This side of Micah piques my interest. What makes a man like Micah Reed soft?

"First and foremost," —he finally meets my eyes— "I want to apologize."

Is this *the apology*? An apology fifteen years overdue, but necessary. Is Micah Reed about to apologize for being one of the most epic assholes?

Slow down, Peyton. Best not to assume and get my hopes up. For all I know, the apology may have something to do with Roar.

"For?" I clutch the hem of my shirt beneath the table until my knuckles burn and nails bite my skin through the fabric.

His lips tilt up a fraction at the corners. The smile loaded with sympathy and regret.

This is it, isn't it? *The* moment. Would it be wrong to take out my phone, open the camera, switch it to video, and record this moment for posterity? Would he tell me to not act so childish? Tell me to take the moment seriously?

When you wait for a moment such as this for more than a decade, wanting to document it isn't strange. After living with self-doubt and being taunted for years, wanting to replay the moment one of the instigators apologizes is *not* wrong.

"I think you know what for." He tilts his head and holds my gaze with watery eyes.

"Humor me."

He yanks his hand from the paper placemat that now misses bits of the lower right corner. His hands drop to his sides. And by the way he shifts, I wonder if he now sits on his hands.

"Peyton, I was young and stupid. What I did to you... What those girls provoked me to do to you..." He drags his lips between his teeth and looks to the side for the count of three before meeting my gaze. His eyes red and veiny. "I'm sorry for the things I said to you and about you in high school. They weren't true. It was all a ruse to make a jealous, egotistical *girl* feel better about herself. It was wrong of me to say and I am truly sorry."

Frozen is the only rational term to explain my physical and mental state. Frozen.

Micah Reed just apologized. To me. Of his own volition. He admitted his words and actions were wrong and cruel and hateful. The bidding of a girl—a bully—who would do whatever it took to make those not in her circle feel worthless. But he owned the role he played in it all.

Nervous energy zips through my limbs and begs for me to jump off the seat. To garner the attention of everyone in the diner. To scream at the top of my lungs, *"Micah Reed apologized."* The words *I'm sorry* left his lips and hit my ears.

Weight lifts from my shoulders. My teenage self sags with a sigh in my mind. His apology doesn't wash away all the hurtful words and unkind acts he and his group of friends enacted. But his apology heals some of the old wounds that marred my heart long ago.

I hold his gaze as I stretch out my fingers. His normally bold blue eyes are dull and damp. Lips firmly tucked between his teeth as he fights his body's inclination to cry.

This apology is real. From the heart. Sincere and honest. Exactly what I waited all this time to hear.

"Thank you."

He sucks in a breath, then turns his head to the side. A hand meets the cheek not facing me and swipes. Then a tear rolls down the other cheek and I drop my eyes to the table. Grab my napkin-rolled silverware and unravel it. Toy with the tacky napkin band. Organize my silverware on the placemat— fork on the left, knife on the right, spoon at the top.

I give him this moment. Let him soak it up. Give him a chance to process the reality of what happened years ago, bask in the ownership he just took, and the apology only he could deliver. Couldn't have been easy. Owning the atrocities of your past never should be.

Once he collects himself, though, I have questions.

The server stops at the table, grabs each of our empty mugs in turn, and fills them with coffee. Then sets a thermal carafe on the table and walks off.

Micah tears open several packets of sugar and dumps them in his mug while I add one and some creamer. Our spoons clink the mugs in tandem with each other. Like synchronized swimmers, we both lift our mugs, blow on the steamy caffeine and sip the nectar of the gods. Although, I still don't understand how he tastes the coffee with that much sugar.

He sets his mug in the center of the placemat but doesn't remove his hands. Eyes on his thumbs as he paints them along the rim. Then he meets my gaze. His addictive lapis-blue eyes still a bit dull, but more beautiful. Raw. Real.

I swallow and try to quell the flurry rising and expanding in my chest.

"Now it makes sense."

"What?" I choke out.

"The instant hatred you had for me. It makes sense. I would've acted the same."

Arms at my sides, I lean forward and press my chest against the table, eyes locked with his. "How did you not know?"

"Who you were?" I nod and lean back. He lifts a shoulder, then drops it. "Guess I just forgot. Does that make me more of an asshole? Probably. But it's the truth. With the exception of track and my closest friends, high school is just a blur."

Wish it was a blur for me. Wish there was some way to make all the horrible memories and name calling and stunts vanish. Hypnotherapy. A magic pill. Years of speaking with a therapist helped, but it never made the memories disappear.

But all things happen for a reason.

If it weren't for those girls bullying me and the guys following their lead, I wouldn't be who I am now. Without their hurtful words and acts, I may not have thick skin. I may not be as bold and outspoken. Who knows... I could have ended up as some doormat.

There are no pros to bullying. No justifiable reasons to be hateful. But I found strength and courage and ferocity because of my high school experience. Yes, there were definitely some low points, but I had Mom and Dad to help me keep my head high. To not let me drown in the trenches. And for that, I am a new woman.

"One day, I hope it disappears for me too."

His back stiffens and eyes go wide. "I didn't mean it like that," he rushes out.

"Yeah, I know." He sags against the seat. "What I mean is, I hope enough time passes that I don't let those memories own me anymore." I lift the mug to my lips and sip. "What made you remember?"

"Shelly." I scrunch my brows and tilt my head. "My sister," he clarifies. "She was two years behind me, one behind you. She went to a different school, but her best friend, and mine, attended ours. And friends talk."

"Ah."

"Shelly, my friends, and I get together often. Gavin, my best friend, asked how work with *the blonde* was." I perk up at this. "They were in Roar a while back and noticed us barking at each other." He laughs and I join.

"Our bickering is an art form."

"Indeed. Anyway, I guess neither Cora nor Shelly had paid attention or were focused on the dance floor that night. They never saw your face. But when I said your first name the other night, they probed me for answers."

"That must've hurt." I smirk at him.

"Ha ha." He turns up the corner of his mouth and makes a goofy face. "Then, they took me on a trip down memory lane." His eyes drift to the table, then back up. "If it makes you feel better, it made me sick. Literally."

"It doesn't. But I'm glad you weren't okay with it. Says a lot."

"Peyton, I—"

The server interrupts Micah to set plates on the table. Once the buffet is spread out, the server double-checks the carafe, then leaves.

"Peyton, I may not be the best guy out there. I have done plenty of stupid and horrible shit. Shit I'm not proud of. Haven't we all. But adult me is disgusted by teenage me."

I break the egg yolk, spear some home fries and dunk

them. Micah stares, fascination glittering his eyes as I bring the yolky potatoes to my lips.

"What?" I mumble around my food with zero care for manners.

"That's cute."

Cute? Eating food is cute? Or is he mocking how I eat now?

I grab a strip of bacon and crunch down on it. "Define cute."

He shakes his head with a laugh. "Don't know many other people who do that." He points his fork at my runny egg. "Break the over-easy yolk to dunk their potatoes."

"And toast," I interject.

His head tips back and he laughs before leveling with me again. "And toast." Inch by inch, he leans closer. Face over the center of the table. "Like me," he whispers.

I stop chewing. Stop breathing. My body frozen and eyes unblinking as I stare straight ahead. The gold flecks in his rich-blue eyes twinkle. Is he serious? Or just yanking my chain?

"Are you making fun of me?"

A shadow passes over the line of his jaw. His smile flattens out. But that damn twinkle is still there.

"No. Definitely not." The corners of his lips curve up. "Never again," he states with reverence.

The muscles in my jaw contract as I chew the remaining bacon. "Good." I point the last of the bacon strip at him. "Wouldn't want to hurt you." Then I shove the bacon in my mouth.

"Might like that," he mumbles and sits back.

I drop my focus to the table, pick up my toast and dunk the corner of the triangle in the yolk. Peeking through my lashes, I spy a look I have never seen on Micah Reed's face. A look I never thought him capable of portraying.

Less than three feet away, eyes on his plate, fingers toying with his fork, Micah Reed blushes. At this time of night, others may pass it off as a night of partying or too much alcohol. But the only thing he's had to drink tonight is Dr Pepper and coffee.

Since our food arrived, I noticed slight variations in Micah's posture. Less rigidity. His spine not as straight and arms not as stiff. The fidgeting has also tapered off. As if he carries a new level of comfort. With me.

Other hallmarks I notice… more softness. The ridge of his cheekbone and how it accentuates his masculinity. The plumpness of his lips and the way they transform when he looks me in the eye. Firmer edges. The angle of his jaw, the light dusting of stubble, and the straight line of his nose until just the end where it bends slightly left. A gentleness. The way his lashes splay and stick beneath his eyes when on the cusp of crying.

When was the last time I saw a man cry? Saw them spill their emotions for all to see. I don't recall.

Maybe when I was seven and fell from the tree in the backyard. When Dad rushed from the deck chair, cradled me gingerly in his arms, and asked if there was pain. Was he crying then? The memory is there, but I don't see his face as clearly as I once did. Not without photographs or home movies.

We finish eating in relative silence. But a new tension builds between me and Micah. A tension I never would have imagined possible with this man. A man who currently has one leg between mine while the other skirts the outside. He has yet to touch me, but I *feel* how close he is. All it would take is the slightest move from either of us and we'd make contact. And hell… my skin flames from the near touch.

The server clears our plates and leaves the check. And just like last time, Micah snatches it first. He throws me a boyish, flirty smile and I can't help but smile in return. Once he pays and I leave a tip on the table, we walk toward my car.

Near the hatch, I stop and face him, hands fidgeting with the hem of my shirt. Why does this suddenly feel like the end of a date? This isn't a date.

Keep telling yourself that, girl.

"Peyton…" Micah stares over my shoulder, but his eyes seem out of focus. Then he blinks and brings his gaze back to mine. "Hope you believed me earlier when I apologized. I meant it. I mean it."

I nod. "Thank you, Micah. And I do."

He takes a step closer. Close enough to touch me without effort. "And I hope you can forgive me. Don't expect you to right here and now. But one day. I'd like…"

His eyes drop to my lips and I lick them. He follows the movement but doesn't speak.

"What?" Bright eyes leap to mine. "What would you like?" My voice low and rumbly.

Hundreds of words and phrases flash in his eyes. Across his face. His lips part, he takes a breath then closes them. He does this again and again. Unspoken words on the tip of his tongue. Wanting. Waiting. Hopeful.

"It's been a long time since I've smiled and laughed this much." He nibbles his bottom lip, then swallows. "And I have zero expectations of anything." He shoves his hands in his pockets. "I'd like if we can be…"

If we can be what?

Why am I sweating so much? And in the most awkward places.

"If we can be…" I parrot his words and drag them out.

"Friends." Oh. Friends. Why was part of me hoping he would say something else? Jesus, he only just apologized. He notices my shift and jumps back in. "Unless you're not okay with that."

"No," I answer, too quick and rowdy. "Yes. Sorry." He laughs as I straighten out my thoughts. "Yes, we can be friends."

"Good." He takes another step closer. His eyes all I see now. And then he wraps his arms around me and presses me to his chest. "Really am sorry, Peyton."

My arms encircle his waist as I rest my chin on his shoulder. Do friends hug like this? Opposite-sex friends. Reese and I hug all the time. But Reese is more of a brother, someone I have been close with for decades, and someone I ask for advice. Micah is definitely not in the same spectrum as Reese.

His breath hot on my neck, I close my eyes. Then the breeze cools my cheeks and neck as Micah takes a step back.

"Drive safe, hellcat." Another step back and a wink. "See you tomorrow."

I lift a hand and wave. "Tomorrow."

In the car, I press the ignition, buckle my seat belt and stare out the windshield. The radio plays, but all I hear is white noise. The lights from the dash brighten the cab, but I zone out into the dark night.

Micah drives off and waves as he goes. I mimic the movement but don't focus. Not really.

Tonight, Micah Reed apologized. More than once. Then, just minutes ago, asked for my forgiveness. Said he wants to be friends. But his flirtatious behavior and his arms around me screamed much more than friendship. Those sweet smiles and warm touches and soft tones spoke volumes. Of what happens beyond friendship.

And that nickname. Hellcat. That is new. Well, he muttered it once before, but I don't think he meant for me to hear it.

Damn, am I confused. Thrown off. Flabbergasted.

"What the hell just happened?" The question of the hour. One I have no idea how to answer.

fifteen

MICAH

What the hell was I thinking? Hugging Peyton had not been part of the plan. Not by a long shot. But now that I had, I wanted to hug her again. And with more frequency.

God, she was so warm in my arms. So responsive. Her minty coconut smell, potent and intoxicating and addictive.

How long had I wanted to do that? Hold her in my arms. Inhale her fragrance. Be impossibly close to her. Can't recall a day since she started at Roar where Peyton hasn't crossed my mind. Her fiery spirit wouldn't let me forget.

But I wanted more. More than the borderline friendly hug we exchanged.

What I wouldn't give to trace the tip of my nose along the bridge of hers. Taste her plump lips and impassioned tongue. Feel her soft skin under my fingers, her hot breath on my neck. Her gasp at my ear. And those brilliant violet eyes… I want them on me. Everywhere.

"Hey, big brother."

I jolt on the barstool at the high-top table as Shelly rounds it and parks across the table. Judgment billows off her as she narrows her eyes.

"Hey," I choke out, then clear my throat.

"Everything alright?"

"Yeah. Of course," I answer too quickly. "Why?"

Eyes that match mine rake over my face. Study every crease, line, and twitch. Search for clues why I jumped at her presence—something I have never done. But my poker face is strong and she gives up sooner than expected.

She huffs, sets her purse down, and laces her fingers on the table between us. This is Shelly's way of telling me we aren't leaving this table until I speak the truth.

Great.

"Micah, I have known you my entire life." *Here we go.* I roll my eyes. "Which means I pick up on everything. *Everything.*" Her added emphasis makes me squirm in place.

I shift my gaze to the parking lot through the window. Get momentarily lost as the sunlight gleams on the row of cars. When I look back to my sister, her brows lift and lips purse.

"Can we at least order lunch first?"

"Fine."

She snatches a menu from the metal clip on the table caddy. Not that she needs to read it. This bar and grill is a regular destination for our group. More during the evenings for karaoke, drinks, and laughter. But if I have more than half the menu memorized, she has the entire thing etched in stone. She, Cora, and Jonas ate here once or twice a week before Gavin moved back. Now, it's half that—which is still more often than my attendance.

A guy sporting a black polo with the bar logo sidles up to the table. He sets glasses of ice water in front of us. "Hey, Shelly."

The flush on my sister's cheeks poses new questions. "Hey, Tom."

He glances my way. "Micah." I give a polite smile and lift my chin. "What can I get you guys?"

Shelly and I place our orders. Tom scribbles them on his small notepad, tosses a stellar smile at Shelly, then walks off.

"What was that?" I gesture over my shoulder with a thumb.

With a slight shift to the left, she peers over my shoulder, then straightens. "Tom and I have gone on a couple of dates."

"Really?" I ask with humor in my tone.

She narrows her eyes and jabs the air with a finger in my direction. "Don't try to distract me from what's going on with you." I mentally sag but show no emotion. Both her forearms rest on the table as she leans closer. "What *is* happening, Micah?"

Sometimes, I wish I hated talking with my sister. Wish we weren't as close as we are. Don't get me wrong, I love Shelly. Would walk through fire for her. But when the more intimate topics come up—my dating life and hers—we both tend to clam up. There are just certain topics and details siblings shouldn't discuss. Right?

No matter how much I dance around answering her, she won't let up. Like when we were kids and she followed me on her bike. I had told her I wanted to play with boys my age, not my little annoying sister. But she never backed down. She pedaled faster. Kept pace with me. Told me boys and girls can play together. And her refusal to play with only girls led to us bonding more each year. If two years didn't separate us, people would swear we connected like twins.

Unwrapping the straw, I jab it between the ice and take a sip of water. Desperate to swallow past the nervous clump in my throat. This is Shelly. My sister. The one person I can spill all my truths to. She may be judgmental a moment, but once she processes, that harsh criticism falls away.

"I apologized."

She tilts her head and regards me for three, two, one. A light kicks on in her thoughts as her eyes grow wide. "To Peyton?" I nod and take another drink from the glass. "How'd that go?"

"Better than expected."

When I don't expand, she lifts a brow. "Elaborate for me, big brother."

Conversations with Shelly will never be basic. Will never be brief. We come from the same parents, were raised the exact same way, and will always want more details. To understand all the ins and outs in full description.

So, I lay it all out for Shelly. Tell her how I mulled over what to say all week. How I didn't say anything unnecessary to Peyton until last night. That I asked her to Teddy's after work—which piqued her interest and created a slight detour. A detour where I tell her we had gone there once already.

When I veer back to the original topic at hand, I explain how the apology went down. How I only remembered what happened all those years ago after talking with my sister and her friend. How my behavior made me physically ill.

"Shell, she accepted my apology with such grace. Made me feel worse."

Reaching across the table, her hands wrap around mine. "If you'd actually taken the time to know Peyton years ago, you would've learned then that she's pretty great. But everything happens for a reason. Cora said she kept to herself and had a small circle of friends. And that she was always with a tall guy with dark hair." I lift a brow and Shelly reads my curiosity. "Reese, I think. Her best friend. Anyway... my point is Peyton is kind and genuine. Your reaction is normal. That's called guilt, big brother. And feeling it, owning it, admitting it is a step in the right direction."

Is Reese the guy who occupied her attention in Roar last weekend?

The eight days since I watched Peyton smile and laugh with that guy feel more like months. Never-ending, nails-on-the-chalkboard months. I had never seen her so relaxed and carefree as I did that night. The way she leaned his direction. How easily she gave him the smile I wanted from her. Her comfort with another man made my skin crawl and blood pressure rise. Made my thoughts scatter like fall leaves on a windy day.

But if they were friends… well, that changes everything.

Did he come into Roar to intentionally provoke me? Was the idea hers or his? The answer makes all the difference. If it was his, I would venture to guess he was making a statement. Flaunting how incredible Peyton is and how easy it is to *not* have her. To say *see what I have and you don't, asshole.*

But… if it was Peyton's idea. That opens a whole new door.

If she asked her friend to fake flirt with her all night to piss me off, it says I cross her mind more than inside those four walls. That thought alone has my ego high above the powdery clouds.

Best not to get ahead of myself, though. Not without answers. Shelly is right. First, I need to absorb what my apology to Peyton means and where it leads us next.

"Have I told you lately how much I love you?"

She brings a finger to her lips and taps, eyes skyward to the left. "Hmm." Tap, tap, tap. "I'm drawing a blank, big brother. Better tell me again."

"You're ridiculous." I ball up my straw wrapper and fling it at her. "But you know I love you."

Her mouth drops open as she picks up the offending paper projectile and launches it back at me. "Love you, too."

Just then, Tom reappears with burgers and fries. His eyes dart between us and he sets our plates down with too much ease. Soon as his hands are free, he shoves them in his back pockets and gives Shelly a sheepish smile.

"Anything else I can get you?" His voice shakes.

"I'm good." Shelly smiles at him, then looks to me. "Need anything, brother?" The word brother leaves her lips louder than the rest.

Does this guy think Shelly is on a date with me? By definition, this is a date. Between two siblings. Zero romanticism going on here. But the fact she needed to clarify who I was says this guy is not only insecure, but has no clue who I am to Shelly. Yes, he knew my name because I frequent the place. But his knowledge doesn't extend much further.

When his shoulders drop and eyes land on me, he appears less concerned. I may not be of romantic interest for my sister, but *who* I am should bother him. Shelly is my baby sister. Which makes me her overprotective, overbearing big brother. That should make him shake in his Nikes, not sigh in relief.

So, I pull an asshole move. Because that is what big brothers are for.

"Thought I asked for a side of barbeque." Tom's brows pinch in the middle and Shelly huffs.

Tom goes from at ease to freaked out in point five seconds. "Shoot. Sorry, man. I'll go grab that." He scurries off to the kitchen without another word.

The moment he's out of earshot, I laugh. Shelly throws a fry at my face and I dodge it. "Not funny, asshole." I laugh harder. "And you didn't ask for a side of anything. Why are you being a dick?"

I pick up the fry she hurled and toss it in my mouth. "Because that's what big brothers do."

Tom rematerializes and deposits a full dipping cup of barbeque sauce on the table. "Sorry again. Anything else?" I bite my tongue at his shortness of breath.

"We're good. Thanks, Tom," Shelly answers. The guy flashes her an award-winning smile then leaves us to our lunch.

"What's going on with you and him?"

Rather than answer me, she scoops up her burger and takes the biggest bite possible. She did this to avoid speaking for the next however many minutes, but I pick at my fries and wait for her to finish chewing. Once she swallows down the last of it, she takes a sip of water and pretends I'm not waiting on her answer.

"Shell?"

She shakes her head. "Ugh. Why can't you just move past this?"

"Because I'm your brother. Why do you want me to?" If that guy so much as laid a hand on her without permission, I will kick his ass.

"No reason." She sighs and hangs her head. "Tom is nice. Like I said, we've been on a couple dates." Picking up a fry from her plate, she swirls it in the ketchup over and over.

"But…" I drawl out the word. "Has he… done something you're uncomfortable with?"

Twin eyes bolt to mine. Her head shakes furiously. "No. No, Micah." She drops the fry and wipes her hands with the napkin. "He's actually been sweet. Never makes me feel pressured."

"Good. 'Cause I'd kick his ass."

"I don't know. It's just..." She trails off and I give her a moment to collect her thoughts. "Have you talked to Mom in the last week?"

I search my memory for the last time I spoke with either of our parents. Last I remember was a few weeks back. "No. Why?"

"Well, she called me a couple nights ago. Said she'd call you, too. Anyway, she wants to start regular family dinners. Like scheduled dinners once a month or every two weeks. I don't remember the specifics."

"Okay… is that a bad thing?"

Shelly speaks with and sees Mom and Dad more often than I do. But I don't see anything wrong with spending more time with them. Maybe I am missing something.

"Normally, I'd say no. But Mom started dropping hints."

"Dropping hints?"

"Shelly, your father and I aren't getting any younger." She mocks our mother's voice. *"Would love to have more Reeds to love."*

"What?" Not sure if Mom is insinuating what I think she is, but I sure as hell hope not.

"Yep." She pops the *p*. "Mom basically told me she wants grandbabies. Seeing as neither of us is in a relationship" —her eyes dart across the bar to where I assume Tom stands— "that's not happening anytime soon."

"Are you not in a relationship with Tom?" I whisper-ask, unsure of his presence.

A huff leaves her lips. "He's nice. Treats me well. And I can tell he wants more." She looks over my shoulder again. "But I don't."

"Then you need to end it. Don't drag it out. It'll just make it worse."

"Yeah, I know." She stares down at her plate and shoves a fry in her mouth. "After that talk with Mom, it got me thinking." She peers up and winces. "Please don't be weirded out."

I place a hand over my heart. "Promise I won't be."

Shelly takes a deep breath, places her palms flat on the table, and looks me in the eye. Her lips twitch every other second as her eyes dart between mine. I have never seen her like this. Concerned about sharing her feelings.

"Micah, I haven't…" She takes another deep breath as I wait patiently for her to finish in her own time. "I haven't been with… anyone."

Setting down my burger, I tilt my head and study her expression. The way she bites her lip to stop the occasional twitch. How her eyes dance around the room every few seconds to be sure no one eavesdrops on our conversation. And how she keeps stretching out her fingers, then balls them again. Her actions have me on edge.

Is she still a virgin? Not that I ever want to imagine my baby sister with any man, but how? How is it possible my thirty-year-old sister is still a virgin?

"Ever?"

She shakes her head. "Hasn't felt right."

Before this conversation, there's no question I classified myself as a whore. Now… is there such a thing as a mega-whore?

Shelly has had zero sex. None. I, on the other hand, have lost track of how many women I have bedded. Hell, it's only the beginning of May and I have gone home with more than a dozen women this year.

"Not sure what to say, Shell. But don't let Mom's need for

grandchildren pressure you into something you don't want." I toss a quick thumb over my shoulder. "If you don't want to be with him, cut it off. When the right guy comes along, you'll know it. You'll feel it. And if you don't want kids, there is nothing wrong with that. That's your choice to make. Happy, romantic relationships don't always equal marriage and children."

"Do you want kids?"

Do I? At some point, when things were good between me and Rochelle, I considered the idea. But Rochelle was past the safe age of bearing children and I dismissed it. Would I give it more thought now? Couldn't be sure. With the right person, anything is possible. But I don't dream of picket fences and children's laughter. Not like some people do.

I shrug. "Not sure. Haven't put much thought into it."

"I don't think I do." She shoves another fry in her mouth.

Reaching across the table, I take her hand. We hold each other's gaze a beat. "Then do what makes you happy, little sis."

We finish lunch and pay. Shelly waves bye to Tom and we go separate ways in the lot after a hug and promise to see each other Sunday. On the way home, I replay our lunch together. My confession and Shelly's. And the fact our mother is practically guilting us to fulfill her own desires. Something I will chat about with Mom soon. Need to nip that in the bud.

Difficult enough to find a partner you love and trust. Going balls to the wall with commitment plus family is a whole other realm. One I am not ready for.

~

Sean texted when I got home from lunch with Shelly and asked everyone to come in early for a staff meeting. No details, just a *be here an hour early*. So, here I am. In the office. Waiting to hear what is going on.

Peyton shuffles past the office. I jump up from the chair, jog out, and call her name. She stops and assaults me with a smile. *Damn.*

"Hey," she says.

"Hey, yourself. Sorry you had to come in early."

Her shoulders bounce up a beat as she gives me a lopsided smile. "No worries. It happens every now and again."

We take a seat at the same table after greeting a few others. Ani and Sean walk in soon thereafter and the room goes quiet. Too quiet. My knee bounces beneath the table and I mentally yell at myself to stop.

"Thanks, everyone, for coming in early," Ani announces, with Sean at her side. "Wanted to touch base with everyone. Maybe start having staff meetings similar to this once a quarter, so we're all abreast of how things are going." Unscrewing the cap, Ani drinks from a bottled water then continues. "Foot traffic and sales have been on the rise since last quarter. And we're looking into ways to keep the momentum going."

Shit. I was supposed to search ideas for the slower nights and send them to Ani. A task I started but never finished. That is priority number one as of now.

"That being said," Ani continues. "Sean and I will be looking at staff changes." Several sets of eyes go wide. "Sorry, let me clarify. We will be adding more staff. So, if you know anyone in need of a job who would be a great addition to the family, pass along the news."

For the next fifteen minutes, Ani carries on with sales numbers and I tune her out. I see the sales numbers for Roar on a nightly basis. Business has been on the rise. Not sure if the themed nights are a hit or if the new apartment complex blocks away has brought more foot traffic. Either way, the influx in business is a good thing.

Out of the corner of my eye, I spy how attentive Peyton is of Ani. How she hangs on her every word. Glued to sales totals from the fourth and first quarters. Giving a nod when Ani mentions the uptick in patron count. Or a subtle smile when Ani looks her way.

Peyton seems more invested than a typical bartender. While most of the staff zones out, she zeros in. This minor detail makes me question Peyton and Ani's relationship, and what her attentiveness means.

What am I missing here?

sixteen

PEYTON

"Let's end this quarter with a bang," Ani cheers as she wraps up the meeting. Then she claps her hands and everyone parts like the perfect comb over.

Those who aren't working tonight share hugs or goodbyes before heading out the back. The rest of us shuffle off to our designated areas to prep for another busy night. Just as I remove fruit from storage to slice and add to the condiment trays, Ani sidles up to me.

"Before you get bogged down, let's chat."

I nod, set the fruit down, and wipe my hands clean. Ani leads me around the bar and toward the hall. As we pass Micah and Sean, I don't miss the way Micah follows us with his eyes. *Great*, something else I will need to handle. Micah's curiosity.

In the office, Ani closes and locks the door. She ambles to the couch, lowers herself onto the worn leather and gestures for me to do the same. Without hesitation, I join her.

"Been a little bit since we last chatted. How are you?"

I sink into the cool leather more, rotate to face her, and

tuck a foot under my bottom. "Oh, you know. Much the same."

"And Micah?"

My head teeters left, then right. "That has improved. Surprisingly."

Ani rubs her hands together in front of her mouth. "Do tell."

I wouldn't say Ani and I go way back. But we have known each other coming up on seven years. We met three years after my father died. At the time, my mother still suffered severe depression and was having trouble making ends meet. I still lived at home when Dad passed and refused to let my mother live alone. So, I stayed, stepped up and got another job when one wouldn't cut it.

That is how Ani and I met.

During the day, I scanned groceries at the local supermarket. The job was dull and monotonous, but it paid a decent wage and provided benefits. I met plenty of interesting and odd people, drummed up conversations about random items they purchased and smiled until my cheeks burned.

Ani came through my checkout line with a barrage of alcohol. Red and white wine, tequila, whiskey, vodka. You name it, she placed it on the belt. Along with soda and fruity concoctions. Beep after beep, I stared down at each bottle and assumed this woman was throwing one hell of a party. I'd asked, *"Where's the party. I'd love to tag along."*

It had been a joke. Something to make my customer laugh. A way to spark conversation. But Ani jumped on board and invited me to her place. At the time, she and Sean were engaged. The wedding a couple months out. They'd met late in life. Both established in running their own business. Both ambitious. They also fell instantly and madly in love.

In their lavish home, we partied and laughed and I made them the grossest mixed drinks ever. We laughed harder. Ani said she and Sean were thinking of buying a bar and that I should work for her. She'd train me, of course. The job sounded fun at the time, but I was worried about leaving Mom home alone.

So, I got a second job at a fast-food place on my days off from the supermarket. Ani and I still kept in touch. Text messages. Random girly days at the salon. The occasional trip to the beach.

As time moved on, Mom got better. She also met Harold. Once I knew she was happy, I moved on too. Moved out of my childhood home and rented an apartment with Reese. It felt amazing to finally be on my own. To be my own woman.

Time after time, Ani begged me to come work for her. Told me all the lavish details when she and Sean bought the club in Tampa five years ago. It wasn't in the best part of town, but it wasn't horrendous either. And the neighborhood was cleaning up. The club was always busy and they saw larger profits each year.

When she begged me again, just over a year ago, I caved. I had never seen her so giddy.

My first night working, the first time I laid eyes on Micah since high school, I spilled our shared history with Ani. From day one, she has known it all.

"He apologized."

Her jaw drops as she smacks the air between us. "Shut up. Are you serious right now?"

"Wouldn't joke about it."

"How did that come about?" I recount the story as she sits back and stares at me in awe. "Who knew? Don't get me wrong, I was hopeful things would get better soon."

"Me, too. I've about had it with his constant antagonizing bullshit."

She reaches across the space and pats my forearm a minute. "You know I love catching up, but we should talk business too. For at least one minute."

I roll my eyes. "Always such a party pooper," I tease.

"Never," she gasps. "I'll address that later. Did you come up with any ideas for Mondays and Tuesdays?"

"Yes." I inch closer and share a list of ideas that may drum up more business for the slower nights.

Ani leans an arm against the back of the couch. A hand at her chin and forefinger over her lip. Her attention focuses solely on me while I talk animatedly. Ani is my friend first and boss second. Which may be one of the reasons she values my opinion more. Years ago, she met *me*. Got to know and bonded with me before business was added in the mix. When she asks my opinion, it isn't only a business transaction. She *wants* and values my input.

Ideas fly from my lips. Charity bingo nights. Karaoke. Bar Olympics. Trivia nights. Plenty of bars do these things. Some nearby, others across the Bay. But we have the space to accommodate more bodies. Yes, we may need to invest in more tables, chairs and equipment. But the profit some of those nights would bring to Roar is endless.

Most bars offer food. Roar does not. But I toss out the idea of offering small options. Food that doesn't require a kitchen. Either that or connect with local businesses and have them serve or cater food. They pay a fee to set up and split their profits between them, Roar and the charity if we chose to offer bingo.

Of course, drinks would be offered. Maybe special drinks

for different nights at a different price point. Again, splitting profit with charity.

When I finish, Ani claps her hands and presses them to her lips. "I love this, Peyton. Thank you. When I'm back at my computer, I'll mull over what days will work best for each. Make some calls and create a marketing plan." She reaches forward and takes both my hands in hers. "Still on board with—"

A knock at the door cuts her off and I nod in answer. "Yes," I say as the door handle clicks, but doesn't open.

Ani rises from the couch. Her heels clap against the concrete as she nears the door. Lock disengaged, she twists the knob and opens the door. From my seat on the couch, I spot half of Micah past Ani's petite stature.

Once, twice, thrice, his eyes dart between me and Ani. Brows pinched and eyes narrowed. Countless questions written on the lines of his face. Questions he will surely ask once Ani leaves. Questions I need to avoid answering until Ani gives me the go-ahead.

Hello, awkward party of one. Especially since Micah and I are trying to heal our past.

"Hey, Ani. Just wanted to let Peyton know I did most of her prep, but there's some left before open." Dark-blue eyes glimmer at me across the room.

With a shake of her wrist, Ani glances down at her diamond-encrusted rose gold watch that cost more than my monthly rent. "Shit, Peyton. Sorry. Didn't mean to keep you so long."

I have never been envious or bitter toward Ani and Sean and their obvious wealth. Simple things make me smile. Not to say I haven't wondered what it would be like to live a lavish lifestyle. Would my purchase habits change? I'd like to believe the change would be subtle. That I would maintain my same style, just purchase better quality items.

I rise from my spot on the couch and walk to the door. I rest a hand on Ani's shoulder and turn my attention to Micah. "No worries. I'll head out."

Squeezing between Ani and Micah, I head down the hall and out to the bar. A moment later, Micah strolls out with Ani on his heels. She looks my way and winks. Micah doesn't miss the interaction. His brow twitches before he joins Sean and Ani. They chat another minute before Ani shoulders her purse and hooks herself on Sean's arm.

She guides him over to the bar and they both say goodbye before leaving through the back door.

Micah's eyes burn my profile, but I don't spare a glance in his direction. Now is not the time to answer all his questions. Ani and I agreed not to share what's coming until she and Sean are ready.

I finish prepping the bar. Cut the last of the fruit, fill condiment bins and stash the extras in the fridge beneath the bar. All the while, Micah leans his hip against the counter and watches me like a predator.

Neither of us says a word. A battle of wills. But my will is stronger. And he will cave long before me.

"Whatever," he grumbles and pushes off the counter. He stomps across the club and checks in with everyone working tonight before unlocking the doors.

The doors open and the masses flood the bar within minutes. Worries of Micah giving me the death stare for the next seven hours vanish. One after another, I focus on the crowd. On pouring shots of whiskey and tequila. Filling mugs from the keg taps. Mixing fruity froufrou drinks and blending daiquiris. Spreading smiles and jokes and laughter.

At some point, I sense Micah behind the bar. I keep my eyes on the task at hand, but catch him out of the corner of my eye. He slings drinks on pace with me. Muscles stretch his black button-down taut while he works. Forearms and biceps flex as he shakes and pours martinis. Jaw more defined by the light layer of stubble and his occasional smile. And every once in a while, he dances to the music while working.

I hate and love how I notice him now.

Before our first night at Teddy's, I was aware of Micah. Knew where he was—to avoid him. Didn't seek him out, but stayed attune to his whereabouts. Of when he walked the floor or stepped behind the bar.

Now, I am much more cognizant.

Years ago, I saw Micah with rose-colored glasses. Dreamed of a boy my mind construed as appealing. Soft hair, long muscular legs, strong arms, and stare-at-them-all-day eyes.

Although he still acts immature, Micah is very much a man. A man my eyes refuse to shift away from. A man I notice now more than I care to admit aloud.

The way his slacks hug his long, thick, muscular legs and rest low on his hips. How his broad chest tugs at his shirt when he stretches or reaches certain directions. The flex of his forearms that makes me bite my lower lip. Far too often, my eyes trail up the exposed skin of his neck. From the hollow of his throat, up over his Adam's apple, to the sharp line of his jaw. From there, his lips garner my attention. Pink and plump and soft looking.

Fingers snap in front of my face. I blink and look to my right.

"Sorry, what?"

Two striking blue irises search my face. "I called your name three times."

"You did?" Someone needs to slap me from my damn daydreams.

"Yeah." He steps closer. Close enough for me to smell his sweet, woodsy amber cologne. Close enough for me to identify the gold flecks in his eyes like stars in the night sky. "Everything okay?" His eyes dart between mine, on the hunt for answers.

I don't trust my voice or my words right now. So, eyes locked on his, I nod. In my periphery, his hand twitches at his side. Balls into a loose fist, then flattens out. Inches forward, then lands back at his side.

He licks, then captures his lower lip before setting it free. "You sure?" He inches closer. So very close. My breasts centimeters from grazing his chest.

Heat slicks my skin. My pulse hammers in my ears as my breath comes in short, shallow bursts. He licks his lips again and my eyes drop to witness the action. I swallow and mentally whimper. My tongue eager to taste him.

"Yep," I choke out, then clear my throat. "Everything's fine." My voice cracks on the last word like a pubescent boy. *Great.* 'Cause that will convince him.

"If Ani gave you a hard time earlier" —he jerks his thumb toward the office— "I'll speak with her."

I shake my head. "Not necessary. We were just catching up."

His brows pinch. "Catching up?"

"Mmhm. Girl talk."

Micah steps back and goose bumps prickle my skin. He squints but relaxes his eyes just as quick. Then he throws me a smile. Not the one that makes me want a second helping. But the one painted in hard lines and artifice and bullshit. Before I say another word, he shifts his gaze elsewhere and walks off.

Tempting as it is to rake my eyes over Micah's broad shoulders and ample ass, now is not the time. Instead, I focus on the actual retreat. On the tension in his shoulders. The hand rubbing at the back of his neck. The rush in his stride and flat expression on his face when I glimpse his profile once more.

He weaves between the tables and heads for the outskirts of the room. At the wall, he glances back to the bar and sees me staring after him. He crosses his arms and widens his stance. His body stiffens. Lips form a flat, tight line. Then he simply shakes his head.

One, two, three breaths. His eyes hold mine captive. My thoughts a prisoner to him. Until he breaks contact, mouths what looks like *whatever,* and gets lost in the crowd.

Just as things were on the upswing with Micah, I ripped it to shreds. "Whatever," I mumble to myself. Soon, it all changes anyway. Best to keep things as they have been. With Micah at a distance.

seventeen

MICAH

Fourteen days have passed since the meeting at Roar. Fourteen days since I knocked on the office door and waited for Ani to unlock it. Fourteen long-as-hell days since I asked Peyton what she and Ani were discussing in the office. And nearly just as long since she gave me some bullshit answer.

An answer I have done my best to ignore and move past. An answer my gut tells me isn't all lies. But it isn't all truth either.

Peyton and I, since the night before the meeting, aren't the same people. As individuals or within feet of each other.

For more than a year, Peyton was at my throat. A lioness out for blood. Claws extended and ready to attack. She did her best to ignore my advances, but I never backed down. Never cowered under her snarl.

Now, she teases me. Eggs me on with her smart mouth and mischievous smile. Has switched from calling me Micky —*thank god*—to starlight. Which isn't any better, but sounds less creepy.

And I have taken the liberty of calling her hellcat—a

name I reserved for when I was alone with my fist and thoughts—more openly.

But fourteen days ago, some other force in the universe shifted. Made Peyton look at and talk with me in a way unlike our previous interactions. Yes, she still has that feisty edge I live for. But now, it has softer edges. And not knowing if Ani is the reason behind the change irks me.

At the end of the bar, Peyton delivers two beers and two fingers of whiskey in a tumbler. A man with dark hair and a protruding belly hands her a bill, flashes a toothy smile, then walks off with the drinks. The moment he disappears, she spins and catches my eyes on her.

In one, two, three strides, Peyton stands less than five feet away. "You looking at my ass, starlight?"

The corner of my mouth curves up and I waggle my brows. "What's it to you, hellcat?"

She steps closer. So close her breasts brush the starched cotton of my button-down. "Maybe I don't want your eyes on my ass."

"No?" She slowly shakes her head. "Then where *do* you want them?"

A millimeter at a time, her lips form a wicked smile. "Get more creative."

I press us impossibly closer. Her breasts flatten against my pecs. One of my legs between hers. Lips a breath apart. *Fuck.* In one move, my lips would crush hers. But damn if the foreplay doesn't turn me on.

"Creative, huh?"

She hums and the vibrations ripple through my chest, my abdomen, my balls. "Yes, creative." Her breath hot and damp on my lips.

Jesus fuck.

I lick my lips—almost lick hers—then unwillingly inch back. "I'll work on that."

She turns to the register, rings up the drinks, cashes the tab out and puts the excess in the tip jar. "Good. Creativity is the spice of life." She winks, then sashays down the bar alley to the next waiting customer.

Screwed. One word and the definition of my current existence. But I wouldn't want it any other way.

The rest of the night goes much the same. We work and tease and laugh. She provokes and bats her lashes with a wicked smile on her lips. Bets me she mixes and serves better drinks. Draws attention from the crowd as she challenges me to a face-off. My hesitation widens her smile and she pushes harder.

"What's the matter?" She leans in, her breath hot on my ear. Her sweet scent in my nose. "Afraid to lose?"

I lean away, lock on to her radiant violet irises and shake my head. "What do I get when I win?"

"Ooh, confident." Her eyes drop to my lips and I stop breathing. "Who says you'll win?"

"Can't deny facts." I lick my lips and her eyes follow the movement. Her breathing hiccups once. But once is more than enough.

"We'll see." She spins to face the crowd. "Ladies and gentlemen," she shouts with hands in the air. "Can I have your attention?" Everyone within earshot faces the bar and falls quiet. "Boss man and I are having a little showdown." The crowd hoots and hollers and whistles. "He says his drinks are better than mine," she yells. Men boo at this and she laughs. "So, I challenged him to a duel of sorts. Who wants to be the judge?"

Cheers erupt from the crowd and three people slap a

twenty on the bar top.

I sidle up to her, my hand brushing hers. "Three people, three different drinks."

"Agreed."

Over the next few minutes, we decide on rules for the challenge. One—the customer selects their preferred drink. But it cannot be premade or from the tap. Two—they don't watch us make or serve the drinks. They will be blindfolded. Three—they will blind taste test the drinks and choose the winner before removing the blindfold and meeting the maker. Four—best two out of three wins.

The three people shuffle up to the bar and take a seat as the crowd steps back. Becky and Jake—two of the servers— step up between them. After the rules are explained, makeshift blindfolds made from Roar tank tops are put in place.

Contestant one requests a mojito. Peyton and I dive for shakers and get to work.

I pinch a cluster of mint leaves from the bin, toss them in the shaker and muddle them with a pestle. Then I measure rum and lime juice before pouring it in. I glance over and spot Peyton adding fresh lime and crushing it with the mint. *Fuck.* Should have used fresh. No going back now.

Simple syrup and ice go in next. I cap the shaker and make a show of blending the ingredients. Several shakes later, I swap the cap for the strainer and pour the drink in a glass, adding a splash of soda water. I place the drink on the bar and Becky helps the first contestant find the glass.

As I rinse the shaker, I peer over at Peyton. She pours her drink, unstrained into a glass, adds soda water and garnishes it with sugar crystals and a mint leaf. Good thing these people aren't basing the winner off of appearances, because mine is nowhere near as fancy as Peyton's liquid art.

The man sips mine. Swishes it around in his mouth. Lets it sit on his tongue a moment. Then swallows. He asks for water, takes a sip, then moves to Peyton's drink. Follows the same taste test routine. And then, silence. After seconds that mirror hours, he raises an arm for the drink he preferred.

Peyton. "Damn it," I mutter under my breath.

The crowd roars as the man removes his blindfold. While we move on to the next contestant, the man throws Peyton a wink and sips his mojitos.

Contestant two orders Sex on the Beach. I bite my cheek to restrain the dirty joke on the tip of my tongue.

We both grab high ball glasses and get to work. This go-around Peyton measures with a jigger. And I don't measure at all. I have made Sex on the Beach thousands of times over the years. Enough to know how much to add without measuring. Enough trial and error to know women suck it down and request another.

Cranberry and orange juice, vodka and peach schnapps, a small scoop of ice and an orange slice and cherry to garnish. Peyton and I add straws and stir at the same time and deposit the drinks in front of the woman. Jake guides her to the glasses and she tastes each one.

Without hesitation, her hand flies up and declares me the winner. Like a child, I stick my tongue out at Peyton and she mocks me in return.

We step over to the last contestant. A lumberjack of a man —inches taller than me, thick beard and more muscle than necessary. His appearance intimidates me. Thankfully, this is all about the drinks.

"White Russian," he announces after Becky taps his shoulder.

A simple drink. Also a drink that is easy to fuck up if not

measured correctly. Of course, the drink with fewer ingredients makes me sweat the most.

While Peyton grabs the vodka and coffee liqueur, I fetch the cream from the fridge. I measure out the vodka while she measures the liqueur. Then we swap. I let her add the cream to hers first, then pour it in mine as she hands over her drink.

Cream swirls like storm clouds as it blends with the alcohol. The man stirs the drink, then lifts it to his lips and tastes. Every person within ten feet of the showdown remains deathly quiet. He sets the glass down and repeats the process with mine. His poker face as hard and unforgiving as stone. Then he tastes them both again.

Dampness coats my skin and stains the armpits of my shirt. My palms clench and unclench as if the muscles glitch. My foot bounces and knee taps the cabinet beneath the bar.

Why the hell does the outcome have me on the edge of a cliff?

I peek over at Peyton and see her biting her lower lip. Watch her pick at the bottom hem of her shirt. When she notices me checking her out, she throws me a half smile.

Her apprehension is cute as fuck.

The bar erupts in cheers and I shift my eyes back to lumberjack man. Who has a hand in the air. The hand that says I just fucking won.

"Hell yes!" I shout as Peyton pushes her lower lip out to pout. And fuck if I don't want to suck on her lip.

"What's my punishment?" she asks as we clean up and business returns to normal.

My bicep grazes hers as we clean glasses and I freeze. Heat starts as a low simmer at my elbow and burns hotter as it nears my chest. A peek down at her still hands tells me she feels it, too.

"Have to think on it," I rasp out. "I'll let you know before we leave." Once everything from the *Micah makes the best drinks* contest is cleaned up, I dry my hands. "Going to do paperwork," I tell her, then walk on uneven legs to the office.

Behind the closed door, I adjust myself and groan as I sit. The worn, stiff chair does me no favors as I shift to find a more comfortable position. Damn, I was on edge. Her pouty lips and punishment inquiry… my dick grew ridiculously painful beneath the zipper.

I close my eyes and her face pops up behind my lids. The occasional flyaway lock of blonde hair on her cheek. How her violet irises glow when she gets excited and the gray flecks enhance the darker rim. Her not too thin, not too thick button nose. And her perfect fucking lips. So pink and fleshy and suckable.

My eyes fly open as I curse and adjust myself. Again.

I wiggle the mouse to wake the computer and open the invoice spreadsheet. Dragging the wire basket across the desk, I get to work plugging numbers and updating inventory. Spreadsheets… a surefire way to kill arousal.

Peyton enters the office as I pick up the last invoice. "Last call," she informs me.

My eyes dart to the upper right of the screen and note the time. Almost two in the morning. "Well, shit."

She laughs. "Time flies when you're having fun."

I wave an invoice in the air. "Were you a math nerd?" Only numbers people get excited over this kind of stuff. Not that I failed math, but when they added letters with the numbers to equations, I questioned everything.

"Wouldn't say *nerd*. But me and numbers are good friends."

She spins and starts for the hall. "Peyton."

"Yeah?" She eyes me over her shoulder.

"Hang out with me tomorrow."

"Sorry, what?" She backtracks and faces me again.

"Call it your punishment. Hang out with me." A wince stretches her lips. "My friends will be there. And my sister."

"Uh…" Her eyes dart around the room a moment then land on mine. "That sounds…"

"Fun?"

"Actually, I was going to say awkward."

I raise my right hand, then lay it over my heart. "Swear it won't be."

"Says the man who knows everyone attending."

"Cora remembers you. And by proxy, Shelly."

"No, they remember high school Peyton. The loner girl who preferred dark spaces and hidden alcoves."

"Don't you still?" I tease.

"Shut the hell up." I laugh. "Micah, we've hung out a couple times. Yes, things are less shitty between us now." I wipe away a nonexistent tear and she flips me the middle finger. *You wish.* "But I don't think we've reached the 'let's hang out with other people together' phase of our friendship yet."

"At least you admit our friendship." She rolls her eyes. "C'mon. Please?" I exaggerate my plea and aim for my best sad-puppy expression.

A groan rumbles in her chest and spills from her lips. "You are so annoying."

"Before the contest, you agreed to winner's choice," I remind her with a smirk.

"True. But I didn't think it would be you forcing me to hang out with you and a group of people I don't know." I give her a look that says, *really?* She narrows her eyes as she tries

—and fails—to give me her most menacing expression. "What?"

"Don't you pretty much do that every night we work?"

Once again, she presents me with her middle finger. "It's different and you know it."

"Please, Peyton," I say, softer this time. "Promise not to make it weird."

Peyton hangs her head. She stares at the floor and taps her thigh with her fingers. When she lifts her head, the look in her eyes stops my heart. Veiny damp eyes stare back. Her chin wobbles as she clamps down on her lower lip.

The chair legs scrape the concrete floor as I bolt up and dash over to her. I halt in front of her, desperate to frame her face in my hands and soothe her. But I don't know if she will shirk my touch. Only one way to find out.

One at a time, and with slow precision, I bring my hands to her face. She doesn't shy away from my touch and that small action has my heart galloping in wide-open pastures.

"Hey." I tip her head little by little until our eyes meet. "It'll be okay."

"You can't know that."

"I'll make sure of it," I vow.

"I-I just can't…" She swallows and gathers her thoughts. One deep breath, then another. "I just can't go through that again." She holds my gaze. "How people were all those years ago."

"You won't. I promise." Fuck, I want to kiss her. Seal my words with our joined lips.

She nods. "Okay. But if shit goes south" —she gestures between us— "this is done."

"Then nothing will go wrong." She takes another deep

breath and I reluctantly release her. "Give me your number and I'll text you the address and time."

This snaps her back to reality. "You want my phone number?"

"Yes," I drawl out. "To text you the info. And in case you get lost, you have my number."

That sounded like a legit reason to ask Peyton for her number. Right? Not that I couldn't get it from the employee contact list. But I'm not that much of a dick.

"Fine," she huffs out. I hand her my phone and she texts herself from my phone. When she hands it back to me, I read the screen.

"Couldn't resist?"

"Nope." She starts for the door again. "Need to go finish up. See you tomorrow."

Sunday. "Tomorrow," I parrot.

~

"You did what?" Shelly shouts in my ear. I yank the phone away and rub my ear.

"Shell," I drag out her name with a groan. "It's too early to yell."

"I don't care," she yells louder. Thank fuck the phone is still a good six inches from my face. "When you text your sister that you invited Peyton Alexander to our Sunday night get-together, what did you think would happen?"

"Maybe that you'd text me back with shouty capitals. You know I work until three in the morning. Cut me some slack."

She laughs some twisted, maniacal sound. "You want *me* to cut *you* some slack?"

"Please." I bring the phone closer, hopeful she got all the yelling out of her system.

"Micah…" she huffs and I picture her eyes rolling. "What possessed you to invite her?"

A question worth asking since Peyton and I don't have stellar history. But we decided to be adults. I extended my long overdue apology for labeling and shunning her during high school. For intentionally getting under her skin at work. For every single pain she endured with the ripple effect of my words.

More than anything, I hold immense gratitude for Peyton.

Peyton didn't have to accept my apology. But she did. She didn't have to agree to Teddy's the first or second time. But she did. She rose above and acted more mature than most. We aren't children anymore, but plenty of people our age refuse to grow up. Thankfully, that doesn't apply to us.

"Shell, please don't make this weird."

"It is weird. You don't agree?"

"I don't," I say with an air of confidence. "Was I an asshole to her more often than not? Yes. But we talked it out. Laid everything on the table. I apologized, Shell. And she has slowly let me in. We're friends." Although, I hope to one day be more than friends with Peyton. After wrapping my arms around her, after inhaling her sweet scent up close, I want so much more.

For now, though, I plan to keep that secret locked up tight.

"I just… how?"

"It's not something I question. She's willing to give me another chance. Willing to be friends. And if it doesn't work out, then it ends." I refuse to fuck up with Peyton again. Refuse to not have her in my world.

"It's still weird."

"Only if you make it that way." I take a deep breath, then rest my forearm over my eyes. "Both of us are trying. Can you do the same? Maybe let Cora and Gavin know too. They're the only other people in our circle that know her."

The line goes quiet. Too quiet. I lift my arm and pull the phone away to see if the call dropped. Nope. Just my sister in her head. And for someone who preaches love and fate and all that cosmic mumbo jumbo, she fights my friendship with Peyton hard.

But I give her a moment. To gather her thoughts and formulate her words. To swallow down reality and move forward with a smile on her cute face.

"Fine," she huffs out. "I'll talk to Cora and Gavin. But I make no promises on how they'll behave."

"You're my favorite sister."

"I'm your only sister, dumbass."

"Which is why you're my favorite." She growls on the other end. "Love you, Shell."

"Guess I love you, too."

The call disconnects and I toss my phone on the comforter. I roll over, bury my face in the pillow and groan.

When I asked Peyton to hang out tonight, I didn't realize I would have so much prep work. To tame my sister and spread the word to the other two people who knew Peyton. To ask them to be cordial and *normal*. But I should have expected it.

Bringing new people into our circle is a big deal. And not something we do often. But the invitation has already been delivered and accepted. Now, I need to do my part. I need to make sure tonight feels like every other Sunday. Just friends hanging out and enjoying life.

'Cause that is all Peyton is… my friend.

eighteen

PEYTON

I fling a shirt across the room and Reese laughs. "Not helping," I say as I poke my head out of the closet.

Reese lays across my bed, feet dangling off the side, and holds up the most recent flying article between his thumb and forefinger. Then proceeds to twirl it like a lasso. Definitely not helping.

"I have never seen you so nervous about hanging out with a *friend*?"

I storm out of the closet, stomp across the lush carpet and stop in front of him. Hands on my hips, I pin him with what feels like my *shut up* glare. And what does he do? He laughs harder.

I snatch the shirt from his hand. "And I've never seen you be such a jerk. But here we are."

"Ouch." He sits up and presses a hand to his heart. "You wound me."

"No." I smack his bicep and a hiss leaves his lips. "But now I have."

He rubs the red palm print on his arm and inspects it far too long. "That really hurt."

"Then I hope you never get into any physical altercations." I riffle through the shirts on the bed in the hopes one will stand up and say *pick me*. But shirts don't stand up. Nor do they speak. "Will you please help me?" I give Reese my best pouty lips and sad eyes.

"Peyton…" He rests a hand on my shoulder. "We aren't teenagers anymore. This is not a date. Quit thinking you need to look perfect. He said it's a group of friends hanging out. Right?" My eyes on his, I nod. "Just be comfortable. Throw on your favorite jeans and graphic tee. Pick a hoodie to take, just in case."

"Ugh." I fall face-first into the mountain of shirts. Inhale the lavender detergent and dryer sheet scent as I take a deep breath. The smell does little to calm me. "Why did I agree to this?" My voice garbled by the cotton.

A warm hand rubs up and down my back. Slow and steady and rhythmic.

Reese has always had the touch. A way to soothe me without effort. If he felt like less of a sibling, our relationship could have been much different. But I love Reese how he is and who he is in my life. He has been my foundation for years. The friend who walked home with me in middle school. Who shared corny jokes and never held anything back. The friend who took my hand in high school, came to my defense and never let me down. Who let me cry in his arms while he stroked my hair and reassured me everything would work out.

Even now, while he razzes me, it isn't meant to be serious. More like an icebreaker. A joke to lessen the anxiety wreaking havoc in my veins.

"Because you're a glutton for punishment," he muses. I lift my head and give my best death stare. "Joking." He lifts his hands in defense. Then his expression turns more serious. "Honestly, you always try to see the best in people. Even those who have wronged you." He shrugs and toys with the shirt in his hands. "You talking and hanging out with Micah, that's you giving him another shot. A chance to make amends."

I hate when Reese is right. When he turns somewhat philosophical on me. Makes me see the truth behind my actions. They aren't bad truths. But speaking them aloud can be jarring.

I wiggle into a sitting position and lift my eyes to his. "Guess you make a valid point." He opens his mouth and I slap my palm over his lips. "Don't you dare."

"Wha—?" he mumbles against my skin.

"Say I told you so." I pull my hand away.

"I wasn't—"

"And don't lie." My finger jabs his direction, inches from his face.

Reese's booming laughter echoes off the walls. "Fine, I was. Can't help myself."

My palms slap against his chest, then shove him back. "Always such a pain in my ass."

"You love me." He winks.

I sit back on my haunches and stare at the mess on my bed. "And if you love me, you'll just tell me what to wear. Isn't that what besties are for?"

"Like a fifth of the time." He sticks his tongue out and makes a face at me. "But sure, I'll help." Searching the hurricane of cotton on my bed, he plucks a shirt from the pile. "Wear this with your black boyfriend jeans and all-black Chucks."

The shirt lands on my head and shields my eyes. "Hey."

Reese just laughs. The bed shifts as I tug the shirt off. I jump up and follow him to the door. "Thank you." His eyes soften. "I know this isn't a date, but I've never felt this nervous about hanging out with people. And you always make me feel better. So, thank you."

Reese lifts a hand, clutches my hair and gives a slight tug. "You're welcome. That's what friends are for." He flashes his sweet smile. The one that only appears on rare occasions. "If he hurts you, though…"

"He'll answer to you," I finish.

"Damn straight."

Reese all but shoved me out the front door and latched the security chain so I would leave.

Once I was dressed, he suggested I leave my hair down and put on minimal makeup. That was how I spent most of my days not at the club anyway. But when it actually came time to leave, I had second thoughts. Argued all the reasons I should stay home, slip on pajamas and eat pizza while watching Netflix. Reese wasn't having it.

Nervous as I am, him shoving me out the door was a good thing. Sometimes, I need that push. And he knows when to deliver.

The music quiets in the car as the Australian male Siri voice chimes in and tells me to turn left in a quarter mile. Something about that voice makes cell phone navigation much more pleasant. I turn onto the street and the voice takes over the speakers again, telling me my destination is a hundred feet on the left.

But I don't need to guess which house it is. Nope. Because

there is only one house on the street with an overflowing driveway, cars in the yard and cars on the street.

Spectacular.

Two houses down, I park my SUV on the curb. Micah's gray pickup is in the driveway, which can only mean he has been here quite some time. I tap my phone screen and check the time. Only ten minutes after he told me to arrive. Would have been here sooner if I hadn't stopped up the street for bottled water.

One last deep breath. I grab my hoodie off the passenger seat, exit the car, and shove the fob in my pocket. Unlocking my phone, I type out a quick text to Reese.

> Why am I here? There's like 10 cars.

> Exaggerate much 😼

Since I can't smack him, I send him a picture of all the cars.

> Sorry 😼 Stay an hour at least.

> Fine 😼

Phone tucked in my back pocket, I trudge for the house. A black Bel Air sits next to an off-roading Jeep in the driveway. "Black Dog" by Led Zeppelin belts out as I step closer to the door. Just as I lift my hand to knock, a dog barks from inside the house.

I step back and glance at the window. A husky has his snout shoved between the blinds as he rattles the slats. He barks again before someone shushes him.

The door swings open and I feel like I stepped back several decades. A petite brunette smiles at me as she wrangles the dog. Her hair swept up in a ponytail. A bandanna knotted in a headband atop her head. Denim hugs her legs and a graphic tee depicting hot rods is tied above her navel.

Not only is she pretty, she also makes me feel welcome when I know only one person here.

"Hi." She extends her free hand and I shake it. "Please, come in. I'm Autumn. And this" —she points to the husky currently licking a little girl's face— "is Spartan and Clementine."

"Peyton," I say and step inside. "Thank you."

"Hope you're hungry." Her red-painted lips curve up farther. "Sometimes we get carried away at the store."

My stomach grumbles at the mention of food, but I'm thankful she doesn't hear. Don't think I can eat right away. "Smells wonderful. Thanks for having me."

"The more, the merrier. Follow me." She starts for another door. "Everyone's out back." My feet stick to the floor and I swallow. Autumn peers over her shoulder, then comes back to my side. She wraps a tattooed arm around my shoulders. "No need to be nervous. Everyone here is family. If anyone fucks with you, they'll answer to me."

I may have only just met this woman, but I like her already. "Appreciate it."

"If you want, when we get outside, I'll introduce you to everyone."

I sag under her arm. "That'd be great."

The door opens and Spartan bolts out with Clementine on his heels. "Sparty, wait." She chases after him and disappears into the yard.

"Simple Man" by Lynyrd Skynyrd starts playing through a speaker off to the side. Two steps down, we land on a paver patio. Hickory and oak drift in the air from a smoker. Tables span the side of the house with paper goods, drinks, and food filling every inch.

Autumn takes my hand without hesitation and tugs me toward the smoker. And several men. None of them Micah. But I feel his eyes on me.

Here we go.

"Jonas," she calls out and a man spins to face us. Roughly the same height as me, he has messy brown hair that's long on top, but buzzed short everywhere else. He sports a Black Sabbath shirt, loose jeans and bare feet. And the way he smiles at Autumn makes me feel as if I'm interrupting their privacy.

"Yes, scarlet." I look to Autumn and she mouths *nickname*.

"This is Peyton. Peyton, this is my boyfriend, Jonas."

He steps closer and extends a hand. "Nice to meet you, Peyton." We shake and it feels more welcoming than awkward. "Burgers, brats, and chicken should be done soon. Help yourself to whatever." He gestures to the buffet.

Tonight will be an abundance of handshakes and *thank yous*. But I don't mind. From the overall vibe, everyone here seems nice.

Next to the grill with Jonas, I meet Reznor, Rex, and Trevor. Reznor and Rex work at the same tattoo shop as Autumn. Both decorated in tattoos and have a few visible piercings. Reznor seems the quieter of the two, only talking when he has something to say. Trevor is introduced as Jonas's best friend. They have known each other since girls were gross, as Jonas puts it.

"Alright, let's go meet some other faces," Autumn suggests.

Maybe it's the fact I meet new people and have random

conversations weekly that has kept me from freaking out so far. The panic I felt before arriving has cooled and now simmers in the background. Autumn, being a gracious hostess, might have something to do with it. Whatever the reason, I'm grateful the urge to puke has tapered off.

The next cluster of people are more of Autumn's tattoo family. Penny—who has bubblegum-pink hair and pops chewing gum more often than not—jumps up and hugs me.

"Pen, don't scare the girl. Jesus," Autumn scolds.

Penny steps back and smiles. "Sorry." She glances at Autumn. "If the guys didn't scare her, no one will." *Pop.*

"Let's not test it."

Then, Autumn introduces Tatyana and Ashton—Reznor's girlfriend and son—and Iliana. We exchange greetings and chat a moment. Penny pops her gum twenty times in less than ten minutes. She speaks with animated hands and doesn't care what anyone thinks. I love her automatically.

Autumn wraps up our conversation with them and prepares to shift us to the last group outside. Where Micah sits with three other people and talks. Where he has kept an eye on me since the moment I stepped outside.

I may not have looked directly at Micah, but I have known exactly where he is from the moment Autumn led me out back. Felt his eyes roam my untamed hair, my face, my body. Heard the occasional falter in his words as he spoke with friends. Caught him staring out of the corner of my eye as I interacted in his world.

"Hey, guys," Autumn says as we approach. "Cora, Gavin, Shelly, this is Peyton."

Familiar names. My eyes dart between their faces as I shove my hands in my back pockets.

The woman next to Micah bears the same eyes and blonde

locks, and I assume this is his sister, Shelly. Makeup paints her eyes and face with perfect lines and strokes. And she wears pink as if she would own no other color, but it doesn't look bad on her. Micah mentioned her the night he apologized to me at Teddy's, but she seems otherwise familiar.

Across from Micah and Shelly is a woman and man who I presume to be Cora and Gavin. Both have black hair—hers cut to her shoulders and his almost just as long, but only on the top of his head. Gavin has his arm around Cora in a way that says they are a couple. A swift glance at her left hand tells me they're married. And god, do they make a beautiful couple.

Shelly pops up from her seat and steps up to me. I expect another handshake and generic greeting. Instead, she surprises me. Her arms wrap around me and squeeze tight. "If he hurts you, I'll kick his ass," she whispers, then steps back and holds me at arm's length. Her eyes don't leave mine until I nod. "You may not remember me. We went to different high schools, but I saw you near the track when I'd stop by to watch Micah run." I stiffen. "We were a year behind you." Shelly points to Cora and Gavin.

Cora rises from the lounger and offers her hand. "Nice to formally meet you, Peyton." Gavin follows suit and shakes my hand.

Just as I open my mouth to return the sentiment, Autumn hollers after Spartan—who just stole food off the table—then excuses herself.

Awkward, party of one?

"Shell, scoot over," Micah says. For a split second, I silently beg her to move closer to Micah and leave me the open end of the seat. But my plea goes unanswered as Shelly slides farther from Micah. He pats the cushion. "Come sit."

I shuffle between Shelly's legs and the unlit fire bowl to sit on the lounger. When my butt hits the seat, I lay my hoodie over my lap and tuck my hands underneath, where I fumble with the threads without prying eyes.

"How's your Sunday been?" Micah asks.

All eyes land on me, and I remind myself to inhale every other second. Cora and Gavin look at me with kindness as they curl into each other. Shelly practically bounces next to me. Everyone appears genuinely interested in my answer.

I can do this. Have nonwork conversations with Micah and get to know these people.

"Somewhat boring. Reese and I hung out."

Micah's whole frame goes rigid at the mention of Reese. Is that jealousy I detect? Interesting. May have to keep that tidbit in my arsenal.

"Reese Triggs?" Cora jumps in.

I peer up at her and smile. "Yeah. You know him?"

"Just remember him from high school. Nice guy."

"The best," I say, with dreamy eyes.

"You two still attached at the hip?"

"When we're home. We both work odd hours, but try to have at least one day off together."

The lounger shifts beside me and I turn to see if Micah is getting up. He isn't. Instead, he inches forward, leans closer with his eyes on me, rests his elbows on his knees and clasps his hands. "You live with him?" The growl behind his words doesn't go unnoticed by anyone.

I bite my cheek to resist smiling. His jealousy flashes like a neon sign in a porn shop window. It's amusing and annoying at the same time.

"Yep." I pop the *p*. "For years. Did I not mention that?" Not that I *need* to mention anything to Micah. We are just friends. My inner circle—not that I have much of one—and romantic life aren't his business.

"Can't say I remember you telling me," he says with too much bite for my liking.

"Well, he does. He also happens to be my best friend. If that's a problem for you…" I lift my brows in question.

"It's fine," he mumbles.

Beside me, Shelly shakes with silent laughter. And for a beat, I wonder if she and Cora tag-teamed to rile up her brother on purpose. If that's the case, we will be friends in no time.

Ready to jump on the 'terrorize Micah' train, I open my mouth to add gasoline to the fire. But Jonas cuts me off as he yells the burgers, brats, and chicken are ready.

The vultures flock to the buffet, but Micah and I stay seated a moment longer.

His vibe has gone from antsy to excited to irritated in minutes. Not sure what he expected when he invited me here, but I won't sit around and be the reason he pouts. He either needs to accept who I am and how I live or leave me be. I refuse to change who I am for another person. Especially Micah Reed.

I bump his shoulder. "You good?"

He rotates his head, but doesn't face me fully. Licks his lips. Eyes on the fire bowl a moment before his gaze meets mine. In those bold blue depths, I see more than expected. Curiosity and confusion. Regret and fear. But most of all, desire.

The ground wobbles. My heart beats faster, harder. My breath all but forgotten.

It's no secret I thought Micah lusted after me. Hell, as much as I despised him, his eyes continued to visit my dreams. By now, I had memorized the constellation the gold flecks formed in his eyes.

But that was all fantasy. All in my head. Right?

Apparently not.

"Sorry for my reaction. It was juvenile," he admits.

"Yes, it was. I forgive you." The blue in his irises brightens. "Don't do it again." His brows pinch above his nose. "Act jealous."

"Peyton, I—"

I hold up a hand and stop him. "I will let you finish as long as you don't say you're not jealous." My arm presses against his as I lean closer. Our lips inches apart. "Do not lie to me," I whisper.

The chatter and music around us fades away. All I see are his twinkling blue eyes, guiding me like the North Star. All I feel is the heat of his body and breath on my skin, on my lips. If either of us pressed forward, our lips would meet. Soft and hot and ready.

"Peyton, I was jealous. Am jealous," he confesses, only loud enough for my ears. His pupils dilate. Breath comes in bursts. He licks his lips and I *feel* his tongue ghost the edge of my lower lip.

I close my eyes but don't dare move. "Why?" The single word loaded with several questions. Why are you jealous? Why me? Why does it matter?

Micah remains tight-lipped until I open my eyes. And when I do, I swallow at the intensity staring back. The swirl of fire and hunger in his eyes.

"Thought it was rather obvious," he declares, voice gruff.

"Humor me," I whisper.

The corner of his mouth kicks up. "Peyton, how can I not

be jealous of any man who sleeps under the same roof as you?"

"I live in an apartment. Sure there's more."

"Smart-ass." I smile. "Seriously, though. If I haven't made it obvious enough, I kind of have a thing for you."

"Kind of have a thing?"

He rolls his eyes and shakes his head until our noses bump. "No, not kind of. I *have* a thing for you."

The attraction between me and Micah has been plain as day for weeks. Not sure if his feelings go beyond then, but that's the first time I really paid attention. Neither of us can deny the spark. The ever-expanding ache between us.

But we have history.

Yes, I accepted Micah's apology. Forgiving him, on the other hand, may take more time. It's easy to let the words leave my lips. *I forgive you.* Feeling them, though, is a completely different wall to scale.

"Micah..." I inch back from him. Drag in a deep breath and hold it for five, four, three, two. "I... I don't know how to respond to that."

In my periphery, I follow his hand as it moves from his space to mine. And then he rests it on my thigh. Not too high, but somewhere in the middle, at the edge of the hoodie. Warmth radiates through the denim and heats my skin. I forget, for the umpteenth time, how to breathe.

"Don't need to. Just wanted you to know." He gives my thigh a slight squeeze, then rises from the lounger. I already miss the scent of his cologne in my nose. "C'mon." He holds out his hand. "Let's grab some food."

I take his hand and we shuffle over to the table. We fill our plates with too much food and each grab a bottle of beer. Once we resume our seats, conversations shift to lighter topics. Autumn regales us with stories of outlandish tattoos. Jonas shares his mechanic wet dreams about working on a 1965 Shelby Mustang. We all hem and haw, but don't appreciate it the same as he does. Gavin and Cora talk about upcoming photo shoots—she photographing a wedding and he's modeling a new line of exercise gear.

I listen as they all carry on. In comparison, my life seems boring. Yes, I meet people from all walks of life in Roar. But I interact with them for maybe a few minutes. It's pure coincidence if I pour all their drinks for the night.

Sometimes, though, boring isn't so bad.

When everyone cleans their plates, Reznor, Tatyana, and Ashton say their goodbyes. With a little one to tend to, they still have plenty to do once they get home. Penny, Rex, Trevor, and Iliana leave next. As each person leaves, I get hugs instead of handshakes.

I take my phone from my pocket and check the time. Almost nine.

Micah taps my foot with his. When I look up, he tips his head toward my phone. "Hot date?"

With a shake of my head, I tell him, "No. Just don't want to be out too late. I'm at the ALF tomorrow."

"Finish your drink first?" He poses it as a question. Leaves me the opportunity to choose.

I lift the beer and swirl the contents. Two, maybe three, sips left. "Yeah."

For the next fifteen minutes, the ladies chat with me. Ask what it is like working at Roar. If I deal with a bunch of pervs. I joke and tell them the only perv in Roar is Micah. Everyone but Shelly laughs. She merely slaps him.

When my bottle empties, I toss it in the trash, gather my hoodie and start my goodbyes. Shelly gives me a more exuberant hug than the one I received upon arrival. She also reminds me she will kick her brother's ass if he hurts me. Cora and Gavin hug me next. Their embrace warm and friendly. Autumn and Jonas are next in line. After hugs are exchanged, Autumn says she hopes to see me again.

As weirded out as I was before I arrived tonight, leaving feels more nerve-racking. Like I am leaving behind family. Such a strange sensation, burning in my chest.

Micah trades hugs with everyone after me. "I'll walk you out."

"You don't have to."

"I know. But I'm heading out too. Plus, it's late and I hear there are some crazy old men in this neighborhood."

I laugh with a shake of my head. "Whatever. Let's go."

The front door clicks behind us as we step onto the porch. And suddenly, every sense amplifies.

I shiver as Micah's cologne gets caught on the breeze and drifts up my nose. Cicadas sing alongside the occasional whoosh of a car driving on the cross street a hundred feet away. I jump when the motion light kicks on and beams down on the driveway. Then heat flushes my skin when Micah rests his palm on my lower back.

Breathe, Peyton.

Thirty-seven steps later, we reach my car. I reach into my pocket and press the fob to unlock the door. But I don't open it. Instead, I stand there, frozen, staring at Micah like I'm broken.

"Thanks for inviting me," I finally squawk out then clear my throat. "I had a nice time."

Micah takes a step closer. The toe of his shoe inches from mine. "Glad you came. I had a great time, too."

Before the words good night leave my lips, he steps forward and snakes his arms around my waist. And then I feel him toe to top. Pressure and heat and… desire. I drag my fingers up his arms, lace them behind his head and close my eyes as I breathe him in.

His lips hover near my ear. Breath ebbing and flowing and heating my skin. If he kissed me right now, I wouldn't stop him. Don't think I could. Not with how good he feels flush against my front.

A hand trails up my spine and halts at the base of my skull as his fingers comb through my loose strands. "I love this. Wish you wore your hair down more often. But know why you don't."

My head swirls with want versus need. An internal battle of whether I should take a step back or press my lips to the spot beneath his ear. In the end, my rational side waves a flag in attention and I ease back.

"Thanks again," I whisper, inches from his lips. "Talk to you later."

He licks his lips and nods. Which is the perfect time for me to go. Before I launch myself at him and kiss the hell out of his soft lips. Then question my sanity.

I open the car door and slip inside. "Let me know you got home safe." He closes the door then taps the roof and walks to his truck with steady steps.

My eyes drift low in the side mirror and zero in on his ass. His jeans hang low and loose, but the definition of his glutes more than noticeable. When he reaches his truck, he unlocks the door but doesn't open it. No, he peeks over his shoulder at me. Well, my car.

The motion light on Jonas and Autumn's house kicks on and creates a halo around his frame. His face unreadable. But his body language begs for more. Tells me way more than his unspoken words.

My heart pounds, pounds, pounds in my chest until he gets in his truck, cranks the ignition and drives off. My knuckles burn and whiten as I fist the steering wheel and watch his taillights in the rearview. Then he turns and disappears into the night.

I gasp and relieve the fire in my lungs. Take a few deep, methodical breaths and cool the burn in my chest. Once my heart slows, I put the car in gear and drive home with one question swirling like a cyclone in my head.

What the hell is happening between me and Micah Reed?

nineteen

MICAH

Peyton sits parked on the street as I turn and she disappears from view. Why hasn't she left yet? Did I freak her out? I half expected her to bolt the second she got behind the wheel. But her headlights hadn't even come on before I turned the corner.

I jolt when my phone rings through the truck's audio. Shelly's name flashes on the screen and I tap the answer button on the steering wheel. Had I forgotten something?

"Hey, Shell."

"Don't hurt her."

Jesus. Hadn't been gone ten minutes and am already on her shit list. Suppose that's how it is between siblings. Always keeping each other in check. Or trying to, at least.

"I won't."

"I'm serious, Micah." Micah, not big brother. Serious is an understatement. "I saw you."

She saw me?

"What does that mean, Shelly? You saw me."

A huff of irritation rustles through the phone line and I picture her rolling her eyes. She doesn't say anything as my knuckles stretch and pale against the steering wheel. My thumb hovers over the disconnect button, but I pull it back. Shelly may annoy me at times, but she would have to commit genocide for me to ignore her.

"Outside." She blows out a breath as I sort through my thoughts, but come up with nothing of substance.

"Be more specific. We were all outside tonight."

"Why is this so difficult?"

The question is meant to be rhetorical, but I answer anyway. "Because you won't spit out what you want to say."

"Argh," she groans. "Fine. You want me to just come out with it?"

"Would make this call a little less one sided."

"Outside. At her car. I saw you… holding her."

I pinch the bridge of my nose and thank the traffic gods for a red light. Irritation spreads like the molten searing of a branding iron. Scalding at the epicenter, but distributing the sting in an effort to temper the pain.

"Were you spying on me?" I bark into the truck cab.

"No," she counters with a fevered pitch. "Not intentionally. I was a couple minutes behind you. When I stepped out the door and saw your truck, I was confused. So, I looked for you—from the porch—and saw you at Peyton's car."

Can't remember the last time I felt stabby toward Shelly. Compared to friends who had siblings, Shelly and I had a great relationship. Sure, we didn't always see eye to eye, but no one does. When she admitted to seeing us, I assumed she followed us outside all ninja-like. Seeing us by accident… I can't be mad at her.

"Sorry I snapped at you."

"You're forgiven, big brother. Still doesn't change things. Don't hurt her."

Bless my sister and her need to look out for others. Any other time, I would deem the trait admirable. Mom and

Dad did their damnedest to raise us as respectable and responsible. *"Lead by example."* Those three words spoken by Mom or Dad at least once a week during our childhood. With the exception to high school and my whore habits post-Rochelle, I have done my best to uphold said qualities. To be an example.

But we all get tested from time to time.

"I love how protective you are, Shell. And I have no intention of hurting Peyton."

On the other end of the line, a beep echoes, followed by a soft thump and electronic dings. After a beat, she speaks up and sounds farther from the phone speaker.

"You may not intentionally. But your life has been a hot mess for a short while. Don't let that bleed into her life."

Hot mess doesn't remotely describe the path my life has taken since Rochelle fucked me over. Literally.

The day I walked in on Rochelle and the young stallion she mounted, in the bed we shared no less, I lost my shit. I have never been physically violent toward women, but furniture and picture frames and inanimate objects were fair game. I'd flung them across the room. My fists so tight, blood spilled from the crescents in my palms. Holes littered the hallway drywall—a smarter alternative than jail after beating the guy's ass.

The worst part of it all… she wasn't sorry. Rochelle had zero regrets bringing another man—who looked barely old enough to be a man—to the bed we shared and fucking him. Not a single ounce of remorse. How had I become so blasé about who she was and her predatory ways?

Because I was a fool.

We hadn't been living together full time—thank fuck. But once I kicked her to the curb, threw all her shit outside, along with the mattress, I made a pact with myself. To never let a woman so close to my heart again. To never let a woman take the reins and steer me down an unknown path.

Not bedding the same woman night after night helped solidify my pact. But these last few weeks, Peyton has me second-guessing said agreement.

"Swear I won't hurt her. Not intentionally."

"Good to hear." The relief in her voice filled the truck cabin. "Will I see you at Mom and Dad's party?"

Ah, yes. The parents' thirty-fifth wedding anniversary. Our parents don't always insist on our appearance, but if we missed this occasion, we wouldn't hear the end of it.

"Wouldn't miss it."

"Cool." A car horn honks in the background. "Well, I'm on my way home. Talk to you later."

"'Kay. Love you, Shell."

"Love you, too, big brother. Night."

The call disconnects as I turn into my driveway. I cut the lights and engine, then stare at the tan-painted single-car garage door. Let my eyes lose focus as I watch tree limb shadows dance over the house. House, not home. The only way it would ever feel like a home is if I wasn't alone.

In my mind's eye, I pictured what having a home would be like. How two people blended their lives together and became one. Similar to Gavin and Cora. On so many levels, I envy my best friend. Not that his and Cora's journey was an easy one. Life ripped them apart. Obstacles stood in their way. But they persevered. Because they wanted each other more than anything else.

I would kill for that type of love. Love that bulldozes

walls and eviscerates loneliness. Love that pulls you in, wraps its arms around you, and never lets go. That crushes all insecurities and makes you feel safe in your vulnerability. That is the love I want.

But after the bullshit with Rochelle, letting another woman near my heart scares the shit out of me.

Without realizing it, Peyton has unintentionally wiggled her way in. Staked a claim on my heart. And fuck... here I am, handing it over. No resistance. No second-guessing. Just willingly plucking the scarred organ from my chest and presenting it to her, in the hopes she will know how to handle it.

Fuck.

I exit the truck, check the mailbox—then remember the mail doesn't run today when I see the box empty—before I amble inside. I flip the kitchen light on, empty my pockets, and grab a beer from the fridge. I pop the cap, chuck it in the trash and take a long pull from the bottle. After flipping the light off, I snatch my phone from the counter and wander down the hall to my bedroom, bottle at my lips.

Plopping down on the mattress, I don't bother with the light. It isn't long before I polish off the beer, strip my clothes, set the phone on the charger, and slip under the covers.

Alone in bed, the silence is deafening. I close my eyes and images of Peyton flash behind my lids like an old movie reel. In the last two weeks, I had seen her smile more often than not. And her smile is magnificent. Like sunshine after the rain. Blinding, yet you can't seem to look away. Marry that smile with her radiant violet eyes and golden hair, she rendered me speechless more often than not.

When had Peyton become such a fixture in my head? In every waking—and sleeping—thought I had?

For more than a year, we were at each other's throats. The constant back and forth. Her yelling at me and vice versa. She did it out of disgust and a hatred for her high school bully. I did it because I loved to work her up, to ruffle her mane. Can't speak for Peyton, but for me, taunting her is the best version of foreplay. A lead-up to where we are now.

Unfortunately, I have no clue where we go from here.

Do I really want another relationship? Dates and intimacy and late nights filled with laughter. Shared time and small tokens of appreciation. A voice buried deep in my psyche screams, *"Yes, idiot. We want all those things."* But another voice—one closer to the battlefield, one more recent—speaks up and reminds me of what I went through last time I traveled down that road. *"You'll just end up here again. Hurt and alone."*

My eyes snap open and stare up at the ceiling I am all too familiar with. "No," I whisper into the darkness. "Peyton and Rochelle are nothing alike." Peyton would never hurt someone she cared about. Not after all the bullshit she has dealt with.

Question is, does Peyton care about me? On any level?

Without a second thought, I blindly reach for my phone on the nightstand. I squint at the screen and open up the messaging app. Before I stop myself, I tap on the text history with Peyton and type out a message. Seeing as she works at the ALF tomorrow, she probably won't answer. But this can't wait.

> Is this too much?

I stare at the blue bubble on the screen. The word delivered beneath it. Then I lock my phone, toss it on the bed and press the heels of my palms to my eyes. "I'm a goddamn fool."

The words are barely out of my mouth when the phone vibrates the bed. I pat the blanket until I locate the phone and see a text alert. From Peyton.

> Is what too much?

How do I translate my thoughts into simple terms? My brain knows the words, but my fingers forget how to type them. My lips forget how to say them. But I do my best to spell it out.

> Me. Us. Hugging earlier.

I hit send and close my eyes. The text is ridiculous. It explains nothing and probably confuses her further. Why does my brain turn to mush whenever Peyton Alexander is in the mix?

> The hug threw me off. But I won't lie and say I didn't like it.

Peyton Alexander just admitted to liking my arms around her. My body pressed to hers. My lips near her skin.

> I liked it too. More than expected.

> Oh yeah. How much more?

Is she flirting? Or does my bewildered brain have me misconstruing her message? It's late and she is probably in bed, half asleep.

Enough that I still feel your heat on my skin.

Fuck. I slip a hand beneath the blanket and grip my hardening cock. Eyes on the screen, I take a deep breath as the dots dance inside the little gray bubble.

Where do you feel it?

Fucking hell. Is this seriously happening? In five simple words, Peyton has me virtually on my knees, begging for relief. Without hesitation, I would worship her like no other.

You really want to know?

Humor me.

I laugh into the darkness. Those two words. We toss them back and forth to lighten the moment. But those two words weigh heavily each time they are said.

Fisted in my hand.

And just like that, my innocent inquiry has flipped to sexting. Well, suggestive sexting. Will my response freak her out?

And how does that feel?

This woman will be the death of me. Via text messages or her smart mouth. Either will do, though.

Nowhere near enough.

Sometimes, not enough makes the end
result that much sweeter.

What end result would that be?

I will not put words in her mouth. Other things, perhaps, but not words. With our history, Peyton needs her voice. Needs to use it to guide me. To guide us. I won't mislead her, but I also want the same in return.

My crystal ball says that still remains to be
seen.

Hmm. Think your crystal ball may need to
be cleaned.

Really?

Yep. I offer up my ball cleaning services
to you.

Oh lord. I really need to think before I type and hit send. And I'm not drunk. Maybe a little buzzed, but not drunk.

I bet you do.

Sorry. Was that too much?

I'm a big girl, starlight. I handle balls just
fine.

And now my vision fills with images of Peyton and the ways she could *handle my balls*. I am so fucking screwed.

You really are a hellcat.

You wouldn't want me any other way.

There are several ways I wouldn't mind having Peyton

Alexander. But it is too early to put those out in the open. Even with both of us braver behind our screens.

> True. Question… why do you call me starlight?

Her new nickname for me is quirky and cute, but it also feels childish. God, I hope it isn't something so inane.

> Really want to know?

> Humor me.

Seconds drag on for minutes as the dancing gray bubble pops up and disappears again and again. Either she is typing a novel or she deletes her words and starts over. The wait is gruesome.

> Because of your eyes.

Not a novel. And definitely not what I expected.

My eyes? What about my eyes made her come up with starlight? I picture Shelly's twin irises. The rich blue with lighter hints. But nothing makes me think of starlight.

> What about my eyes?

> Hidden in the blue, you have these little gold sparks. Like stars.

Like stars. I read those two words over and over. Sift them through the confines of my mind. Interpret the fact she has studied my eyes hard enough to notice small gold flecks. *Like stars.* That every time she uses the nickname, it has more meaning than other pet names people share. That she sees deeper than surface level. *Like stars.*

I never noticed.

The screen dims after no response for a couple minutes. I tap the screen and it brightens. Then I note how late it is. Seeing as she has to be up earlier in the morning, it wouldn't surprise me if she fell asleep.

Night, hellcat. Sweet dreams.

I lay my phone back on the charger and stare up at the ceiling. After texting Peyton, staring at the slight texture above the bed seems less interesting. Worth less of my time. So, I close my eyes and let my imagination wander.

Images of Peyton from earlier in the evening pop up from my memory. Of her relaxed attire and loose strands. Of her easygoing smile and breath an inch from my lips. How at ease she was around my friends, my family. And how perfect she felt flush against my chest, my hips. Most of all, I recall the way her brilliant eyes studied mine.

Like stars.

twenty

PEYTON

Small waves crash along the shore. Salt licks my skin. Cocoa butter and the distinct smell of seaweed float through the air. Seagrasses ruffle in the wind between the parking lot and white sand. The sun bright and high in the cloudless blue sky.

I peek up from my romance thriller as Ani exits the water and treks back to our spot in the sand. For a woman in her late forties, Ani is smoking hot. I have never been sexually attracted to women, but will openly admit when they steal my attention. Ani works hard for everything in her life—physically, emotionally, and financially—and it shows.

Our friendship is one of the greatest gifts, and I thank my lucky stars she entered my checkout line years ago.

Ani has given me so much. More than I ever expected. She provided me with opportunities I wouldn't have easily come by without her. But she is also a great friend. Without a doubt, one of my best friends—after Reese, of course.

Over the years, my tally of female friends has remained small. One—I don't have time for petty nonsense. Drama happens, but I don't need women who provoke and promote drama in my circle. Two—I enjoy the more laid-back nature of guy friends. Plus, guy friends give better hugs when you need them.

But Ani is the exception in my circle. Her drive and no-bullshit attitude make her admirable. She busts her ass for what she wants and ignores everyone who tells her she can't have something or accomplish her goals. As a woman who wants more from life, I hold Ani in high esteem. With her guidance, I have the opportunity to become a better version of myself too.

Women empowering women tops crushing them beneath your heel any day of the week.

Ani flops down on the lounger next to me, slides her sunglasses into place, and sips her water. "The water feels amazing today. We need more beach dates."

I bookmark my page and set the book in my bag. "Agreed." I stare out at the water and how the sun shimmers along the surface like stars. In a blink, my thoughts drift to Micah and his starry-night-sky eyes.

Two weeks have passed since I hung out with him and his friends. Since he wrapped me in his arms and touched me more like a lover than a friend or coworker. Since he texted me from his bed and our conversation went from concerned to heated to confessional.

And since that night, Micah Reed has texted me daily.

Random and not-so random messages. Texts asking how my day was at Gulfside. A barrage of questions in an obvious attempt to learn every fine detail of who I am.

"Favorite style of music?"

"Favorite movie snack?"

"Last show you binge watched."

"Place you want to visit, but haven't."

A different question hit my messages every day. Even

days when we would see each other at work. Some I answered within minutes. Others I left unanswered for hours. Not because I didn't have an answer, but because there is something thrilling about delayed gratification.

"You ready for tonight?"

Tonight... I have been ready and waiting for this day for ages. The day I become more than just a woman behind the bar. The day I take the next step.

"Yes. Already adjusted my schedule at Gulfside."

"I love that you'll still be there one day. They're lucky to have you."

When Ani called me last weekend and said things were moving forward at Roar, I spoke with human resources at Gulfside. And Ms. Jenkins. HR accepted the change without complication. They understood the younger staff wouldn't stick to the same routine. But they were excited when we stayed. Ms. Jenkins, on the other hand, was a bit peeved. Not that I would only be at Gulfside one day a week, but that I'd still show up.

The woman loved me as much as Nana did. Wanted to see me thrive in the world. Wanted me to not be "one of those people that works more than lives." I promised her this change would help me do that. But I still need Gulfside. Need the solace it provides when life is hectic. Need the conversations and interactions with Ms. Jenkins that parallel to those I shared with Nana. Moments I miss more than anything.

"The feeling is mutual." I take a deep breath and lose focus as I stare out at the water. Then twist to face Ani. "How's this going down?"

Her legs sweep over the edge of the lounger as she looks my way. A hand pushes her sunglasses into her hair. Eyes survey my face. "Are you nervous?"

Am I nervous? I scrutinize my own feelings. The expanding flutter beneath my diaphragm. The one that sparked to life when Ani called last weekend. But it was the same sensation when I agreed to work for her. Delight. Exhilaration. Having the chance to be more.

But I also can't ignore the lump in my throat. The one I woke with this morning when realization kicked in. When I stared at the text notification on my phone.

"Morning, hellcat."

It wasn't necessarily the text that had my body in slight hysterics. Micah started texting me that same message following the night I hung out with him and his friends. And I love seeing it each morning.

Today, though, his message sent a wave of panic. Has me second-guessing what happens next. Not about the overall change at Roar, but how Micah will react with the announcement. Will he be pissed? Or will he praise me? For some stupid, girlish reason, his reaction matters. Suppose that's what happens when you get closer with someone.

"Yes," I answer honestly. "What if this pisses people off?"

"And by people, you mean Micah." Ani poses it more as a statement than question.

I huff out the irritation I have with myself. Irritation over the fact that I am worried what a guy thinks. "Not just him." Half-truth. "But also Gina and the others who have been there longer."

Ani reaches for my hand and clasps it between hers. "This is happening because I want it to. It isn't just about you. The move is also smart for business. Sean and I always mull over business decisions before putting them into action. Hard and heavy. This decision wasn't made because we're friends or on a whim. I believe in you and what you have to offer. And that's why I'm doing this."

My breath comes easier. "Thank you. Didn't know I needed to hear that."

"You're welcome." She drops my hand, then shifts to lie back on her lounger. "How do you think he'll take it?"

She doesn't have to say Micah's name for me to know who she's talking about. "Wish I knew. Things have changed between us. But I don't know him well enough to answer."

"Well, don't let it worry you. He's a grown man. If he can't handle it, that's his problem. Not yours."

Every rational part of me knows Ani is right. That if Micah gets upset with tonight's announcement, it is on him. But part of me still feels as if I am betraying him. Betraying the friendship—or whatever the hell -ship—we formed. Things between us get better with each passing day. I don't want all that to go down the shitter.

I only hope he takes the news with a managerial mindset and does not let it bruise his ego.

You can do this, Peyton.

I stare at the back of Roar from the comfort of my car. The aged brick more red than brown today. A fresh coat of paint over the club name adds an extra pop. Large string lights near the roofline already lit, although the sun doesn't set for another two hours.

Parked two spaces to my right is Ani and Sean's Tesla. Another space down is Micah's truck. Both vehicles empty of passengers. Seeing both adds a new layer of nausea.

Get out of the car. Go inside.

"Ugh." I grip my hands at ten and two on the steering wheel and rest my forehead at twelve. "Why is this eating at me?" What I wouldn't give for a couple saltines right now.

Leaning back, I press my head into the rest and drop my hands. I take a few steadying breaths. *In through the nose. Out through the mouth.* When my pulse settles and the compulsion to vomit wanes, I step out of the car, shoulder my purse and head for the employee entrance.

On any other day, if I were to walk in Roar two hours before open, it would be quiet. A radio may be on, quiet in the background. But otherwise, the space would be still. Peaceful. The calm before the storm.

But today is a new day. And new days come with music at normal levels and the chatter of several close people. I stroll past the office, skipping the time clock or stashing my purse. When I enter the main area of the club, the space seems smaller. Claustrophobic. Restrictive. The walls inching closer to the tables.

All eyes shift my way as I step out from the hall. Smiles and waves and greetings I don't hear beyond the white noise in my ears. I pinch the front of my shirt, pull it off my chest, then push it back rapidly, over and over.

Is it hot in here?

Ani pats Sean on the shoulder, then strolls over to me. "Peyton?" I hold her gaze. "You okay?"

I nod. "Just need some water."

She shuffles me over to a stool and forces me to sit. "I'll grab you some. Sit tight."

Ani waltzes over to the bar as Micah takes her place at my side. Brows drawn together, he bends at the knees so we are eye to eye. For one, two, three breaths, he doesn't speak. Then he reaches for my hand. His warm touch a partial balm to my anxiety.

"You look like you've seen a ghost." He lifts a hand and lightly brushes my cheek with his knuckles. "If you need to go, they'll understand."

My eyes dart between his and memorize each gold fleck against their inky sky backdrop. Certain I may not see them this close again, I etch them into my mind to recall when I am alone.

"I'm fine," I choke out as Ani approaches with water. "Just have a lot on my mind."

Ani sets the glass on the table and winks before going back to Sean. She whispers in his ear—a signal the meeting is about to start. My stomach churns and I sip the water in the hopes it will settle.

"Want to talk—" Micah starts, but is cut off when Ani speaks up. He shifts to stand beside me. Hand on the back of my chair. Thumb absently drawing small circles between my spine and shoulder blade.

"Thank you all for coming in early or on your day off." Ani and Sean flash bright white smiles to everyone. "We called this meeting to update you on new changes with Roar." A mix of excitement and concern mar some of the faces in our group. Others remain impassive.

I grip the edges of the seat until pain shoots up my forearm. The next words out of Ani's mouth will be the ones I have waited to hear for far too long. Words that will change *everything*. I relish and fear the change. But I won't let anyone snuff out what I worked hard to achieve.

Not even Micah.

"First announcement… Roar has a new manager on staff." Micah freezes beside me and Gina, two tables over, looks ready to puke. *Right there with ya, girl.* "Everyone, please join me in congratulating Peyton on her promotion."

Applause and cheers erupt and echo throughout the room. But one clap stands out more than the rest. The one less than a foot from me. Slow and exaggerated and far from congratulatory. Each time his hands smack together, I twitch in my seat. Jump at the vibration of anger each strike sends my way.

This is exactly what I expected would happen. That Micah would go off the emotional deep end. Instead of smiles and hugs and overall happiness for what I achieved and earned, I had a feeling the opposite would happen. My assumptions weren't wrong.

Without hurry, I peek to the right. Prepare myself for the sight that will undoubtedly make the pain beneath my rib cage worse. But no amount of preparation will ease the anger and hurt I see on Micah's face.

His nostrils flare. Eyes cold and distant as he meets mine. A measured headshake full of disbelief. And then he breaks contact. Not just his eyes, but also the hand he'd had on the back of my chair. With each harsh breath I take, he takes a step away.

Asshole.

Fuck him. If me achieving success pisses him off, he can crawl in a hole and weep like a toddler. Alone. I will not lower myself so he feels better about himself. Fuck. That.

I sit up straighter, pick up my water, and sip it as Ani continues.

"Gina, we'll be switching you to Tuesday through Friday. Micah, your days will remain the same. Starting next week, Peyton will work Monday through Thursday. We will also add three new bartenders, two servers and another doorman." Light chatter kicks up, then dies down when Ani continues.

"They will be arriving for introductions in a half hour. I wanted to give the original Roar team this moment before they joined us."

Micah leans forward, his breath hot on my ear. "Can we talk later?" he growls.

I purse my lips and meet his gaze as he rights himself. "Sure." My mouth stretches into a tight, forced smile before I face Ani again.

Over the next fifteen minutes, Ani shares the changes coming to Monday through Thursday. All the ideas I tossed out at her plus drink specials for each night. She drones on about contacts who are eager to partake in charity bingo night and companies who want to host trivia night for their employees. With each new idea that leaves her lips, Micah grows more frustrated and tense.

More than a month ago, Ani asked Micah for ideas to boost the slower nights. Asked for his input because of his role in the company. She'd also asked Gina, who suggested board game night, speed dating, and painting parties. Some of which Ani plans to incorporate once or twice a month. But Micah never responded. Never gave a single suggestion.

Maybe it had something to do with me and the distraction I provided. Or maybe his head was elsewhere. Distracted with other things I was unaware of. Either way, he didn't hold up his end of the bargain. And now, he has to deal with what Ani and Sean decided. Without him.

The new employees arrive and introductions are made. Josiah, Caleb, and Mable will join Adam and Kaylynn behind the bar. Charity and Dylan will be new additions to the tables with Becky and Jake. And Julio will work with Dan and Ted. The new cliques chat among themselves and get to know each other. All of the new additions will be working with us tonight, so management will get more time with them.

Before long, Ani announces everyone needs to start prepping for open. She shoots me a worried look, but I wave her off. Micah may be upset, but that is his burden to carry. Not mine. As the meeting carried on, this sank in more and more. That I should not be wrung tight because Micah cannot handle life and the positive things happening in mine. If he can't step off his pedestal one minute and allow others to shine with him, I don't need him in my life. Period.

So, I let it go. Enjoy the bliss of promotion and all the possibilities in my future. And later, I will celebrate with a drink and the people who cheer me on. Life is too short. I don't have the time or patience for someone not in my corner.

Fuck Micah Reed and his piss-poor attitude.

twenty-one

MICAH

No way this happened overnight. No way Peyton did not see this coming before today. Yet, she never said a goddamn word. Not once. None of our conversations hinted this colossal change was coming.

Manager.

Peyton just got promoted to manager after working at Roar for one year. One fucking year.

How hard had I slung bottles before Sean and Ani considered me management material? The first time Sean broached the subject had been three and a half years in. *"We need to see more professionalism,"* he'd said. *"You have what it takes, but need you to step it up. Show us you want it."* Those days, Sean and Ani spent more time at Roar than not.

But they rarely set foot inside nowadays. Not unless they were meeting with me or Gina or an event happened during the day. Yes, they kept tabs on their business. But they were less involved with the actual day-to-day functionality. They left that up to management and staff, only stopping by if things were amiss.

So how did Ani know Peyton was management material?

Without working side by side with her a single night, Ani had no idea how Peyton worked inside these walls. And I hadn't received any calls, texts or emails asking my opinion on Peyton's work ethic. Only the occasional generic inquiry when Ani stopped by to grab bank deposits or paperwork for the accountant.

The only reasonable explanation is Peyton and Ani's friendship. But I had to know. I need answers from the source. Peyton.

As the meeting came to a close, Peyton stood from her stool and took a step toward the bar. The color had returned to her cheeks. Her skin less clammy and gray. Eyes more alert and chin held higher.

Before she stepped out of reach, I took her elbow. She jerked to a stop as her eyes flashed to mine. Lips are a brutal flat line. A crease between her brows. If she had claws, I'd be shredded to bits by now.

"Can we talk?" My voice low as my eyes dart toward the hall, to the office.

She drops her gaze to my hand, then brings it back to my face. The ferocity in her stare makes me drop my hand and take a step back.

"Please," I add in a softer tone.

Am I angry? Absolutely. But not for the reasons Peyton presumes.

"Fine. But make it quick. I need to do prep."

Behind the bar, Adam and Kaylynn get to work with Josiah, Caleb, and Mable. Without being asked, they went into instructor mode. Showing their new coworkers how Roar operates. By the time Peyton and I finish our talk, the bar prep will be done with time to spare.

Without another word, I storm toward the office. The *tip-*

tap, tip-tap of Peyton's heeled boots clacks loud in my wake. I step into the office and move off to the side. Once she steps in, I slam the door and lock it.

"What the hell, Micah?" Her tone is fire and rage and trembles slightly.

Feet away, I huff out a laugh. "You're angry at me? Seriously? Seems a bit backward."

Her nostrils flare as her chest expands and contracts in rapid succession. The muscles of her jaw flex and tighten. Fists balled at her sides. "How so?"

"Shit like this doesn't just happen overnight, Peyton." I wave a hand in the air. "This type of change gets planned. Weeks and months ahead of time."

"Your point?"

I take a step in her direction. "You think I'm mad at you? Mad about the promotion?"

She waves a hand in the air, up and down the length of my body. "Body language speaks volumes. As soon as it was announced, you retreated from me."

I had pulled away from her. Stopped touching her. Stepped out of her bubble. Only because I felt betrayed. Betrayed by my bosses. And betrayed by Peyton, a woman I thought I had a connection with. I needed to hear everything without distraction. Needed to absorb the words being spoken. And I couldn't do that with Peyton so close.

I take another step in her direction. "I'm not mad at *you*. More like the situation."

"Not a fan of me being on the same level," she bites out.

A smaller step. Her body close enough for me to touch. "That's not it either," I say with a shake of my head.

"Then what is it, Micah?" She cocks a brow. "Humor me."

The corner of my mouth twitches, then relaxes. "Do you know how long I've worked here? How long it took me to step into a management role?" She doesn't answer or react. "Longer than you. I busted my ass for three-plus years before it was even a possibility. And even then, it came with stipulations."

Peyton's shoulders lift, then drop. Her lips puckered and eyes unyielding.

"Not to sound petulant, but it feels like I had to bust my ass for something that landed in your lap."

Her spine stiffens, the action inching her closer. "You think I haven't paid my dues, Micah? You think Ani just handed me this? Goes to show, you don't know shit." She spins to face the door. "This conversation is done."

Before she takes a step, I grip her elbow and twirl her back around. "No. Uh-uh. Not done yet."

Peyton steps into me. The tip of her nose a millimeter from mine. "What else is there to say?"

My hand drops from her elbow and lands on her hip. Her lips part just enough for me to notice. I rest my other hand on the opposite hip. Her breasts brush my chest as her breath coats my lips. Her violet irises sparkle and don't deviate from my pinned stare.

"Why did you hide the news? All the texts and times we've talked, you never mentioned it. Why?"

She exhales and I briefly close my eyes. *God, I want to taste her lips, her skin.*

"Nothing was set in stone. Ani and I talked about it here and there, but she never gave a timeline. Until last weekend. As in four days ago."

I fist her hips, but not enough to bruise them. "Still could've told me." The words practically inaudible.

"Micah…" My name rolls off her tongue and lights a fire beneath my sternum. "I wasn't trying to hurt—"

My lips crash to hers. Hot and aggressive and hungry. For one, two, three beats of my pulse, she doesn't kiss me back. I start to back away as defeat and mortification form a dark cloud overhead.

Until she fists my shirt and hauls me closer. Fuses our lips together again and licks the seam of mine. I part my lips and she dives in. We lick and taste and wage war with our tongues. Peyton tastes of sweet cream and something distinctly her.

A groan builds in my chest, rises up my throat and spills from my lips. I snake my arms around her waist and draw her impossibly closer. Her hands trail up my chest, my neck, my face until her fingers fist my hair.

An inferno blazes around us as I walk her backward. Her back hits the wall, the bulge behind my zipper pressing hard against the junction of her thighs. I run a hand down the side of her leg, then hoist it up to hook my hip.

My hips circle once, twice, and she moans against my lips. Sucks them between hers. Dives back in and siphons my tongue like a succubus. Devours me whole. My dick on the cusp of tearing my slacks.

Bam, bam, bam.

"Peyton? Everything okay?" Ani jiggles the door handle.

Our lips break apart on a gasp and I inch back. But only enough for her to speak.

Chest heaving, she looks up and licks her lips. "Fine," she pants out. "Be out in a minute."

Ani jiggles the handle again. "I heard yelling. Don't piss me off, Micah."

I huff out a laugh. "Everything's fine." I lock on to my

new favorite color. Violet. "Wouldn't be in my best interest to piss you off."

Another shake of the handle. Relentless. "If you're not out in five minutes, we'll be having a different conversation soon. An unpleasant one." Not a second later, her heels clack against the concrete and grow quieter with each step.

Without hesitation, I kiss Peyton again. This time, the kiss is less rushed. More tender. Engrossing. And all too soon, with much reluctance, I break the kiss and take a step back.

"We should get back out there," I say, and drop a chaste kiss on her lips.

"Yeah. Okay." She steps into me, hands framing my face, and returns the kiss. "Let's go." Another kiss.

Fuck. If I don't put five to ten feet between us, we will never leave this room. Not that I *want* to, but we need to. We have a job to do and a boss outside this room that will bite my head off if neither of us make an appearance soon.

Peyton steps over to the small mirror beside the door, flattens some of the kinks in her hair and adds a swipe of gloss to her lips from a tube in her pocket. Her eyes meet mine in the mirror as the brightest smile stretches her lips wide. She spins around, then steps into my space. Without a word, she runs her palms up my chest, my neck, then combs her fingers through my hair. And fuck me, I don't want her to stop.

Her hands drop to my collar and straighten the folds. Eyes locked on my lips as she swallows. When her hands fall, her eyes lift to mine again. "Time to work, starlight." She drops one last kiss on my lips before turning on her heel, unlocking the door, and strutting out of the office.

My tongue sweeps over my lips, her coconut gloss sweet on my tastebuds. Tonight may be the most challenging yet, but the test is worth the prize.

~

This has to be the slowest Wednesday in humankind. Slow-est.

Monday to Thursday has never brought in crowds like the weekend, but I don't remember them being this slow in months. With kids out of school, the start of summer usually has mothers stopping by for half-priced cocktails. For whatever reason, tonight is dead.

The new staff left more than an hour ago. They sliced enough citrus to fill the condiment bins for the next three nights. Fifteen minutes ago, I told Kaylynn she could head out for the night as well. Seeing as Roar is only open another hour, Ani wouldn't be too pleased if unnecessary staff stood around with nothing to do.

"Cosmo, please," a brunette says as she parks herself on a barstool.

"Coming up." I get to work on her drink and make light conversation with her. Generic topics such as the weather and asking if she has kids.

I pour the drink, place it on a napkin in front of her, and slide my hands back to my side of the bar. She plucks a bill from her purse and goes to hand it to me. When I reach for it, she takes hold of my hand and keeps it prisoner.

"If you're not busy after—"

"Micah," Peyton barks from the other end of the bar. I glance her way and smile. "How's the rash?"

Dear god, woman.

I sincerely hope Peyton has no concerns about me picking up other women. Not when I kissed the hell out of her three hours ago. But the way she marks her territory without it being obvious to outsiders has me biting my cheek.

"Better since the cream."

The woman quickly removes her hand. "Never mind." She hops off the stool. "Have a good night." And then she waltzes over to a table of women, whispers something to them and they all look my way with wide eyes.

I wipe down the bar top and head toward Peyton. She restocks the disposables—one less thing to do tomorrow before open.

"Did you enjoy that?" I ask when I reach her.

She bats her lashes excessively. "Whatever do you mean?"

"Cute."

"What's cute?"

I love how she plays coy. Goes toe to toe with me or lips off. But this new possessive side… I think I love this side the most. The spunk and bite and territorialism. The unspoken claim only I hear when she fends off other women. Her silent, *"He. Is. Mine."*

Fuck. The ownership makes my dick swell.

One year ago—hell, two months ago—I would never have imagined this raw hunger I harbor for Peyton. Or vice versa. But damn, do I love the energy vibrating through my body. The extra bounce in my step. The constant compulsion to smile. The rapid beat of my heart and expansion of my lungs.

Never imagined I would feel like this again. That I would want more than friendship or meaningless sex with a woman. That I would want to caress and taste a woman more than once.

But Peyton… she changes everything.

twenty-two

PEYTON

"Hang out with me tonight."

"At Teddy's?" I ask, unsure what his definition of hanging out entails.

Micah shakes his head. "We can get food, but that's not what I mean."

I seriously hope after one kiss—a really fucking great kiss —Micah doesn't think I will sleep with him. No doubt the man holds me captive with his looks alone. But I am not like one of the floozies he has taken home time and time again.

Never once have I given up the goods easily. I make men work for more. Make them woo me and prove their loyalty. One and done is not my style. Never has been, never will be. And Micah Reed will not change this.

"What *do* you mean?"

A small step brings him close enough to touch. His eyes drop to my shoulder as he reaches up and toys with the end of my ponytail. "Come back to my place." I wince. "Or yours. The place doesn't matter. I'll order pizza and we can watch a movie."

From point A to B in no time. For a short time, he had me

fooled. Had me believing he could be more than a douchebag. The occasional brush of his skin on my arm. Confessions in softer tones. The way his eyes searched mine —deeper, harder. Guess I read the signs wrong. Read him wrong.

"Um." I stall a moment to find the right words to let him down. "Not sure what you thought would happen tonight after that." I point toward the office. "But I don't hook up."

Bright, wide eyes fly up and take me captive. "Peyton, that's not what I meant. Wasn't my intention to suggest—"

"Then tell me your exact intention."

He takes another step closer. A knee comes between mine and knocks them apart. Heat licks my skin—could be his, but I know it comes from within. With each erratic breath I take, he inches closer. Close enough to taste, but I fight the urge. Remind myself we are at work. And kissing Micah behind the bar is not a good idea.

"Pizza, a movie and you sitting on the couch. Believe it or not, I can behave. May take a bit of effort, but it's possible."

No sex. Possibly no making out. Sounds like a solid plan. Although kissing Micah again, away from prying eyes, is definitely on the to-do list. Not that I plan to share this news. For now.

Dinner and a movie and couch time with the man I just kissed. The first man I kissed in more than a year. And damn, what a kiss it was. One for the record books.

If I agree, will either of us keep our hands—and lips—to ourselves? Better yet, which of us will cave first?

"Okay, I'll hang out. But the moment you start sneaking bases, I'm out."

Micah tips his head back and laughs. The rumble loud and deep and unrestrained. Has he ever laughed like this around me? Not to my recollection. But I love the way it shakes his frame. The way his throat reddens and his Adam's apple bobs.

"Noted." He fetches the broom and starts sweeping behind the bar. "Let me know where you want pizza from? I'll order when we leave and pick it up on the way."

"You got it, starlight."

Over the next half hour, we do all the end-of-night tasks. Jake leaves once he wipes down the tables and stools, then cashes out. After Micah takes the tills to the office, we do one last sweep of the club and shut everything down.

On the way to our cars, I tell him where to order my ham, pineapple, garlic and onion pizza from. He makes a face but doesn't insert his opinion. Smart man.

"Mine or yours?" he asks.

My mouth goes dry. I work to hide my sudden need to excessively swallow. "Yours," I choke out.

The hint of a smile twitches at the corner of his mouth. "I'll text you my address, in case we get separated. See you in a bit." Then, as if second nature, he presses a chaste kiss to my lips before going to his truck.

His truck starts up, but he doesn't leave the lot until I drive off. For most of the drive from Tampa to Clearwater, we ride in line with each other or side by side. I feel like a fool with this painful smile stretching my face most of the ride. But no one sees or judges it. So, I leave it in place as the wind whips my hair and the radio plays loud rock tunes.

When I hit the first red light after crossing the Bay, I plug Micah's address into the map app and connect it to the car audio. After I turn off the main road, I scope out the area. This stretch of town is slightly unfamiliar. The map tells me to take the next right.

My brows pinch in the middle. *I cross this exact street almost daily. A couple miles down the road.*

A left turn, then another right. "Your destination is on the right," the navigation announces.

I park on the street and stare out the window at a quaint house. The streetlight one house down illuminates the yard more than the dual lamps on either side of the garage. From the front, the khaki and rich green house appears small. But the extended roofline past the tall wood fence indicates otherwise.

A tall oak, with a trunk too round to hug, occupies a hefty section of the yard to the left of his driveway. Thick branches with lush foliage extend over the house, driveway, and street. On the right of the driveway, white flowers highlight two mature crepe myrtles.

A short distance from the left of the garage, three small steps lead up to a screened-in porch. Soft white light brightens the lanai enough to see a wood bench swing at the end, pair of Adirondack chairs and small table.

As I lean forward and squint to see the flowering shrubs along the porch front, headlights flash in my rearview mirror. I lift a hand to shield the light and drop it as Micah's truck turns into the driveway.

I open the car door and Micah jogs over before I step out. "The street isn't busy, but it's probably best to park behind me."

"'Kay."

In the thirty seconds it takes me to start the car and park in his driveway, my body sprints into panic mode. Sweaty pits, clammy hands, stomach in knots. The whole shebang.

Before I exit the car, I remind myself Micah and I have already hung out. Eaten after work a couple times. I joined him and his friends at a get-together. Hell, I kissed the man like no other only hours ago.

So why the sudden freak-out?

Because we have never been truly alone.

Dining out came with the steady flow of patrons and restaurant staff. Hanging out with his friends… well, that explains itself. And earlier tonight, when we couldn't keep our mouths off each other, people stood less than twenty feet from us—the office walls and door our only form of privacy.

But inside the four walls of Micah's home, it would only be me and him. No one to stop at our table to interrupt conversations. No one to jiggle door handles and inhibit us from touching. Or kissing.

Micah strolls over and opens my door, two pizza boxes balanced in his other hand. "C'mon." He jerks his head toward the house. "Let's get inside and eat."

He shuts the door and I press the fob's lock button. I follow his sure steps on slate pavers. Slow down as we approach the screened porch. Stop breathing as he opens the front door and gestures me inside. He flips a switch beside the door and warm light filters through the space.

"Make yourself at home." He sets the pizzas down on the coffee table and starts unbuttoning his shirt. "Be back in a sec." He disappears down a short hallway.

I step farther into the room, the scent of Micah's cologne and lemon float in the air as my eyes scan every square inch. The house isn't small but feels big for one person. Has Micah always lived alone?

Light oak planks the open floor plan. The exterior wall to the right has more windows than concrete or drywall. During the day, I picture the living and dining area bright and warm and serene.

An earthy-brown couch with a chaise faces the front wall of the house. A natural-edge, wood coffee table with wide iron legs sits within reach, a television mounted feet from the front door. Warm light spills from a lamp between the television and wall of windows, and a second lamp near the corner of the couch.

Across the room, near the windows, is a dining table—the same natural edge as the coffee table—with two chairs on either side. Large round bulbs hang at uneven lengths from thick black cords. In the dark, I bet they glow like stars. Like Micah's eyes. Beyond the table, a large, sepia-tone world map is pinned to a corkboard. A collage of photographs surrounds the map and I step closer to view them.

I reach out and stroke a finger over a younger version of Micah. One I remember from years back. When life was simple and not so simple. In the photo, he has an arm around Shelly and who I assume is their mother. All three of them smiling without a care in the world.

"That was in the Smoky Mountains."

I jump and slap a hand over my chest. "What are you, part secret agent?" He laughs with a shake of his head. "Don't sneak up like that."

"Didn't mean to." Another chuckle leaves his lips. He presses his front to my back as his arms snake around my waist. "Just saw you here and didn't want to disturb you." Warm, soft lips press against the skin beneath my ear. "I like seeing you in my space."

I wiggle out of his arms and twist to face him. "And how many other women have you delivered that exact line to?" The question is meant to be a joke, considering all the women that have left Roar on Micah's arm.

But guilt swirls like a waterspout beneath my diaphragm as his face pales. *Shit.*

"The women I left the club with… they never set foot in this house." His eyes close as he inhales deep. On the exhale, his eyes reopen. "The last woman to step foot in this house brought another man." Dark, starry irises swallow me whole. "You being here… let's just say it's a big step."

Wow. Just wow.

Way to make an ass of yourself, Peyton.

"I didn't—" I fumble over my words. Unsure how to pedal back and fix my mistake. "Sorry."

A hand brushes mine before our fingers intertwine. "Let's eat." He nods toward the couch.

We plop down on the sofa and I open the pizza boxes as Micah scans a list of movies on the television. When I look up, he selects *Pulp Fiction,* presses pause and sets the remote on the table.

"Want a drink?" He rises from the couch and ambles toward the small, yet spacious kitchen. Whoever designed the kitchen knew how to make the most out of the limited space.

I follow Micah with my eyes. Take in his relaxed demeanor and attire. Drop my gaze down his backside and swallow. Something about gray sweats and a snug cotton tee…

He fetches a pitcher from the fridge and sets it on the small island while getting glasses. The island sits askew in the open space, three barstools on the side facing the living and dining area. The overall vibe of the kitchen is a blend of dark wood cabinets, stainless steel appliances, and light granite counters. A large window over the sink faces the backyard. For someone who doesn't cook, his kitchen is dreamy. I would cook in it.

Wait. What?

Why does being here—in Micah's space, his home—feel so natural? So comfortable? Why does it conjure thoughts of us wrapped up in each other? Laughter and flour handprints and water fights with the sink sprayer.

"Water, please," I croak out and turn to face the television.

Snap out of it, Peyton.

When half of my pizza—and all of Micah's—vanishes, I set the box on the table and pat my belly. Micah scoots over until our arms bump, and then he rests a hand on my thigh. The contact is simple and non-suggestive. Yet it warms me more than the summer evening.

I rest my head on his shoulder and do my best to focus on the movie. Which works out... until Micah kisses my hair. Then does it again. And again.

His hand on my thigh takes on a new weight. Feels heavier and hotter.

Before I overthink what happens next, I lift my head and rotate to lock on this softer side of Micah. I hold his gaze for three breaths before dropping my eyes to his lips. I lean closer, slowly eradicate the space between us, and kiss him.

A low frequency hum purrs in my bloodstream when our lips collide. The kiss is soft and chaste at first. A slow buildup to the fiery kiss we shared earlier, but equally soul stirring.

Our tongues stroke with languid movements. Hands and fingers explore uncharted terrain but don't cross the line. A hand slips under the back of my top and guides me back to lie on the couch. One of his legs wedges between mine. His weight above me is welcome and constant and perfect. The planes and lines and musculature of his frame mold to mine as the kiss picks up tempo.

My hands trail up his chest, his neck, and fist his hair. He moans and rocks his hips forward, grinding his thick erection against the junction of my thighs. Lust clouds every rational thought, and I do it again. He breaks the kiss with a gasp. Teeth nip along my jaw, my ear, the column of my neck, the base of my throat. Then he licks leisurely up, tasting me, until our lips crash together.

We kiss like horny teenagers. His erection rock hard between my thighs. My panties drenched and clit throbbing. But neither of us leads the moment beyond heavy kissing and light petting. Micah staying true to his word—that nothing further would happen tonight—makes my heart happy and body frustrated.

As if my thoughts were broadcasted aloud, he breaks the kiss and gasps. "You'll be the death of me."

Before I get a word in, he shifts us both so we lie on our sides and face the television. His front to my back. His hips lined up with mine, I'm acutely aware his erection hasn't calmed whatsoever. And I love that he doesn't hide his body's reaction.

He reaches for a throw pillow and tucks it beneath our heads. His hand on my hip dips as his fingers trail the faint line of exposed skin between my shirt and pants. Fingers skirt beneath the shirt hem and splay over my belly. Although his hand doesn't move, the tips of his fingers paint small circles near my navel. I feel every whirl and loop and stroke, at the point of origin and throughout my body.

I close my eyes. Forget about the movie. Forget about everything except the tingles rippling over my skin from his touch. How can something so simple feel so damn good?

Then he licks up my neck from the curve of my shoulder and I moan. Press my ass against him. Lose myself in the intoxication of it all when his free hand clutches my throat. Squeezes enough that I see his starry irises behind closed lids.

"You have it wrong," I choke out.

He licks and nips his way to my ear. Sucks my lobe between his teeth. "What's that?"

I lift a hand over his at my throat and hold it there. "You'll be the death of me first."

twenty-three

MICAH

Bzzt. Bzzt.

Peyton twitches in my arms, then relaxes. Her chest rises and falls in a steady, rhythmic tempo. I nestle more into her neck and curl my arm tighter around her midsection. Hold her closer as I drift back to sleep.

Bzzt. Bzzt.

I shake half awake. Peyton groans, twists in my arms, snuggles closer to my chest and burrows her face near the base of my throat. My leg drapes hers as our lower limbs tangle. I draw her impossibly closer. Kiss her hair. Cradle her against the length of my torso. Her warm breath at the hollow of my throat soothes and settles me back to sleep.

Bzzt. Bzzt.

Peyton grumbles against my chest and I tighten my hold on her.

Bzzt. Bzzt.

"Who is that?" I complain, my words like sandpaper.

Peyton shifts in my arms and I open my eyes. I look down at her as she peers up. Inch down to press my lips to hers. Her phone buzzes on the coffee table again. For the umpteenth time.

She stretches an arm behind her and slaps the table until it lands on her phone. When the screen lights, she bolts upright. "Oh, shit."

If I wasn't awake a minute ago, I am now. "What's wrong?" I scrub a hand down my face and blink several times to shake off the sleep.

"It's after eight." I stare at her and patiently wait for the reason why this is a bad thing. That was the best sleep I have gotten in weeks. No sense in complaining. "In the morning. As in, I stayed the night at your house."

"This is a bad thing?"

Unlocking her phone, she opens her text messages and starts typing. "No. Yes. No."

My hand draws lazy circles on her lower back. "Take a minute to wake up. I'm sure everything is fine."

She drops the phone in her lap, then gives me her profile. Stares at the ceiling as her weight presses into my side. "It is. But Reese is freaking out because I didn't come home or let him know I was staying out."

I wiggle to the cushion edge and rise from the couch. Head toward the kitchen for water before I say something irrational about their close relationship. The water staves off an inkling of my jealousy. So, I drink more.

Last thing I need to do after sleeping with Peyton in my arms all night is to piss her off. My unjustifiable green monster needs to sit the fuck down and chill the fuck out. I have no right to be jealous over a friendship she's had for decades.

Peyton saunters into the kitchen, steps up behind me, and

wraps her arms around my waist. Her arms crisscross over my chest as she presses her palms flat to my pecs. God, I love the feel of her body against mine. No awkwardness or mismatched placement. She fits every angle and curve as if meant to be there.

"He's not mad because I stayed out," she whispers along the curve of my neck. "Just wanted to make sure I wasn't lying in a hospital. We usually text or leave notes when staying out late. He was worried. That's all."

My rational brain processes this and shakes a finger. *Don't be a dick. They are just friends.*

I rotate my head and drop an innocent kiss on her lips. "Glad you have someone who worries. Sorry."

"No need to be sorry." Her arms form parallel lines on my stomach and constrict. "All this between us…" Warm lips trail up my neck and my eyes roll shut. Fuck, every touch Peyton gives feels amazing. "Is new. For me and you."

I twist in her grip and wind my arms around her. Drop my lips to hers, but don't deepen the kiss. When we break apart, I tuck loose tendrils of her hair behind her ear. Study her freshly woken features—hair in a messy topknot, pillow crease lines on her cheek, brows a bit shifty, eyes bright but not yet alert.

If I woke up next to her each morning, it would be a great life.

I kiss the tip of her nose. "Gonna go brush my teeth." Her eyes widen as a hand covers her mouth. As if she just thought about her own morning breath. "Probably have extra toothbrushes in the bathroom." She lifts a brow. "From the dentist goody bags." I kiss her forehead, wrap her hand in mine, and lead her to the bathroom.

After we get the bathroom to ourselves a moment, I dig out a spare toothbrush. We hover near the sink, squeeze paste from the tube, and brush simultaneously. And it's so bizarre. How scrubbing our teeth together is the most normal my life has felt in a long time.

"Confession," I say as we enter the main space of the house. "Although I fail at cooking most foods, breakfast is not one of them. So, you're in luck." She laughs as I guide her to the barstools. "Have a seat, hellcat. I'll whip us up something. Promise it'll be edible."

Peyton parks herself at the breakfast bar, props her elbows on the counter, and rests her chin in her hands. Her violet eyes sparkle as they follow my every move. And damn, I love how good it feels to have her eyes rake over my backside. To survey my body without shame. Heat my skin and drive me wild.

From the fridge, I collect eggs, milk, cheese, and butter. Sausage links from the freezer and the loaf of bread on the island. I set a pan on the stove, crank the heat to medium-low and add some oil. Next, I crack eggs in the bowl, add milk and whip them together. All the while, Peyton watches me in mesmerized silence.

Domesticity has never been something I pictured in my life. Mom and Dad have it down to a science. A natural flow whenever they are together. Synergy. Anyone in their presence sees it, feels it. Obviously it exists, but I never considered I'd have the same simplicity in my own life. Not even with Rochelle.

But as Peyton's eyes follow me around the kitchen, watch me season and mix and flip, my mind considers new possibilities.

I drop bread in the toaster, then add shredded cheese to scrambled eggs as the sausage finishes. After I grab plates from the cabinet, I fish a butter knife from the drawer. The toaster clicks and the bread pops up. I butter, then cut the slices in half and add them to the plates. Followed by the eggs and sausage.

"Your breakfast, m'lady." I deposit a plate in front of Peyton and hand her a fork. "Coffee, milk or juice?"

"Coffee, please."

I brew us both a cup from the Keurig, then join her at the breakfast bar. We eat in relative silence. Her knee bops mine a few times until she leaves it there. Until our plates empty, we find some way to keep physical contact. Knee or foot or elbow. The contact has my chest fluttery and limbs tingly.

"Really should head home," Peyton says as she sips the last of her coffee.

She slides down from the stool, ambles to the couch, and puts her shoes on. Usually going separate ways from a woman gives me relief. But as Peyton collects her purse and phone, an ache builds beneath my sternum.

"Would it upset you if I said I don't want you to leave?"

A soft smile tugs at the corners of her mouth. "Quite the opposite. But I need to shower, put on fresh clothes, and do errands before work."

I follow her to the door, but neither of us moves to open it. "Know it wasn't intentional, but I'm glad you stayed." Inching closer, I plant my hands on either side of her and box her in. "Haven't slept like that in a long time."

Her palms flatten on my pecs. "Oh, yeah. And how's that?"

My head lowers, lips an inch from hers. "Solid. Restful." I drop my lips to hers and taste the coffee on her lips. "All because you were in my arms."

Pink paints her cheeks as she swallows. Her reaction

sends a rush throughout my body. "Me, too," she admits with an unfamiliar level of softness.

I dip down and take her mouth again. She fists my shirt and I drop my hands to her hips, heaving our bodies closer together. Her lips part and our tongues duel. Hands trail up my chest and dive into my hair, clenching the strands and tugging. A growl rises in my chest and spills into her as she deepens the kiss. Mouth fucks me near my front door.

Then she breaks the kiss, pins me in place with her vibrant irises, and inches back. "Really should go." Her breathy words lack oomph.

I drop a kiss on her lips. Then another. "Okay. I'll walk you out." After a quick adjustment, I unlock the door, take Peyton's hand, and lead her out the door.

The car beeps when she presses the fob, but she doesn't get in immediately. We exchange a few more chaste kisses before she opens the door and slips behind the wheel. The engine starts up and she rolls down the window.

"Best unintentional sleepover," she says, leaning out the window. I bend and kiss her one last time. "See you tonight."

"Tonight." I tap the roof of her SUV. She rolls up the window and backs out of the driveway. Within seconds, her car vanishes from sight.

I trudge my way to the front door and stumble inside. Flopping down on the couch, I rest my head on the pillow we shared not long ago. Inhale her lingering coconut and mint scent on the throw pillow. And bask in the simplicity and tranquility I felt—still feel—with Peyton in my space. In my arms. In my world.

~

Lost fucking cause. Might as well etch it on my skin now.

I straight up pouted when Peyton arrived at Roar fifteen minutes prior to open. With all the extra prep done yesterday and Kaylynn showing Mable and Caleb more tonight, Peyton didn't need to rush. Which means I got zero alone time with her beforehand.

And now, I stomp around the club with a permanent frown and childish demeanor.

"Someone's not having a good day," Peyton teases when I step behind the bar.

I bump our shoulders together. "Hmm. Wonder why?"

The corner of her mouth kicks up in a playful half smile. "Maybe someone needs a nap or caffeine." Her tone pouty and mocking. Makes me want to bite her lip.

"Or..." I drawl the two-letter word out as an idea sparks. "Maybe I need to take someone in the office." Her violet eyes go wide. "To show you how the invoices need to be cataloged, of course."

Her frame sags a hair, but her eyes don't leave mine. Unspoken questions on whether or not sneaking off to the office is a good idea. The fact I won't see Peyton every night at Roar is the perfect reason. Although, we are most definitely seeing each other outside these walls again. Often.

I approach Kaylynn as she explains the non-serving aspects of the job to Mable and Caleb. Both listen with rapt attention. "Hey." Kaylynn shifts her gaze and pauses her instruction. "You all good out here if I teach Peyton management tasks in the office?"

Kaylynn scans the club. Still early, the place doesn't have much activity. The Thursday crowd usually picks up in an hour. "Yeah, boss. I'll come get you if it's busy."

Peyton hesitates until I round the corner of the hall. Her

heels clap on the floor in quick succession as she catches up. Not a breath after the office door closes, and the lock flips, I smash her against the wall. Kiss her hard and rough. Grind my stiffening cock to the junction of her thighs. Moan as her taste hits my tongue.

We kiss like brutal beasts ready to shred the other's clothes. Fingers fist my hair and yank hard. I bend at the knees and rub my pulsating cock over the seam of her pants. A sweet whimper exits her lips and I swallow it down.

All we have done is kiss and dry fuck. If she gets this turned on and desperate with our clothes on, she will no doubt ravage me when we are skin to skin.

Presumptuous of me to assume Peyton and I will have sex, I know. Although I plan to take my time with Peyton, not jump the gun and ruin the foundation we are building, our relationship will go next level. And beyond.

I break the kiss, take a step back, and smash my palm to my dick. "Fuck, hellcat."

She bends at the waist, drops her hands to her knees and gasps. "Back at ya, starlight."

It takes a hot minute, but once our breathing levels out, I guide us to the desk. "We really should do some work. Can't drag you in here constantly and leave you still not knowing what to do." I chuckle.

Peyton drags a chair from the guest side of the desk and parks it next to the one reserved for the manager on duty. For the next hour, I slip on my leader mask and focus on the task at hand. Peyton hangs on every word as I go over payroll, inventory, invoices, and scheduling. Watches my every move as I key figures into the spreadsheets. Asks questions to clarify how often we do full inventory and handle the cash each night. In my unbiased opinion, Peyton learns and catches on quickly. Which is great for two reasons.

One—I don't have to repeat myself. Not that I wouldn't have if necessary. And two—I get more alone time with her while I show her the ropes. It's a win-win.

twenty-four

PEYTON

Everything has fallen into place. Work. Life. Both feel more on track than any other time in the past. For once, I am headed in the right direction.

Can't remember the last time life flowed so smoothly. Had this level of comfort. Streamlined without effort. Maybe with Chad?

Chad Lark—the first guy I dated, post high school. Guys in high school weren't worth my time, effort, or energy. But Chad was different. Mature and kind and gentle—although he knew how and when to be rough and harsh. In our two years together, we were inseparable. A team. He was the marrying type and I would have said yes.

Unfortunately, Chad never got to ask.

One morning, Chad didn't wake up. The coroner said a natural defect caused the chambers of his heart to not contract as normally. He died peacefully in his sleep. He was twenty-two. We had started planning for the future. Hinted at taking the next step. Neither of us aware that his heart had a sooner expiration date.

They say you never forget your first love. The sentiment is true. I will never forget Chad.

Sadly, I have dealt with enough heartache to last multiple lifetimes. One can only hope I have met my quota.

Life is on an upswing. Work is taking steps along a positive path. I busted my ass—contrary to what Micah believes—to get here. Learned so much about the business and have done my fair share of hands-on. Ani groomed me little by little over the span of our friendship. Long before the announcement of my promotion, she pegged me as her go-to person. Someone she trusted. Someone she wanted to help run her business. I was more than thrilled to be chosen by her. Ani will always be more than my boss. She's the sister I never had growing up.

Outside of work… well, that seems to be pretty damn good too.

In a matter of months, I went from loathing Micah Reed to fantasizing over our next kiss. The way his lips devour, the way he puts every ounce of passion into each kiss… my body quivers. Trembles and whimpers, imagining the idea of more. Of his bare chest against my breasts. Of his hands and fingers tracing lines and peaks and valleys as he maps my body. Of his lips on my breasts, my abdomen, and between my thighs.

"Hey." Micah sidles up to me behind the bar. "Everything alright? You're flush." Starry eyes survey every exposed inch of my skin.

I pour a glass of water and drink it. "Fine. Just got warm."

When the glass empties, Micah inches closer and brings a hand to my cheek. "Sure you're alright?" I knock his hand away and he has a light bulb moment. Leaning closer, his lips and hot breath brush my ear. "Were you thinking about me just now? About us?"

I breathe in short, quick bursts. My breasts rise and fall and graze his pecs. Heat blooms from my chest, paints my skin, my neck, my cheeks. Fingers trail up the side of my thigh, stop at my hip bone and squeeze.

Part of me worries what our interaction looks like from an outsider's perspective. Are we the center of attention? Can people not look away? Not that Roar has brought in a crowd tonight.

The other part of me doesn't give a damn and aches to drag him closer. Smash my lips to his. Kiss him like he is my last meal. Ignore the audience and take what I want.

"Yes," I answer, breathy. No sense in skirting around the truth.

"What were you thinking about?" His tongue licks the shell of my ear. My eyes roll shut as my bones turn to putty. "Tell me, Peyton."

Jesus fuck. Now is not the time for this conversation. Roar —among employees and patrons—is not the place to have this conversation. But with each passing second, my will to steer this talk in another direction becomes more difficult.

I hook fingers in his front pockets. Eager to pull him to me, but keep him rooted in place. "Was thinking about last night." I lick my lips. "Kissing you."

"Kissing me then?" He nips my earlobe. "Or kissing me now?"

"Both," I admit, softly. "How I want your hands on my skin."

His chest vibrates as a growl tears up his throat. A hand fists my hip. "Come over again tonight."

It isn't a question. More like a directive. I hate the way I love his subdued demand.

"We aren't having sex," I whisper, in the hopes no one

hears this not-safe-for-work conversation.

The hand on my hips tightens and releases. "There're other ways to enjoy each other without sex. Figured you'd know that, hellcat." He inches away. "Come over."

The lights and '80s music flood back in as cool air smacks my face. My eyes scan the club, behind the bar, but no one pays us any attention. At least not now.

"Yeah, okay."

A bright, toothy smile lights up Micah's face. I love this smile. "Perfect." He smacks my ass. "Now, get back to work."

The rest of the night goes as slow as last night. Weekdays during the summer can be hit or miss for places like Roar. Hence why Ani wanted fresh ideas. New attractants to draw in the same crowd and maybe new people. With Ani, her market research, and how she wants things perfect from the get-go, the new changes will be great for business.

As the night wears on, the crowd thins and Micah lets the staff leave early, one by one. With thirty minutes until the door locks, Kaylynn and I start stocking and cleanup while Micah serves.

Sweeping the floor behind the bar, I peer down at the opposite end as a blonde woman steps up. In a blazing-red dress that leaves nothing to the imagination, she smiles at Micah and leans toward him. A shiver rolls down my spine as he returns the smile. Although it's forced, I recognize the familiarity between them.

He says something and grabs a shaker, ready to mix her a drink. But she shakes her head. With each stroke of the broom, I inch my way down the bar and closer to them. Micah's face reddens as he works his jaw, then says something else. Their conversation too quiet for me to hear yet. So, I sweep down the line faster.

"I just want to talk," she complains as I pretend not to hear.

Still far enough away, Micah might not realize I hear the exchange.

"Before we hooked up, I told you there'd be nothing else. What's there to talk about?"

Not that I didn't know Micah was a manwhore. But hearing him verbally duke it out with some desperate floozy is insane. Another reason to resist temptation and not have sex with Micah yet.

"I really don't want to do this here," she shoots back with a huff.

"No one's stopping you from leaving." Micah waves a hand in the air.

I step closer after sweeping the same square footage for too long. Micah has to know I am within earshot now.

"Why are you being such an asshole?" she shouts.

Now is when I opt to turn around. Time for me to get acquainted with my managerial role. We don't get a ton of bullshit in Roar, but every now and again, we have to deal with the belligerent and physically violent.

"Ma'am." Her eyes snap to mine and she stiffens. "Not sure what the problem is, but you need to calm down or leave. Your choice."

She crosses her arms and forces up her breasts. "I'm not leaving until I talk with him."

"And I already said, not happening," Micah states as I sidle up to him and form a stronghold.

"Fine," she huffs out. "Don't want to go somewhere private? We'll do it right here." My brow pinches at the middle, and Micah rolls his eyes. "I'm pregnant, asshole. And you're going to be a daddy."

A Love So Bright

BOOK TWO

Thank fuck.

For the first time in what seems like hours, I breathe. I turn to face Peyton and notice she hasn't moved. At all. Is she breathing?

Shit.

"Hey," I say and lift my hands to frame her face. She doesn't respond. Her eyes vacant and off in the distance. "Peyton?" I step in front of her, crowd her, so she will look me in the eye, and stroke my thumbs over her cheeks. "Peyton, look at me."

I stop breathing. My eyes refuse to deviate from hers. Then, she blinks several times as if waking from a deep sleep. Her usual fiery violet irises are duller as they refocus. My thumbs continue to stroke her cheeks as she starts to shake her head. When her chin wobbles, my pulse jolts.

"I need to go," she mutters.

"What?"

"Micah…" Her eyes glaze over as she tucks her lips between her teeth. "I… I need to go."

Go? What does she mean she needs to go? Go where?

Maybe she needs to sit down and breathe a minute. Shake off the crazy bitch that flew in and stormed out. If I were her, I would need time to process what just went down.

"Why don't you go sit in the office. I'll finish up out here. Then we can head out."

Glassy violet irises whip to my starry blues. "No, Micah." Her breathing picks up. Lungs heaving as if they can't pull in enough oxygen. "I need to go *home*. Knew this was a bad idea."

She starts to step away from me, but I catch her elbow. "Peyton." Her name is a plea for mercy on my tongue.

"Please, just come back to my place. We can talk about this." I point toward the door. "There is no possible way that woman is pregnant by me. Or any woman, for that matter."

Realization of how loud this conversation is has my eyes sweeping the club. I breathe easier when I see everyone has left. Well, the patrons are gone. The remaining staff has scattered to give us privacy.

"How can you be so sure? I'm no rocket scientist, Micah, but even I know the tiniest pinprick can lead to pregnancy."

Jesus fucking Christ.

Why is she on this other woman's side? Is it the whole "women band together" thing? Because in this situation, that is complete and utter bullshit. Not when one of the women is shady as fuck.

If Peyton walks away from me now, I have a feeling I won't stand a chance in the future. Again. No matter what, we can't go separate ways tonight. Not with this fake ass shit lingering in the air. Not without talking this through and seeing reason.

"Peyton." Her name is a whisper on my tongue as I step back into her space. "This whole situation is a clusterfuck. But I know, without a shadow of doubt, there is no possible way that woman is pregnant with *my* child. Not a chance. So, please…" I fully invade her space. Bring my lips to her ear. Feel her tremble beneath me as I rest my hands on her arms. "Please, don't do this. Don't walk away. Don't shut me out. Not without giving me a chance. Not without giving *us* a chance."

For day-long seconds, she remains a statue in my arms. Stoic and silent. Her hot breath on my neck the only reminder this is real. That this isn't an epic nightmare—at least not the type to vanish when you open your eyes. This nightmare is manageable. It would be more manageable if Peyton took my side. If she believed the truth. *My truth.*

Do pregnancies happen when condoms are worn? All the time.

But I am no damn fool. Maybe off my rocker at times, but not a fool. The guy in the contraceptive aisle inspecting the condom boxes with hardcore scrutiny… yep, that would be Micah Reed. The guy who opens the box when he gets home and examines every wrapper for any cuts, tears or holes. That would also be me. Condoms don't go in my wallet unless I am one-hundred-percent sure they are tamper-free. Hell, I even buy the ones with spermicide.

Don't care what the woman said, her baby—if she is actually pregnant—doesn't share my DNA.

Peyton fights an internal battle. Her fingers ball into fists, then relax, over and over. Much as I don't want her to walk away from me tonight, she gets to make the decision to stay or go. What is happening between us is fresh, new. Wouldn't surprise me if she took a step back and told me to fuck off. That she didn't sign up for this.

But I really want her to step up and fight. Stick with me as we navigate our feelings. Then, give in to those emotions. Allow me to give in to mine.

For far too long, Peyton has consumed my thoughts. I suspected the moment I had a chance with her, I would shred her clothes and relish my name on her tongue.

The moment my lips crashed down on hers, though… it was as if my synapses fired right for the first time. Pieces fell into place and life started to make sense. And if I felt all that after one kiss, I fantasize what life may be like after I taste more than her lips. More serious and intense. Addictive and engrossing. I won't be able to stay away from her.

Which is why *I'm* not ready to have sex with Peyton.

Hands brush the sides of my torso and snake around my waist to connect at my lower back. I inhale deeply for the first time in minutes. Let the cool air fill my lungs and settle my anxiety. Allow my body to relax and melt with hers.

"I'll come back to your place under one condition," she whispers in my ear. "We talk. That's it. Tonight will not be a rerun of last night."

I nod. This, I accept… with one slight variation. "Can we at least grab food?" I lean back, sweep wayward strands of hair from her face, and brush my knuckles down her cheek. "Microwave meals from the store or order delivery. Don't care which. But we should eat."

"That's fine." She looks to the broom on the ground. "We should finish up and close."

I don't want to free her from my hold, but we will never leave otherwise. So I loosen my grip and step back. I drop a kiss on her forehead, take a deep breath and nod.

We get back to work and finish our nightly tasks. Twenty minutes fly by faster than expected and it isn't long before we say good night to the staff walking out the door with us. I tell Peyton I will order Chinese and pick it up on the way to the house. After she gives me her order, she hops in her car and drives out of the lot.

As her taillights disappear, an odd sensation slithers up my spine, spreads through my limbs and I shiver head to toe. The sensation eats me alive like a microbial plague. Makes me second-guess Peyton's reason to come over tonight. Acid rises in my throat and I swallow to stanch it from exiting my lips.

It's all in your head, man. Don't make something out of nothing.

After several deep breaths, I call the Chinese joint near my house. I order more than either of us will eat, but plan to have leftovers for another meal or two. Once the order is placed, I take one last deep breath, death grip the steering wheel, and drive off.

When I hit the bridge, I pray the salty air whipping my face and filling my lungs will untwist this knife in my gut. Will loosen the knot gradually getting tighter with each mile my truck eats up. Will vanquish the overall bad feeling swallowing me whole.

No matter how many breaths I take, no matter how I steer my thoughts, the pang beneath my diaphragm doesn't fade. If anything, the knife twists deeper. Grinds my bones and digs into the marrow.

Please, let this be my imagination running wild. Don't let the beginning of what we have go to shit. Not over this.

I repeat this again and again. A dictum to reign over what will come of tonight. A precept to dictate the future, regardless of the irrationality steering my thoughts. Because if you repeat something enough times, if you put the energy out into the universe, it becomes truth. Not like prophecy. More like guidance down the path of my choosing.

The red-dress woman made an attempt to derail my life, my future, tonight. Tried to trap me with a pregnancy scare. But she won't rattle me so easily. She won't cuff me at the ankle and drag me beside her. Not without hard proof. And until that day arrives, I will live my life. On my terms.

Who knows what my future holds. If Peyton is a part of said future, I will be forever indebted to her and whatever celestial being grants me the opportunity. An opportunity to right the wrongs I have committed. An opportunity to see where our connection leads.

"Thank you," I mutter into the wind. "Whoever is looking out for me, thank you."

I won't let you down.

two

PEYTON

Why the hell am I here? Why did I agree to this?

Agreeing to meet Micah at his house after what just happened is not a good idea. Especially with my mind all over the place. I don't know which way is up or whose truth to believe. Anger and frustration and anguish claw me up one side and down the other. My guardian angel has one hand on her hip while she wags a finger from the other in my face. The words *I told you so* on the tip of her tongue.

I want to heed her advice and drive off before Micah gets home. Save my heart from another walk down Shitty Life Lane. Yet, here I am. Waiting. A glutton for punishment.

I press the heel of my palm to my breastbone and rub. Do my best to sooth the ache and simmer the heightened sting. One by one, my heart leaks every ounce of hope and joy and possibility I had for Micah. Spills it at my feet. And I simply watch it puddle before it seeps into the earth.

Fuck.

When it comes to me, Micah Reed breeds misfortune.

As a young woman, I pined for him. Watched him from afar on the track. Peeked his direction whenever he was near.

Even after he crushed my soul with his words, even after he made a mockery of me in front of half the school, I still yearned for his affection. For his attention. For any fondness he would bestow upon me.

Then, I grew up.

The memory of him always sat in the shadows of my mind, but I moved on. Found people who knew my worth. Knew I wasn't just some loner girl with a crazy obsession for all things black. Knew I had more to give. And those people surrounded me with smiles and laughter and love. They lifted me up and brought me back to life. Showed me real friendship and what it meant to care for others. I owe them more than I will ever be able to give.

So why the hell am I here?

Why did I willingly choose to walk into the lion's den? Why am I setting myself up for more pain? More pain inflicted by Micah Reed.

"Because I'm a fucking idiot," I whisper into the dark cab of my SUV.

Unlike last night, Micah's house holds no interest. I don't stare at the shrubs and flowering plants along the front and try to guess what they are. I don't stare at the wood fence and wonder what setup he has beyond the wall of windows. I don't have the energy to care. Not tonight. Not after the wake-up call from Little Miss Red Dress.

Not focusing on anything in particular, I stare toward the end of the street. Let my eyes glaze over as they land on the yellow diamond sign that reads *no outlet*. Space out and let my mind blank as I wait.

Before long, Micah's headlights beam around the corner and blind me in the rearview mirror. Once he parks in the driveway, I move my car to park behind him. He hops out of his truck with two hefty bags of food and waits for me to join him.

Here we go.

The thirteen steps from his driveway to the front door feel like miles. Neither of us says a word as he unlocks the door, flips the light on and gestures me toward the couch. He sets the bags on the table, kisses the top of my head and wanders down the hall to what I presume is his bedroom.

Twenty-one breaths later, he settles on the couch, his leg brushing mine. Silence dominates the room like a deprivation chamber. And with each passing tick of the clock, a new pin gets pushed into the voodoo doll made to inflict me with pain.

Cursed. That's what this is. My life curse. If not, I am all ears for some other logical explanation. Some magical reason as to why I can't seem to hold on to... love, happiness, anything worthwhile.

I don't *love* Micah. It is way too soon to feel such a powerful emotion. But I do like him. More than I imagined possible after all the hurt he caused.

But every person I get romantically close to... the relationship always goes south. Every. Single. Time.

Am I destined to be a loner hag? A cat lady minus the cats. Always just me, myself and I as my hair turns gray and wrinkles define my face more than my expression.

As a little girl, I don't remember a time when I played dress-up, pretended to marry the boy up the street, and have babies in our perfect house with the perfect yard. I never fantasized about a prince sweeping me off my feet and rescuing me from tragedy. I didn't dream of a happily ever after and forever love. It just wasn't who I was.

But as years passed, my perspective on life shifted. I see things in a different light and with occasional filters. I wonder what would happen if I took a leap, tried something new, explored all the possibilities.

I don't want to spend my life alone. But I also don't want the heartache that comes with giving your all to another person.

And with Micah's history, heartache has an open-ended invitation.

Carton by carton, he pulls the food from bags. Sets a small container of shrimp egg foo young, rice and gravy in front of me on the coffee table. Places a fork and chopsticks on top.

"Hungry?" I choke out as Micah removes another four cartons and a container of soup.

He gives a timid smile. "I like leftovers. Makes my life easier."

Life probably won't be so easy for the next however many months. I want to say this to him. Want to tell him just because he says the baby—real or not—isn't his, doesn't make it true. Only science will prove one way or the other. And as crazy as the woman was in Roar, I don't picture her backing down. She will return, with a smug smile on her face. She will be a constant smack in the face, a constant reminder of who Micah was before.

I open the cartons and poke at the food. Eat a few small bites. Taste the egg, shrimp and vegetable pancakes, but don't savor them. Not like I usually do. When I peek at Micah from the corner of my eye, he appears to be in the same predicament. Half an egg roll eaten, some missing lo mein noodles, and a few slurps of egg drop soup gone.

"Micah..." He sets the egg roll down on the wrapper, wipes his hands clean, then meets my gaze. His eyes are veiny and damp. The starry flecks less visible in his dark-sky irises. "We have to talk about this."

Have to, versus want to, are two different animals.

I don't *want* to talk about the possibility of some random woman being pregnant from the guy I just started spending time with. We just sorted out our differences. He apologized and I mentally forgave him sometime over the last two weeks. Things between us were headed in a good direction. And now we *need* to talk about this.

We need to talk about the *what-ifs*.

"Yeah, we do." He huffs and sags into the couch. "For the record, though, this sucks."

This does suck. Hairy, sweaty, nasty balls.

He sits back up, plants his elbows on his knees, then leans forward and hangs his head. His broad shoulders stretch the cotton of his shirt. Put the definition of his muscles and stress on display. I swallow at the sight. My fingers itch to reach out. To trace the lines of tension in his neck and upper back and soothe his suffering. I lift a hand, then hesitate. Resist temptation. Drop my hand, curl my fingers into fists at my sides and force them to stay put.

Micah may need comfort right now, but so do I. This situation may not be directly impacting me, but it impacts me nonetheless.

"What if she is pregnant?" I pose the first of many questions.

He sits straighter. "She might be." He twists to face me and our knees knock. "But I won't believe anything without proof."

This I understand. If I were in his shoes, I would want hard evidence too. To be present as the tests are performed. Receive my own letter of proof when the results become available. Micah may have slept with his fair share of the female population, but I believe him when he says he practiced safety measures.

"What if tests prove the baby is yours?" I wince as the words leave my lips.

My reaction may give the vibe I don't care for children. Couldn't be further from the truth. I love their chubby cheeks and chunky legs. Love their expressions and laughter when you make faces or speak in different tones. Love how soft they are and how good they smell. Their innocence and untainted view of the world. Babies and young children are just happy.

But the idea of potentially dating someone while another woman carries his child... not sure I have the strength to handle it.

Micah reaches for my hand and I let him take it. He cocoons it in both of his. I focus on the warmth of his touch. The way his thumbs draw small circles over the top of my hand. And how he stares at our joined hands as if scared they will disappear if he looks away.

"Don't think it will." He lifts his red eyes. "But if the baby is mine, I'll take responsibility." I jerk my hand back, but Micah doesn't release me from his grip. "That doesn't mean anything changes between us, Peyton."

I love and hate that he won't let me go. That he refuses to surrender to outside forces. That he plans to fight for what he wants, but will still do the right thing in the end if need be.

The Micah in front of me isn't the same from my teenage years. Teenage Micah was more selfish and did whatever benefited his life the most. Adult Micah still has some of these same tendencies, but knows when to step up and be a man. When to do the right thing, but not let anyone rob him of life and the prospect of love.

"I want to believe you. God, Micah, I really do. But you can't deny a baby would flip your world upside down."

"Not denying it. But life is what we make it. If this woman *is* pregnant with *my* child, I will do my part. Doing my part does *not* equal being in a relationship with her." Fingers brush the underside of my chin and lift. Our eyes lock. Neither of us breathes. "If I haven't made it obvious yet, I want a relationship with *you*."

You know what they say about assuming... and I am definitely not going to assume with Micah Reed. Not when it comes to matters of the heart. Not when he has the ability to squash me like a bug and walk away unscathed.

His fingers drop away from my chin. Then his knuckles brush along my cheek. I sigh, and my entire frame caves forward. There will always be a piece of me that is weak for Micah. A part always ready to crumple to his demands, his will. This doesn't necessarily make me weak as a woman. Just weak when it comes to making informative, clear-minded decisions regarding him.

And I cannot afford to be weak.

"Let's eat," I suggest. My appetite may not have returned, but I hate food waste.

Micah flips on the television, but neither of us pays attention as our food slowly disappears. Dinner tonight is riddled with silence and anxiety and stress over what the future holds. Not only *my* future with Micah but also his if he becomes a father. Like it or not, fatherhood will change his life more than he realizes.

When I can't eat another bite, I close up the containers and put them in one of the bags. "I should go."

I need time alone to process this evening's news. And maybe some best-friend time to mull it over. When too close to a situation, it's always better to talk with someone not in the thick of it. Someone you trust and will listen to when they give advice.

"Sorry," Micah mumbles as we rise from the couch.

"For what?"

"Fucking this up. Seems to be my specialty." He laughs without humor as I lead us to the door. "But I'll make it better. I swear."

I don't doubt his proclamation. Micah is the type to go after what he wants. If what he wants happens to be yours truly, it will happen. Doesn't mean I won't make him work for it, though.

Before I get out the door, before I stop him from stepping closer, Micah crushes my lips with a smoldering kiss. And for one, two, three vicious beats of my pulse, I remain stone cold. Frigid as he tries to coax a kiss in return. The softness of his lips, the warmth of his arms circling my waist, and the sweet woodsy scent of his cologne... the triple whammy makes me surrender. I fist his shirt and haul him closer. Kiss him as if this may be the last time—because who knows what tomorrow will bring.

My body says to never let go. But my mind tells me to stop, take a step back, and leave. To get out of here before my feet refuse to go. Difficult as it is, I break the kiss. I unclench my fingers and turn my back to Micah.

"I should go," I mutter and twist the knob.

From the door to the car, the only noise to fill the silence is the clack of my heels and the soft thumps of Micah's bare feet hitting the ground. No buzzing insects. No wind gusts to rustle the leaves. No chatty neighbors or rumbling car engines. Nothing but undiluted silence. An awkward, unbearable silence until I unlock the car.

I start the car and roll down the window. "Thanks for dinner."

He reaches forward, his knuckles brush down my cheek. "Sorry it wasn't as great as last night."

God, this is so weird. Why does this have to be so fucking weird? "I better go."

With a solemn nod, he takes one, two steps back. "Drive safe. See you tomorrow."

I roll up my window, back out of the driveway, and watch as Micah disappears in my rearview mirror. The moment he vanishes, a fist tightens around my heart as the floodgates open and spill down my cheeks. I drive the short distance home in a mental and visual blur. The minute I walk through the front door and Reese takes one look at me, two warm arms engulf me.

This annihilates the dam wall on my emotions. My frame shakes as I drench Reese's shirt. He hugs me impossibly tighter, rubs a gentle hand up and down my spine, and shushes me as we rock in place. My purse hits the floor with a thump, and my keys clang when they land next. At some point, without me realizing, Reese walks us to the couch and sets me in his lap.

After hour-long minutes, the tears form dry salt lines to my chin. Snot clogs my nose and stains Reese's shirt. My throat withered; eyes puffy and achy. My heart an ashy mold waiting for the breeze to blow it to dust.

Reese holds me close while his one hand continues its journey up and down my spine. Every other stroke up, he stops to tuck a strand of hair behind my ear or run his fingers through the strands.

"Talk to me, sunshine," he whispers, his breath warm and comforting at my temple.

I inch back and stare into kind brown eyes. Eyes full of love and sincerity. More times than I can count, Reese has held my hand. Been my stronghold or lifted me up. Been there for me without judgment or conditions. No matter what bullshit life throws at either of us, our friendship never crumbles. As if fate knew I needed someone to love me in every way except romantically.

Reese is my person, and I am his. Day or night, through thick and thin, we are there for each other.

I spill every unsettling second about tonight. About the woman and how Micah reacted to the whole situation. How the entire scenario felt like a dull knife pushing into my rib cage. How the knife twisted each time Micah denied the possibility. And how the knife gutted me when Micah wanted to go about things as if the woman never stepped foot in Roar.

"My sweet Peyton." Reese hugs me close again. "I understand your pain and frustration with all this." He releases me and leans back to look into my eyes. "But if I were in his shoes, I'd be equally defensive. Especially if I took every precaution."

"Are you seriously taking his side?" I whine and narrow my eyes.

Warmth wraps my hand as Reese takes it in his. "This isn't about sides, sunshine. First of all, you'll always be number one. Always. Second, stop and really think about it. Put yourself in his position. If someone approached you and told you something equally life changing, wouldn't you question it?" I teeter my head left and right. "The answer is yes. We've known each other too many years to say otherwise."

He has me there. For obvious reasons, I can't put myself in Micah's shoes. Me impregnating someone is impossible.

But if someone accused me of something heinous that I felt was inconceivable, I would deny it without evidence too.

"This is one of a long list of reasons why I need you. You know me. You explain it from different views until I have more than one perspective." I huff out a deep breath and my shoulders cave inward. "Not that it resolves how I feel, but thank you."

Reese pats my hand. "Don't drive yourself crazy thinking about it. But don't let it go without giving it genuine thought. It's a big deal, but not the end of the world. No sense in worrying over something that may not hold merit."

I rise from his lap and he stands too. "Thanks for always being here. Don't know what I'd do without you." I wrap my arms around his neck and hug him hard.

His arms circle my waist and hug with equal strength. "Live a boring life, I'm sure." I drop a hand and poke his ribs. "Argh! It was a joke. Geez."

"Ha ha," I deadpan. I pick up my purse and keys from the floor and start for the hall. "Going to try and get some sleep. Night."

"Sleep tight, sunshine. I'll make us French toast in the morning."

I press a hand to my heart. "With extra powdered sugar?"

"Always."

After changing into a knee-length nightshirt, I slip under the covers and close my eyes. Sleep doesn't take me quickly, like usual. Instead, my brain clicks on and evaluates every possible outcome to several scenarios. An hour of mental torment passes, and I have no viable answers. I can't.

Because I don't know Micah well enough to know what he would do. Nor what the truth is when it comes to the red-dress woman.

So, I do my best to let it go. Let go of an outcome I have no control of. Let go of a future I can't predict. Let go of the what-ifs and fabricated scenarios my mind created.

~

"You look like shit."

Nothing like bluntness when you need softer edges. "Thanks, Aunt Leanne. I love you, too," I say with a dash of sarcasm as I slide into the booth across from her.

Monday has always been our day. Lunch after I leave Gulfside. An hour or two of girl time as we catch up on life. My weekly dose of Dad's side of the family. But with the new change in my work schedule and last night's bullshit, I need to see her today.

"Don't get your panties in a bunch. All I meant is you seem exhausted."

Exhaustion is a good word to explain how I feel. My limbs are heavier than Corinthian pillars. Eyes swollen, veiny and dry. My mind spends so much time in the fog, I'd swear we lived near the San Francisco Bay rather than Tampa Bay. And my heart... well, my heart currently teeters on barbed wire. Sleep was a joke last night; or should I say this morning. I may have slept three hours max as I tried my damnedest to let go. Easier said than done.

"Yeah, yesterday was rough. Glad you could meet up."

Aunt Leanne reaches across the table and covers my hand with hers. "Me, too. Now let's get some food and talk."

We study the menu and pick out lunch as the server approaches the table. Once we place our orders, I sip my water while Aunt Leanne lifts a brow and waits for me to spill every detail.

In so many ways, Aunt Leanne reminds me of Dad. Her bluntness and no-nonsense attitude. But also, her never-ending patience and practical mind. Whenever life feels off-kilter, Aunt Leanne uses her saintlike restraint and listens to every word. Just like Dad did. She lets me spill all the crazy details, then sits quietly for a bit and lets my words marinate. Figures out which parts are most important and starts there first.

"Remember the guy at work I told you about?"

She studies my eyes a beat. "Mmhm."

"Well, a couple nights ago, we kissed. And not your basic peck. More the hot and heavy kind."

Just like Dad and Aunt Leanne, I don't beat around the bush either. Some conversations are tougher to have, but they spill out sooner or later.

"Why do I get the feeling this kiss was great then, but isn't now?"

I take a deep breath and hold it to the count of five. "Because last night at work, some woman came in and claimed to be pregnant with his baby."

Aunt Leanne chokes on her sip of water. *Jesus, Peyton. Could you not have waited until she swallowed first?* I jump up from my seat and smack her back over her lungs. She waves me away as the coughing slows.

"Damn, girl. Trying to kill me?"

I purse my lips and raise my brows. "Hope you're being sarcastic, 'cause that's not remotely funny."

"Sorry." She coughs one last time, then takes another sip of water. "Of all the scenarios I expected, that was definitely not one of them. Took me by surprise, is all."

"Just be glad you didn't witness it firsthand."

The corners of her mouth turn down as her lower lip juts

out slightly. Some may confuse the look with pity, but I recognize the fraction of heartbreak she has for me in this moment. With all the painful tragedies of my past, adding another to the list sucks.

"It probably hurts, but tell me everything. From start to finish."

So, until our lunch arrives, I regale her with the events of the last forty-eight hours. Tell her the good news with work, Micah's reaction, and mine in turn. The kiss in the office and later at his house. I share how happy and weightless it felt to be around him, and the potential of what the future holds.

Then, I go into the bomb drop. How worked up this woman was about Micah not accepting her word. I share how the woman looked ready to party, and take another random man to her bed. And then, how I went back to Micah's house to talk. Our awkward silence and kiss before I said good night. How I felt empty and broken the moment I drove away.

Our plates slide in front of us and I snag a fry from my plate to munch on. As per usual, Aunt Leanne goes quiet after my story. She eats her BLT and I eat my fish sandwich. I pick at my fries and she eats her pineapple coleslaw. When our plates are empty, Aunt Leanne pushes hers aside and clasps her hands on the table.

"I assume you asked me here today because you want advice."

Mimicking her movement, I push my plate aside and lean forward. "That and to see if you think I'm overreacting. Is it weird for me to presume she's telling the truth? To think Micah should act differently?"

Taking my hands in hers, she rubs back and forth. "No reaction is wrong, Peyton. We all see and hear and feel and react to things in our own way. Just because it's different than someone else's reaction doesn't make it right or wrong. Your reaction is your own."

"I hate that instinct has me leaning away from him instead of standing closer."

She releases my hands, but doesn't stray far. "Sweetheart, you two have history. One that has messed with you for years. I'd find it odd if you *didn't* feel the way you do." My brows shoot to my hairline. "Just because you played tonsil hockey with the man, it doesn't erase history."

"Tonsil hockey? Seriously?" Feels like I'm a kid again.

Laughter floats in the air as tears spill down Aunt Leanne's face. "Would you rather I say sucking face? Or swapping spit? Canoodling, perhaps?" I drop my head in my hands. "Doesn't matter what you call it, you've had your tongue down the man's throat."

Jesus. Heat surges up my chest to my neck and face. No doubt my cheeks look more like pomegranate skin. I lift my gaze enough to see no one is paying us any attention. Thank god. Then sip my water in the hopes it will cool down the heat of embarrassment.

"Where were we?" I ask once I drain the water glass.

"Having good weeks with a person doesn't erase the bad years in your memory. You may enjoy his company now, but you still have barriers in place. Protection measures, in case he messes up again. By the sounds of it, you've already got the razor wire in place and the gate closing around your heart."

The waiter stops at the table to check on us and clear our plates. A thirty-second break in our conversation. Enough time to ponder what to say next. The moment he walks off, Aunt Leanne perches her chin on her hands and waits with eager eyes.

"If you were me, what would you do?"

"Obviously, I never experienced *your* pain years ago. But if I were in your shoes, I'd give myself a little time. Nowadays, everyone feels decisions have to be made immediately. That no one should have to wait. In some situations, this may be true. But in others, time is what you need. Especially when it's personal."

"So, I should give it time?" Time to sink in? Or time apart? This is so damn confusing.

This is why relationships are a pain in the ass. Don't get me wrong, I love sharing a connection with someone. Love not wanting to be apart from them. But drama and uncertainty are not qualities I want to embrace in a relationship.

"Give yourself time to really grasp the situation. Look at it from your perspective. Then, look at it from his. Write down your feelings on each. Imagine how you'd feel if someone threw news like this in your face and expected you to halt your life and cater to them. Let yourself *feel* what it'd be like to be in that scenario. Then make a decision from there."

Wise beyond her years, just like her brother had been. This is the reason—among several others—why I ask Aunt Leanne all the hard questions. Why I bring up the life-changing stuff with her. Not that Mom wouldn't give sage advice. Mom's advice just happens to slant toward whatever is easiest. And easy isn't always the best choice.

"Thank you. You always know how to make me see situations with fresh eyes."

"Glad to help." She pats my hand and scoots out of the booth. "Now let's get out of here. You need to nap before work."

I chuckle at her vague way of telling me I look like shit again. But I wouldn't want this woman any other way. There are few people in this world whose opinions matter to me. Aunt Leanne gives it to me like it is, straight and to the point, and I appreciate it each and every time.

We hug near my car. "See you Monday?" she asks.

"Yeah. My schedule changed, but lunch is still good. Maybe an hour earlier?"

She kisses my cheek. "Sounds good. Keep me posted until then. Love you."

"Love you, too."

I hop in my car and press the ignition. For a moment, I stare out the windshield and lose focus. *"Look at it from your perspective. Then, look at it from his."* Call it my homework assignment, but I need to sit down and really evaluate us and both sides of the coin.

No matter what happens in the end, no matter what I choose, I trust my intuition won't lead me down the wrong path. Not again.

three

MICAH

The longer Peyton is silent, the more I wither at the seams.

Yesterday, she walked in the back door of Roar, set her belongings in a locker, threw me a half-assed smile, and got to work. I had sent her a text in the morning—like I had for weeks—and got no response. All night, she slung drinks behind the bar and laughed with patrons. But the moment she glanced my way, an impossible wall erected between us.

I hate walls. But she needs space. I get it.

Does space equal zero interaction? No standard greeting or cordial exchanges. Fuck if I know. But her avoidance is the slowest, most torturous death. Like getting thrown on the rack, limbs bound at the wrists and ankles, torso stabilized, and, inch by inch, my starfished body gets stretched to its limit.

"Hey, boss," Ted says as I approach the front. "You good?"

Irritates me to no end that people read my emotions without a word. It isn't my nature to flaunt my feelings. Yet, I don't shut down or dodge them. But having my heart on my sleeve—at work, no less—is an open invitation for questions. Questions I have no desire to answer.

"Yeah, man. Just got a lot on my mind is all." The two seconds I pause to take a breath, Ted opens his mouth to speak. But I beat him to it. "Things good here?" I point toward the door.

He nods, then prattles on about the few people who tried to get in without paying cover or were underage. His voice hangs in the atmosphere, but I don't absorb a word. Not when I spot Peyton across the club, smiling and laughing with two guys.

How many days had passed since she smiled at me with gaiety? Two. Two decades-long days. And I hated every single, solitary second of those two days.

Ted stops talking and I have enough sense to notice. I pat his shoulder, force a smile, and leave him to stroll the perimeter of Roar with Peyton in my periphery. Her champagne locks secured in a high ponytail, I recall the silky gloss of the strands. Her laughter floats across the club as flashes of her under me as I tickled her ribs invade my vision.

Fuck.

When was the last time I focused so much attention on one woman? Let her occupy my every waking and sleeping thought.

Sadly, the answer to that question comes too quick. Rochelle.

Rochelle Cook was the only woman I let consume me. In every way possible. She lured me in and sank her perfectly manicured claws into my heart until every drop of blood dried at her feet. I hadn't realized it at the time, but my entire life revolved around her and her needs.

Until the day she drove her five-inch heel through my heart and left me a fraction of a man.

Is the same happening? Am I setting myself up to suffer all over again? Maybe, but I don't think Peyton has a malicious bone in her body. I don't picture her hurting me on purpose.

As I step behind the bar, I approach Peyton like a scared animal. I plant each foot forward with care. Keep my frame relaxed and expression neutral.

The extended silence between us has run me ragged. Sleep has been shit. Two nights ago—when she sat in my living room and occupied my space—was the last time I ate. And the constant nausea has my throat raw.

I sidle up to her but leave inches between our arms. "Need help?"

She peers from the corner of her eye, then tucks her lips between her teeth. Just when I think she may say yes, she shakes her head. "I'm good. Thanks, though."

I don't want to walk away. Can't force my feet to move. "Ready for Monday? We can do one last walk through." At this point, I am throwing darts in the dark and hoping something sticks.

"No. Ani went over most of it with me." Of course she did.

"Well, if you need anything, I'm here."

Ugh. This fucking sucks.

I exit the bar without hurry. Send voiceless wishes to the universe Peyton will stop me as I head for the office. But my wishes go unanswered as I enter the hall and turn into the office. I drop into the chair, plant my elbows on the desk, and drop my head in my hands.

Only two days have passed, yet I don't know how much

more of this I can take. Peyton's silence is a life sentence on death row. Years in solitary confinement with my arms in a straitjacket and soiled floors beneath my feet.

I swallow down my personal agony and bury myself in work. Distract myself with every possible task. Stay in the office until closing time and wallow in my new personal hell.

When Peyton and I go our separate ways at the end of the night, I say nothing. Not good night or goodbye. No "talk to you later" or "good luck on Monday." Nothing.

The worst part… she does the same. And after she drives out of the lot, I open my car door and spew the empty contents in my stomach across the concrete. No relief comes. Just the same emptiness I have felt since Thursday night.

I need to fix this. Fix us.

"What's up with you?" Gavin knocks me in the shoulder with his. "You've been scary quiet."

I am not in the mood to deal with questions or criticism. Life is shitty enough, no need to add another helping to the heaping pile. "Nothing," I grumble.

"Bullshit." I tilt my head to face Gavin and narrow my eyes. "We've known each other almost twenty years. Your lame, short answers don't fly with me, bro. You don't spill, I'll spew some bullshit to Shelly to make you talk."

Jesus fuck. Can a man not get one goddamn night without diving headfirst into the dark? All I want is one night. One. One night where Peyton doesn't own every other minute in my head. Is one night too much to ask?

Seems as if tonight will *not* be that night.

"Please don't."

"Then you better start talking."

This whole situation has repeated so many times in my head, new trails have been worn into my brain. Bone tired doesn't touch the fatigue in my muscles or the weariness in my bones. Each day moves in a blur as I go with the motions.

I flip into robot mode and reiterate the last week with Gavin. The good and bad. Moments I never wanted to end and the minutes that have yet to end. My best friend listens without interruption. Nods and winces and pinches his brows at all the appropriate times. Then he turns introspective as he processes it all.

"First things first. I'm on the same page as you." I scrunch my eyes. "Shit happens with condoms, but I wouldn't believe anything without proof. Sucks to think like that, but there's some crazy bitches in the world."

"Thank you." I take the first deep breath in days. "For days, I've felt like *I* was the asshole for being skeptical. Don't know how else to explain it other than saying *I just know.*"

"Know what?" Shelly says as she steps into view and plops down on the lounger across from us.

Great. Obviously, we weren't *alone* in Jonas and Autumn's backyard. But I hoped Gavin and I would be able to finish this conversation without other ears or opinions in the mix. Looks like that isn't happening.

"Nothing," I mumble.

"Uh-uh." Shelly wags her finger in the air. "You don't get to be in some serious secret conversation with Gavin and not me. I'm your sister."

"Shell..." I hang my head. The second I tell her everything, she will rip me a new asshole. Guaranteed.

"What did you do, Micah?" Irritation laces her tone.

I lift my head and lock on to her familiar irises as mine

glass over. Saliva floods my mouth as a boulder expands in my throat. I open my mouth, but nothing comes out. Gavin slaps my back when I don't say anything, then fills in the blanks for Shelly and the others lingering nearby.

"Told you not to hurt her." Her words are a growl on her lips.

"Yeah, I remember. Not like I predict the future. And this… do you think I did this on purpose?"

"Of course not. But how did you not see this coming? You've probably banged over a hundred women in the last year. Did you expect *nothing* would happen except sex?" She crosses her arms over her chest and shakes her head. "If you say yes, you're dumber than I thought."

"Ouch, Shell. Tell me how you really feel."

"Maybe you need a reality slap, big brother."

"Well, consider me slapped. Punched is more like it, though. I know I fucked up. That's nothing new." I close my eyes, inhale deeply, then reopen them. "Now that we've discussed my shitty life, maybe you can help me fix it. Because…" I tip my head back and blink rapidly. Swallow, again and again. When I drop my eyes to meet Shelly's, hers glaze over too. "I don't know how. I fucked up and have been lost since."

Shelly hops up and comes to sit beside me. Her hands take mine and squeeze painfully tight. "Sorry I yelled." A tear rolls down her cheek, but she doesn't wipe it away. "But I knew messing things up with Peyton would be bad. Not just for her, but you too. You flaunt a hard exterior, but I know you, big brother."

Only around Shelly and close friends will I admit to being a softy. Not that there is anything wrong with not being a burly man twenty-four seven. That just isn't me. Hell, majority of the population walk around with phony fronts. Always splashing the best of the best. Do I want a good life with nice things? Sure. Who doesn't? But I don't give anyone a false sense of who I am. Have I made shitty decisions since Rochelle fucked me over? Definitely. Any self-respecting person would have lost their shit the same as me. Not everyone would fuck their feelings away, though.

"Shell, tell me what to do. She won't talk to me. She doesn't answer my texts. I'm trying to give her space. But if I give too much, will she walk away?"

I don't mean for Shelly to answer the last part, but she will. It's in her nature. In both of ours.

"Hate to say it, big brother, but you need to give her time." I drop my head in my hands and groan. Her hand finds my back and rubs the length of my spine. "In this instance, time sucks. But she needs to be able to form her own thoughts without you interfering. If you give it time, I'm sure she'll speak up sooner rather than later."

"This fucking sucks," I grumble against my palms.

"Yes, it does. What about this other woman?"

I straighten my spine, meet Shelly's gaze, and shake my head. "Told her to leave and not return without proof."

"How would she prove it's yours without DNA?"

"I meant that she's actually pregnant and can take a paternity test with me present." I close my eyes for three breaths. "Shell, I know my life has been out of control. That I have made such horrible choices. But I would never put myself in a situation like this. I have no plans to father children. At least not without being committed to someone and we both decide we want that."

She leans back and looks to the sky in deep thought. Her

particular brand of silence is one I can handle because I know she's mulling over ideas.

Please let her have some solution to this.

Fatherhood may not be something I have given much thought, but if a paternity test proves—without a doubt—this woman is carrying my child, I will step up. I may not be ready to parent, but it doesn't mean I won't do my part. You do the deed, you take responsibility. Period.

"I have no absolute answers for you," she says with a pout, pushing out her lower lip. "But I'd suggest you quit fucking around, try not to worry over it until you have to, and just have patience." My eyes shut as I drop my head back to rest on the lounger. "Sorry, big brother. Not much else you can do at this point."

"Thanks, Shell," I whisper into the night.

She means well, I know this. But, fuck. I hoped she would say something—anything—that would lift me up. That would flip on the light bulb in my brain because I can't quite reach the cord. Her advice is solid. Just not what I want to hear.

What I really want is to text Peyton. To grovel and beg for her to talk to me. For her to tell me she needs time to herself, but she will be there in the end. Just some words to let me know all is not lost.

Because right now, all I feel is lost. I have never felt so alone and in the dark as I do now. Like I have no way out. Like each breath may be my last.

And I have no one to blame except myself.

four

PEYTON

I have never hated silence and distance. Not until now.

When one day bleeds into the next, when your mind never shuts off, gauging reality is a feat. And reality has been one gigantic blur since the woman in the red dress walked into Roar. Since I pretty much shut Micah out.

In the two weeks since she walked up to the bar and dropped the ticking time bomb, I have noticed a significant change in Micah. Not just physically, but also in his demeanor. With my new schedule, we see each other less. Which makes the changes that much more dramatic.

Across the club, I spot the purple crescent moons beneath his eyes. Notice the looseness of his shirt on his shoulders and chest, and the bagginess of his dress slacks. Every smile he flashes to the employees or guests is forced and brief. And he hasn't looked my direction in days. Too many days.

Seeing Micah like this, slowly sinking without a life preserver, wrings my insides to no end.

Is it the woman who has him gaunt and a shell of himself? Does the idea of becoming a parent scare him this much?

Our in-depth conversations prior to this never revolved

around serious topics, such as marriage and children. Sure, we have both been in serious relationships and the idea of next steps may have crossed our minds. But obviously, ideas are where it ended since we are single and childless.

Or am I the reason for his frail frame and sullen disposition? Has my standoffish attitude and silence whittled him to this state? My eyes trail over his caved frame and dulled irises. Study his timid, forced smiles and the minimal energy he exerts with everyone—staff and patrons alike.

Micah and I share a horrid history, but we were headed in a new direction. To a positive place. A place full of second chances and possibilities, genuine affection and his lips on mine.

What if he hurts me? *What if he doesn't and this turns out to be what you've been waiting for?* The voice in my head has me backpedaling for the hundredth time in days. Has me seeing both sides of the coin. The same voice keeps me from making a sound decision. Because that voice belongs to my heart and it continues to argue with my brain.

"Making my rounds," I tell Mable as I exit the bar. Mable has been doing exceptional. Slaying Monday and Tuesday with me and working Wednesday with more hands on deck.

I wander through Roar, doing my best to steer away from the karaoke stage setup in the middle of the dance floor. Out of the corner of my eye, Micah stays opposite me and heads for the hall. He lengthens his stride and his feet tread quicker. Before I fully turn my head to see him, he darts inside the office and closes the door.

Finishing my circuit around the club, I check in with the staff and patrons, then head to the office. Being away from Micah has given me time to think. More than enough time. At this rate, I am surprised my brain hasn't swollen or some form of self-combustion hasn't occurred with all my thinking.

But I am done thinking. Done seeing him suffer. Done asking myself questions I don't have answers to. Questions neither of us have answers to. Now, all that's left is us, suffering. And I hate it.

Although unnecessary, I knock on the door before turning the handle and entering. One, two, three steps into the room, Micah finally lifts his head from his hands. His starry eyes are puffy and lackluster and rip my heart to shreds. The dark marks beneath his lashes are more noticeable this close up. A vise squeezes my middle and holds me captive at what he has dealt with. Alone.

"Hey," I choke out and close the door without taking my eyes off his.

He licks, then tucks his lips between his teeth. His head tilts slightly off-kilter as he breaks eye contact and stares down at the desk. "Hey," he says almost inaudibly.

I flip the lock on the door, then walk across the room. Wood scrapes concrete as I drag the guest chair around to park it beside Micah. He remains frozen as I sink into the chair and stare at his profile. Aside from the horrendous singing outside the room, silence consumes the space.

It eats me alive.

"Micah…" His breath stutters and, without second thought, I reach for his hand. "Please. Look at me."

Soft blond lashes dust his skin as his lids close. I give his hand a gentle squeeze and wait him out. Give him whatever time he needs. Life has changed so much—for us both—in the last two weeks.

Waiting, I focus on my breath. Count each inhale, each exhale. Concentrate on the warmth of his hand. The occasional callous where his fingers meet his palm. How his fingers twitch—just the slightest bit—every other heartbeat. And when his breathing calms, mine does too.

As if in slow motion, he tilts his head my direction. The muted-gold flecks over his dark-blue irises remind me of dying stars in distant galaxies. Their light fading and swallowing the darkness around them. Seeing them this close, seeing him this close, is a punch to the solar plexus.

Life-altering information was hurtled at him and I abandoned ship for my own selfish needs. I harbor no guilt for wanting to keep my heart safe. But I do foster guilt for not supporting him or lending an ear or shoulder. Especially when he needed me most.

"Sorry," I say, although the five-letter word doesn't feel adequate.

He laughs without humor. "Why are you sorry?"

My free hand comes to his cheek. Thumb brushes the arch of his cheekbone. Fingers comb through his hair. His eyes close as he leans into my touch. And the pang beneath my breastbone wanes slightly.

"Of all the times for me to go tight lipped, it's when you need my voice most. So, I'm sorry. For ignoring you and not being there when you probably needed me most."

He shakes his head and I drop my hand. His legs swing around and weave between mine as he scoots closer. "I did need you. But you needed space to think too." Fingers brush over my temple, down the angle of my jaw and to my chin. "Not gonna lie. Your silence, your distance, it sucked. But I respect it."

"Thank you."

His fingers continue to trace the ridges and valleys of my

face. I close my eyes and bask in the trail of tingles his touch leaves behind.

"Missed you."

"Me, too." My eyes meet his with a list of questions, but I start off with a simple one first. "When's the last time you ate?" I probably sound like a nagging partner, but I don't care.

His momentary silence speaks volumes. "Haven't had much of an appetite. Been snacking here and there."

This jacks my guilt up to level ten. "Please eat." I grip his biceps. "You've lost weight." Not in a healthy way either.

"I'll try." His thumb swipes slow over my bottom lip, his eyes following the movement. "Maybe we could hang after work. Make sure I eat." Doubt and hope lace his voice as he lifts his eyes to mine.

My first thought is to tell him yes. The last two weeks have been shitty. For both of us. But I don't want to give the impression that this is an easy fix. A supposed pregnancy won't just disappear. Not for weeks or months. But I also want to support him… and more.

"Can I think on it?" His gaze drops as he nods. "Let you know soon." I rise from the chair and bend to kiss his hair. "You do paperwork. I've got the floor."

After depositing the chair back in its place, I head for the door. Just as I reach for the knob, Micah's voice stops me. "Peyton?" The rough scrape of his voice fiercely hugs my heart.

I pinch my eyes for two breaths before peering at him over my shoulder. "Yeah?"

"Thank you." My brows scrunch. "Even if you don't say yes, this" —he gestures at the now vacant space beside him— "I needed it."

"Sorry it took me so long." I unlock the door and twist the knob. "Talk to you in a bit." And then I walk out.

Karaoke Night is in full swing. Beer pours from the taps and fruity cocktails fill fancy glasses. Laughter and cheers and the occasional perfectly tuned voice belts out over the sound system. Since we made the changes and Ani has advertised the hell out of Monday through Thursday events, the bar has seen an uptick in guests and income.

After another circuit around the club, I help Mable and Kaylynn behind the bar. The next two hours bring interesting versions of Miley Cyrus's "Wrecking Ball" and Alanis Morissette's "You Oughta Know." The one to grab everyone's attention was the middle-aged woman dancing provocatively while singing Madonna's "Like A Virgin."

Yeah… I will never unsee that.

The crowd starts to thin as the evening wears on. Most people need to get home for decent sleep before work tomorrow. Mable and Kaylynn start cleaning up behind the bar and I help clean tables on the main floor. With the majority of the work done, I leave Charity to finish up while I check on Micah.

After a light knock, I enter the office. Micah sits studiously behind the desk, entering invoices. It takes him a minute to look up from the screen. But when he does, he rewards me with a smile I haven't seen in weeks.

Damn, I missed that smile.

"Almost done?" I ask.

"One more after this. Everything good on the floor?"

"Mmhm. Should be able to close on time."

The urge to laugh at our avoidance of whether or not we will meet after work takes center stage. I bite the inside of my cheek and resist.

"About after…" Micah, on the other hand, comes right out with it.

"I'll come over." Feet away, I catch the stars in his irises as they glimmer. Just from my agreement. Who knew Micah Reed's soft spot was the girl he picked on as a teenager? Certainly not me. "But only if food is involved."

"Bossy," he teases. That he jokes at all is a step in the right direction. "Think I like you bossy."

Well, that shifted quick. If the erratic thump beneath my sternum is any indication, I rather enjoy his response. I miss our banter. The constant teasing. And the way his eyes eat me alive.

I shrug a shoulder. "What can I say… I like taking charge."

"Hmm. You in charge sounds… fun." He licks his lower lip. "I'll order food as we leave and have it delivered."

Narrowing my eyes, I point a finger. "No weird shit."

"Says the woman who eats pineapple on her pizza."

"What's wrong with pineapple on pizza?"

"It's a fruit," he says as if that concludes the debate.

"Technically, tomatoes are fruit too. And you smear that shit all over the crust. So…" My lips pucker and brows lift. Let's hear your response now, fruit boy.

"Fine, I concede." I give him a snide smile and he sticks out his tongue. "And I promise nothing weird."

"Good." I start for the door and stop just as I step through. "I'll finish up out here. Then we can close up."

Before he answers, I head down the hall and back into the club. Most people have left and the few that linger appear to be finishing their drinks. Karaoke is being packed up as tables get shifted for tomorrow night's Bar Olympics.

The last of the stragglers leave and I lock the door. Mable,

Charity, and Kaylynn wrap up the last of their closing duties and wish me good night as they head out the back together. The overhead and bar lights go black as I flip off switches. My heels clap down the hall as I head to the office.

Behind the desk, Micah scrolls on his cell phone and doesn't see me straight away. I lean against the doorframe and, for a moment, take him in.

The last two weeks have been rough, for him more so than me. Guilt still eats at me for ignoring him so long. But then I recall Reese and Aunt Leanne telling me to do what felt best for my well-being. If I wasn't strong enough to handle the situation, there was no way I could deal with it and stand strong beside Micah. I needed to work through some things in my own head. Decide whether or not it was possible for me to take this on. To date and stand beside a man who may or may not become a father to someone else's unborn child.

In the end, I changed my viewpoint. Looked at the entire scenario as an outsider.

Nowadays, people have children outside of wedlock all the time. Most of those people aren't in committed relationships. Some try a relationship for the sake of the child, but end up parting ways. Sometimes, what is best for the child isn't always the parents together. Especially if love doesn't exist between them. A forced relationship only adds more stress—for the parents and child.

This realization changed everything. Just wish it didn't take me so long to figure it out.

"Ready?"

Micah looks up from his phone. A soft, lopsided smile dons his face, and my heart rate spikes. God, I missed his smiles.

"Yep." He nods, taps the screen, then locks his phone.

"Just ordered food. Should arrive about the same time as us." His voice is still scratchy, but less melancholy than hours ago.

I shuffle into the office and dig my purse from the desk drawer. "Perfect. 'Cause I'm starving."

Rising from the desk, Micah turns off the computer monitor. I flip off the light as we walk out. The trek to our cars is short, but filled with silence. A comfortable silence that has been missing between us for too many days.

"Drive safe." He leans in and I stop breathing as he presses his lips to my forehead. "See you at the house."

"'Kay." It's the only word I manage to get past my lips as he ambles to his truck. My heart squeezes a little tighter and I take it as a sign.

This may be the best thing—a relationship with Micah—to happen to me. Or I purchased my own one-way ticket to hell. Hopefully, it isn't the latter.

five

MICAH

I scoop up the bag from the porch and punch in the front-door code. Peyton, less than a foot behind me, has my heart beating with purpose for the first time in weeks.

She's here. We are talking again.

Within hours, my life feels less daunting. All the craziness weighing me down—the possibility of fatherhood and an unhinged ex-bedmate—is pounds lighter now. Because Peyton is here. Her presence alone gives me a boost I didn't know I needed. Our relationship—the weird place between friendship and next level—may never be what it was pre–bomb drop, but Peyton approaching me tonight was a step in a favorable direction.

Over the last thirteen days, I had my doubts. Questioned whether she would speak to me again. With each passing day of silence and her obvious avoidance, I closed off more and more. Every time my phone alerted me to a text, excitement soared in my veins. Only to fizzle out a second later when I didn't see her name on the screen.

Work was worse. Ten times worse. Because of her promotion and the schedule changes, we spent less time in the same space. Her not stuck behind the bar all night changed things, too. Before her promotion, she stayed in one place all night. I could count on her proximity by stepping behind the bar. Could easily keep my eyes on her. But now, she is as mobile as me and almost impossible to pin down.

Until tonight.

Tonight, Peyton opened up to me again. Took initiative. Gave us another shot. And I won't waste the opportunity. Won't do anything to fuck this, us, up again.

We settle on the couch and I take containers out of the bag and set them on the table. "Hope you're good with Italian."

"Let me just get this out of the way." Shit. Does she have food allergies? I mean, she eats pizza. Practically devours it. Figured Italian was a safe bet. "I haven't met a food I *don't* like. Not yet, anyway."

Thank fuck.

"Good to know for future reference."

I open boxes to reveal cheese ravioli, meat lasagna, salad, and garlic knots. I hand her a paper plate and a package of plastic cutlery from the bag. We portion a little of everything onto our plates before scooting back on the couch, cross-legged, and digging in. Well, I eat a bit slower since my appetite was absent for too many days. Last thing I need is to run to the bathroom and embarrass myself at the throne.

"Still working at the ALF?" I ask to spark some form of conversation. Although the quiet has been mostly comfortable with Peyton, I miss talking with her. More than expected.

"Mmhm," she mumbles around a bite of food. "Only on Sunday for a few hours, though." The corners of her mouth turn down slightly.

I love that Peyton is doing well for herself, but hate that her promotion has taken away something she enjoys. I may not know the entire backstory or understand her reasons, but working at the facility brings her joy. Spending time and chatting with a group of elders makes her smile. That is what matters.

"Sorry you don't get to visit as often."

"Thanks." The corners of her mouth tip up in a halfhearted smile. "Knew being there less would be a side effect to the promotion. Ms. Jenkins is happy with the change."

"Ms. Jenkins?"

"An older woman I visit with regularly. She's always telling me to move on and quit visiting the old folks. I tell her it makes me happy to see her."

"Does it?"

"Does it what?"

"Make you happy?"

Without an ounce of hesitation, she answers. "Yes. It's probably weird, but it reminds me of when I spent time with my Nana. She passed a few years back. I visited with her often. We talked for hours about my life and hers. She'd ask about my goals and how I'd accomplish them. I traveled the globe with her stories of adventure. On lazier days, we played cards or sewed cross stitch. Life with Nana was simple and peaceful and full of love. Every memory of or with her squeezes my heart." She places a hand over her heart and pats. In a blink, her eyes glass over and I see and feel every ounce of love Peyton had for this woman.

Her spending time at the facility makes more sense now. And I am more in awe of the woman beside me.

"Your Nana sounds like a wonderful woman."

"She was," she says with a sniffle.

"Sorry." Peyton scrunches her brow as she wipes under her eyes. "For upsetting you."

Peyton waves me off. "I love talking about her and reliving those memories. Please don't apologize."

"I'm sorry for two weeks ago. For what went down. I'm sorry it happened and you had the stress on your shoulders, too. I would never want that for you and it wasn't—isn't—fair."

"Not like you knew it would happen," she states.

"True. Still sorry. This whole ordeal shouldn't be yours to take on. Not the stress or concern. None of it. And I get why you needed time to sort through it all and how you felt."

Peyton jabs at her lasagna, her eyes darting left and right, then left again. When serious matters come up, I love that Peyton doesn't word vomit her feelings. She digests them and sorts through them before speaking her mind. She carefully crafts her words before opening her mouth. Because once out in the open, words can't be taken back.

"I didn't mean for it to take so long," she mumbles before lifting her gaze to mine.

A zing flares in my chest. My heart does a little dance, knowing she didn't want to be apart as long as we were. But the jubilation is quickly replaced with a pinch. I hate the melancholy in her voice, the slump in her shoulders, and the downturn of her lips.

Between the two of us, only I should be riddled with guilt. Not Peyton.

My knee grazes hers and I delight in the connection. "I know. But we all do things in our own way and time. Please, just don't shut me out again. I'll beg, if necessary. If you need space or time for yourself, just tell me. But check in from time to time."

Her eyes glaze over as she nibbles her lower lip. *Damn, I*

want my lips on hers. Unhurried, she nods and frees her imprisoned lip.

"I will."

Unable to resist, I reach forward and brush the wetness off her cheek. "Please, don't cry." I lick the lone, salty tear from my finger. "Things were good between us. Then, my past barreled in and threw us in reverse." Closing my eyes, I inhale deeply, then meet the violet irises I have missed dearly. "And I'll understand if you want nothing more than friendship. For however long. I don't like the idea, but understand and respect it, if that's what you need."

Peyton stabs the middle of her lasagna with the plastic fork, then sets the plate on the table. Her fingers fidget in her lap. Her eyes downcast, watching the movement.

Why did I do this? Every good person or situation to enter my life… one way or another, I always fuck it up.

The few long-term relationships I had, Rochelle was the only person I envisioned a future with. A life beyond dinners, nights on the town, and sex. I had never fantasized about children or gray hairs. Just years—decades—spent loving each other.

The two women prior to Rochelle… the first wanted more when I wasn't ready. The second—we just grew apart. Both women were lovely, but never made me weak in the knees.

Early in my relationship with Rochelle, I felt that spark moment. The one where your heart flutters every time you think of the person. When your skin breaks out in a sweat seeing them. When your world wobbles a little because she is near. At the time, I thought fate was telling me she was the one.

Obviously, I was a gullible guy wearing rose-colored glasses.

Rochelle was my first real love. The woman who opened my eyes and heart to things I never knew. She was also my first heartbreak. The pain of her betrayal had nothing to do with the sex. It was more about my naivete and how someone I trusted completely stabbed me in the back.

I never wanted to experience pain like that again. Which led to my nighttime escapades. It was a way to vent my frustrations and fulfill my primal needs. Without getting attached. My philosophy—if I didn't form attachments, I would never suffer heartbreak again. Great philosophy for my mind. My heart didn't get the memo.

What I felt for Rochelle—during the best parts of our relationship—is nothing in comparison to what I feel for Peyton.

With Rochelle, my heart did this odd flutter. Nothing more.

With Peyton, my heart charges forward like an Olympian sprinter. Pound, pound, pounding in my chest. A fanatical swirl of energy sparks to life beneath my diaphragm. A passion that feels bigger than either of us. Powerful. Life altering. And more often than not, I forget how to breathe. Forget how to speak or function. My world doesn't just wobble with Peyton, it flips on its axis.

She may need us to dial it back a notch before jumping in the deep end. If so, I will understand and heed her wishes. I will tone down my feelings. A little. At least the emotions I put on display. The idea terrifies me, but I will do whatever it takes and keep my promises.

"Not that we titled our relationship weeks ago, but let's just call it friends," she says, voice shaky. An audible exhale leaves my lips as I sag deeper into the couch. "Until I mentally wrap myself around everything."

I should be grateful for any form of Peyton in my life. Not

pouting like a petulant child. Hopefully, the shadow over my heart isn't flaunted on my sleeve.

"Long as I have you in some way, I'll call it a win. Thank you."

Friendship may not be what I want with Peyton, but time without her is out of the question. So, I take it and plan to do everything within my power to set things right. To show her I am not that guy anymore. That I am someone worth having as more than a friend. Not just a lover, but also a true companion. Someone she can rely and depend on. Someone she deserves and wants in her life.

We finish eating dinner and watch an episode of *Supernatural* on Netflix. With each passing minute, she inches closer to my side of the couch. Midway through the episode, she curls her legs under her butt and leans into my side. Head on my shoulder and hands clasping my bicep. Her breath warming the cotton of my T-shirt. Legs brushing my thigh.

If this is her definition of friendship, I take it tenfold.

When we evolve beyond friends again—because let's face facts, we will—I look forward to more cuddle time with Peyton. And what happens beyond first base.

Each time Peyton puts her lips on mine, she kisses me as if it will be the last time. Kisses me as if it's her dying wish. Full of heat and passion and frenzy. I only imagine what it will be like when I kiss her elsewhere. When I taste the saltiness of her skin and arousal on my tongue. When I watch her come undone with my mouth alone. Or when she learns about my… accessories.

A wicked smile threatens and I bite my cheek. *Shift your focus, Reed.* Now is not the time to sport a hard-on.

All too soon, the episode ends. If it were up to me, I would let it roll right into the next. Keep Peyton curled up on my left. The last thing I want is for Peyton to leave. But bidding her good night is inevitable. For now.

"I should head home," she says and lifts her head from my shoulder.

Inch by inch, I trace a hand from her ankle to knee. When I reach the top, she shivers and the energy at my center swirls to life.

"Yeah. Okay." Although, what I want to say is *"no, don't go."*

Baby steps, again. Baby steps.

She starts picking up the trash from dinner, but I shoo her away. She puts her shoes on and I internally laugh at the pace. Slow. As. Fuck. Seems I am not the only one who doesn't want her to leave. My heart does a backflip.

Rising from the couch, we amble to the door. Those ten steps go far too quickly. Maybe it is time to rearrange furniture. Make the walk to the door twice as long. Who cares if it messes with the open space and feng shui. If it equals a few more seconds with Peyton, I am more than game.

"Thanks for dinner." Her violet irises closer to indigo when our gazes lock. She licks her lips and swallows. "Was nice being here again. Spending time together."

Unable to resist, I lift a hand and reach for the loose strands at her shoulder. She sucks in a breath. Her body freezes on the spot. I stare at the tendrils. How the indoor light accentuates her champagne locks differently than the morning sun. Study the natural wave that stands out enough to be noticeable.

I'd love to see her in a dress. Nothing fancy. Perhaps a sundress. Yellow, like daffodils. Hair down her back with more wave. Her bright smile across the table from me as we enjoy dinner by the water.

"Couldn't agree more," I say, voice scratchy.

Without warning, Peyton leans in and presses her lips to mine. The kiss innocent. Nothing more than a peck on the lips. But I don't dare move. Not to breathe. And certainly not to deepen it.

This kiss may be much tamer than previous ones we shared, but it is the most intimate yet. This kiss speaks volumes. Tells me she forgives me for my past discretions. Says she doesn't quite know how to do the friendship thing either. At least not with me.

Of all our kisses, this one is my favorite. This one, I will tuck away and keep safe.

Our lips break apart and she takes my hands in hers. "See you tomorrow." She spins and opens the door.

It takes a beat for me to notice Peyton is out the door and halfway to her car. I jog outside, down the steps, and catch up to her a second later. Her headlights flash before she opens the door and hops in. Once the engine purrs softly, she rolls down the window.

I want to kiss her again, but tell myself to stand down. Until she is ready for more than friendship, Peyton should initiate intimacy going forward. I won't ruin us. Not again.

"Drive safe." I tap the roof and reluctantly step back. "Tomorrow."

After a gentle smile and finger wave, she backs out and drives away. Watching her drive off sucks. But I was lucky to have had her here at all.

I press my fingers to my lips and smile. Until I see her again, the tingle her kiss left behind will remain on my lips.

six

PEYTON

Was last night a mistake?

I asked myself the same question for the umpteenth time since leaving Micah's house. The question distracted me the entire drive home. Cars and landmarks had passed in a blur. I vaguely remember saying good night to Reese as I zombie-walked to my bedroom. But the question kept me wide eyed in bed more hours than desirable. Woke me after maybe five hours of fitful sleep.

And now, as I lie in the comfort of my bed and stare at the ceiling, the question still haunts every synapses.

Was going to Micah's house and kissing him a mistake?

Over the last two weeks, I watched Micah morph into a shell of himself. Watched him turn into someone unrecogniz-able. More sullen. Frail. Lackluster. Each day, his posture slumped farther forward. The shadows under his eyes grew darker, more purple. And he refused to make eye contact with anyone longer than necessary.

Going to Micah's after work felt like the right thing to do when he asked. Agreeing to a friendship with him did too.

Then I blurred the lines less than an hour later. What a disaster I am.

I don't regret kissing Micah. Not one bit. I am, however, pissed at myself for sending mixed messages. If I say I want friendship, I shouldn't kiss him. Friends don't kiss. Well, not the way I kiss Micah.

"Damn it," I huff out as I slap a pillow over my face. Too bad smothering myself won't fix the situation. Too bad I don't know how to separate what I *should* do from what I actually feel.

Friendship with Micah is important and a major component of our relationship. Having a foundation—learning more about our backstories, what makes us tick, our individual mannerisms—matters. Doesn't need to be life altering facts. Small pieces build up. Like whether or not he picks his nose. Does he prefer the toilet paper over or under? Cats or dogs? Animal preference says a lot about a person. No matter, I don't want to enter a serious relationship without a history between us; even if the history is short.

Micah and I definitely have history. A path we navigated together and worked to improve. Then a tree snapped and fell over the path. Blocked us from moving forward. While Micah stood in front of the tree and tried to move it, I retreated. Stepped back into the brush and tucked myself away. Stayed hidden until comfortable enough to step into the light again. Now, we are back at the start. Trying to get around the tree and learning how to be a team again.

Starting over isn't easy. Not when you want to skip steps.

Hours had passed and I still feel the softness of Micah's lips on my lips. The scrape of his stubble along my chin. His taste on my tongue. It is too much and not enough.

A shiver rolls up my spine. A thin sheen of sweat blankets

my skin. Heat blooms at the base of my tailbone and pools between my thighs.

"Ugh." I groan at how fast my thoughts went from point A to B. How I went from telling myself I need a friendship with Micah first to fantasizing about him. Am I a lost cause or what?

Peeling my arm away, I squint at the morning sunshine brightening the room. Sleep will have to wait. I throw back the covers and drop my arms in a huff.

Shower time.

Staying in bed any longer is not an option. My wayward thoughts are the last thing I need.

I make quick work of washing my hair and body. Then throw on lounge pants and a tank top. In the kitchen, I spy a folded paper on the counter. Unfolding it, I chuckle at Reese's scratchy script.

Morning Sunshine,
Stop laughing at my handwriting.
Anyway... leftover breakfast casserole in the
fridge.
Xo

I amble over to the fridge and retrieve the casserole dish. Scooping out enough for two, I plop the egg, sausage, and potato concoction on a plate, put it in the microwave, and press the two-minute button. I pour a tall glass of orange juice and toast a slice of bread while I wait. Settling at the breakfast bar, I eat and scroll through new emails, deleting the junk and scanning the keepers. Then I clear the other notifications. Same stuff, new day in social media land. No surprise.

After cleaning the dishes, I stretch out on the couch and distract myself with a few episodes of *Supernatural*. As the intro credits come to an end, my mind wanders to Micah. Until I suggested it, he had never seen the show. This seemed absurd. The show has fifteen seasons for crying out loud. As for me, I have rewatched the show. Not difficult when it is my "I don't have anything to do, so I'll watch TV" show. But Micah doesn't need to be privy to this information.

When the episode ends, I turn off the television and rise from the couch. "Lazy time is over," I mumble as I enter my room.

Since the promotion, I dress slightly less provocative for work. My tops are still a bit snug with a dash of cleavage. But my bottoms are less second skin and more loose skinny dress pants. After wearing snug, curve flaunting pants for so long, dressing in looser attire has been an adjustment. The pants are growing on me more each day.

I twist left, then right as I check myself out in the full-length mirror. The yellow top has wide straps on the shoulders, forms a *V* at the start of my cleavage, flows over my breasts and hangs loose a few inches below the waistline of my black pants. The more I stare in the mirror, the more I evaluate myself. And the more I tell myself I look like a sunflower.

"Why is this so difficult?" I tug at the shirt hem. Contemplate switching out the top for a different color. "Ugh." I give up and stick with the yellow.

In the bathroom, I add enough makeup to be noticeable but not take an hour to apply. Brush my hair and opt to leave it down for once. Since I no longer dart like a madwoman behind the bar for nine-plus hours a night, I worry less about

my hair in my face or drinks. Plus, not having my hair strangled in an elastic band all night is a nice change.

With my hair styled into soft waves, I exit the bathroom
and slip on a pair of heeled boots. Grab my purse and phone,
then head for the kitchen. I whip together a quick lunch, eat,
then pack some snacks in my purse for later. One last trip to
the bathroom, I lint brush my pants and swipe gloss over my
lips before tucking the tube in my purse.

The sun beams down as I drive toward Tampa. Temperatures are too hot to ride with the windows down on the way to
work. But I look forward to the salty wind in my hair on the
drive home.

It isn't long before I park behind Roar, next to Micah's
truck. How long has he been here?

I check the time on the dash—thirty minutes early. Either
he arrived early to set up the rest of the Bar Olympics or in
the hopes we would have more time alone. I have no qualms
about spending time alone with Micah. But I am, on the other
hand, still kicking myself for blurring the lines last night.

"Get it over with already," I coach myself as I exit the car.

Soft music echoes in the hall as I step through the
employee door. I squint at the overhead lights as I reach the
main floor. Scrunch my nose at the artificial lemon-scented
cleaner in the air. I don't mind most cleaning product scents,
but whoever decided this one was lemon is sorely mistaken.

I take a deep breath and enter the office. My brave face
falls when I discover it is empty. I release my held breath and
stow my purse in the desk drawer. Then I set off in search of
Micah.

I exit the office, the click of my heels loud on the
concrete. *Clap. Clap. Clap.* The sound thunderous compared
to the music in the main room. The hall shrinks and my foot-

steps slow. At the end of the hall, I stop and scan every square foot of the club. It takes seconds to spot Micah.

Micah is across the room with his back aimed this way. He shuffles tables around and sets up the various games and events. Leaning on the wall, I observe him a moment. Take him in while his attention is elsewhere. Study the flex of his arms. Rake my eyes down his broad shoulders, defined back, and firm glutes. Call me piggish, but I want to enjoy this blip in time. To ogle the man without him giving me a ration of shit for doing so.

Then, I take a breath. Sooner than desirable, I shut the moment down and snap back to reality. Time to work.

"Hey," I say as I waltz in his direction.

He spins around, eyes me head to toe, and flashes me with the best smile. A smile I haven't seen in weeks. And I can't help but return it. Micah licks his bottom lip and I swallow.

"About finished with setup. If you want to lay out the beer pong cups." Micah points to a nearby banquet table.

I lay out the cups and set the balls in a bowl at each end. We don't fill the cups until people start playing. And the cups are changed out between each player rotation. Health code and all.

It isn't long before Roar fills with countless bodies. The deejay now takes requests on Thursday nights and plays upbeat music between those songs. Bar Olympics night—along with the other new themed days—has only been going for two weeks and already brings in a decent crowd. Roar easily makes double profits on Thursday nights since we changed it up. Adding fresh ideas was a smart business move for Ani and Sean. Each night continues to bring in new faces.

On the nights Micah and I both work, we trade off who gets paperwork duty. It eases me into my new role, but gives us the chance to not stare at a computer monitor and rows of numbers all night. The monotony of filling in spreadsheets, filing paperwork, writing schedules, and updating payroll doesn't bog me down. At times, I enjoy the simplicity and repetition. But hours later, my eyes grow weary. My mind a bit sluggish.

I tap Micah on the shoulder and he turns, giving me his starry gaze. A brilliant smile plumps his cheeks and brightens the room. And once again, I question whether or not kissing him last night was smart. Too late now. Turning back time only exists in fiction. Now, I just put one foot in front of the other and trek forward.

"I'm doing rounds, then going in the office."

Micah steps forward, stopping inches from me, close enough to touch without effort. And I forget how to breathe.

Son of a bitch. Breathe, Peyton. Deep breath in. Then exhale.

I inhale a deep breath, doing my damnedest to keep the action undetectable, and shuffle back an inch. But it's too late. The scent of his sweet cologne hits my nose and the room goes foggy. I beg my legs to move, my feet to carry me away from him, but nothing happens. My legs grow heavy and bury themselves deep in the earth like tree roots.

I am so screwed.

Perspiration slicks my skin and I send a silent prayer to the air conditioning gods, pleading for the cool air to kick on. Micah locks me in place with his magnetic eyes; the gold flecks sparkling with more intensity. I want to look away. I want to flee to the office and use the brick walls and industrial metal door as a barricade.

But I can't. Breaking eye contact feels impossible. A fool's errand.

Neither of us says a word, but I need space. And air. Air that doesn't smell of Micah and desire. I clear my throat and he blinks as if I woke him.

"I'm going to…" I circle my finger in the air and step around him.

One, two, three steps and I take a breath. A burst of cool air hits me, clears some of the Micah-induced fog, and allows me to think clearly. I take another breath and drop my shoulder, thinking I'm home free. Then a hand grips my bicep.

Without looking, I know whose hand is secured around my arm. Every sensory organ in my body alerts me to Micah's proximity. Even through the hate-filled years, I was aware of all things Micah Reed. Always.

I peek over my shoulder and flash my best work smile. "What's up?"

A tingle ripples from his touch down to my fingers and up my shoulder, neck, and chest. I conjure up any and every thought to distract me from the sensation. Public bathrooms, cottage cheese, scooping the litter box as a kid. And it works… until his grip loosens and his fingers traipse down my bicep, my forearm, my wrist. Then he steps into me again. Invades every molecule of air within breathing distance.

Damn it. Damn it. Damn it.

Why must this be so difficult? Why am I torturing myself? For what?

It would be so easy. To take his hand in mine. Lace our fingers together and curl them tight. To feel the callouses on his warm skin as he strokes my thumb with the pad of his. To get lost in euphoria as sparks travel from my fingertips, my forearm, up and across my chest, to coil around my heart.

Believe me, I want to hold his hand. Want him so close, all I see and feel and breathe is him.

Should I, though? Let him invade me completely. Should I jump back in without reservation? My subconscious screams to slow down and use the time to learn more about Micah and the years we didn't know each other. Meanwhile, my heart beats erratically and begs me to cave. To give in to my desires; come what may.

Argh!

"Thank you," he says and steps closer.

My skin buzzes under his touch. God, I want to feel him everywhere. "For what?" I rasp, then swallow.

Get ahold of yourself, Peyton.

"Last night." A finger draws small circles over my pulse and I fight the urge to close my eyes. If he picks up on my galloping heart rate, he doesn't let on. "It may not have meant much to some, but it meant the world to me."

I will myself to respond. Tell my brain to part my lips and let the words flow freely. But nothing happens. My lips go on lockdown as I stare foolishly at Micah. When I manage to string words together, I sound like a bumbling idiot.

"Yeah. Sure. No problem."

What the hell is wrong with me?

Since when do I get tongue-tied around men? Around Micah? This isn't high school. A boy isn't asking me to a damn dance. I am an extroverted, grown-ass woman who doesn't take shit from anyone. My step has never faltered. Neither have my words.

Until recently.

One more circle on my wrist and Micah releases me. My skin prickles where we were joined. I want to wrap a hand or glove or bandage around the area. Trap the sensation so it will stay put. But I fight the urge.

"You look beautiful." The soft edges of his voice warm

and soothe the wild organ beneath my breastbone. "See you in a bit," he says, then turns back to the bar and helps a waiting customer.

I shake off the daze that is Micah Reed and exit the bar alley.

Once I check in with the staff, I enter the office and lock the door. If I were the only manager on duty, the door would remain unlocked. But with us both here tonight, locking isn't an issue. Plus, I need solitude.

After catching up with the paperwork, I busy myself with straightening the office. Organizing drawers and tidying shelves. Rearranging the folder icons on the computer desktop and shifting furniture in the room. I do any possible thing to avoid exiting the office.

It sounds cruel—ignoring Micah—but I don't know what else to do. Last night, we agreed to friendship. But shortly thereafter, I kissed Micah. Jumped right over the friendship line. Possible presumptions were made. Thoughts strayed—at least mine did.

For now, I need this—us—to slow down. I need time to marinate in the idea of more with Micah. Again. Need time to consider how I might feel if Red Dress *is* pregnant.

I won't ghost him again. But with the weight of the situation hanging overhead, it only seems fair for me to be a little selfish. Right?

I scrunch up my nose and swat the air. Dust or a bug or hair tickles the tip of my nose. Pinching my eyes tighter, I rub the heel of my palm over my nose. As I drift back to sleep, whatever it is tickles my nose a third time. Bolting up in my bed, I flail my arms.

"Ow!" Reese belts out as I make contact with him.

My eyes fly open and I squint at the too-bright sunlight coming through the blinds. Reese sits on the edge of my bed, rubbing his arm.

"What are you doing in here?" I groan out and fall back on the mattress.

"Well, I was trying to wake you up. Thought we could have breakfast out before my shift at the rec center."

I sit back up and stare at his faux wound. "Maybe you should wake me like a normal person. Nudge my shoulder. Call out my name." I purse my lips and lift a brow. "Not tickle my face and wait to get hit."

"Where's the fun in that?"

Throwing the covers off, I scoot out of bed and point to the door. "If you want to go out, I need to get dressed. Which means you need to exit, mister."

"Grumpy, sunshine."

"Yeah, yeah."

When the bedroom door clicks shut, I slump forward, press the heels of my hands to my eyes, and sigh. I love my best friend. Wouldn't want anyone else as a roommate. But sometimes, he really knows how to get under my skin. And laugh at my expense.

Fumbling through my dresser and closet, I go for easy and comfortable. It's early and I give no fucks about my appearance. Not after Reese woke me via tickle torture. Once my jeans are zipped, I drag a brush through my mane to tame the scary, then twist it up in a topknot. I slip on my black Vans, grab my phone and keys, and meet Reese in the kitchen.

Reese and I agree to take separate cars so he can go

straight to work after. We meet up at a local breakfast and brunch restaurant not far from the apartment. Thankfully, since most morning people have gone to work and it's the middle of the week, the place isn't jam-packed.

We get seated and order coffee while we peruse the menu. The server returns with a carafe and fills our mugs. Reese orders as if eating for two while I get biscuits and gravy with a side of hash browns and fruit.

With our orders scribbled down, the server takes our menus and wanders off. Silence stretches over the table as we fix our coffee how we like and take the first sip. No good conversation happens before this moment. At least not with me. I have no shame in admitting this.

"You sleep better?" Reese asks as he toys with the empty stevia packet.

I take another sip of coffee, then nod. "Yeah. Like a rock, actually."

"What changed?"

"Good question. Maybe it's all the office cleaning and rearranging I did last night to avoid Micah." I shrug a shoulder.

Reese's jaw tics as he glances out the window next to our table. "Thought things were better between you two," he growls, then meets my gaze.

"They are," I say in a rush. "It's just..." I pluck the creamers from the bowl and stack them into a pyramid to buy myself time.

"Just spit it out, Peyton."

"I may have confused him." After I stack the last creamer, I knock them down and start again.

"How so?"

The more I ponder this over, the more I question if I am

overthinking the whole situation. Am I the only one focused on the fact I kissed Micah? Am I the only paranoid one reading too much into the moment? Probably. And also not surprising.

I stop stacking the creamers to look up at Reese, the corners of his mouth slightly upturned. His eyes bright as they stare back, as if he knows something I don't. *Feel free to share with the class, Mr. Triggs.*

"I told Micah I wanted to be friends again. Give things between us time, then go from there."

"Okay," he drawls out the word.

"I told him this two nights ago. And then I kissed him. More than once." I drop my head in my hands and groan. "Wasn't hot and heavy. But still…"

"Hey." Reese reaches across the table and jostles my arm. "Look at me." This feels like a parenting moment, one of those annoying times you get told what you did right and wrong. I don't want to look up, but I do. Reese lays his hand on the table, palm up, and I place mine on top. The warmth and slight curl of our fingers is a comfort I have only ever gotten from Reese. "You didn't do anything wrong. Can't help what you feel."

"Ugh. This sucks." He squeezes my hand. "I need things to slow down. Me kissing him counteracts the whole purpose."

"Why?"

"Why, what?"

"Why do you need things to slow down?"

My brows pinch at the middle as my head jerks back. "Are you serious?" Reese nods with the most somber expression on his face. "Did you forget what happened two weeks ago?"

"No. But I don't think Micah should be punished for something out of his hands and which may be false. Without proof, it's all hearsay."

Since when did my friend jump off the Peyton wagon and on the Micah train? Not cool.

"So, I'm supposed to forget it ever happened? Act as if his world is hunky dory and may not flip upside down in months? Seems idiotic, if you ask me."

Reese shifts his gaze out the window and loses focus. A few breaths pass and he gives my hand a light squeeze as his eyes drift back across the table. "What if all this stress you're taking on is for nothing? What if the woman isn't pregnant? And if she is, what if it isn't his? Then you put yourself through all this for nothing."

Does he not think I have considered this? God, I have thought over every possible scenario. Problem is, I have no clue which way to go or how to feel until the truth comes to light. I want to believe this outcome—that Micah has nothing to do with this woman's pregnancy. But I should also be mentally prepared for the possibility of it becoming a reality. And I need Reese to see both sides of the coin.

"What if she is and it is his? If I don't prepare myself for that, how will I cope? How will I know if I can have a relationship—in any capacity—with him? If I don't consider the possibilities of what our future may look like, how will I know?"

"Sunshine…" He sandwiches my hand between both of his as the most endearing expression touches his face. "There's no way to know what the future holds. But you impact it." I tilt my head and narrow my eyes. "If you constantly focus on the potential negative outcome, that's all you'll see and think." I open my mouth to rebut and he holds a hand up. "I'm not saying to discount the possibility. What I am saying is you shouldn't focus all your energy on the bad. If you like him, really like him, do what feels right *for you*. If that means time apart, so be it. But if it means time together, don't second-guess it." He leans down and kisses my hand. "Life is too short to miss out on the good. You of all people should understand this."

This is why I love and hate conversations with Reese. He tells me like it is and doesn't sugarcoat a damn word. And that last part… god, that hits home. Hard.

Far too often, I questioned if I'd ever find and hold on to love. Whether familial or romantic. Because the universe has thrown a lot of shitty cards for my hand. And it's difficult to believe anything else.

Reese releases my hand, sits back in his seat, and gives me time to process. To mull over what it is I want with Micah. To decide what steps I should take next. A decision only I can make.

Before I get too deep in thought, the server steps up to the table and delivers plate after plate. I unwrap my silverware, lean over my plate and inhale, and sag at the hearty scent of sausage gravy and fresh biscuits. Forks clink the ceramic plates as we eat in companionable silence. The entire time, I dissect everything Reese said. Take it apart, one word at a time, then restring it together to see if it makes better sense.

As his words cycle through my head for the hundredth, two questions pop up. Questions I need answers to, but fear what they will be.

Am I wrong to keep Micah at a distance? Or am I sheltering my heart so I don't lose someone else? Sadly, only I have the answers. If only I knew where they were hidden.

seven

MICAH

Why did I agree to this? Why did I let Shelly talk me into coming here?

Naturally, Shelly is running late. Which is why I am still in my truck, with the engine and lights off, waiting for her arrival. Because I refuse to walk into the lioness's den without her. Okay, I may be exaggerating a bit. But after what Shelly said the other day, I can't muster the energy to enter my childhood home without her as a buffer.

So, while I wait, I stare at the only home my parents have owned. Picture perfect. I love everything about this house. All that it stands for and the love that resides in each square foot of the property. It irks me I haven't quite reached this comfortable stage as a homeowner yet. It's a marathon, not a sprint. Mom and Dad have worked their asses off for what they own. Have spent countless hours on every little detail, inside and out, to make their home shine. I remind myself of this each time I upgrade a room in the house or update the backyard and patio. All good things come with time. And patience.

Including love.

I stare at the two-story, natural brick home. The pristine white trim, decorative shutters and modern double front doors with large stainless fittings. Grass cut three inches tall. Hedges manicured and colorful flowers blooming along the front and down the walkway. Twin maple trees taller than the house rooted on either side of the long drive leading to the three-car garage. The house surrounded by an acre of land, an iron-and-brick fence and a gate.

The house wasn't always this gorgeous. All the hours and labor my parents have put in are an inspiration. It energizes me to take on the next project in my own home. Baby steps eventually lead to full strides.

Shelly pulls up and I breathe easier. We exit our vehicles and converge to walk to the house as a unit. We both love our parents, had a happy and healthy upbringing, but have zero excitement about tonight's dinner.

"You ready for this?" she asks.

"Not in the slightest. You?"

"No. Last thing I need is a reminder of my singledom. Or my lack of offspring."

Same. Although, if I play my hand right, I plan to not be single much longer. No comment on the offspring. But Mom and Dad won't be privy to either bit of news. Not yet. No need to have them barrage me with questions I can't answer. Nor do I want them to nag or ask to meet Peyton. Our relationship hasn't crossed that bridge yet.

Shelly opens the front door and leads the way. We toe off our shoes and set them on the rack past the foyer. Less than ten feet inside, the scent of pork, citrus, garlic and herbs wafts in the air. Soft jazz notes echo throughout the house. Mom says something about opening wine and I assume she talks to Dad.

We round the corner and spot our parents canoodling at the stove with their backs to us. Before we disturb the moment, I take it all in. How after thirty-five years of marriage—and seven years unmarried—they still hang on each other and kiss like teenagers. Dad has his arms locked around Mom's waist, her back to his front, as he whispers in her ear and she swats the air near him as she giggles. My heart swells seeing them so in love. The simple touches and secret conversations give me hope I will one day have a similar happiness.

"Hope we're not interrupting," Shelly pipes up as Dad kisses Mom's cheek.

They spin around, smile wide, and stop what they are doing to come hug us.

"How's my baby?" Mom asks as she wraps her arms around my neck. I circle my arms around her waist, lift her off the ground, and squeeze her.

"Good, Mom. Miss you."

When I set her down, she takes a step back and frames my face with her hands, eyes soft as she regards me. The lines on my forehead, the arch of my brow, the light in my eyes, the scruff on my jaw. "Miss you, too. Both of you." She peers over at Shelly, then swaps places with Dad.

"How's work been?" Dad asks as he hauls me to his chest and knocks the wind from my lungs.

"Good," I say once he releases me. "The owners have made some changes and it's been great for business."

"Like what?" Dad guides us farther into the kitchen, where he and Mom resume cooking.

I prattle off the new changes—leaving out all things Peyton-related. When I finish, Shelly looks at me like she did the one time I stole her clothes and towel from the bathroom forever ago.

"What?" I ask, scared of her answer.

"Why am I just learning about Karaoke Night?" Her brows shoot up and eyes widen.

Damn it. How the hell did I forget that my sister, Cora, and Jonas are karaoke buffs? Probably because I haven't hung out during the week with them in a while. After learning this new information, though, I bet I will see them Wednesday nights. Often.

I love my sister—and my friends—but seeing her at work feels a bit much. Maybe I am overanalyzing, but I like having time and a place that is just mine. Kind of.

"Uh…" Dad stands far enough behind Shelly she doesn't notice his *yikes* face. "Because I don't talk about work with you," I answer in staccato.

She rolls her eyes, then slaps a hand over her sternum. "Wound me, why don't you. If karaoke doesn't make you think of me, I feel like we need to bond more."

Oh, Jesus.

"Throwing it on a little thick there, Shell."

"What do you expect? My feelings are crushed." She play weeps and Dad bites his fist to resist laughing.

"Oh, please." I laugh and Dad joins in. "Work on your weeping skills, little sis."

"Alright, you two," Mom intercepts with hands on her hips. "Time to plate up and eat."

We line up beside the counter near the stove, grab a plate, and pile on the food. Mojo pork tenderloin, oven-roasted red potatoes, steamed green beans and homemade rolls. Needless to say, I put too much on my plate.

Mom and Dad lead busy work lives, but always make time

for what matters. Family. Mom still works forty hours a week as a corporate marketing manager. She has the ability to retire in a few years without worrying, but she won't. That's what happens when you love what you do. Dad owns an insurance company that handles mostly vehicles, vessels and property. For a short time, he dipped his toes in the health and life side, but it became too taxing. Dad hit retirement age earlier this year, but said he plans to run the business a few more years before selling.

Both my parents have done so much in their career lives. They started at the bottom, put in their time, learned more about what they love, and worked hard for their career dreams. As a child, Dad often said, "Micah, you should never expect your dreams to be handed over. You have to put in the effort. Bust your butt until you get what you want. If you don't earn it, you won't respect it."

And I guess that applies to anything you want in life. Not just your career.

We sit in the same chairs we have since I was a child. Mom to my right, Dad on the left, and Shelly across from me. Dad fills glasses with sauvignon blanc while Mom lights the two candles in the table centerpiece. Nothing fancy. Just the norm.

Quiet consumes the first few minutes around the table as we taste the meal. I sample a little of each before the silence is broken.

"Excellent as always, Nicole."

"Agreed," I follow after Dad. "Really wish I had your cooking skills, Mom."

Mom eyes Dad across the table as her cheeks pink. "Thank you." Eyes that mirror mine shift my direction after breaking contact with Dad. "And you, too." She cuts and pierces a piece of pork loin. "We can try cooking lessons again. If you want."

One trait I love about Mom… she never gives up. I may burn or undercook every dish I attempt, but Mom still holds on to hope. I love how she feels I am not a lost cause.

"Maybe." I reach over and rub her forearm. "Might be best to start with recipes written for kids, though."

The entire table erupts in laughter. Years have passed since I cared whether or not I got teased in the cooking department. Can't be good at everything. May as well own it.

"I'd love that, Micah. Let me dig up some recipes and we'll plan a day to get together."

"Sounds great, Mom."

So far, tonight has gone smooth. Shelly had me frazzled for days. Worried about conversations over relationships and grandchildren. But the night has been normal. Good food, smiles and laughter. Everything I love about my parents and where we grew up. Couldn't be more perfect.

"Shelly," Dad starts and she turns to face him. "Still seeing that nice young man from the Italian market?"

And… I jinxed us.

Thank goodness she swallowed her bite before he finished speaking. Her eyes flit to mine and beg for help. But I have nothing. The second I come to her defense, Mom will jump on me with a similar question. Then we will both sweat under the spotlight. Better to let her go first, then I will follow. Cruel, yes. But that's what older siblings do.

Shelly stabs a potato with pent-up aggression. "No, Dad. We went on one date and I felt really uncomfortable." I widen my eyes at her and she shrugs. "He didn't *do* anything wrong. Just a vibe."

Dad takes her hand and consoles her. "Never be upset for

turning down someone who makes you uneasy. I will always be in your corner. You mean the world to us, Shelly Bear."

"Same," I say. Speaking up and agreeing with Dad is right. I will always be there for my sister and family. In a heartbeat. And they will do the same.

The seriousness of the moment fades and we all breathe easier. Then, Mom shifts her attention toward me and whips out her inquisition claws. *Damn it.*

"What about you, Micah? Is there a special lady in your life we should know about?"

Why? Why did I agree to this? And why are our parents pestering us about our romance lives? Well, lack of romance.

What spurred this on? Dad had his annual birthday checkup with Doctor Harris not long ago. Hopefully, it all went well and this isn't Mom and Dad's way of saying they don't have much time left. I don't enjoy their nosiness, but I would take it over bad health any day of the week.

"No, Mom. Can't seem to nail down the right one." Which is not a lie. Mom just won't hear my words how I mean them.

We all quiet and go back to eating. I chew the pork and potatoes way longer than necessary. Keep my mouth busy in case one of my parents decides to pry further. I pray the relationship talk will stay where it is. In the past. And once again, I should quit thinking. It's as if Mom or Dad have a sixth sense, as if they hear my every thought or pick up on the exact vibe of my mood.

"With the massive population in the area and technology, I figured my kids would've married by now," Mom mutters before biting her roll.

Why didn't I put a contingency plan in place? Should have asked Gavin to text or call. He does owe me a favor, after all. Or have Cora do the same with Shelly. Both of us came here knowing our parents were on a mission. To marry us off and make us baby factories. Not really, but that is how it feels under the current spotlight.

Part of me wants to counter Mom's comment. But if I open my mouth, it will fuel the fire. So, I bite my tongue. My sister, on the other hand, didn't get the memo to keep her mouth shut.

"You'd think with the massive population and all the dating apps, there wouldn't be thousands of creepy guys in the area." Shelly shrugs, then stabs the pork loin on her plate with pent-up anger. *Shit.* "But most only want one thing. And it isn't commitment." She shovels the bite in her mouth and doesn't look up.

My blood boils that Shelly feels the need to defend herself like this. Especially to our parents. Are they aware of her lack of sexual experience? Doubtful. If they were, there is no way they'd be so eager to push her into the arms of a random guy. All for some picture-perfect idea they have in their heads.

"Surely, they're not all bad."

That's it. Conversation over. "Mom!" I bark out. Her fork freezes halfway to her mouth. "Drop it."

"Micah, don't speak to your mother with that tone."

My eyes dart to Dad. "Don't mean to be cruel. But this conversation… it's uncomfortable. For both of us."

"Sorry, sweetheart." Mom rubs Shelly's forearm. "Just don't want either of you to miss out on the opportunity to have a family of your own."

I turn back to Mom, softening my tone as I speak. "I get it. But have you given thought as to *why* we aren't with some- one? Sure, I could stay with a random hookup—"

"Micah," Dad grumbles.

"No, Dad. Hear me out." I set my fork down, wipe my

mouth, and fold my arms across my chest. "Is it so wrong for Shelly to be picky? Shouldn't she wait for the guy—or girl—that makes her happy? She has her own reasons for being single." Shelly's eyes widen. "Which are none of our business unless she wants to share."

"Okay, we're sorry," Dad says with sincerity. "Hope you understand this conversation came from a place of love." He and Mom look at each other, then us.

"We do," I answer. "And as soon as either of us wants to introduce someone, we will. So, please, can we not bring this up again?"

Mom scoots potatoes around her plate, her eyes following the motion. Dad does the same with the last of his green beans. *Jesus.* They act like pouty children. I love my parents, always, but this is ridiculous.

Chair legs scrape the wood floor as I rise and grab my plate and head for the kitchen. I scrape the last of my food into the trash, rinse the plate and put it in the dishwasher. I drag my fingers through my hair and tug.

Shelly prepped me for what was coming tonight, but I had no idea it would set me off. Not like this. I don't typically lash out at my parents. Tonight, though, feels different. The weight, the pressure… an expectation I have never dealt with from them fists my heart in painful ways.

And I don't know how to handle it.

"Micah?" Mom calls out, her voice soft as she approaches.

"In the kitchen."

She rounds the corner, sets her plate on the counter, walks straight to me and wraps her arms around my waist. My arms wrap around her waist as I haul her closer and rest my cheek on her head.

"Sorry," she mumbles against my chest.

I rub a hand up and down her back. "It's fine, Mom. Just please, respect our choices. And privacy. We'll tell you when the time comes. Promise."

She drops her arms and steps back. "Okay." Matching eyes hold mine as a gentle smile curves up her lips. "Just want you both happy."

Shelly and Dad shuffle into the kitchen and clean their plates. The thorny topic gets dropped and we dish out dessert —mixed berries and chocolate cake with fresh whipped cream. Shelly and I hang out a while longer once our plates empty. Fortunately, everyone but me has to be up in the morning. So, the evening ends early.

Hugs are exchanged on the front porch as Shelly and I step out to leave. Mom says she will reach out to us both for the next get-together.

On the way to our cars, Shelly mutters, "Thanks for the save earlier."

I bump her shoulder with my arm. "Always, little sis. They mean well, but their persistence frustrated me."

"Yeah, I picked up on that." She chuckles as we reach her car and she opens the door. "Remind me to never pester you."

"Whatever." I play shove her in the car. "Drive safe. Love you."

She blows me a kiss. "Love you, too, big brother. Talk to you later."

I drain the last of my beer. The *Peaky Blinders* episode ends and I shut off the television. Silence engulfs me as I turn off lights, close blinds and curtains, and check the door locks.

The short distance to my bedroom is a mile long tonight. My usual solace with solitude has taken a back seat.

I strip my clothes, toss them in the hamper, pull back the bedding and slip under the covers. For a moment, I lie in the dark with an arm tossed over my eyes. Take a few breaths as all the relationship talk filters back in from earlier tonight.

My parents mean well, but don't grasp the example they set for us. Shelly and I will never just settle. Not for some random person who we check *some* boxes off with. No, whoever we choose will have to check off all the boxes. Will have to fill all the cracks and seal old wounds. Make us see the world with new eyes. Make us *feel*.

We aren't emotionless people, but Shelly and I don't give away love freely. And letting someone new get close is a feat. Years ago, I let people in easier. Loved more openly with family, friends, and romantic interests. Then Rochelle fucked me over and my trust in the opposite sex fizzled. At least when it came to love.

Until Peyton.

I slap a hand in the direction of the nightstand and locate my phone. Tapping the screen, the background lights up. A picture of me and Shelly smiles back at me from my birthday this year. I unlock the phone, open the message app, and tap on Peyton's name.

Too many days have passed since we texted back and forth. As of recent, the texts have been one sided. From me. She needs time, I get it. But I reject the idea of leaving her alone altogether. Out of sight and all that.

Before the idea dies, I type out a message to her and hit send.

> Awkward dinner with the parents tonight 😒
> You'd think that'd end when you're an
> adult.

I lock the screen, lay the phone on my stomach and stare at the wall. The shadows from the oak tree and streetlight dance over the cream-painted wall opposite my bed. Leaves flutter on the branches and I try to create other shapes out of their combined shadows.

I jolt when my phone vibrates. Fumble as it slides off my chest and hits the sheet. Scramble until I locate and unlock it.

> Probably wasn't intentional.

For a moment, I stare at the screen and forget to breathe. *She answered.* That has to mean something. Right? Probably best to not read into it too much. Not yet, anyway.

> Nah. They want us happy, but approached
> it all wrong.

> What happened?

I scoot closer to the headboard, toss the second pillow on the one under my head, and inch upright.

> Asked if either of us is dating. They're
> worried we'll miss out.

> What'd you say?

Her response makes me smile. I may read into it more than intended, but it seems she wants to know if I told my parents I was dating someone.

That when either of us wants them to meet someone, they will. It got a little heated. Which isn't normal.

Sorry you had a crazy night.

Thanks. Better now.

Is that so?

I read the last text with her voice in my head, imagining her hands on her hips and brow perked up. *Fuck.* How I miss this side of her. The snark and banter and sass. The side that has me crawling like a bumbling fool.

Damn straight.

And why is that?

Hmm 😏 Maybe because a certain someone is awake.

Do you have a pet?

God, she makes me laugh. Lifts away the heavy and provides incomparable comfort.

No. Do you?

No, but I want a cat.

Good to know.

Are you allergic?

No. But it's always good to know the competition.

For the next hour, we text back and forth. Talk about

randomness. Some with substance, but not much. By the time we say good night, a peculiar bouncy sensation ping-pongs beneath my rib cage. I press the heel of my palm to my sternum, take a deep breath, hold it until my lungs burn and relish in the bliss Peyton delivers.

I have no clue what this is between us. But I plan to do whatever it takes to keep it. To keep her. Who knows… maybe in the not-too-distant future, I will have dinner with my parents and tell them about Peyton. Introduce her to them. One day…

eight

PEYTON

How do so many people know this much random shit?

When I first suggested Trivia Night to Ani, I figured it would revolve around movies, television and basic geography. Questions like "what is the capital of Arkansas?" or "name the show with a woman who performed magic with a twitch of her nose." or "who crushed on Penny first in *The Big Bang Theory*?"

What we got instead was some serious nerd action. Super. Nerd. Action. And it's kind of hot. I never pictured myself interested in highly intelligent men—the nerds of my youth were… odd—but I have a newfound appreciation for them. The women too.

"What's the diameter of Earth?" the trivialist asks.

Bzz.

"It's 7,917.5 miles," Mr. Rolled Sleeves answers.

"Name the largest sea on Earth."

Bzz.

"Philippine Sea," Mr. Tall and Lanky states.

"List three Wonders of the Ancient World."

Bzz.

"Great Pyramid of Giza, Hanging Gardens of Babylon, Lighthouse of Alexandria," Ms. Hot Librarian says as she straightens her spine and pushes glasses up her nose.

Gina sidles up to me and fans herself with a coaster. "Damn."

Tipping my head back, I laugh. "You and me both, girl. Never saw this day coming." She lifts a brow. "When intelligence ranks in the top three traits to tick off." At this, Gina laughs with a shake of her head.

"Speaking of guys…"

Over the last six weeks, since my promotion, Gina and I have bonded. We aren't to the point where we hang outside Roar. But it has been nice forming this new relationship. Having another woman to shoot the shit with. Someone I can vent with or tell dirty details to.

She hadn't been blind to the chemistry between me and Micah. Neither has most of the staff. My stomach constricted when she let me in on this non-secret. Guess I had been willfully blind to the staff and everyone else setting foot in Roar. Now, I notice every little detail. Pay attention to the way they watch us on the nights we work together. Pray our interactions don't disrupt work.

Because things between Micah and I could definitely disrupt.

"Yes?"

Pulling down on the tap, Gina fills a pint glass and hands it to a shorter man with shaggy brown hair. He scurries back to his chair, sips the beer, and holds his hand over his buzzer. This crowd stirs the best belly laughter and intriguing inquisition. Trivia Night was one of the best ideas, hands down.

Hands on her hips, mouth in a firm, straight line, Gina shakes her head. "Don't play coy."

I put on my best poker face while I laugh internally. *But it's fun.* "Well" —I wipe the bar— "you didn't ask a question."

A sharp sting bites my skin after Gina whacks my bicep with a bar towel. "Smart-ass." Rubbing away the sting, I shrug. "How's things with starlight?"

Gina has no idea why I call Micah starlight. One night, she overheard us talking and my casual use of the nickname. Since then, she throws it out on occasion when we chat. I have no intention of telling her the meaning behind the name. All that would do is add another twenty questions to her mile-long list. For now, she believes it's just me teasing him. I have no intention of changing her opinion.

"Good."

With Gina, I give vague answers. One—it drives her crazy. Two—I don't feel the need to divulge my entire life. Our friendship fairly new, I choose to keep some parts of my life private. Only one friend gets all the dirty details. Reese. Our bond wasn't always what it is today, but we have been tight for years.

"Good?" she deadpans.

"Yeah. Good."

"Remind me to never ask you for detailed opinions in the future."

I laugh and mix drinks for an order Charity drops at the bar. "You got it." Setting the Jack and Coke, Cosmo and IPA on the tray, Charity flashes her award-winning smile, then walks off to deliver the drinks. "Things have been good," I say once Charity is out of earshot.

The staff may be aware Micah and I are friends—or more than friends, no definitions have been laid out. I don't make a point to ask their opinion. What Micah and I have should not interfere with Roar. All workplaces are different—some lenient on personal relationships outside work, others not so much. Seeing as Ani is a friend and I tell her quite a bit, she is cool with whatever Micah and I have, so long as it doesn't interrupt business.

For the most part, we maintain our managerial persona when on the floor. Sporadic flirting and banter are good for business. What we do away from the crowd is a different story.

Things with Micah haven't veered back to steamy kisses and hands under shirts. Yet. But we seem to be speed walking the same path that led us there before. Part of me jumps at the idea of kissing Micah again. Ready to feel his soft, warm lips pressed to mine. Taste his hunger on my tongue. Thinking about it makes my mouth water and thighs clench.

My phone vibrates in my back pocket and I snap out of my wayward thoughts. Slipping it from my pocket, I glance down at the notification and snort. Micah's ears must have been ringing.

"What's funny?"

"Micah." I shake the phone in my hand. "Like he knew we were talking about him."

"Creepy." Gina wanders down the bar, chats with customers not playing trivia, and leaves me to read the text in privacy.

Come over tonight 🙏

In the last month, Micah and I have hung out after work more. Gone to Teddy's on occasion, but spent more time in his living room with take-out boxes and episodes of *Supernatural*. Last week, he introduced me to *Peaky Blinders*.

Although he watched three of the seasons, he swears starting over is fine.

> I don't know. These trivia guys are kind of hot.

You want to play twenty questions, hellcat?

I bite my lower lip and fight the grin begging to come out. I spin to face the wall of liquor bottles and hide the heat on my cheeks. Don't know what it is, but the nickname he gave me makes me hot, bothered and goofy.

> Depends...

On?

> Mood. Food. Booze.

Why did I press send? It isn't only my brain that forgets how to properly function around Micah Reed. Obviously, my fingers have a mind of their own as well. *Swell.*

Really?

> Yep.

Best get your ass here after you say good night to the trivia BOYS.

I laugh out loud and Gina shoots me a *that good, huh?* With a shake of my head, I wave her off and resume texting.

> They are definitely MEN. Who knew nerds this good-looking existed?

Now, this is fun. Something about banter with Micah

makes my chest lighter. Tugs at the corners of my lips. Makes my heart stutter. My breathing stammer. I dish it out and he gives it right back. It's who we are, only the context has morphed over the last two months.

You want nerdy?

I mean…

Be here after work 👀

The urge to drag this out further tempts me, but I cut the conversation short. If I head into the office, paperwork will occupy me long enough for the night to end soon.

I like it when you're bossy 😊 Later.

I stow my phone in my pocket and ignore the final buzz. Passing Gina, I signal toward the office and she nods. Behind the closed door, I slump down in the desk chair and eye the stack of work. Most of it is menial, but necessary. Never expected to be a number cruncher. Someone who sits behind a desk and fills in spreadsheets. But here I am, squeezing the armrests on the chair while tucking myself closer.

And I love it.

nine

MICAH

I read the last text I sent for the tenth time.

She hasn't opened the text, but she will once work wraps up.

My connection with Peyton over the last month has been this force. Gradual yet powerful. Strong yet gentle.

After the night we agreed to give friendship another try—let's not forget the kiss, I sure as hell won't—our relationship has bloomed. Neither of us has titled the relationship beyond friendship. Yet. But the chaste kisses from week one have morphed into longer kisses and frequent caresses. No suck-your-soul kisses or groping of parts, but my crystal ball indicates we are headed that direction.

I order pizza online and schedule it to be delivered around the time she typically arrives. Then I surf through movie options. Usually, we watch an episode or two of my show or hers. But after her snarky comments earlier, a change of plans seems in order.

After I choose the movie, I peel off my shirt on the way to the bathroom. Ditching the last of my clothes, I crank the shower and step under the hot spray. I wash up in record time, towel off, and sort through my wardrobe for the perfect attire.

I wander from the bedroom into the kitchen and dig out the candle lighter and jar candles. Next time I see Shelly, I must thank her for the obscene number of candles she gifted me over the years. Most of them have been decorative dust collectors for years strategically placed in the main space of the house.

Tonight, though, they will be put to good use.

After I light enough candles to heat the house, I stow the lighter, then grab a bottle of wine from the fridge. I pop the cork, set the bottle on the counter, and let it breathe.

Mood. *Check.*

Booze. *Check.*

And any minute… the doorbell chimes. "Food."

I open the door and am greeted by a smiley young man that hands me two large boxes and a bag. The moment he exits the porch, Peyton parks in the driveway. She cuts the ignition, hops out, and practically skips to the front door.

Fuck, she's adorable.

"Hey," Peyton singsongs as she openly ogles me. "Look at —" She freezes as she takes in the main room of the house. "What's this?" Spinning around, a crease forms between her brows.

"Mood, booze" —I set the pizza, salad and garlic bread on the counter— "and food."

"And this?" Peyton lays her palms beneath my collarbones, then, inch by inch, drags her hands down my abdomen. Her thumbs brushing the column of buttons.

"Going for the nerdy look." She lifts a brow. "Didn't find the fake glasses before you arrived."

Her arms sweep around my waist and rest on my lower back. "You don't need them."

Hands on her hips, I secure Peyton in my grip. If I leaned forward an inch, her lips would be under mine. But anticipation is everything. And I love the push and pull between us.

I lean in and she gasps. Instead of kissing her, I brush my cheek along hers and stop at her ear. "Time to eat," I whisper, then nip her lobe. Her body shudders beneath me and the corner of my mouth twitches. My fingers drift along the inside of her forearm and lace with her fingers. "C'mon."

I guide her to the couch, park her in the spot I dubbed hers and go back to grab the food, wine and glasses. Everything on the coffee table, I sort the boxes while she pours the wine. I turn on the television and hit play on the movie as we dig in.

"Really?" Peyton asks on a laugh-squeal as the intro of *The Princess Bride* pops on the screen.

"What? It's a classic."

"Never pegged you as someone to watch *The Princess Bride*. That's all."

"Well…" I cock a brow at her. "I'm full of surprises."

The movie starts and we settle back on the couch, cross-legged, with salad and pizza in our laps. For a bit, we focus on the movie and dinner. Several years have passed since I last watched this movie and I forgot its greatness.

Around the time when Iñigo talks with Westley about the six-fingered man, Peyton leans forward to set her box on the table. Her knee brushes mine in the process. And when she sits back with her wine, her leg presses and remains butted to my thigh. The motion natural, leisure. As if it wouldn't be any other way.

And I no longer want to hold back. No longer want to resist the one person I want. Her.

I set my box on the table, reach for her glass and put it down. "Hey," she contests.

But before she gets another word in, I lean back, twist in place, frame her face in my hands and bring my lips to hers. She freezes for one, two… then her lips move with mine, soft and sweet at first as her hands snake behind my neck. It isn't long before her lips part and she sucks on my lower lip. She tastes of tangy grapes and herbs and something distinctly Peyton.

My hands drop from her face to her hips as a growl rips from my throat. Her fingers trail into my hair and fist the strands.

Fuck. She will unman me on this couch.

As the thought takes residence, she shifts and slowly lays back, bringing me down with her. I hover inches above her, my arms framing her face and weight pinned between her thighs. Our lips and tongues dance in sync as we give in to the desires we stowed for too long. Her back bows off the cushion and her breasts press to my pecs as she rubs my dick with her pelvic bone.

God, she is fucking perfect.

My hand skims down her shoulder, along the curve of her breast, and she pushes into my touch. I continue my venture down her torso, graze her abdomen, and slip my fingers under the edge of her top. The heat from her skin ripples up my arm and undulates across my chest. Jolts my heart. Expands my lungs. Gives me life.

A hand trails down my back to my elbow. Her fingers drift down my forearm to my wrist and rest on my hand. I am ready for her to stop me, us, from taking this moment any further. Our mouths continue their assault, my hand still on her skin. What I don't expect is what happens next. Peyton guides my hand up her body. Skin to skin, my fingers float over her abdomen, her stomach, her lacy bra cup.

A moan spills from her lips and I swallow every thrum. The resonance vibrates against my palm. Drives me wild. Urges me further.

I shove her top up, tug it over her head, and toss it to the floor. Dropping down, I kiss the spot beneath her ear while I unhook her bra from behind. Peeling the lacy fabric off, I take in her bare breasts for three jagged breaths. Not too big nor too small. Dark-pink areolae with pert nipples in the center. "Perfection."

My mouth crashes down on her lips with another vicious kiss. My hand palms her breast while I twist the nipple between my thumb and forefinger. She rocks her pelvis and rubs my cock with flawless precision. I snake a hand around the back of her neck, comb my fingers through her hair, fist the strands and yank her head back.

Her gasp breaks the kiss and I trail my lips down the front of her throat, past the hollow and between her breasts. Lick my way left, suck the stiff bud between my lips, add a little teeth.

"Micah," she breathes out. "Fuck."

"You like that?" I ask and circle her nipple with my tongue.

"God, yes."

I pay equal attention to her right nipple. Peyton claws at my scalp, tugs my hair, mewls as I lick my way down, down, down her abdomen. When I reach the hemline of her pants, I lift my gaze to meet hers and ask permission.

"Yes," she says, breathy.

My lips drop back to her belly, kiss her sweet flesh, lick her navel. I unbutton her pants and tug down the zipper. I sit up, scoot back and drag the fabric down her thighs, her calves, then drop them on the floor. As badly as I want to rip her panties off, I leave them in place. For now.

"So fucking perfect."

I lift her leg, drop her ankle on my shoulder and kiss the lower inside of her calf. Drag my fingers up the length of her leg as I lick a trail up the inside of her knee, her thigh. Mid-thigh, I suck the skin there. One hand at her hip. The other trails up her belly to her breast and pinches the nipple.

Peyton claws at my shirt. Tears at the buttons. Rips the fabric apart and sends buttons skittering across the room.

"I want your skin on mine."

Hooking her leg on my hip, I wrench the shirt off and toss it behind me. Drop my weight over her, crush my lips to hers, smash her breasts with my chest, and grind the bulge in my pants against her apex.

My hand snakes around her backside, my fingers trailing up her spine. Peyton lined up with my body... damn, this woman was built with me in mind. The lines of her neck and swell of her breasts. The planes of her abdomen and angles of her hip bones. How her lips move in synergy with mine. Her tongue dances the same familiar tune with mine.

Peyton and me, we are perfection.

I clutch the back of her neck, break the kiss, and make the trek back down her body. Taste the saltiness of her skin as I trail down her breastbone, her abdomen. Inhale her coconut mint scent with each new area of skin my lips touch. Trace the soft flesh along the outside of her thigh with my fingers as I drop low, low, lower.

Peppering kisses on her lower abdomen, I peer up at her

and lick along the low hemline of her panties. She fists my hair and shoves me lower.

"Something you want?" I mumble over the thin strip of fabric separating her skin from my lips.

"Teasing time is over."

I blow gently over the apex of her thighs and she trembles. "Is it, though?"

She props herself up on an elbow, clutches my chin and tips my eyes to hers. Her violet irises glow with hunger and I swallow. For a beat, her eyes drop to my lips as she licks hers.

"Taste me," she moans out before dropping her hand and shoving my face between her legs.

Jesus fucking Christ.

Until both of us are bone tired, I do exactly that. Taste her. Give her one orgasm after another. Torture her in the best possible ways. And when she offers to return the favor, I decline. At least for tonight.

Peyton needs to know I want more than one thing from her. That I want more than casual sex with her. That I want the whole package. Her smart mouth and brilliant mind. Her shapely body and sutured heart. All of it. The only way I know to show her this is to deprive myself of the one thing I am synonymous with—sex.

It may not be the perfect answer to show her I care. But it is the only way I know. For now.

And she doesn't seem to mind. Not one bit.

ten

PEYTON

Last night feels like a dream. A really fucking good dream. One of those dreams you never want to wake from, but inevitably do. The ones you can't revisit, no matter how quickly you fall back asleep.

Being known as a town whore isn't always the best title for anyone—man or woman. But the experience Micah has gained from said relations… let's just say no one will hear me complain. Not once.

The man weaves witchcraft with his tongue. Spins gold with the tip. Just the tip. And could make my shower singing voice Grammy-worthy in just one night. That is pure talent.

My experience with men—as far as number of partners— is minuscule in comparison to Micah. The few relationships I had were long term, the shortest a year and a half. Each man had his own talents or mannerisms I loved—a specific maneu- ver, the way he touched my cheek, how he looked at me like no one was in the room. Each of them sweet in their own way. Each of them someone I cared for deeply at the time.

But none of them shared similarities with Micah. Which strikes me as odd. Looking back at my past relationships, all the men shared identical physical features and comparable ways of thinking. All of them were the complete opposite of Micah. Part of me wonders if it was my brain's way of sheltering me from the past. Steering me away from men like the one I crushed on, but crushed me in a different way.

Compared to the men of my past, Micah Reed is wild. Untamed. Unrestrained. With the words that leave his lips and the tricks he performs with his tongue.

But Micah has also displayed a tender side; a side he keeps hidden from those not in his inner circle. This is the side of Micah that holds my gaze as if nothing exists but me and him and the moment shared between us. This side remembers my food preferences and what shows I watch and the spot to kiss that makes me melt. The playful side that spurs me on for fun, makes me laugh and puts a smile on my face.

Micah Reed is a true anomaly. A mysterious man with countless layers to unfold. A man who puts on a decent front, but harbors much more within himself. With what happened with his ex, I get not allowing your heart to be vulnerable. But at some point, if he wants more out of life, he will need to expose himself emotionally more than ever. Especially if he wants our relationship to evolve.

"Hellcat!"

I snap my head up from the glass I cleaned for the last however many minutes. Surprised I haven't scrubbed the bar logo off in the process. Glancing down the bar, I spy Micah looking my way with a cocked brow.

Great. I will never hear the end of this.

After I set the glass down, I spin to face him. "Yes?" I draw out the one-worded question.

"Been calling you the last five minutes. Need a break?"

Five minutes? No fucking way have I been washing the

same glass, spaced out, for five minutes. I narrow my eyes. He is messing with me, right?

Rather than holler down the bar, especially with every set of female eyes in the club on us, I walk the short distance and aim for a quieter conversation. Well, as quiet as a conversation can be with karaoke playing in the background.

"One," I say when I reach him. "You have *not* been calling my name that long." He opens his mouth to interrupt, but I hold up a hand. He snaps his mouth shut and flashes me a lopsided smile. "Two, what makes you think I need a break? We've only been open an hour."

The other corner of his mouth curves up and presents me with the most wicked grin to don his lips. A grin that trickles a thrill in my veins and dampens my panties. A mischievous smile that hints at secrets only we share and heats my skin from crown to root.

He shrugs, then tilts his head. "You look a little tired. Like you were up past your bedtime."

Smart-ass.

I step closer. His starry eyes playful as his tongue darts out to lick his lips. Taking another step in his direction, I inhale his cologne and refuse to exhale until necessary. The scent dances in my nasal cavities, swirls in my lungs, then takes up residence in my memory. It has me begging for more of him. Another taste of his lips, his tongue. But I won't tell him that. Not here. Not yet.

"I'm a big girl, starlight." I toss a smirk his way. "And I go to bed when I'm ready." My tongue sweeps over my lips and I bite and hold the lower for one, two, three breaths before releasing. Micah shifts his weight from right to left as I lean in, my lips less than an inch from his ear. "Maybe you should've offered me yours."

Micah sucks in a sharp breath, then releases it. Heat paints my skin as his breathing spikes. I startle when fingers tug at the hem of my shirt. Claw at my hip bone. Neither of us takes a step back. The bar may be packed with women wanting fruity cocktails and countless people hoping to make it big on stage, but they all vanish.

Right now, all I hear, all I see, all I feel is Micah.

Memories of last night play on a repetitive loop. The gentle and hungry ways his fingers caressed my skin. How he worshiped me with his lips. And how he took my body to places I never knew existed.

Yes, I have orgasmed with other partners—and myself. But what happened last night… that was not just oral and orgasms. Something else simmered beneath the surface. As if a dormant piece of me woke up and opened her eyes for the first time.

And I can't get enough.

"Best be careful what you ask for, hellcat." He kisses beneath my ear and a shiver rolls up my spine. "I make good on my promises. Do you?"

Before I open my mouth to respond, a female voice grabs both our attention. "Well, don't you two look nonproductive at work."

We simultaneously inch back, but stay within reach. A twin pair of starry eyes stare at us. When I broaden my view, six other sets of eyes leer at us. Their expressions range from *way to go* to *that's interesting*. No matter how they regard me or us, I don't want to be seen like the other women Micah has been with. Easy and replaceable.

Thankfully, none of them look at me in this manner. Perhaps because they never met any of the women Micah bedded. Works in my favor.

"What's up, Shell?"

She rolls her eyes and points to the makeshift stage as if the answer is obvious. "Karaoke, big brother. It may be out of our way, but we're here for it. Plus, we get to see you."

Although I have hung out with everyone opposite us, I remain quiet. Not that I feel uncomfortable in their presence or sparking conversation. My personal relationship with each of them is still new. With new people, I tend to be more reserved and less of an open book. Talkative, but not open.

Cora and Autumn smile, the corners of their eyes lifting with the gesture. Cora nudges Shelly. "Let's grab a table." Then Cora returns her attention to me. "You guys able to sit with us for a song or two? Or does it get super busy?"

I open my mouth to tell her we have other stuff to do, but Micah beats me to the punch.

"Sure." He glances my way. "Give us a few to wrap up paperwork in the office."

Shelly nods at her brother, but I see the *sure you have paperwork to do* glint in her eye. Because in what universe does it take two of us to plug numbers into spreadsheets for an average-sized nightclub/bar? Simple answer—it doesn't.

Do I correct him? Nope. Because after our conversation moments ago, I am dying to have his lips on mine again. Dying to taste and tangle tongues with him.

"Sure thing, big brother."

The group wanders to two vacant tall tops and scoots them closer together. Jake greets them and takes their drink order. Before Jake brings over the order, Micah starts popping off beer lids and mixing drinks. He knows his friends—family —well.

"Why don't you head back to the office," he suggests. "I'll be there in a few."

"Micah…" I start with a laugh. "Do they honestly believe we both need to do paperwork? It takes one of us a couple hours, at most, to get through it."

He stops shaking the drink, sets it down and steps into my personal space. "They have no clue what our job entails. Even if they did, I wouldn't give a fuck." Another step in my direction and we are toe to toe. Heat radiates off him and is like a match to my libido. "Go. I'll be there soon."

I drop the towel I picked up at some point and start for the office. As I pass the group, I give a courteous wave and smile. Seven return my way. When I reach the hall and step out of sight, my stride kicks into high gear. Once in the office, I shut the door but leave it unlocked.

With no idea when Micah will waltz in or what he had in mind, I plop down in the desk chair and get to work. Whether or not it is his intention for us to actually work, invoices and orders still need to get done.

Thirty minutes later, I input the third invoice and set it in the "to be filed" pile. As I pick up the next, the office door swings open and Micah strides in. He studies me behind the desk, licks his lips, and locks the door.

Dear lord, someone help me with this man.

"Almost done," I croak out as he saunters across the room.

"Good. Means we have more time."

"More—"

Before I finish the question, he spins the chair so I face him, bends down and smashes my lips with his. Stunned, it takes me two swipes of his lips over mine before I react. Then I fist his shirt and haul him closer. The chair slides back, smacks into the wall, and we laugh.

Micah loops his hands under my arms and stands me up. He brings his lips back to mine, snakes his arms around my waist, and walks us toward the couch. Carefully, he lowers himself to sit on the couch, then hauls me forward so I straddle him.

Fingers grip my hips, my ass as I rock against him. Lips and tongues and teeth assault each other, hungry. Starved. Downright famished. He breaks the kiss and licks his way down the column of my throat. A hand palms my breast, pinches my nipple between the material.

Fire and ache and titillation course through my veins, awaken every nerve ending, and scorch every square inch of my skin. If we were anywhere else, I would rip off my shirt then his. Press our bare flesh together and taste him.

But we aren't somewhere else. And I will *not* take this next level at work. At least that is what I tell myself.

"Micah." His name jagged and breathy on my tongue as I grind against his erection. "We have to…" God, this feels so fucking good. "We need to…" He nips at the skin along my collarbone and my eyes roll back. "Stop," I pant out. "We need to stop."

He licks from the thick strap of my top to the hollow of my throat. I rock against his hips and moan in his ear.

"You want this to stop, hellcat? You're gonna need to stop doing that," he mumbles into the crook of my neck.

Did I say I *wanted* this to stop? The word *want* never left my lips. No. Because I *want* this to continue. More than anything. But we *need* to stop. Not that she has in quite a while, but Ani—or Sean—could waltz into Roar at any moment. Last thing either of us needs is to have just-fucked hair and rumpled clothes.

I inch back and lock eyes with Micah. The starry gold flecks in his dark irises smolder. Burn hot and beg for more as he continues to fist my hips.

"Never said want," I say, my voice gruff and wobbly.

His brows pinch above his nose. "Huh?"

"You said if I *wanted* this to stop… I never said want. Need is what I said. That we need to stop."

He drops his forehead to my shoulder and groans. "Why do you have to be right?" And I love how his whiny and muffled words vibrate my skin, my chest. I comb my fingers through his hair, scrape his scalp with my nails. The pads of his fingers dig into my hips as a groan rumbles up his throat. "Better stop doing that or we won't stop."

Huffing out a breath, I lean away and force myself off his lap. I offer my hand once upright. "Come on, starlight. If you want to hang with your friends, we need to get some actual work done."

Micah takes my hand, rises from the couch and adjusts himself. "I'll finish with the invoices if you'll work on ordering."

"Deal," I tell him.

When we keep our hands to ourselves, work actually gets accomplished. Over the next hour, we wrap up the invoices, file them away, and input a supply order. Everything done and back in its rightful place, we head for the door.

But before I unlock it, Micah whips me around and pins me to the door. He clutches my chin between his thumb and forefinger. Eyes locked on mine. Lips a breath away.

"Kiss me. Before we leave this room and have to force ourselves to maintain a distance, kiss me."

This side of Micah is so new. His urgency to have me. To taste me. Feel me. Possess me. It calls out to my baser instincts. Wakes me up and revitalizes parts I didn't know were asleep.

As for his steady demand for me to kiss him…

With his grip still on my chin, I lean closer. But rather than give him the kiss he craves, I lick up the stubble on his chin, over his lips and stop at the top of his philtrum. He reacts with unfathomable speed.

Micah wraps his fingers around my wrists and pins them over my head. Presses his hips to mine and locks me in place —not that I planned on moving. Slides a foot between mine and kicks my feet out. Then leans in and traces the tip of his nose up the column of my throat, stopping just below my ear.

"Tsk, tsk, hellcat. Really should be mindful of your actions. You wanted me on my best behavior, but that… you just handed over your one-way ticket. There's no going back."

My chest heaves, nipples taut and chafing the material of my bra and shirt. With the taste of him on my tongue, his scent invading my nose, his body pressed to mine… fuck, I am tempted to provoke the beast. Within him and me.

"One-way ticket?" I wheeze out.

He gyrates his hips, his erection unyielding as it rubs my clit through my pants and his.

"Mmhm." A hand trails down my arm, the side of my torso and lands on my hip. His tongue darts out and licks the spot beneath my ear. And I don't fight the shiver that rolls through my body. "Best hold on, hellcat."

Before I ask what he means, he drops to his knees in front of me. Deft fingers make quick work of the button and zipper on my pants. Two breaths later, my pants are at my ankles as he traces his nose along the fabric of my panties. Inhaling deeply, his palms slide up my thighs, grasp the thin straps of my underwear and wiggle them down, down, down.

We shouldn't be doing this. Not at work.

Then his tongue drags leisurely over my lower lips and I forget everything. The office, the fact half my clothes are missing, the club and people outside this room. All of it… gone.

Micah shimmies a foot out of my clothes, spreads my legs wider, hikes one over his shoulder and devours me like his last meal. One of my hands fists his hair while the other clutches the door handle. I grind myself on his mouth, moan as he slips a finger inside me, then another, and revel in the abrasiveness of his stubble against my sensitive skin.

The back of my head smacks the door as I tug his hair. Grind harder. Faster. Unladylike moans crawl up my throat and spill from my lips. His fingers pick up speed as he sucks my clit between his lips. My legs tremble and breaths come in short bursts. I slam my eyes shut as the room spins.

Then Micah performs sorcery in a one-two combo with his tongue and fingers. Stars light the back of my lids. Shock waves surge through my body as the orgasm pulses over and over. My legs give out and he grabs my hips to keep me upright.

Again and again, he licks up my seam. Feasts on every drop of my orgasm as I quiver atop him. Slowly rises to his feet then slams his mouth down on mine.

The taste of me on his tongue does libidinous things to my body. I fist his shirt and drag our bodies flush. Suck his tongue like I plan to his dick when given the opportunity.

"You taste like fucking nirvana and sin," he groans against my lips.

"Wait until you experience it too."

"Fuck," he whisper-hisses. "How the hell can I leave the room now?"

I laugh, haul his lips back to mine, and kiss him with unrestrained aggression. As his hands glide from my hip up my abdomen, I break the kiss and shove him back a step.

"We should stop." I say the words, but they hold no umph. Because right now, all I want to do is shed his clothes and drop to my knees. Worship him in ways I never have, in ways he has never known.

Who knew Micah Reed would turn me into a craved vixen? Certainly not me. But here we are.

He palms his cock as I reach for my panties and slip them back on, followed by my pants. Zipper up and button in place, I walk over to the small mirror in the office and work to make my hair resemble what it did prior to Micah entering the office. In the end, I twist it in a topknot and say fuck it.

After I swipe a fresh coat of gloss on my lips, I spin to face Micah. "You know we can't walk out of here at the same time."

He lifts a brow as the corner of his mouth kicks up. "Why?"

"One—I look freshly fucked." This garners a bigger smile from him. "Two—it would just be odd. We're never both in here together this long in the first place. To walk out of here at the same time would definitely bring unwanted attention our way."

"Who says it's unwanted?"

"Me," I say on a sigh. "Micah, the last thing we need is the staff thinking we're acting inappropriately. And that they can do the same." I shake my head before dropping my gaze to the floor. "I've worked hard to get here. If anyone even remotely believes I slept with my boss to get promoted…"

"Hey." Micah steps up to me, pinches my chin between his thumb and forefinger, and lifts until our eyes lock. "That is not what's happening here." The edge to his words sharp enough to sever any doubt.

"You and I know that." I point toward the main part of

the club. "They don't, though." My eyes glaze over. "Please, can we just go back out there? You first and I'll follow in a few."

"Under one condition." He steps closer and we stand toe to toe.

"What?"

"I don't want to hide this. Us." He trails a single fingertip from the hollow of my throat to the v of my shirt. "Working here isn't the same as a corporate job. Rules are different. More flexible. Besides, I think Ani knows about us and she doesn't seem bothered by it."

Considering Ani and I have been friends for years, she definitely knows more about Micah than he realizes. Nothing outlandish. I do keep some things private. But I shared our history with her. And where our relationship resides now— minus the intimate details. Gossip over such personal aspects of my life will never happen. No matter how close I am with someone. In my opinion, certain things should stay between the two people involved.

"She knows."

He shifts to hold my gaze easier. "Yeah? And she's cool with us?"

My entire frame sags. "Yes," I mumble.

"What's that?"

"You're such a pain in the ass." I straighten my spine and roll my eyes. "Yes, she knows about us. Kind of. Not the nitty-gritty, but that we've been hanging out."

"And?" My brows inch up as I look away. "She's fine with it, isn't she?"

Micah Reed lives to drive me insane. I just know it. Of course, Ani is fine with Micah and me being together. As long as our relationship doesn't interfere with work or cause future problems, Ani has no issue with us being together. In any capacity.

"Mmhm." I nod.

"Then why are you so worked up?"

He doesn't get it. Either that or he doesn't comprehend how other people may perceive the situation. Anyone with eyes would have seen me and Micah close prior to the official promotion. It wouldn't matter that the job had been offered to me months back. Some people may still assume I slept my way up the ladder.

And that… is not acceptable.

"Have you ever been a woman?" I ask the question knowing I will get a smart-ass answer. But I hold up a hand before he gets a word out. "No, you haven't. So, you don't understand what it's like. To have to bust your ass ten times harder for the same opportunity. To work extra just to show you're worthy of the same pay. It isn't our fault we were born with different parts between our legs and on our chest, but our part of the world was founded by men. And most of society doesn't see men and women as equals." I close my eyes, take a deep breath, and reopen them. "So, please… do this for me. Straighten your clothes and hair, walk out of here, and pretend like we were working back here and nothing else."

Warm hands engulf mine as Micah erases any remaining space between us. He lifts my hands and deposits them on his shoulders, then snakes his around my waist.

"Sorry," he whispers, inches from my lips. "I have no intention of flaunting what you and I do behind closed doors. But Peyton?" I meet his starry night eyes. "I won't hide our relationship. Not saying I plan to walk up to everyone and tell them. But this…" He presses his lips to mine briefly. "You aren't some dirty secret or sidepiece. For you, I'll walk out of here alone. But make no mistake, if someone asks about our relationship status, I won't lie. We haven't defined us, but there is an us."

He kisses me once more, steps back and walks out the door. No tension or awkwardness lingers. Just Micah giving me the space I need while fulfilling my request. When the door shuts after him, I take a deep breath and collect myself—physically and mentally. Organize my thoughts on what happened over the last thirty minutes and stash them for later conversation, when we are alone.

I take one last glance in the mirror, brush my hands down my outfit, and head for the door. Each step away from the office weighs heavily. But the moment I hit the main club floor, spot Shelly and Cora on the karaoke stage making asses of themselves to Wreckx-N-Effect's "Rump Shaker," I breathe easier.

No eyes dart my direction. No whispers or pointed fingers. Everything is just… normal.

After checking in with the staff, I join Micah at the table with Gavin, Trevor, Erin, Jonas, and Autumn. Cora and Shelly still dominate the karaoke machine while the crowd cheers them on. For a moment, I sit beside Micah and enjoy myself. Enjoy the laughter of the people nearby. Enjoy the ease at being with this group of people and with Micah.

Cora and Shelly skip off the stage when the song ends, park on their stools, and sip their drinks. A fifty-something woman picks up the mic and preps for her song to start. When the intro of the song spills from the club speakers, everyone at the table goes wide eyed. Cora and Shelly set their drinks down and spin to face the woman on stage who breathes heavily into the mic with the intro of "My Humps" by Black Eyed Peas.

"Thought Karaoke Nights at our hangout were great, but this…" Cora points to the stage. "This is gold."

Micah leans in and kisses my temple. "You good?"

My eyes do another scan of the club, the staff, the group at the table. No one bats an eyelash my way. No one curls their lip or rolls an eye. Life continues to exist around us as if this is normal. As if *we* are normal. And I have never loved the feeling more.

"Yeah."

"Peyton!" My gaze darts to Shelly, who all but bounces on her stool. "Hang out with us on Sunday."

I scan the two tables, take in the other sets of eyes peering my way. Cora leans into Gavin as they both give me a content smile. Jonas wraps his arm around Autumn's shoulders before they both nod. Trevor and Erin smile my way before she rejoins a conversation with Cora and he looks back at his phone.

How many years did I want this form of acceptance? To have my own people. Yes, I have Reese and love everything he brings to my life. But I always felt like something was missing. I always wanted more. Like dreaming of the big family you never had but wished you did.

Is that what this is? An opportunity at my own family. Maybe.

"I'll be there."

Beneath the table, Micah rests a hand on my thigh and squeezes. Our eyes lock and something new passes between us. An unnamed emotion. A flicker. The start of something more.

The start of us.

eleven

MICAH

"That's a lot of meat."

I peer over my shoulder at Shelly and laugh. Did she really leave that comment wide open? My sweet baby sister. Naive and not in the same breath.

"That's what she said."

Shelly slaps my bicep. "Shut up, asshole. Seriously, though. Who's going to eat it all?" She points to the grill where Jonas flips burgers, brats, chicken, and ribs.

It is a lot of food, but Sunday always involves this much or close to it. Our Sunday get-togethers have slowly evolved into a massive gathering and tend to last several hours. The food gets eaten. If not, Autumn packs it up and ships it out with us as we leave. Which is a win for me since my kitchen skills still suck.

"Considering close to twenty people will be here, it won't go to waste. Why're you freaking out? You're never this antsy."

Shelly isn't the quietest person among us, but also not the most exuberant. That award goes to Penny. But I know my sister. Her fretting over the amount of food is… weird. Then again, she has her moments. I find it best not to question the change unless instinct tells me otherwise.

Her hands plop down on her hips. "I'm *not* freaking out." Then she storms into the house where Cora and Autumn work on side dishes.

"Dude, what's up with your sister?" Gavin asks as he grabs a beer from the cooler.

Sipping from my own bottle, I shrug. "Who knows. Probably something or someone irritating her and I'm her scapegoat today." If she continues with the theatrics, I will pull her aside later and ask more probing questions.

Gavin, Jonas, and I shoot the shit while the ladies are inside. Still early, only the six of us here, we catch up on monotonous stuff. Work, homelife, day to day boring stuff.

Gavin tells us about an upcoming photo shoot for sportswear. No travel is involved, which makes him and Cora both happy. Before coming back to Florida, Gavin traveled extensively for work. But once he and Cora reunited, they don't leave each other's side often. Can't say I blame them after spending so much time apart.

Jonas says his dad continues to hint at working less. His dad working less at the garage equals him slowly taking over the business. He always knew the day would come, but the fact it is happening has him slightly on edge.

I share how busy work has been since the changes made in early June. It sucks not seeing Peyton at work four nights a week, but we would never get things done if we worked every shift together. But with each passing week, we spend more and more time together outside of work. And I want more.

As if my thoughts summon her, Peyton walks out the back

door and down the steps. Arm hooked with Shelly's, they laugh at something I wasn't privy to hear. No doubt, Shelly told her an embarrassing story of my younger days. I expect nothing less.

"Hey," I say as she approaches and unhooks from Shelly. "Glad you made it." I kiss her temple and wrap an arm around her waist. "Drink?"

"Please. And did you think I wouldn't show?" she asks with a chuckle.

With reluctance, I drop my hand from her waist, set my beer down, fetch one from the cooler for her, pop the top and hand it over. "I never want to assume anything when it comes to you." I guide us over to the loungers and sit. "How was Gulfside?"

Her face falls as her frame caves. "Good. I miss being there as often."

Peyton went from working two weekday shifts at the assisted living facility to one. Then, two weeks ago, she cut it back to every other Sunday. Roar doesn't interfere with her days at the facility, but the extra hours at the club and spending time with me have stretched her thin.

Wrapping an arm around her, I stroke up and down her spine. "Sure they miss you too."

Before either of us get another word out, cacophony erupts as Penny, Rex, Reznor, Tatyana, and Ashton walk outside. Clementine steals Ashton from his mom and they run into the yard with Spartan hot on their heels and laughter in the air. Greetings and hugs are exchanged before new conversations start.

Three rock ballads later, everyone has a plate in their hands and is piling it high with a little of everything. I tease

Peyton at the excessive amount of food on her plate, even though I don't give a fuck. I simply love our banter. She tosses me the middle finger, then shoves a coleslaw-covered brat between her lips.

Fuck me.

I groan and bunch the cotton of my shirt near my zipper in an effort to disguise my stiffening cock. Sensing my hopefully not obvious discomfort, Peyton brings her lips to my ear. "Need help?"

Of all the things I expected her to say, that was not one of them. A tease, yes. Offering assistance with my *dilemma*, no. I choke on the heaping forkful of potato salad I shoveled in my mouth seconds ago.

Peyton sets her plate and mine on the table, lifts my hands over my head, then slaps my back. My face turns red—not only from inhaling food but also embarrassment—as tears spill down my cheeks. The cough doesn't quit and almost has me laughing.

Rising from the lounger, Peyton takes my hand and hauls me inside. "Be right back," she tells everyone as we head for the house.

Inside, she steers us into the bathroom, shuts the door and locks it.

"What are you..." My cough, lighter this time, cuts me off. Before I finish the question, Peyton reaches forward and grabs me. More specifically, my cock.

"Offering to help." She bats her lashes and strokes me through my shorts.

I grind against her and growl. "No chance in hell I'm letting you get me off in this tiny-ass bathroom."

Her grip tightens. "Why not?" she asks, breath hot on my neck.

"The first time I get off with you will be after hours of foreplay." *Holy hell.* If she doesn't stop, my shorts will flaunt evidence of our bathroom escapade in no time.

"Foreplay, huh?" she purrs in my ear and my eyes roll back.

I grip her hand and stop her teasing. "Yes." Unwillingly, my fingers peel hers away. "Lucky for you, we have hours ahead of us."

She lifts a brow. "You speak as if *tonight*, here, is foreplay."

I bring her hand to my lips and kiss each knuckle in turn. "She gets it," I whisper. "Hope you're ready, hellcat."

Dropping her hand, I adjust myself then waltz out of the bathroom with an ear-to-ear smile. Not until I reach the door do I hear Peyton rushing to follow me out.

When we return to our seats on the patio, half the group looks our way. We weren't gone long, but definitely longer than necessary. I don't give a fuck, let them think of all the possible things we didn't do that we could have.

After no one says a word for too long, I tap my throat. "Potato got stuck." I shrug, pick up my plate, and act as if nothing happened.

Peyton, on the other hand, has rosy cheeks. *Way to put our bathroom rendezvous on display.* I love it.

The next ten minutes pass uneventful. Beer, food, music and good conversation occupy the group. Peyton turns her attention to Penny and Autumn as they talk about weird tattoo placement. Penny recants the story of some guy who had the word *sweet* tattooed on his right ass cheek.

As Peyton goes to respond, I set my hand on her thigh and slowly trail it toward her midline. She sucks in a breath and doesn't say a word. Penny drones on about Mr. Sweet Cheek, not realizing I cut Peyton off.

Peyton doesn't move. Doesn't shift her attention. She keeps her eyes forward and pretends to listen, nodding at the appropriate times.

Inch by inch, my fingers dance over her skin. Slide over the exposed flesh and toy with the frayed hemline of her denim shorts. The action hidden from observation by the empty plate in her hands. The tip of my pinkie slips under the denim and she shifts her weight. The outside of her thigh presses firmly against mine as her thighs part imperceptibly to anyone looking. But I feel the change. Her breath hitches and skin pinks.

Much as I love the reaction, I remove my hand and bring my lips to her ear. "Dessert?"

She huffs out a laugh. "Yes." The huskiness in her voice pauses my rise from the lounger. I take my plate and hers, deposit them in the bin, and load up a single plate with sweets.

Most of the night at Jonas and Autumn's continues much the same. Me toying with Peyton while she tries to carry on as if I don't affect her. A brush of the arm. Graze of the thigh. Breath near her neck. Hand on her lower back. With each touch, I pick up on her twitches and startled moves. Subtle enough no one speaks up. Obvious enough, I detect every single one.

Then I switch gears. Drape an arm over her shoulders and draw circles on her skin with my fingertips. Drop my lips every few minutes to her hair, her temple, the angle of her jaw and leave chaste kisses. Toy with the ends of her hair or the hemline of her top.

Reznor announces their departure. While hugs get

exchanged, I lean closer and whisper in Peyton's ear. "Want to go?" My thumb strokes her shoulder. "To my place."

Twisting enough to face me, Peyton's eyes dart between mine. Two dazzling violet irises glitter in the dim light of the tiki torches. The way she regards me, the way she searches for answers to questions left unspoken, brings doubt to the surface. With Peyton, I never want to presume. She may have forgiven me for past discretions, but that doesn't mean she has forgotten.

Her tongue darts out and licks her lips, slow and calculated. The corner of her mouth kicks up when my eyes drop and follow the action. After a beat, I bring my eyes back to hers. Study the intent behind her stare since she has yet to answer.

Reznor and Tatyana step up to the lounger, ready to bid us good night. But I want Peyton's answer before they do.

"Promise to behave," I whisper, hoping it will provoke a response.

At this, she cocks a brow. "What if I don't want you to?"

Hello, hellcat.

"Then maybe I won't." I nudge my head toward the door. "Shall we."

She tips her head left and right as if pondering the idea. As Reznor all but begs for a goodbye hug, she answers, "Yes."

One word is all it takes and my mind goes through all the steps we need to take to leave like civilized people. We rise from the lounger, say good night to Reznor and Tatyana. Then we go through the process with everyone else. I do my best to act casual. Behave as if there is no rush. When, in fact, my feet won't move fast enough and the hugs seem to never end.

Finally, we escape out the front door and I walk Peyton to her car. "See you in a few." She nods.

I hop into my truck and crank the engine. As I throw the truck in reverse, I coach myself to not speed on the way home. Traffic violations will only add misery to the evening. But damn, am I eager to have Peyton all to myself. Eager to see how this night ends. Because once she is in my bed, there is no going back.

twelve

PEYTON

A few blocks from Micah's house, I text Reese while at a stoplight.

Might not be home tonight. FYI

I expect details.

I don't respond. Last thing I need is an endless back-and-forth exchange with Reese before possibly taking my relationship with Micah next level. Reese is the brother I never had. And who talks with their brother before making out—or more —with someone. Certainly not me.

Micah parks in the driveway and I pull in behind him. Turning off the headlights, I cut the engine, stare out the windshield, and take a deep breath.

"This is Micah," I mumble to myself as I watch him exit his truck. "The man you've been kissing for weeks. The man who's gone down on you." He steps closer to my car and I take another deep breath. "Don't go acting shy now."

One last deep inhale through my nose, then I open the door on the exhale. I lock the car before he takes my hand and guides us inside. Neither of us says a word, but the silence is pleasant. Tranquil and a little energizing.

With each button he presses to unlock the door, my pulse thumps a faster rhythm. A thin layer of moisture slicks my palms and I pray to whoever hears my call to not let Micah notice.

As we step into the house, I expect him to maul me. To slam me against the door and crush my mouth with his. Pin my hands over my head and grind his erection against the junction of my thighs. Moan my name and bite my lip.

But none of this happens.

We step inside and he guides us to the couch. Gives me a chaste kiss on the lips, lets go of my hand and goes to the fridge for water. After a sip, he offers me one. I take it in the hopes it will cool off my immeasurable fever and wake my rational side.

Does he sense my low-level anxiety over what might happen? God, how embarrassing. I feel like a trembling virgin. Who knows why? My virginity flew out the window more than a decade ago. And I haven't exactly been celibate —although, it has been a while.

When he turns the television on and starts an episode of *Supernatural*, I start to second-guess every thought from tonight. We kick off our shoes and settle into the couch. When he tugs me closer to him, I stop thinking and sag into the warmth of his frame. After fifteen minutes, my anxiety vanishes and I curl into his side and rest my head on his shoulder.

Three-quarters through the episode, Micah kisses the top of my head. The gesture sweet as his lips linger for a beat. I tip my chin up to return the kiss. The act natural and innocent.

Until the kiss evolves. Grows from chaste pecks to the

delicacy of tasting lips. Slow and gentle mixed with heat and the occasional scrape of his stubble.

A hand cups my cheek. Fingers weave through the hair at the base of my skull as he draws me closer and keeps me in place. A match strikes beneath my breastbone when his tongue traces the seam of my lips. The chambers of my heart pound, pound, pound against my rib cage as I gasp and his tongue slips in and tangles with mine.

And then everything explodes. Detonates like a ticking time bomb.

I fist his shirt, throw a leg over his lap, and straddle him. Rock my hips and rub against the thick bulge beneath his zipper. Tangle his tongue with mine before I suck it like a popsicle.

He clamps down on my hips hard enough to bruise me for days. Adds more pressure where I stroke him through our clothes. Sits up straighter, trails a hand up my spine until he reaches the base of my skull, wraps my hair around his fist and jerks my head back.

The motion stings my scalp as I gasp for air. He sucks and bites his way down the column of my throat. Kneads my hip with his other hand. Paints his tongue along my collarbone. My hands glide up his chest, snake around his neck, take hold of his hair and yank. Hard.

His lips break from my skin in a hiss. "*Fuck.*"

Before I voice a comeback, he scoops under my ass and stands. His lips back on mine as we move through the house. Greed and hunger taste so fucking sweet on his tongue.

And then I am airborne. But not long.

In the dark room, I land on a cloud. Micah crawls up the bed and reinstates our kiss. His hands at the bottom hem of my shirt inch up my body—slow, too slow—as they tug the material away. Lips and teeth and tongue imprint my skin as he unclasps my bra. The skimpy fabric gets tossed aside and replaced with his mouth.

I thread my fingers through his hair as I arch my back and press my breasts into his hungry mouth. He grips my wrists, breaks my hold on him, and pins my hands to the mattress. Clamps down on my nipple before popping it from his lips and paying equal attention to the other.

"Micah," I whisper-moan into the darkness.

He releases my nipple and hovers above me. Stars burn white hot in his dark irises as he holds my gaze. The intensity in his irises slicks my skin, and I swallow.

"Keep your hands here," he commands in a thick baritone. I nod and he shakes his head. "No, Peyton. In here, you need to use words."

"Yes," I whisper. "Won't move my hands."

"That's my hellcat."

He drops his lips back to mine, kisses me one, two, three times before sucking my lower lip between his. Then his lips leave mine and kiss a trail of fire up the line of my jaw. Nibble on my earlobe as my eyes roll back. Suck the tender skin beneath my ear as I grind my clit against his erection.

As his lips move down my neck, he releases my wrists. Skims the tips of his fingers along my forearms, my triceps as he kisses his way down. Fever flares over my body as he tattoos my skin with his tongue. Marks me as his with his teeth. Bruises my flesh with his mouth.

His hands squeeze my breasts, graze the sides of my abdomen, then land on the button of my shorts.

And then he freezes.

I lift my head and glance down my midline. I lock eyes

with him as he watches me, studies me, questions me. As he silently asks for permission. As he waits for consent.

"Micah?"

"Yes, hellcat," he purrs, his breath hot on my skin.

"Take my clothes off."

He cocks a brow and tilts his head. "Anything else?"

I love and loathe how he wants me to say the words aloud. I am not a shy lover, but Micah and I haven't traveled this road yet. And I get his need to hear me verbalize what I want.

Sitting up—which causes him to do the same—I come face-to-face with him. Inches separate our lips. My bare breasts a breath from brushing his cotton shirt. I hold his gaze. Read the carnality in his eyes. It adds fuel to the roaring fire beneath my skin. Possesses me. Makes me ravenous.

Without moving my hands, I lean forward, bite his lower lip then growl as I release it. A breath between us, I whisper-hiss, "Fuck me."

Unexpectedly, his eyes widen a beat. A growl rips from his chest and spills from his lips. Then his hand wraps around my throat and constricts as he shoves me back to the mattress. My oxygen is cut off enough to make me dizzy, but not knock me out and I roll my eyes before closing them.

The button on my shorts pops open seconds before he bites the fabric and separates the zipper teeth. Cool air stings my lungs when he removes his hand from my throat. The mattress shifts before his hands scoop my ass cheeks and he shimmies my shorts and panties down my thighs.

Completely bare on his comforter, he stands at the foot of the bed, palms his cock, and licks his lower lip. My hands itch to reach down, not to cover myself, but to touch myself too. But I resist the urge and let him visually devour me.

Micah traces his fingers up my shins, then slides them

back down to my ankles, takes hold and yanks my ass to the edge of the bed before dropping to his knees. He hooks my left leg over his shoulder, followed by my right. Lips press to the inside of my thigh. Teeth nip their way up, up, up my thigh, tongue tasting me along the way.

When he reaches the apex of my thighs, he licks everywhere but where I want him. Teases me with slight touches. Tortures me with occasional bites. Makes me moan as he marks my flesh on the upper part of my inner thigh.

Then he licks my lips, bottom to clit, and hums his appreciation. "Fuck, I love how sweet you taste." Before rational thought forms from his words, his mouth is on me. Lapping and sucking, tasting and devouring. He adds a finger, rubs that sweet spot inside me. Flicks his tongue over my clit again and again before inserting a second finger.

I fist the comforter as my back bows off the mattress. Thighs clamp the angle of his jaw. Ankles hook behind his head and force him into me as I rock against his mouth. Against the scrape of his stubble. Against the perfect strokes of his tongue and drive of his fingers.

Heat builds between my legs, curls up my spine, blooms across my chest, up my neck, over my cheeks. Consumes me in every possible way as Micah picks up speed. Curls his digits and pumps faster. Sucks my clit between his lips and performs voodoo on my body.

In the past, I had never been a vocal lover. Never moaned or screamed or cried out a name in pleasure. But with Micah, I whimper. Mewl for more. Beg him not to stop. Moan his name like it pains me not to.

He makes me wanton. Carnal. Hungry for only him.

And the way he looks at me now—eager to consume every part of me—sets me off. Has me fisting the comforter and cursing at the ceiling. Tremors rock me head to toe. Blind me in the darkness. Steal my breath and stall my heart.

"So fucking sweet," he says on a moan as he licks the orgasm from my skin.

As the shaking settles, I shift to my hands and knees. Crawl to where he stands at the foot of the bed, shorts tented by his erection. He grins down at me lasciviously.

"Whatcha going to do, hellcat?" He cups my cheek and tips my chin up so we are eye to eye.

I lick my lips, rock back on my haunches, and reach out to drag him closer. Still fully dressed, I slip my hands under his shirt, force it up and off him. Before the cotton hits the floor, my fingers unbutton his shorts, then slide down the zipper. A low thump sounds in the room as his shorts drop to the floor.

Eyes locked on his, I lean forward and drag my tongue from his navel to his nipple. "Taking what's mine," I state.

"Fuck," he whisper-hisses. He fists my throat, locks me in place, and crashes his lips to mine.

But it is my turn.

I slide a hand up his abdomen, over his pec, and land on his throat. When my fingers tighten, as my nails bite his skin, he releases my neck. Moans in my mouth.

I crawl backward on the mattress and he follows. He plants his knees on the mattress and I shift our positions. Drop my hand to his chest, shove him down and straddle him. Grinding myself against him and soak his boxer briefs.

His eyes roll back briefly as he grips my hips. "Confession."

I wiggle my way down his body and reach for the band of his boxer briefs. "This isn't church, Micah. But feel free to worship me."

I yank his briefs down and off, then toss them aside. I rake my gaze over him and stop when I reach his cock. *Sweet fucking Jesus.* The size makes me stutter mentally, but that isn't what has me praying for mercy. No, what makes me swallow and crawl closer are the three barbells.

When my eyes flash to his, a smirk kicks up the corner of his mouth. He tucks an arm under his head and fists his cock with the free hand. "As I started to say—"

"You're building a ladder," I interrupt and tilt my head. "Lucky for you, I'm into construction."

As he opens his mouth with what I bet is a witty comment, I bend down and lick the length of him.

"Dear god," he hisses out as he fists the comforter. A hand comes to the back of my neck and tightens as he hauls me up his body.

"Wasn't done," I mumble against his lips.

He flips me over. "Don't care." With a rock of his hips, he rubs the piercings over my clit. My eyes roll back as I dig my nails into his obliques. "Fuck." Another hiss from his lips. "I need to be inside you."

"What's taking so long then?" I lick along his jawline, then bite the angle of his jaw.

Fingers comb through my hair, fist the locks and yank to the side. He nips and peppers kisses over my cheek, my jaw, my throat until he reaches my ear.

"I need to *feel* you, Peyton." He lifts enough for our gazes to meet. "I'm clean. Got tested weeks ago. Haven't been with anyone in months."

"I'm on the pill."

Although more than a year passed since my last boyfriend, I continued birth control. The other benefits were a perk, but I also continued taking them in case someone else came along. Figured no harm, no foul.

In this instance, my indifference paid off.

"Thank fuck."

My hair still in his grip, Micah rocks his hips again and teases my lips and clit with the barbells. I carve new crescent moons into his flesh and bite down at the curve of his neck.

Holy Christ. He hasn't put it in yet and I am ready to claw my name on his back. "Micah." His name a moan on my lips.

"Patience, hellcat." He lowers his lips to mine. "I want to take my time with you. Savor you. Own you."

Dear baby Jesus. Not sure what I did to deserve this delicious torture, but thank you.

Micah continues to take his time. He worships every inch of my body. Focuses on places I never knew I wanted a lover to pay attention to. Places that spark cosmic pleasure. After my body convulses a second time, he finally shows me what sex with ladders is all about.

Needless to say, I will never look at a ladder and not blush. Micah may have slutted around town more than a year, but I reap the benefits in the end. Because no chance in hell anyone else in the future will enjoy the Micah Reed adventure. Not on my watch. Not after I felt him bare and engraved my name in his flesh with my nails.

It's quite possible I had an out-of-body experience when my third orgasm hit. Or I blacked out. To be honest, the likelihood of both happening is conceivable. I won't discount the chances.

What I do know with certainty... Micah more or less just staked his claim. Marked me as his. Not only on my flesh, but also on my soul.

Micah Reed has no idea what it means to be mine. But from this moment forward, I plan to show him.

thirteen

MICAH

How long can I get away with watching her like this? With thin lines of sunlight highlighting her hair and skin. With soft blonde lashes fanned out just above her cheekbones. And champagne wavy locks spilled over my pillow.

I don't dare move or breathe too heavily. Don't reach out to brush to wayward strands out of her face and tuck them behind her ear. Don't trace my fingertips over her skin and write secret messages only I can decipher.

That would disturb this moment. And this is solely mine.

Instead, I bask in the sight of her. Her fair skin and peaceful expression as she sleeps. The soft snores from her lips as she dreams, hopefully, of me or us. Relish the memories from last night. Every line and curve of her body under my hands. How she reacted to my touch—the bow of her back, quiver of her muscles, moan of my name. How we exhausted ourselves, yet it was nowhere near enough.

In the early morning hours, we collapsed in a pile of loose limbs and sated souls.

For more than a year, I have yearned for Peyton. Watched her from the sidelines while I took my frustrations out on nameless and faceless women. Taunted her so I had her atten-tion. Because every second she paid me attention, she gave it to no one else. Even if the attention was negative, I wanted it all to myself. Her irritation and poutiness was, is, such a turn-on. In the beginning, I craved something strictly carnal with Peyton. To blow off steam and get her out of my system. Fulfill a need clawing at my insides.

But now… my need for her is so much more. An unquenched hunger. A deep, primal demand. A vital compo-nent of my existence. She floods my veins and occupies my marrow. Spins an endless web beneath my sternum that encases my heart and refuses to relinquish its hold.

It steals my breath and awards me life simultaneously.

My fingers twitch beneath the sheet. Itch to feel the warmth of her skin again. But softer this time. Delicately trace the arch of her brow, the bridge of her nose, the swell of her lips. Twirl her soft hair around my finger and toy with the strands in the sunlight. Kiss her until her our lips or tongues tire, whichever happens first.

Her nose twitches, followed by her lips. A gentle pinch of her lashes as she slowly stirs awake. I train my eyes on every tweak her face and body make as she leaves the land of dreams.

Damn, she's gorgeous.

Lucky doesn't begin to describe how I feel as her violet eyes flutter open and lock with my blues. Countless breaths pass and neither of us says a word. She tucks a hand beneath her cheek as a soft smile brightens her face. Waking up with Peyton in my bed, her angelic features the first thing I see in the morning, is the best way to start the day.

"Morning," I whisper and reach for the fallen hairs on her cheek. Her eyes close at my touch. When they reopen, gray flecks dance against the violet backdrop and render me breathless.

"Good morning." Her voice raspy and soft and sexy as hell. Another trait to add to the long list of characteristics I like about her.

Morning breath be damned, I want to kiss her. Feel her beneath and above me in the early morning hour. Well, early for us.

I quit resisting my need for her and eliminate the space between us. Press my lips to hers, light and tender. Skim a hand down the side of her breast, her waist and stop when I reach her hip. The subdued kiss turns hungry as she throws her leg over my hip. Rocks herself against my cock as her fingers comb my hair and fists the locks.

Within seconds, she has me on my back and straddles my waist. Long champagne locks curtain us as the kiss turns ravenous and she coats my erection with her arousal. On the next circuit up, she shifts so the tip of my cock presses between her lips.

Up and down and up and down. She teases the head of my cock over and over. As I open my mouth to tell her to quit being a tease, she pushes back and fills herself to the hilt.

"Dear god, woman." I fist her hips and keep her in place. "You give religion new meaning."

She sits up, tosses the hair from her face and plants her palms on my chest. "Won't stop you from worshiping me," she says with a rock of her hips. Her hooded eyes look down and pull me into her orbit. "Welcome to heaven."

Peyton rides me like the goddess she is. Head thrown back, tits pushed out, lips parted as her whimpers mingle with the slapping of our bodies. Nails bite my skin to mark me as hers. Marks I will gladly own and flaunt whenever possible.

When her moans and whimpers escalate in pitch, I tighten a hand on her hip and wrap the other around her throat. Piston harder into her sweet, tight pussy. Groan when her walls tighten around me and her claws dig deeper. Revel in the blotchy flush that decorates her breasts, her neck, her cheeks.

And the moment she can no longer hold herself upright, I flip her on her back, hook her legs over my shoulders and drive into her. Skin slapping and grunts echo off the walls as I grip her shoulders and pound her pussy. The violet of her eyes a thin rim around her glassy dilated gaze.

A hand claws its way up my chest and wraps around my throat. Her grip slight as she tugs me down to her lips. Kisses me until her body climbs, climbs, climbs back toward that delicious peak and she gasps for breath.

My pace kicks into fifth gear as I all but slam her body into the headboard. Slide one hand from her shoulder to her throat as I beat her clit with my pelvic bone.

Slap. Slap. Slap.

Her pussy slowly tightens around my cock. Sweet, stuttered cries of pleasure spill from her lips. Nails dig so deep, I swear she pierces my flesh. And it all just adds to the intensity of the moment. Wakes the beast inside me.

Tingling manifests in my balls. Liquid fire slithers up my spine, then winds its way back down. Converges low in my abdomen. Immense pressure and the need to come makes me dizzy, breathless, a slave to the act.

But I hold off. Wait until Peyton gets there first. Wait until her body convulses and milks me.

Hand still on her throat, I lean down and lick her chin, her lips, her cheek. "Let go, hellcat."

I crush my lips to hers. Slam my hips forward and adjust my angle to hit her sweet spot better. Annihilate her clit with my pelvis. Her nails dig deeper. Our bodies slick and hot and on the brink.

Then her walls fist my cock with ferocity. A lyrical staccato of moans echoes in my ears as she trembles beneath me. My next thrust forward ends in a detonation of euphoria as my balls draw up and I release inside Peyton.

For a split second, I feel invincible. On top of the world. Atop the tallest mountain peak, howling at the moon. An incomparable high. A high that dissipates much quicker than Peyton's; her eyes rolled and back arched as her body continues to grind and writhe.

When both our bodies settle, I lower her legs and massage her hips. Then I kiss the fuck out of her. Aggressive at first, then almost submissive and more emotional. She tangles her legs with mine. Wraps me in a full-body embrace. Lightly runs her nails up my back and into my hair.

This single moment more intimate than any other. And it is in this exact moment a warmth builds beneath my sternum. Expands and contracts, conforms and comforts. Takes me prisoner and sets me free.

Much as I want to keep her in my bed all day and night, I can't. Much as I want to kiss her for hours and never release her, I can't. Although early, she needs to start her day before work. And I have to learn how to not be selfish and hoard her from the world.

"C'mon." I break the kiss, slowly sit back on my haunches and offer my hand. "Let's shower. Then I'll make you breakfast."

Peyton takes my hand, scoots off the bed, and holds on to me as her noodle legs give out on the way to the bathroom. She walks all wobbly like a newborn giraffe and I bite back laughter as I crank the shower and we step under the spray.

After soaping each other up for longer than necessary, we rinse and towel off. I hand her a pair of my sweats and a T-shirt, and don the same.

I admit I never thought a woman would look sexy in my clothes, but fuck me running because I never want to see Peyton in anything *but* my clothes. None of it snug on her frame or exposing skin other than arms and above the collar.

Just damn.

Reaching out, I fist the shirt near her belly and tug her until our bodies are flush. Drop my lips to hers, clutch the back of her neck and kiss the hell out of her. Then cut the kiss short before I get carried away.

"Really need to leave the bedroom and feed you," I mutter, my lips still on hers.

Slender arms wrap around my waist and pin me to her. "Probably right. Although, I'd rather stay exactly where we are."

"Ugh," I huff out, grab her hand, and stumble out of the bedroom. "C'mon. Time to eat."

Peyton plops down on a stool at the breakfast bar as I get to work in the kitchen. I pull out all the ingredients for French toast, bacon, and sliced fruit. Within minutes, the scent of maple and cinnamon fill the room as I flip the bacon one last time and add the final pieces of French toast to the pan. When the last piece turns golden brown, I plate it, add fresh fruit and bacon on the side, and top the French toast with powdered sugar and whipped cream.

"A girl could get used to this," Peyton states as I set a plate in front of her and hit the brew button on the Keurig.

"Is that so?" I set down our coffees, park on the stool beside her and kiss her temple. "Good to know."

Breakfast with Peyton gives life a new definition of

comfortable. With her, I am more at home than I have been in years. I don't second-guess myself or wonder what comes next. There are no absurd expectations or the need to be someone I am not.

With Peyton, I get to be myself. Not the guy who put up a front and bedded any willing woman because he felt empty and sad. I haven't been me in so long, haven't felt comfortable in my own skin with anyone else, and I love how she has guided the old me back into the light.

All too soon, our plates empty and Peyton prepares to head home before work. I don't let her change back into her clothes—the idea of her out in the world in my tee and sweats is a major turn-on.

"Talk to you later."

"Damn right you will," I say as I frame her face and kiss her one last time. "Have a good night at work, hellcat."

Peyton gets in her car, backs out, and drives off. I walk back into the house, go back to my room, and plop down on the bed. Hints of her coconut mint scent hit my nose and I close my eyes.

It may be too soon—what the hell do I know—but I more than like Peyton. But because I have been burned, I still fear the word that comes with the next level of emotion. So, I ignore the anxiety-inducing four-letter word and just think of her. The woman with golden hair and violet eyes. The woman who has bewitched me in every way possible.

~

Poorly sang rock music pierces my eardrums in an attempt to ruin yet another classic. As great of an idea as karaoke was for Roar, I may have to suggest some songs stay off the list of options. Peyton, on the other hand, snort-laughs her ass off next to Shelly and Cora. The sound equal parts disturbing and adorable as fuck.

My hand on Peyton's thigh under the table gives a gentle squeeze. Turning to face me, her laughter pauses a beat as my favorite smile lights her face. A smile that screams happiness and affection and gratitude. This single glance spreads heat through my chest. Gives me a sense of weightlessness. Fulfills me in an unfamiliar way, but one I don't want to end.

"You seem all too happy these people are trashing classic songs," I tease.

Peyton play smacks my bicep and shakes her head. "Not happy. Plus, I can forget their rendition, if I choose to. But c'mon." She waves a hand toward the stage. "You can't tell me this isn't hilarious to watch."

I narrow my eyes at her, then shift my gaze to the makeshift karaoke stage inside Roar. Karaoke always seems to bring in the oddest mix of people. Every age group and a wide array of music. Current and classic and everything in between. The man with the mic to his lips right now, he slaughters "Ramble On" by Led Zeppelin. Every muscle inside me cringes, but I suppose it is for entertainment.

"Whatever." I shrug. "Gonna go work in the office." I lean closer, so only she hears my next statement. "Join me in a bit."

"Yes." She inches back. "I'll hang here a bit longer, do rounds then be there."

Pressing a kiss to her temple, I rise from the chair and excuse myself. "See you guys later."

I don't rush to the office. My stride is a hair slower than usual as I nod and smile to patrons on the way. I make my way inside the office, shut the door, and drop down in the chair behind the desk. Get to work and don't fret over when Peyton will join me. Although most have inferred we are a couple, we don't need people believing either of us slacks off on the job.

In the middle of ordering, the door opens and in walks Peyton. Hair half up in a messy bun with the rest trailing down her back. Black dress slacks snug on her thighs, her sculpted ass partially visible under the tail of her mint-green top. A top that allows me an occasional view of her cleavage.

"How's it coming along in here?" Peyton asks as she saunters over.

"About done." I spin the chair to face her, lean back and tilt my head as I bite my bottom lip. "Things good out there?" I avert my gaze to the door momentarily with a nod.

"Mmhm." She braces herself on the chair arms, slips a leg between mine and closes the space between us.

When our lips meet, I sit up straighter. Snake my arms around her waist. Awkwardly lower her to my lap; the two of us a fumbling mess of limbs. She shifts her leg and scoots forward as I do the same. My hands slip up the back of her shirt and press her impossibly closer.

It would be so easy to strip her bare and take her on the desk. Swipe my arm across the oak and send paperwork flying. Fling pens to the floor and bend her over. Slap her ass and take her from behind. Press her cheek to the grain and tug the loose strands of her hair as I pummel her over and over.

God, would it be easy. Which is why I won't go through with it.

Much as I would love to fuck Peyton every waking minute of the day, we need rules. Rules that include behaving—minus the occasional kiss—at work. If rules aren't set, we will spend every Wednesday and Thursday in this office doing R-rated acts. Ani may be Peyton's friend, but she would not be too pleased to pay us to make out or fuck like horny teens on the clock.

I break the kiss and lean back into the chair. "We should work." The jut of her lower lip and batting lashes is adorable as hell. And damn, it begs me to break every rule put in place. "I'd much rather kiss you all night, but—and I can't believe I'm the one saying this—we should behave."

She leans back, a smirk on her lips and a knowing look in her eyes. "Who knew?"

My brows bunch together. "What?"

"That Micah Reed would choose to be the responsible one." She rises from my lap, gives me a chaste kiss and adjusts her top as she starts for the door. Twisting the knob, she stops and looks over her shoulder. "I like it." The corners of her mouth kick up. "A lot." Then she waltzes out the door and leaves me to finish the office work. Alone.

For a solid five minutes, I stare at the door. Not in the hopes she will walk through again. The opposite, actually. Because Peyton Alexander is nothing like I expected. She is next level. A commanding force, but also a woman who will submit when asked. An exquisite creature who captivates me at every turn. She keeps me on my toes and surprises me with each step forward we take. She has me dreaming of possibilities.

Of next steps and the years to come. With her.

fourteen

PEYTON

Arriving at Roar early, I park beside Micah's truck with a wide-stretched smile on my face. Neither of us gets here early to do anything untoward. But the free time with no eyes on us is nice.

Before heading inside, I walk the short distance to the mailbox cluster for the plaza, unlock the club's postal box, and retrieve the mail. Thick stack of envelopes in hand, I hike my purse higher on my shoulder and enter through the employee door. Low-volume rock music plays from the speakers in the main room and floats down the hall. I drop the stack of mail and my purse on the desk and stroll out to the main area of the club.

Micah sets up the Bar Olympics, unaware of my presence. As I have on several occasions, I hang back at the edge of the hallway and watch him. Stare at his broad shoulders, thick arms, and dexterous fingers. Fingers that have clenched my throat and pinched my nipples. I swallow and drop my gaze to his trim waist and sculpted ass, snug in his slacks. An ass I have dug my nails into more than once. I lick my lips as he moves around with ease and an air of masculinity.

Oblivious to company, Micah is his true self. More laid back and effortless. Relaxed. No front or phony disposition. No flashy smiles or smart remarks. He is just… him.

And I love seeing this side of him. Love seeing him more himself. Quiet and focused and determined. It is a side not many get to see. Not even his family. I consider myself lucky I get the privilege.

"Gonna keep fawning over me?" he says, barely over the music, with his back to me.

Pushing off the wall, I walk in his direction. "What can I say? I was enjoying myself." When I reach him, he sets the red plastic cups down and grabs hold of my hip. "How long have you been here?"

I rest my forearms on his shoulders and toy with his hair. "Not long. You?"

"Maybe thirty minutes." He presses one, two, three chaste kisses to my lips.

Doing my best to behave, I don't push for more. I will save that for after hours. "Need help?"

He kisses the tip of my nose, then steps back. "Sure."

After the Olympics are set up, we both head to the office. Olympics night has become such a hit in the last few weeks, it ends up being an all-hands-on-deck-while-open event. Micah and I help out on the floor and behind the bar to keep the night flowing as smoothly as possible.

Micah shakes the mouse to wake up the computer as I start opening the mail. A few invoices and payments later, I come across an envelope addressed to Micah. There is a return address, but no company name.

"Here." I hold the envelope out in his direction. "This is addressed to you."

His forehead scrunches as his brows pull together. He

takes the envelope and stares at the return address as if waiting for it to tell him the sender's name. After a moment, he flips it over and tears at the flap. Takes out a folded piece of paper and flattens it out. He scans the paper but doesn't move otherwise.

From where I stand, the words are unreadable. The typed letter appears brief with a printed logo on the top left.

Unable to bear the silence any longer, I speak up. "What is it?"

When he lifts his head and his starry eyes meet mine, I stop breathing. He looks as if he has seen a ghost. Skin gray, eyes dull, lips slightly parted. Frozen in fear.

Nausea rolls in my belly. Has me taking slow breaths and swallowing to settle the sensation. But until he answers, I know the feeling won't vanish.

"Micah?" I walk around the desk and touch his shoulder.

He holds up the letter for me to take. "It's from a clinic." I glance down at the paper. "To take a paternity test." Glassy eyes stare up at me in shock. His jaw shifts left to right, again and again. "Tomorrow."

Oh shit.

How long has it been since the woman in the red dress set foot in Roar and claimed Micah fathered the baby in her belly? More than a month. Hell, closer to two months have passed. Her silence hadn't made me forget her. But I had hoped she would take her accusation train somewhere else.

Who knows… maybe Micah was the easiest guy to pin down because she knew his workplace. Her other rendezvous may have been with random guys in clubs. And if no names were exchanged, she would have no way to find the *actual* father. Unfortunately for Micah, his job made him an easy target in this situation.

I take the paper from his hands and read it line by line.

Mr. Micah Reed:

This letter serves to notify you of a scheduled paternity test requested by Ms. Janine Vallons and her attorney, Kristin Montgomery, Esq.

The test will be performed at Life and Wellness Health Facility, Friday, August 5th at 12:00 p.m.

Please bring one form of government-issued identification and arrive at least thirty minutes prior to the appointment time listed to fill out paperwork.

Regards,

Life and Wellness Health Facility

"How the hell is it acceptable to give a person less than twenty-four hours' notice?" I bark out.

Micah keeps his eyes trained on the desk and doesn't say a word. I swipe the envelope up and look at the date stamp from the post office. Postmarked on Tuesday. Even if it arrived yesterday, the short notice is unprofessional and mind-boggling—especially by mail. I would love to give this facility a piece of my mind. But without knowing if it was them or the attorney acting through them, it would be uncouth of me to do so.

Frozen in place, Micah has yet to look up, react, or speak in regard to the situation. He needs time to process it all, but seeing him like this forms an empty pit in my stomach. But now is not the time to focus on how I feel. Now, I need to pour all my energy into Micah. Help him—us—get past this momentary road block.

Because we will get past it.

I comb my fingers through his hair—slow and gentle. Over and over, without a word spoken. Little by little, he leans into my touch. Closes his eyes, then slowly spins the chair until he faces me. Places a hand on my hip, then the other, and pulls me into him. Rests his forehead on my belly and draws in ragged breaths.

"Don't ask me how, but I *know* this baby isn't mine. But taking a test, having some lab run my DNA against an unborn baby's sample, terrifies me more than anything." His voice trembles as he hugs me closer.

Fingers still in his hair, I continue to comb through his locks and soothe him—and me—the best I can. "I believe you. This letter… anyone receiving this would be nervous as hell. But we'll get through this."

Slowly, he leans back and lifts his eyes until they hold mine prisoner. Red veins crowd the whites of his eyes. The usual sparkle in his irises is absent. "Will you go with me?" Tears well his eyes as he digs his fingers into my hips and awaits my answer.

Seems such a simple question to answer. A short word in response. Weeks ago, my first response would have probably been no. Or that I needed to think it over and get back to him. Not that there is much time, but the me from weeks ago would have made him wait. Possibly until hours before the appointment.

Now, Micah and I are different people. Apart and together. The dynamic of our relationship has changed. Leveled up. It holds power and strength and heart. Isn't solely based on attraction, but something more powerful. Hidden beneath the surface. Deeper. More profound. Something only he and I see and feel and grasp.

I frame his face with my hands. Brush my thumbs over the slight stubble on his cheeks. Hold his starry, constellation gaze. "Yes." I bend and press a kiss to his lips. "I'll go with you."

"Thank you," he whispers, then turns into my hand and kisses the center of my palm.

"Anytime." I press another kiss to his forehead. "Do you want to stay back here tonight? Or be on the floor?"

Unsure how his mood will be around others, I give Micah the option to choose. I would want the choice if our roles were reversed.

"If I stay in here, I'll drive myself mad."

"'Kay." I comb my fingers through his hair again. "Let's wrap things up in here and then we can both spend tonight on the floor. Sound good?"

"Perfect." He gives my hips one last squeeze, drops his hands and swivels back to face the desk. "And Peyton?"

"Yeah?"

"Thank you." I tilt my head at him. "For not running. For agreeing to go with me to the clinic."

I give him a small half smile. "You're welcome." I hold his eyes a beat longer. "Now, get to work, starlight."

"Yes, ma'am, hellcat."

fifteen

MICAH

Fuck.

Can't hold the goddamn pen to save my life. But I will be damned if *Janine* sees my hand—or any other part of me—shake. Hell. No.

I stare down at the stack of papers trapped under the metal prong on the clipboard and lose focus. Zone out as the reality of what is happening hits harder. Black printed letters swirl in a sea of white and yellow and green sheets of paper. The letters jumble and spell new words. Words I refuse to believe until they are proven true.

I am not the father of this child. I am not the father of this child.

In thirty minutes, I have to let some unknown doctor or nurse stick an oversized cotton swab into my mouth and swipe it over the inside of my cheek. Take a sample of my DNA, seal it in a tube, and process it in some random lab to tell me whether or not I fathered an unborn baby.

I lift a loose fist to my lips, close my eyes, take a deep, shaky breath, and fight the bile creeping up my throat.

Then, the sensation subsides. Warmth radiates in my chest

and settles every anxiety-ridden thought. I open my eyes and spy Peyton's hand on my thigh. Her thumb stroking back and forth, back and forth. The small motion and weight of her hand is exactly what I need. An elixir.

She leans in, her breath hot on my ear and soothing for my soul. "Want me to fill it out?"

Peyton doesn't ask because I appear incompetent. She asks because this is one of the most stressful circumstances in my adult life. Although I try to mask my difficulties, she sees the slight tremor in my limbs. The occasional bounce in my knee. Hears the slight hiccup in my breathing. Notices the fact I haven't brought pen to paper and filled out the documents yet.

And this amazing woman—one I am damn lucky to call mine—offers to help. Offers to be my strength when I fear I cannot be.

"No, I got it." I take a slow, deep breath. "Just don't move your hand. Please."

Once I finish the paperwork, which was way more involved than the basic questions a general practitioner asks, I hand it back to the man behind the reception counter and he returns my identification. Janine has yet to make an appearance, but I assume since she set all this up, she completed paperwork ahead of time.

Somewhere nearby, a clock second hand ticks softly behind the generic doctor waiting room music. A muted television plays a home renovation show. Disinfectant mixes with artificial rose air freshener and creates an unpleasant smell. And every five seconds, the man behind reception gives me a sad half smile.

The walls inch closer and my breath comes in short bursts. My nails bite the skin at the center of my palms and form deep crescent moons. I blink a few times as the room seems to bend and flex around me. The need to vomit and pass out hit me simultaneously as I break out in a cold sweat.

Can't say I remember being claustrophobic at any point in my life, but I feel trapped inside myself. Incapable of doing anything, of speaking up, of running away. Is that what claustrophobia feels like? Being a prisoner in your own skin?

"You okay?" Peyton whisper-asks.

I subtly shake my head. "Not so much."

She studies my face a beat. "Shit. You're pale. Don't move." She bolts from the chair and steps into the bathroom off the waiting area. Before the count of ten, she sits beside me and presses a cool, damp paper towel to the back of my neck. "Deep breaths," she whispers. "Close your eyes. I'm here. I got you."

I do as she suggests and close my eyes. Focus on my breathing and her hand at the back of my neck as the other draws small, lazy circles on my thigh. And it helps. Settles my heart rate and breathing. Calms my crazed thoughts of *what if*.

And Peyton is the key. The epicenter of tranquility. If not for her, I would be passed out on the floor.

"Thank you," I say and lay a hand over hers. "Wouldn't be able to get through this without you."

She kisses my temple. "Glad you have me."

"Me too."

"Mr. Reed?" a shorter woman asks as she steps into the waiting area with a file folder clutched to her chest.

"Yes," I choke out. "That's me."

She gives a bright smile, one I am sure she reserves for clients. "If you'll come with me."

Looking at Peyton, I ask, "Can she come back too?"

"Yes." She nods to reaffirm. "She may join us."

We rise from our chairs and head for the door. Just as we reach it, the front door to the clinic office opens and in walks Janine. The first thing I notice is how *large* her belly is. Like way too big to be only roughly three months pregnant, but not quite third trimester pregnant.

But I don't have time to think on it as the woman in the white coat escorts us farther into the lab.

The first thing I notice as we walk down a corridor is how sterile this place looks and feels. Not that doctor offices don't typically appear neat and hygienic, but this place is next level. Bare white walls—no generic health posters in cheap frames or doctorate degrees. Shiny light-gray linoleum floors that reflect the fluorescent lighting and squeak if you stub your shoe sole. And the antiseptic smell… the stinging smell ten times worse back here than the waiting room.

White coat lady leads us into a small room off the hall and directs me to sit on the exam table. Peyton sits in a chair off to the side and remains quiet as the woman explains the process.

"Mr. Reed, the procedure to collect your DNA sample is simple and painless." She points to a paper-lined tray on a rolling cart where sealed tubes and packaged cotton swabs wait to be used. "This tube is labeled with a barcode matching that in our file." She opens my file, then holds up the tube and shows me the matching barcodes. "This is to protect your sample once it goes to processing. Your name will not appear on anything, which keeps the test confidential. After processing, your DNA sample is then destroyed." She sets the tube back on the tray and closes the file. Then points to the sealed cotton swab. "The sterile swab will be used to catch saliva and cells from your cheek. Then it is placed in the tube and a new seal is placed on the sample. Do you have any questions before I collect the sample?"

The test seems pretty straightforward and noninvasive. I expected needles and hair plucking and skin scraping until I searched the web last night. When I learned a ball of cotton on a long stick would be rubbed along the inside of my cheek, I questioned the testing system. Seems too easy. To swipe someone's cheek to learn their internal fingerprint.

"How long will the results take?" I ask.

This is the biggest question of all. First and foremost—gut instinct told me from the start, this baby isn't mine. Second— seeing the size of Janine's belly when she walked into the clinic, instinct went into hyperdrive. The sooner I have the results, the sooner this clinic confirms what I know deep in my soul, the sooner this whole debacle will be over.

And although I swear the outcome will swing in my favor, it doesn't stop the constant, violent buzz from the hornet's nest inside my rib cage.

"Test results typically come back in two to five days, depending on how busy the lab is. With the pregnancy at nineteen weeks, the sample from the mother is easier to attain. As soon as the results are available, we send them to the email address you listed as well as a physical copy via postal mail. Any other questions?"

I shake my head. "No, ma'am." But I do stash the pregnancy time frame away for further thought.

"Very good."

The tech or nurse or doctor—whatever she is—walks over to the small sink and sets the file on the counter before washing her hands. She resumes her position in front of me and goes through a routine she probably does dozens of times per day.

She picks up glove one and works her hand into it. Sweat pricks my forehead and temples.

Repeats the process for glove two. A drop of sweat rolls down my temple and lodges itself in the stubble I have yet to shave.

She breaks the seal on the tube and sets the stopper on the tray. I swallow in an effort to rid the lump in my throat.

Next, she peels open the cotton swab package and removes the largest Q-Tip I have ever seen. My pulse whooshes loud and fast and hard in my ears.

"Open your mouth as wide as possible, please," she instructs.

I follow her instructions and avert my gaze to the ceiling. Bad enough I have to do this, but to witness the process... no thanks. Seconds that mirror centuries pass as the cotton wad scrapes and swirls and gathers from my cheek. My fingers curl into fists as my breathing escalates. I work to focus on anything except the fibrous material collecting my cells.

"All done," the woman states. My eyes open and I watch as she places the swab in the tube, replaces the stopper, peels a red strip off a paper and seals it around the tube and stopper. "This sticker assures your sample is not contaminated before processing. If the sample gets opened, this sticker separates and lets the technician know the sample has been opened and compromised."

She peels the gloves away, tosses them in the red biohazardous waste bin and washes her hands again. She dries her hands with paper towels, tosses them in the bin, collects my patient file and sample, then guides us to the door.

"One last stop before you leave," she states. "If you'll follow me."

We continue down the corridor and stop another twenty feet down beside a smoky sliding window. She knocks on the window and a moment later, it slides open.

"Afternoon, Becca," a man says with a smile.

"Hey, Frank. Sample drop off."

My eyes remain locked on the long tube as she hands it over to the man. He takes it and tosses me a cordial smile. Before another word is spoken, the tube disappears from view and the window shuts.

"You're all set. Let me walk you out to the front." The woman steps in front and leads us to the waiting area door.

Peyton laces her fingers with mine and gives them a squeeze. I glance her way, take in her subtle smile and gentle eyes. How she studies me, reads the words I don't speak aloud. I soak up her quiet strength and tenacious affection. An affection I never expected to receive, but will cherish every day I have it.

No one occupies the waiting room when we step out. The receptionist confirms my email and mailing address and phone number one last time before we leave. He reiterates how and when I will receive the results. Then we leave.

"Hungry?" Peyton asks as she drives us out of the lot.

"Yes and no. Probably should eat."

"I'll find somewhere closer to the house."

For a beat, a small sliver of my brain focuses on how Peyton said *the* house and not *your* house. Call my thought process juvenile, I don't give a fuck, but small differences like that do crazy things to my heart.

Unfortunately, all happy thoughts leave my head as I recycle what just happened at the clinic. Hundreds of what-if questions cycle through my mind. Questions that have no resolute answer until the results hit my inbox. Of course, I can speculate where all this will lead, but without answers, it isn't worth expending the energy or torturing myself.

Then, I recall something else. *"With the pregnancy at*

nineteen weeks, the sample from the mother is easier to attain." Nineteen weeks. Nineteen. Weeks. What is that in months? Just shy of five, and half the normal gestation period of human pregnancy.

Five months seems like too long.

Two months have passed since she came into Roar with her announcement. Call me crazy, or ignorant, but don't most women have some sign or symptom of pregnancy within a month or so? If she is nineteen weeks, that means she was roughly eleven weeks along when she spoke up. Which makes no sense whatsoever.

I think back to months ago. Run through the faces of women I went to bed with and when. A not-so-simple task since I slept with dozens of women in the months leading up to me and Peyton. The moment sparks flew between us, the moment I thought it possible to have more with Peyton, I refused to be with another woman.

When I finally recall Janine's face, my eyes go wide. She was literally one of the last few women I slept with before cutting myself off. At the end of April.

"This baby isn't mine," I say over the radio.

Peyton pats my thigh before leaving her hand there. "I hope that's true, but we won't know until the results are back."

I turn in the passenger seat to face her and all but slice my throat with the seat belt. After I adjust the belt, I continue my thought. My voice stronger, louder, bolder this time. "No. I mean, there is no possible way this baby is mine."

Peyton takes her eyes off the road a split second to narrow them at me. "How can you be so sure?"

I lay my hand over hers and take a cleansing breath. "The

person who took my sample, she said Janine is nineteen weeks."

"Yeah, so?"

"Since the letter yesterday, I've been in my head a lot. One thing I remembered…" I pause for a beat and take a deep breath. "…is when I was with her. Yes, I have been with a lot of women, but I don't forget a face. Ever. And I've been thinking about it, really thinking about it, since that woman said nineteen weeks."

I stare out the driver's side window. Take in the Bay as the sun glistens on the water. Stare after the seagulls as they fight over scraps from an unlidded trash bin. For the first time in less than twenty-four hours, a sense of relief washes over me.

"And? Don't leave me hanging."

"I was with her near the end of April. Fourteen, maybe fifteen weeks ago. Tops. Just before I stopped hooking up."

"You mean, before there was potential for us."

"Yes." I wrap her hand with my own. "Even if the chances were slim, I didn't want to fuck up the opportunity." I lift her hand and kiss her knuckles. "So, without a doubt, I *know* this baby isn't mine."

"Why do you think she came to you then?"

I shrug. "Was probably the easiest person to find. She knew where I worked. If she hooked up with random strangers in clubs or bars, chances are she has no way to find them. Not unless they exchanged numbers or hooked up at the other person's house."

"Are you sure you're remembering the correct person at the correct time?" She peers over from the driver's seat, a smirk on her lips. "You do have a thing for blondes. No doubt they all blend together." Her tone is teasing, but I get her meaning.

With my free hand, I reach over, pinch a strand of her champagne locks between my fingers, and give a slight tug. "Blondes have more fun. I should know, I am one."

"Ha ha." She makes a silly face, but I only catch her profile.

I twirl her hair around a finger and simply watch her as she drives. Can't recall a time in my life where a woman has made me so introspective. Has made me really dig deep and see past the mundane. Has made me want more from life—not because that is what I should do, but because I want more with her.

"Or maybe I wanted one specific blonde and the others were mental distractions."

We reach a red light and she faces me. "What?" She appears genuinely confused by my admission.

"Peyton, it's no secret I pined for you from the beginning. Even the days when you verbally bit my head off, I still wanted you." Laughter vibrates my chest. "For so long, I never knew why you despised me from the get-go. At first, I thought it was your form of banter. But soon realized it wasn't. I didn't want to give up, though."

The light turns green and she faces the road again. We remain quiet the rest of the drive until Peyton parks at a delicatessen near the house. The restaurant somewhat busy considering the time of day.

Unbuckling her belt, she twists to face me fully. I mimic the action, and for a moment, we just sit and stare at each other. Her violet irises hidden behind dark lenses as she holds my gaze. With some, I would shake off their nonstop gaze. But with Peyton, I want her eyes on me as often as possible. Want the attention she gives and the radiance it generates just beneath my sternum and to the left.

"Glad you didn't," she says.

Glad I didn't what? I scrunch my brow. "What?"

"Give up. I'm glad you didn't."

For three breaths, I sit immobile. Then I lean across the console, wrap my hand around the back of her neck, pull her close, and kiss the hell out of her. We make out like teenagers in the parking lot for several minutes. I don't know who breaks the kiss, but I press my forehead to hers when it ends.

"Me too, hellcat. Me too."

sixteen

PEYTON

Rolling over, I curl into Micah's side. Breathe in the scent of him; a faint hint of his cologne mixed with a scent distinct to Micah. Bask in his warmth and comfort, and snuggle his frame. He curls an arm around my waist, hugs me impossibly closer, and eliminates all space between us. Then he kisses the top of my head and I sigh and kiss his shoulder.

"Morning." His raspy tone wakes up more than my mind.

Throwing a leg over his hips, I roll to straddle him and press my breasts into his chest. "Morning."

Since Sunday evening, after hanging out at Autumn and Jonas's place, I have spent every night in Micah's bed. Woken up the next morning with our limbs twisted in new pretzel shapes. Been pummeled by or ridden on his dick after we say good morning. Dug my nails into his skin and bruised it with my lips.

And each morning after we come, I want him again. In the shower. On the couch or kitchen counter or dining table. Against the glass wall facing the backyard. Out back on the veranda. Wherever I can have him. His head between my legs or me on my knees in front of him or both our mouths on each other.

Micah Reed makes me insatiable. A wanton creature. For him, and only him.

How many times per day is considered abnormal? Is too much sex unhealthy? I would think not, but I am no sex therapist. All I know is I have never felt so damn good in my life.

I bury my nails in his pecs. Mark my ownership of him next to the previous marks, now fading. Rock my hips harder as he holds on to them and jerks up into me over and over. The delicious rhythm drives me higher and higher. I tip my head back, hair tickling my tailbone as I close my eyes and gasp at the ceiling. He rams into me as I slam down on him.

Familiar, delicious heat builds low in my abdomen. Spirals up, up, up until it hits between my breasts and disperses like wildfire. Fire crawls up my chest, my neck, my face. My eyes roll back in my head. Panted high-pitch whimpers and throaty grunts ricochet off the walls. The animalistic scent of sex drifts through the air. My body starts to constrict Micah's cock. He clamps down on my nipples—hard—and tugs with a twist.

I sink my nails deeper and shatter around him. My body exhausted yet eager for more. He flips me on my back and pistons hard and fast. The headboard smacks the wall as skin slaps skin. He bruises my thighs with his fingers. Slides a hand up my abdomen, my breast and stops at my throat. His thumb, third and fourth fingers clamp down, making me dizzy and euphoric.

Slap. Slap. Slap.

Stars fill my vision, my breaths come in short bursts, and my body constricts his once more. Micah growls into my neck, crushes my pelvis with his, and releases inside me.

His arms buckle and he gives me his full weight. And I welcome it. Wrap my legs around his waist and arms around his chest. Bear-hug him to my chest and breathe in the scent of our sweat and orgasms. Trace my fingers up his spine and over his scalp.

"Never want to wake up without you," he mumbles into the crook of my neck.

I freeze at his words. Not because they frighten me or make me want to bolt. Quite the opposite, actually. A lightness I have never experienced with anyone slips into my bloodstream. Consumes me. Fashions a new energy in the chambers of my heart and pumps it through my veins. Warms me in ways I never thought possible.

My limbs relax and I comb my fingers through his hair. "Me either."

He kisses up my neck, sucks the sensitive spot beneath my ear, then kisses his way to my lips. "C'mon." He pushes up and scoots off the bed. "Let's shower, then eat." Standing at the foot of the bed, he grabs my ankles and yanks me down. Me and the bedding plummet to the floor and I erupt in a fit of laughter.

When I gain control, I sit eye level with his cock. His not-so-soft cock. I lift my gaze to his and lick my lips.

"Hellcat…" he says in warning. "Shower." I push out my lower lip and aim for my saddest puppy eyes. He growls. "Now." He offers his hand and I take it.

"Fine," I say on a huff, then stomp off to the bathroom.

Little does he know, I have tricks up my invisible sleeve.

By the time we step out of the shower, our skin is wrinkly and legs wobbly. But damn, do I feel like a queen. Micah definitely makes a great devotee and king.

We move around the kitchen like an old married couple.

He whips up eggs, sausage, home fries, and toast while I cut fruit and brew coffee. His task seems more daunting, but it works for us. In no time, we plate up food and sit at the bar to eat.

We push food around our plate more than eat it. Forks scraping the ceramic, occasional chewing, and coffee slurps are the only sounds in the room. Breakfast came out perfect... we just don't have the oomph to enjoy it.

Today is day five. Five treacherous, unbearable days have passed.

And although I haven't seen him on his phone this morning, Micah has probably checked his email several times. Which means nothing has arrived yet. If it had, whatever the result, I would be the first to know—after him, of course.

We finish breakfast in amicable silence, then plop down on the couch and watch a movie until it is time to dress for work. Arms wrapped around each other, we cuddle on the couch and do our best to not pick at our nails or tap our fingers with unreleased nervous energy.

But every now and then, Micah's knee bounces or his breathing picks up. He tries to not let it show, but I notice. I just keep it to myself.

The movie ends and we amble to the bedroom to dress for work. We move slower than usual, but it isn't long before we head for the door. Since I have stayed with Micah the past few nights, we decide to take one car to work on the days we both go in. Why waste the gas?

In this very moment, driving together works out in our favor.

His phone alerts him to an incoming email as we slip into my SUV. He opens the message after buckling his belt. All I can do is stare and wait while he reads the screen.

How can five seconds feel like five years? My heart beats out of my chest as I wait for some reaction from him. The downturn of his lips. A smile worthy of conquering the world. Anything.

Finally, he breaks the silence.

"Hell yeah!" he screams in the confines of the car. "Woo!" His whole body vibrates as the biggest smile I have ever seen brightens his face.

This has to be good news for him. Please let it be good news.

"Not a match?" I ask, just to be certain.

"There is zero probability that the donor tested has any familial relationship," he reads from the email, then faces me. "Zero. Zilch. Nada. I knew it! I fucking knew it!"

Thank goodness I hadn't backed us out of the driveway yet. Micah bounces around like a kid high on too much Halloween candy. No way in hell I would be able to focus on the road with his excitement. Not to mention my own.

Relief I never knew possible hits me like a summer downpour. *Zero probability. No familial relationship.* The sudden weightlessness exhilarates and consoles me. *Jesus.* I didn't realize how badly I needed to hear those words.

Not that I wouldn't have stood by Micah's side if the opposite result was delivered. But this... happy and relaxed are a microscopic percentage of the elation I feel right now.

I unbuckle my belt, claw across the console for him, haul him to me and hug the hell out of him.

"Deep down, I knew it too. Glad the results finally came and were what we thought and hoped they would be."

Strong arms hold me close. "Just glad this is over and we can put it behind us now."

"Me too."

Micah leans back enough to look me in the eye. "We should go, but..." He waggles his brows, his radiant smile still firmly in place. "We are definitely celebrating later."

"Celebrating, huh? And what exactly did you have in mind?"

He shrugs. "Hadn't gotten that far yet. Still have plenty of time to figure that part out."

After I buckle my belt again, I back out of the driveway and head toward Tampa. Micah cranks up the music and sings obnoxiously with the songs on the radio. From the corner of my eye, I watch him every chance I get.

I love his new ease and cheery disposition. The endless smile highlighting his sharp jaw. The additional sparkle in his starry eyes. The happy-go-lucky attitude emanating from him.

I am beyond glad this whole fiasco with the red-dress woman will soon become a distant memory. One we will have no problem erasing.

Now... it is time to build new memories. Better ones to replace all the bad. And I am eager to get started.

seventeen

MICAH

All stress left my body after reading that email. An email I plan to print and stash in the miscellaneous file for years to come. Not that I think Janine will try to pull something in the future. More as a reminder of my idiotic past choices and how they could have ruined what continues to bloom between me and Peyton.

Nothing will ruin what I have with Peyton.

My face hurts from the smile that won't fade. But I will take the pain and smile twice as hard. Brighten the world with my pearly teeth and endless exuberance. This pain is the best pain. And later tonight, I don't care what we do, but we sure as fuck will celebrate.

Peyton pulls into a space behind Roar. Soon as she throws the car in park, I whip off my belt, frame her face with my hands, and kiss the hell out of her. Kiss her until we both gasp for breath. She whimpers as the kiss breaks and it only makes my smile stretch wider.

I love how I leave her wanting more. Love how difficult it will be to resist temptation all night. Most of all, I love how it leads into the best seven-plus hours of foreplay. By the time we get home, her need for me will be ravenous. Even then, I may drag it out a bit longer.

"You head in. I'll get the mail," I say, then smack her ass.

"Best watch yourself, Reed." The way my last name rolls off my tongue does crazy things to my body.

"Yeah? Why's that, hellcat?"

"You're not the only one who likes to play games." Her lips kick up in a devious half smile, and then she winks. "See you inside." She disappears inside Roar and leaves me standing in the lot, bedazzled and horny.

After fetching the mail, I head inside. Peyton has parked herself behind the desk and works on all the monotonous tasks. So, I head out to the main part of the club and prep for Karaoke Night.

Time flies faster than usual and soon the rest of the staff arrives, does their prep work, and we unlock the doors for the evening. Drinks get mixed and poured. Horrible renditions of songs I love get belted out. And my favorite group of people walks through the front door.

Although karaoke had never been a favorite pastime, I love that I see Shelly and my friends more than once a week now. Love that I have a chance to sit with them and catch up more often. With my odd work hours, it hasn't always been easy to hang out.

Before long, Shelly and Cora skip off the stage after their third song. Everyone finishes their drinks, exchanges hugs, and says they will see us Sunday.

Last call is announced and the Wednesday crowd starts to thin. A few patrons linger to slam one more glass before calling it a night. The staff shuffles around the club and rushes to complete their end-of-night duties. Minutes later, the front doors lock and we clean up faster than any previous night.

One by one, the staff clocks out and heads home. In less than thirty minutes, Peyton and I do the same.

"Food from the diner near the house?" I toss out.

"Sounds good. Maybe we can grab dessert too."

It is on the tip of my tongue to tell her *she* is the only dessert I want. But I resist the urge and think of what I may do with said dessert. "Yeah, sure."

I place an order online for burgers, fries, milkshakes, and half a peanut butter pie from the diner near the house. We drive across the Bay with the windows down and the music loud. Salty air licks our skin and whips our hair. Our fingers laced over the center console and thumbs brushing the other's hand.

This right here… this is perfect.

Some of the simplest things in life are the most notable. Like a lover's hand in your own. Listening to them sing with the radio as you drive down the highway. The glimmer in their eye when they give you a side-glance and smile. Those small details are ones I deem most precious. I hug them close to my heart and don't take them for granted.

Lost in thoughts of us, I miss the moment Peyton pulls into the diner parking lot. Miss her pull into a space and put the car in park. But I don't miss her laugh when she looks over at me with raised brows and wide eyes.

"You want me to get the food?"

I break contact with her and stare out the windshield. Bright neon lights spell out *open* in red as the smell of fryer grease hits my nose.

"Oh. No, I got it," I fumble over my words as I unbuckle and exit the car.

In and out of the diner in less than a minute, we head back to the house with growling stomachs. Peyton parks behind my truck and I scoop up the bags. We amble to the front door, hand in hand, without a worry in the world.

We drop down on the couch and I take the food out of the bag, depositing take-out boxes on the table. She moves beside me as she has every night for weeks. And then it hits me. A new version of contentment. The ease at which Peyton and I have fallen into this new routine. Eating dinner on the couch with our legs crossed and knees bumping. Watching movies and television shows together as she curls into my side. Kissing and groping until we land in the sheets and sweat and moan our way toward ecstasy.

And I hope to do this every night and day with her in the future. Enjoy the simple moments. Like a shared meal or making breakfast together. Merge our lives. Become something bigger than who we are individually. Discover a new way to exist together. Find a happiness no one can dull. A happiness brighter than any star in the galaxy.

I finish my burger, set my empty take-out box on the table beside hers, hit pause on the show, then pull her onto my lap and hug her close. Peyton combs her fingers through my hair as I tip my head back and close my eyes. Being like this with her—vulnerable and more myself than ever—is the most freeing moment in my life.

Yes, I want to tear her clothes off and taste every inch of her right now. But the intimacy in this moment—her fingers lazy in my hair, eyes heating my skin, her coconut mint scent in the air, breath inches from my lips—I want it just as bad.

Intimacy without sex is somewhat new in my life. And I never knew how amazing it could be.

Her weight shifts and the heat of her breath hits my lips a beat before our lips connect. The kiss light at first. A tender graze of soft warmth. Her fingers stop in my hair and lightly tug on the strands as the kiss takes a gradual turn. From sweet and subtle to exploratory and eager to desperate and ravenous.

My hands at her knees inch up her thighs without hurry. The inclination to map her body, memorize every peak and path and adventure it takes me on, overwhelms me. To learn every perfection and imperfection and love them equally. To chart her freckles and name them like constellations. Discover each scar and kiss away any pain they cause.

Sex with Peyton is indescribable. Unlike any experience I had with another person. It isn't just the physicality. Being with Peyton… yes, what we share is raw and primal, deep and carnal. But it is also impeccable and disorienting, covetous and euphoric. Our bond makes me weak in the knees. Light-headed and unsteady.

With Peyton, I don't just picture the physical endgame when we have sex. I envision where it will lead us years from now. Sharing the same bed, day in and out. Not just for sex. I picture her limbs tangled with mine. Breath steady on my chest and palm over my heart. Hair splayed on my shoulder and the pillow. Breasts and hips snug to my side.

"Take me to bed," she whispers against my lips, then kisses me softly.

I snake my arms around her waist. "Hold on tight."

Peyton laces her fingers behind my neck. Scooting to the couch edge, I rise and walk us to the bedroom, her ankles locked at my lower back. Every step forward, she kisses my lips, my chin, the line of my jaw. Nips the lobe of my ear. Sucks the spot just above the pulse in my neck.

Every step forward is a match to the fuse only Peyton lights. One she sparks with her heady touch and reverent kisses. Fire and vibrancy and undiluted need spills from my veins. Every nerve ending wakes and begs for more. And deep in my marrow, my soul connects with hers.

The sensation engulfs me. Swallows me whole with no promise to let go.

And I never want it to let go.

I lay her on the bed. Kiss her as if she may crumble at my touch. Unhook her feet and peel away her clothes. Then my own.

Skin to skin, the world around us disappears. For the next several hours, we connect like never before. Slow and sentimental, as if we have been lovers for a lifetime and not weeks. Every touch is special and new and incomparable to any previous connection we shared.

And when we curl into each other, breathless and sweaty and sated, an imaginary bulb lights in my head.

For the first time, I made love to a woman. Linked myself to her. Connected with her on the most intimate level. Bonded beyond the physical. Something I have never done. At this realization, a sense of wholeness engulfs me. Aligns all the little pieces that never fit right with anyone else.

Peyton does this. Straightens all the jagged edges and fixes all the broken parts. Without effort, Peyton makes me whole. Better. A man.

I squeeze her closer to my side, kiss the crown of her head and resist saying the three small words on the tip of my tongue. Words I have never said to any woman. Words I won't be able to resist saying much longer.

Question is… will Peyton reciprocate? Or has my love for her blinded me?

eighteen
PEYTON

Hoots and hollers mingle with the cacophony of hundreds having conversations. Ping-Pong balls and red plastic cups slap tables. Quarters bounce to the floor. Stacked, precut two-by-fours, grow taller with each move and threaten to teeter.

Bar Olympics night is in full swing. Body odor and upbeat music fill the air. People stand on the sidelines and cheer on the players.

Smaller tables host card games or tic-tac-toe with shots. Bowls of peanuts and pretzels on every other table. While most people here play, several just drink and enjoy watching the festivities. Games aren't tracked via Roar, but most of the regulars make note of who leads who in the different games.

In the last two weeks, Ani and Sean hired more staff for Thursday, Friday, and Saturday. Roar has definitely had an uptick in patronage and sales since the changes took place. At first, the newer crowd was easily handled with the current crew. But not long after, it stressed out the former staff. Now, everyone smiles and goes about business as Ani and Sean envisioned—giving time to the customers and engaging with them so they will return. A win-win.

"One more hour," Micah says as he presses flush to my back, squeezes my hips, and kisses the spot beneath my ear.

"Mmm. Did you have something in mind for when said hour ends? Cause we still have to clean up."

His chest vibrates as a groan spills from his lips. "Several things we shouldn't do here." He kisses my neck and steps back as I spin to face him. "Let's get an early jump on cleaning, so we aren't stuck here all night. Then…" He pauses and stares as if he has something to say but isn't sure. "Maybe we can stay at your place tonight."

Stay at my place? Micah has a quiet, cozy house with no roommate. Why on earth would he want to stay in my tiny two-bedroom apartment with my best friend slash roommate? Not sure why, but it strikes me as odd.

"Something wrong at your house?"

He shakes his head. "No. Thought it'd be nice to experience your bed for once."

He wants to *experience* my bed? What does that mean? My imagination wanders in a blink and I picture Micah jumping on my bed like a child. Compared to his king-size bed, my full will be quite the *experience*. As in, snug and sweltering and a fight for covers.

But, whatever. If Micah wants to *experience* my bed, then that is what we will do.

"Sure thing. We'll pick up food on the way. Haven't grocery shopped since I've been staying at your place."

His lips press to my forehead a second before he smacks my ass. "Now, get to work, hellcat. Don't want to be here all night."

Micah saunters off as Kaylynn approaches with a blinding smile. An all-too-eager smile with dozens of questions. Questions I will *not* answer at work.

Kaylynn and I have been acquaintances from day one. But that is it. We never did anything outside these walls. Not because neither of us wanted to; it never came up. And now, I am her boss. Although we still behave somewhat the same around each other, there are boundaries we shouldn't cross. Boundaries *I* crossed before my promotion. But Ani was aware the entire time.

"Hey, girl," Kaylynn says as she sidles up beside me. "So, you and Micah, huh?"

"Mmhm," I mumble, loud enough for her to hear. Grabbing the clipboard beneath the bar top, I inventory what bottles and beers need to be brought from the storage room.

Less than a foot away, Kaylynn vibrates with curiosity. She has never been one to gossip, but I have never been one to spill my private life to people I don't know well. Yes, we have worked together for more than a year. But... I don't really *know* Kaylynn.

Is she single? Married? Divorced? Straight or bi or lesbian? Does she have children or pets? They are all basic questions, but I don't know the answer to any of them. To be honest, I have no intention of asking either. Unless it is generic conversation and not one where we take mental notes of what shampoo we use and what happens behind closed doors.

Because that is where the conversation seems to be headed.

"How long? And how... is it?"

Micah and I have been hanging out for weeks. Hell, two months plus have passed since the first night I went to his house. But it wasn't until this past weekend, a few days after he made love to me for the first time, that we slapped a title on our relationship. That we dubbed each other boyfriend and girlfriend. Granted, we had been in the role already, we just hadn't given it a name.

But with the direction of our relationship, we figured, why not? In all ways, we fulfilled the role. Why not give the title to everyone who asked?

"For a while. Things are great."

The second half of my response left intentionally vague. She didn't outright ask anything specific. All aspects of our relationship are great, so the answer isn't false.

As she opens her mouth to ask another question, a customer steps up to the bar and distracts her. I take the opportunity to walk off under the guise of restocking the bar.

Down the hall, I unlock and enter the storage room across from the office. On the opposite side of the hall, the office and employee lounge divide the space. The storage room, though, takes up the whole length and is roughly twice as deep.

Everything is organized by type, brand, and what sells faster. Beer fills more than half the space with kegs and cased bottles stacked high. Liquor sits on industrial shelves in rows. Paper goods, glassware and miscellaneous shelf-stable goods fill the remainder of the room.

I grab the items jotted down and set them on a rolling cart we keep for larger restocks. Exiting storage, I lock up and push the cart slower than necessary. Not because it has an overabundance of glass or weighs a lot. More because I want to creep out and locate Kaylynn before she does me.

Peering around the corner, I spot her wiping down the bar. With her back to me. As I round the corner, cart in tow, she reaches for the broom and gets to work on the floors.

Thank god.

Kaylynn is nice. Probably had no ill-meaning behind her inquisition. But I hate being in the position to say *no, I don't want to share my life with you.* Especially with someone who I have somewhat known a little more than a year.

Micah locks the door after the last person leaves. One pro Monday through Thursday… we close early. Much as I love the energy in those late-night hours on Friday and Saturday, I don't miss the exhaustion it brings. Yes, I miss the upbeat tempo and bass vibrating my bones. But not much else. If Micah and I still worked Friday and Saturday together, it wouldn't be like the other days. We would both be too busy to stop and say hello, much less wave across the packed club.

Kaylynn finishes the last of her cleanup as Micah and I stash the Bar Olympics tables in the storage room. We wave her off and do one last sweep of the bar and club before leaving.

I shoulder my purse while Micah shuts off the lights. We walk out, hop in my car and drive toward home.

"Stop by the house so I can grab some clothes."

"Sure. What sounds good to eat?"

At the mention of food, Micah quiets for a moment. His focus out the passenger window with his chin resting on a loose fist. From my vantage point, he appears too serious to be weighing food options.

On our side of the Bay, less than a mile from the house, he speaks up. His voice more reserved than usual.

"Sorry. Was just thinking."

"About?"

"This Sunday is family dinner night."

"Okay." I drag out the second syllable.

"And…" He tucks his lips between his teeth, swallows, then meets my gaze. "Mom wants me to bring you." My eyes widen briefly. "But please don't feel pressured to come if you don't want to," he adds quickly.

Have we reached this point in our relationship? Hell, less than a week has passed since we officially declared ourselves a couple. Does official status equal meeting the parents?

A thin layer of sweat blankets me and makes my clothes cling to my skin. White noise blocks my hearing as my heart pounds harder with each beat. My knuckles whiten as I fist the steering wheel.

Thank god we reach his house without me running a light or rear-ending someone.

I don't *think* it is his parents that have my nerves bouncing like live wires. But the step of meeting family is *huge*. It screams the legitimacy of our relationship. That I am no fluke. That Micah plans to have me around for weeks and months, and possibly years, to come.

Don't get me wrong, I love that he feels this way toward me. That I am not a random woman in his bed. He pictures more for us in the future. He *wants* there to be a future.

Me from a year ago—hell, four months ago—would laugh at the idea of a steady, solid relationship with Micah Reed.

Me today… she smiles painfully big.

Meeting the parents is a big deal, but we have overcome so much in the last three months. If I found a way to forgive Micah for his past discretions, I can swallow my nerves and join his family for dinner.

I pull into his driveway, throw the car in park, and shut off the engine. Since he said his parents wanted me to join family dinner, Micah has sat deathly quiet with his eyes on my profile. And I am grateful he allowed me a moment to digest the request without interruption.

"Dinner on Sunday would be nice," I say as I twist to face him.

His bright smile I love makes an appearance as he leans

forward and kisses me. "Are you sure?" I nod. "Okay. We'll talk more about it later. For now, I want to grab clothes, my toothbrush, then some food." He plants a chaste kiss on my lips, then exits the car.

Once he has everything, we drive off and stop at the Chinese restaurant near my place. It is one of the few places that has late hours. One massive bag of noodles, rice, veggies, and meat later, I drive to my apartment.

As I park in front of the building, it dawns on me I didn't warn Reese. Not that an actual warning is necessary. More like I don't want us walking in the door and interrupting anything. Seeing as I haven't been at the apartment much in the last week or two, Reese has probably had his boyfriend over more. And neither of them understands quiet, if you catch my drift.

Like someone on the prowl, I creep up to the door, slowly insert my key and twist even slower. Micah looks at me as if I have lost my mind. I don't care, though. Twisting the knob, I tiptoe inside and listen for any sounds of fornication.

Micah chuckles behind me. "Will you just go." He taps my ass. "No one will jump out and grab us."

I slap the air behind me, straighten my spine, and step out of the way for Micah to enter. "Sorry. Just wanted to make sure the couch wasn't occupied."

Leading Micah to the kitchen, he sets down the food and his overnight bag. His brows pinch together at the same time his lips pucker. "Does that usually happen? Your roommate having sex on the couch."

His ears must have been ringing because, as Micah finishes speaking, Reese strolls into the kitchen. With no shirt on. And sweat dripping down his abdomen.

"Who's having sex on the couch?" he asks and my cheeks heat.

"No one. Working out?" I ask and pray that was what he was doing.

"Sure." He smiles, then chuckles. "All done now, though." His eyes land on the bag of food. "Did you happen to get *me* dinner? I did just burn a shit ton of calories."

I slap his bicep. "Ew! Shut up. And yes, I got you orange chicken."

Reese hugs me against his sweaty chest. "You're the best." I shove him off with a laugh and he steps toward Micah with his hand extended. "We haven't been formally introduced. Reese."

Micah takes his hand and they shake. "Micah, but I'm sure you already know all about me." This time, they both laugh.

"Wouldn't say I know *all*, but quite a bit."

A moment of awkward silence passes and I beg for someone, anyone, to swoop in and make it end. Thankfully, Reese says he needs to wash up. He also asks if I mind his guest joining us. Of course, I agree and tease him about working out again.

We plate up food and get comfortable on the couch. After we select the next episode of *Peaky Blinders*, Reese and his new beau, Trent, join us.

The next hour is more normal than I imagined it would be. We all laugh and gasp at the same parts as we eat dinner. When the episode ends, we clean up, say our good nights and go to our rooms.

It isn't until we step foot in my room and I watch Micah's expression morph that I laugh. My room isn't girly or dirty or cluttered. But the bed is small. Way smaller than his. Literally half the size. In his defense, I didn't really warn him because I thought it would be fun.

"Great for cuddling," I say, his eyes still zoned in on the bed. "Best way to get closer. Don't you think?"

He laughs with a shake of his head. "I can think of other ways to get closer."

"Oh, really?"

"Mmhm. Come here." He curls his finger in a come-hither motion. "Let's see exactly how close we can get."

For the first time in however many years, I love how small this bed is. And I love how Micah knows the ways to use it to his advantage. Every night and day with him is brighter than the previous. Every one a new experience.

And I never want them to end.

nineteen

MICAH

Weekends at Roar don't hold the same level of energy and exhilaration since Peyton switched days.

Yes, the club is packed with bustling bodies. Loud music spills from the speakers and the air reeks of sweat and hops. Flashes of blue and yellow and red lights hit gyrating bodies and casual bystanders. Everything *looks* the same as it always has.

The missing factor, though, is Peyton. Her heart-stopping smile and infectious laughter. How people hung out at the bar more often because she chatted with them. Funny to say, but I also miss watching her flirt with customers.

Yeah, I have that level of confidence in Peyton and our relationship. Her flirtatious nature exists only between us and with the customers inside these walls. With the customers, it is more about retention and tips. She may not collect tips anymore, but she wants the other staff members to get paid well too.

I finish pouring a round of beers, then tell Caleb I will be back after rounds. He, Adam, and Kaylynn handle the bar while Charity and Jake bus and serve tables. I check in with both of them first. Ask if either need help or if they've had any customer issues.

Then I weave my way toward the front to check in with Ted and Julio. Ask about current occupancy and if there is anything I need to know about. Thankfully, we don't get too many people who cause a ruckus. The occasional belligerent person goes berserk and tries to cause problems. But our team is a solid unit and we don't put up with shit.

"Let me know if anything comes up," I tell them and wander the club's perimeter.

A few weeks back, Sean and Ani invested in wireless communication for the busier nights. Walkies with wired earpieces. Makes me feel like a sleuth or retail security guard. On countless occasions, I respond with "over and out" or "roger that." At this point, it is a running joke to see how goofy we all act over the walkies.

I spend the next ten minutes against the wall opposite the bar. Mindlessly scrolling through social media, I look up every now and then to check the crowd. Bored with my phone, I pocket it and wind my way toward the office. Saturday is one of two days Roar only has one manager on staff. The other night being Monday, when Peyton manages Charity Bingo night solo.

Feet from the office door, I jolt as my walkie crackles in my ear. "Hey, Micah?" Caleb speaks a little too loudly into the mic. Probably to be heard over the music.

I press the button on the corded earpiece. "What's up, Caleb?"

"There's a woman at the bar asking for you."

The first person I picture is Peyton, but I dismiss the idea as quick as it appears. One, she wouldn't come here on her night off unless something was going on. Not only that, but

Caleb would refer to Peyton by name. And why would she come to the bar for me. Simple; she wouldn't. Peyton would have texted or come in through the back. She has the means to find me without asking Caleb.

The next person that comes to mind is Janine. Which freaks me the fuck out. There would be no reason for Janine to come into Roar, much less ask for me. Everything with her and the whole pregnancy situation got resolved a week and a half ago. No valid reason would bring Janine here. I expect to never see or hear from her again.

So, who the hell is here? What woman would come here asking for me?

A shiver rolls up my spine at the idea of some other woman claiming some other bullshit.

Nope. Not happening, universe. No more bullshit. You hear me?

"Did she give her name?" I ask, undecided if I want to peer around the end of the hall and look.

"No. When I offered to get you, she paled."

How fucking weird. A woman comes to the bar and specifically asks for me. But when Caleb says he will get me, she freaks. Why? What purpose does that serve?

"Is she still at the bar?" I walk closer to the open end of the hall and stop a foot short.

"No." He pauses, but still has the button pressed. "She's walking toward the door. White dress, brown hair."

From the end of the hall, I scan the crowd between the bar and door, looking for said woman. When I spy the head of brown hair and white dress, my blood turns to lava.

"What the fuck?" I whisper-growl to myself.

Weaving through the crowd is a brunette with a frame I will never forget. Not because she is drop-dead gorgeous. But because the last time I saw her, she was stark naked, riding another man's cock. One never forgets a moment like that.

Rochelle fucking Cook.

The simple fact she stepped foot in Roar has me nauseous. More than a year has passed since I caught her cheating—moaning another man's name in my bed without care—and ended our relationship. Needless to say, I replaced the bed the next day. No way in hell was I touching or sleeping in a bed someone else fucked my supposed girlfriend in.

My entire relationship with Rochelle wasn't bad. The beginning was absolute fire. We laughed and enjoyed each other's company. Went places and had fun together. But… each month of the twelve we were together became less fire and more monotonous. I didn't see it at first; blinded by infatuation and what I thought was love. Once the relationship ended, I saw everything with new perspective.

And through the grapevine, I learned Rochelle had been unfaithful more than once. Each occurrence was a knife to the chest. Hence, my unwillingness to invest myself with anyone else.

Until Peyton.

Peyton is the light I need in life. Sunshine on the darkest, shittiest day. She gives me hope and promise for the life I never knew I wanted until her. Not necessarily picket fences and immaculate gardens and two-point-five kids. But a life filled with laughter and joy, wonder and intimacy. A life of adventure and challenge and thousands of memories.

"Thanks, Caleb. If you need anything else, I'll be in the office."

"Everything alright?"

I turn on my heel and stroll down the hall and into the

office. Closing the door, I flip the lock into place. "Yep. All good." Peachy fucking keen.

~

Be there in ten.

Perfect timing. Pizza just arrived.

On more than one occasion, the word *love* has come to mind when talking with or thinking of Peyton. Oddly enough, it doesn't freak me out. Not like it did past me and guys in my inner circle.

Love is an anomaly. Every life form on the planet experiences love in some capacity. For a parent, friend, family member, or partner. Each type different from the previous. But one difference happens among humans versus all others.

Humans often resist what they feel. Especially when it comes to love. Time and again, they fear voicing emotion for someone. Fear the outcome it may bring. The possibility of rejection weighs heavier than acceptance.

Why?

When did humans start to fear the key to our existence? When did loving someone become something to dread? Wish I had the answers. Right now—as my heart pounds a vicious rhythm and dizziness whirls beneath my diaphragm—answers would be handy.

I park my truck across and a few spaces over from Peyton. Cutting the engine, I stare a moment at her bedroom window. Watch her silhouette haloed by the soft lamplight in her room. Her form, her profile, soft and angelic. Watch as she combs her fingers through her hair and secures it with a hair tie. The move makes me want to run my fingers through her silky, wavy locks.

The times I have been on the cusp of dropping the infamous *L* word, I force myself to resist.

I resist because I don't know if Peyton is ready to hear the word. I resist because I don't want to ruin what we have if my emotional decree isn't reciprocated. Granted, my worries may be all for nothing. But no use in voicing how I feel until the time is right.

And the time hasn't arrived. Not yet.

Exiting the truck, I grab my overnight bag and stroll across the lot to her door. Seconds after I knock, the door swings open and her bright smile greets me. Renders me speechless, breathless. Has me swallowing past the knot in my throat as my heart rattles in my rib cage.

And just like that, all coherent thought goes out the window. That four-letter word scoots a little closer to the tip of my tongue.

"Hey," I croak out, then swallow. Stepping into her, I tug at the hem of her shirt, bring her closer and press my lips to hers. "You look cute." I skim the side of her nose with the tip of mine.

"Cute, huh?" Peyton glances down at the oversized band tee and baggy sweats. *My band tee and sweats.* Fuck, I love her in my clothes. "Do I get to say you look cute when you wear them?"

I tip my head back and laugh. "Sure. If it makes you happy, I don't give a fuck." Then I pull her in, kiss her harder, and close the door behind me.

The night goes much the same as normal. We eat dinner, snuggle on the couch watching an episode of her show choice or mine, then we fall into bed but don't sleep for hours. Everything else in the world slips away.

And that four-letter word begs to be spoken as she wraps her limbs around me and falls into a deep sleep. This right here... life couldn't be more perfect.

Rolling over, cool sheets greet me along with the morning sun brightening my lids. With a groan, I pat the bed in search of Micah's warm body and come up empty. Slowly peeling my eyes open, the room comes into focus.

Why are the blinds not shut all the way? I never forget to crank them closed before bed. But I answer my own question as flashes of Micah's lips and hands and weight on me replay in my memory. His body hovering as he slowly moved in and out of me, eyes always connected.

As of recent, sex with Micah has been different. Better. More… just more.

Some nights feel like a fight to the death. Me ripping off his clothes, or vice versa. Lips smashed together and tongues at war as we try to fulfill our hunger, our insatiable *need* for one another. Growls and screams of pain and pleasure and everything in between.

But… there are also nights filled with tenderness.

A subtle touch of fingertips. Kisses so soft, I question whether his lips met my lips or skin at all. I know they did, though. The prickling tingle they leave in their wake grows,

grows, grows until heat licks my skin from the inside out. Spreads slow and steady until it consumes every inch and I combust internally. Our bodies rock and glide in sync without hurry. Unearth a bond, a force we never knew existed but can't live without.

Now that I have Micah in my life, I don't picture a day without him. Nor do I plan to.

Laughter echoes down the hall and through my door. Laughter from the man missing from my bed. And laughter from the man who sleeps across the hall.

I toss the covers aside and slip on the sweats and shirt I wore last night. Combing fingers through my tangled hair, I pull it back, twist and secure it with a hair tie. After a quick trip to the bathroom to freshen up, I wander down the hall as quietly as possible. Tiptoe to the edge and hope neither of them spot me right away.

Peering around the corner, I catch sight of Micah and Reese. Both in the kitchen, backs to me, and cooking. Not sure who cooks what, but the scent of biscuits, peppers and onions, bacon, and eggs hits me with the first full breath I take.

My stomach rumbles so loud, I am surprised neither of them hear. I press the heel of my hand to my stomach. *Just another minute.*

Micah and Reese carry on a conversation as they cook breakfast. They speak loud enough for me to hear their voices, but soft enough the words are gibberish. No doubt, I have been the subject of their conversation at some point, if not now. And that is okay.

Seeing them like this—talking like old friends, sharing a laugh, existing in the same space—creates this ever-expanding warmth beneath my breastbone. A merriment of my past and future—not that I am getting ahead of myself. I do see Micah in my future for years to come, though.

Unable to deal with my stomach trying to eat itself any longer, I step into the open living space that connects with the dining area and kitchen. Neither Micah nor Reese hear me, so I sit at the breakfast bar until one does.

"You seriously can't cook anything other than breakfast?" Reese asks Micah.

"Don't judge me," Micah retorts on a laugh. "Mom tried. Just didn't stick."

"Trust me, you want to learn." As the words roll off his tongue, Reese reaches for his coffee and spots me. "Morning, sunshine. How long you been eavesdropping?"

Micah peeks over his shoulder and gifts me with my favorite smile of his. He doesn't care if I heard every word.

I stick my tongue out at Reese. "Only long enough for you to learn Micah can't cook. He does make kick-ass breakfasts, though."

"Thanks, hellcat." He winks.

Jutting my chin toward the stove. "Speaking of breakfast. What're we having?"

"Southwest omelets, bacon, and biscuits," Micah answers.

Before I voice my opinion, my stomach groans and responds loud enough both guys laugh. "Shut up." I flip them both the middle finger. "Is it almost ready? I need to get dressed soon."

As if they have worked in kitchens together their entire life, they plate up my food. Micah places the omelet on the plate, then Reese adds three strips of bacon and a biscuit. Micah sets the plate in front of me and hands me a fork. Reese fetches the butter and honey while Micah pops a mug under the Keurig drip and presses the large button.

If they aren't careful, a girl could get used to this. Two guys tending to her. But I keep the thought to myself.

One—Reese and I will only ever be friends. I know that. He knows that. But Micah may still misconstrue the statement if said aloud.

Two—I honestly don't think I would ever be able to mentally handle more than one person in my life. My romantic life, that is. If I were into one-night stands or casual, no-strings-attached relationships, I might consider the idea. But I'm not. So, the point is moot.

Halfway through my breakfast, Micah plops down beside me and starts eating his own. Considering I eat slower than the average person, we will probably finish at the same time. Mine and Micah's plates are almost empty when Reese sits on the third stool.

"You seeing Ms. J today?" Reese asks around a mouthful of omelet.

"Yeah." My fork clatters against my plate. "I hate not being there as often. Seeing her every other Sunday feels wrong. Like I've abandoned her." I pick at my biscuit and eat it bit by bit. "Hope she's better today."

"Me too, sunshine." He swallows his bite. "Having lunch with Aunt Leanne after?"

"Yes." Spending time with Aunt Leanne is one of the week's highlights. "She wants to take me to some new deli. If she says it's good, I'll love it."

Micah bumps my knee with his. "Busy day."

"I love it, though." Busy doesn't cover it, but I love seeing people who make me happy. Hopefully, I will add Micah's family to the list when we have dinner with them tonight.

When I clear my plate, Micah takes both ours to the sink, rinses them off, and places them in the dishwasher.

"He's domesticated," Reese announces with a shit-eating grin. "Does he have a clone?"

I chuckle and scoot off my stool. "Just a sister. But I don't think she's looking for love."

"Boo. Well, let me know if you find his doppelgänger in the world."

"What happened to Trent?" Last I knew, he and his beau were still together. Which is a record for Reese. Long-term relationships aren't high priority for him—not that I judge how he lives his life.

Reese drops his head between his shoulders. "He wanted to take a break while on his work trip. Said he didn't want me to feel tied down." Reese lifts his head and meets my gaze. "But I like it when he ties me down."

"I almost felt bad for you," I say as I slap his arm. "Ass."

"No, seriously. I like him. Enough to make roots. But that's a story for another day and when he returns." Reese slaps my ass. "Now, go get ready for Ms. J. I want my crochet beanie before winter."

In the bathroom, I crank the shower and strip out of my clothes. As the sweats slide down my thighs, Micah steps up behind me, grabs my hips, and peppers kisses along my shoulder.

"Don't have much time," I moan out as he nips the skin below my ear.

"A quickie." *Kiss. Lick. Suck.* "Then I'll wash you."

Will I learn how to say no to this man again? Don't see it happening. And the notion doesn't bother me one bit.

~

Ms. Jenkins has lost weight. A lot of weight. And her skin doesn't seem to bolster the same radiance I usually see. It appears more translucent and wilted. Will she crumble if I touch her?

Seeing her like this—slowly fading—stirs up unpleasant memories. Memories that brought me to work at Gulfside in the first place.

Naturally, death is a part of life. Is unavoidable and happens to every species. Doesn't mean I have to like it. Doesn't mean I need to be okay accepting it.

"How've you been? Feel like I never see you anymore."

Ms. Jenkins stares at the crochet hook and yarn in my hands. "Your cap looks great. Who's the lucky recipient?"

Why didn't she answer my question? She never avoids answers. In fact, she usually tells me what is on her mind without hesitation. Gives me her two cents and a few quarters to boot.

So, why the evasion now?

I set down the beanie project in my lap and lay a hand on hers. Her hand is so cold. Too cold. And her skin feels as if it could peel away any minute. The need to wrap her in a thick blanket and hug her close overwhelms me immediately. Something about this entire situation is off and I don't like her obvious avoidance.

"Tell me what's wrong. Please," I say an octave above a whisper.

Ms. Jenkins sets down her own project—a baby blanket— and faces me as best she can. "You're such a sweet girl, Peyton." A cool hand cups my cheek as she gives me a soft smile. "I'm just an old lady. And my time is almost up. That's how life works."

For a minute, I stare into her warm brown eyes and digest

what she said. Yes, eighty-seven is old. But I have known several people to live well into their nineties. Does she think she won't? Why would she think that?

"Last I saw you, everything seemed good. What's changed?"

Her thumb brushes slowly over my cheekbone. "Not sure. I just feel a change inside me. It isn't painful. More like my body is preparing for the inevitable."

A tear rolls down my cheek. "I don't want you to go."

The corner of her mouth lifts as she wipes away the tear. "I know. But when it's time, it's time. We can't fight what is meant to be. But we can use what time we have left wisely. Pass on pieces of ourselves so we live on in others." She looks down at the crocheted beanie in my lap. "Life has more meaning when we share and enjoy it with someone. That is my wish for you."

"Your wish?"

"Yes, sweet Peyton. Live your life. Seek adventure. Learn new things. Don't live your life in fear. Share yourself with others, so you too can live on through them when your time comes."

I don't want to leave here today. Ms. Jenkins says to live without fear. But how can I do that when I fear what will happen when I walk out the front door today? Why does today feel like *goodbye* and not *see you next time*?

"Why are you saying all this?" I ask through fresh tears.

She lifts her other hand to frame my face. "You know why."

"What if I want to be selfish and keep you?"

Her thumbs wipe at my tears. "As much as you want to, you won't be. It's my time. And Stephen is waiting for me. I won't be alone."

Oh god. Right here, in the middle of the community room at Gulfside, I am about to lose my shit. Weep and wail like a child. Throw a fit because this isn't fair. Life isn't fair.

And yes, it is petty of me to want her to stay when she seems ready to go. But I am so tired of loss. Downright exhausted at feeling it time and time again. Ms. Jenkins may not be my family by blood, but she is my family nonetheless. Not seeing and hugging and chatting with her will rip me apart. Not hearing her stories or crocheting beanies or sitting in the sun with her will gut me.

She drops her hands from my cheeks after one last swipe at my tears. "I have lived a long, happy, and fulfilling life, Peyton. Today will be the last day you cry about me. Understood?"

"How can you ask that of me?"

"How can I not?" She tucks loose strands behind my ear. "Last thing I want is people mopey. Remember all the wonderful moments. The ones that make you smile and laugh. Those are the ones that matter most. Not some morbid ritual where people think only of loss and not all the joy that person brought to others. Remember the joy, Peyton. Then go out and live your life. Experience love and the world. Hopefully, both at the same time. And when you remember me, I want you to think about our talks and crocheting and strolls outside. You hear me?"

I nod and wipe under each eye. "Yes, ma'am."

"Now, let's finish this cap and blanket."

The rest of my time at Gulfside is spent learning all the final touches on my project as well as hers. And when I walk out the front door, I do so with a heavy, full heart. I pray today isn't the last time I see Ms. Jenkins, but know the possibility is there. Not that I will ever be okay with losing someone I care about, but at least we had today. At least, I got to say goodbye.

～

"So, you're meeting the parents tonight, huh?" Aunt Leanne asks before she shoves the club sandwich between her lips.

"Yeah. From what Micah's said, they sound like nice people."

"Then why do you look nauseous?"

Because I am. Because today has a lot happening and my body is on the fritz with how to handle it all.

"Ms. Jenkins pretty much told me she's dying today." It isn't the sole reason for why I feel—and probably look—like garbage. But it is a major player in the game.

Aunt Leanne sets down her sandwich. "Oh, Peyton. I'm so sorry." She moves to my side of the table and hugs me a moment before returning to her seat. "Do you think she meant it? Or is she just losing it?"

This crossed my mind more than once as I finished my shift at Gulfside. The possibility something triggered her to say what she said. A friend in the facility passing. A family member passing. Death changes people's perspectives. It has certainly changed mine.

"Don't know. Part of me *feels* she won't be there in two weeks. But I pray she is." I sip my drink and the cool liquid does nothing to settle the unease in my chest. "She said some pretty profound things today. Things people say when they aren't sure another chance will happen."

Aunt Leanne reaches across the table and takes my hand. "I'm glad you had today with her."

"Me too."

She gives my hand a gentle squeeze, then releases it. "Now, what can I do to make tonight less stressful?"

I shake my head and laugh. "Wish I knew. Not like I've never met the parents in previous relationships."

"So, why the jitters?"

The answer crawls its way to the tip of my tongue. Ready to escape, but I restrain it a little longer. Right here, right now, with Aunt Leanne, isn't the time to confess.

"Because everything is different with Micah." And that little fact excites and frightens me equally.

MICAH

Lifting a hand, I knock on Peyton's front door.

On the other side, a thump sounds. Followed by Peyton saying "shit" and Reese laughing at whatever happened. The lock disengages a second before the door flies open.

"Hi," Peyton huffs out. "I'm not ready."

I step in and shut the door. "No worries, I'm early." I check her head to toe and bite back laughter. "You okay?"

Reese laughs again and Peyton rolls her eyes. "Fine. Just bumped the wall trying to put my shoe on."

Peyton wanders down the hall to her room and I follow in her wake. Inside, I close the door and sit on the bed. For a moment, I track her rapid-fire movement as she plucks clothes from the closet and dresser, then stuffs them in the bag she brings to the house.

Tonight, she put on a golden maxi dress and black flats that peek out when she walks. Her hair is down in thick, soft waves and stops an inch or two below her mid-back. A light layer of gloss makes her lips shimmer. And with each pass in front of me, I inhale my favorite scent—Peyton's coconut mint.

She stops within reach and looks around the room. "Got that and that," she mumbles to herself. She carries on, ticking things off on her fingers.

I lift my hands and grab her hips. "Hey," I say and tip my head back to see her better. She stops and meets my gaze. "Something wrong?"

"No. Just making sure I have everything. I think I have everything. What if I forget something?" The words spill from her lips faster than her movement around the room.

I rise from the bed and pull her into me. Releasing a hip, I bring the hand to her cheek and caress it with my thumb. "Are you nervous about tonight? About meeting my parents?" Her eyes widen just enough for me to know the answer is yes. "You have nothing to worry about. Mom can be a little much at times, but Dad levels her out. Plus, if she says anything *I* don't find appropriate, I'll open my mouth. She gets excited."

"What if they don't like me?"

What a ridiculous question. Who would not like Peyton? Petty bitches of the past, but no one else.

"What if they love you?" I counter, biting my tongue so I don't add *"like I do."*

She huffs and a few strands close to her lips fly up and tickle my face. But I don't brush them away. Instead, I relish all the contacts and connections we share. Leaning in, I press a chaste kiss to her lips and come away with glossy coconut on mine.

"C'mon. If you forgot anything, we'll figure it out." I take her hand in mine and weave our fingers together. With my free hand, I shoulder her overnight bag. "Ready?"

After a deep breath, she nods. "Yeah. Let me grab my purse."

We say good night to Reese, hop in the truck and toss her

bag in the back cab seating. Peyton picks a music playlist from my phone as I steer us onto the highway. The drive is spent with our fingers weaving in and out of each other's and rock music quietly vibrating from the speakers.

Less than thirty minutes later, I park next to Shelly's Beetle in Mom and Dad's driveway. Surprisingly, Shelly isn't in her car waiting like prior dinner nights. Maybe—hopefully—she tames Mom a bit before we step inside.

Inhaling deeply, I open my door then walk around to open Peyton's. With her hand in mine, we stroll to the front door in silence. Peyton may be nervous to meet my parents, but I am nervous too. I am nervous Mom may be too eccentric or Dad too dull. Shelly may be a little extra tonight, too, but I doubt it.

After Mom's declaration of wanting us to find happiness with another person, Shelly and I remain tight lipped when possible. Arranged marriages aren't really a thing around here anymore, but I wouldn't put it past Mom to try.

"Ready?" I ask as my hand hovers over the knob.

Peyton nods. "Ready as I'll ever be."

I twist the knob and the door flies open with Shelly on the other side. "You guys making out?"

Please don't let this be a precursor for the entire evening. "No, Shelly, we were not making out. This isn't high school. I act like an adult when necessary."

"Whatever." She rolls her eyes at me, then gives Peyton a big smile and hug. "Glad you're here. Maybe Mom will be less… maybe she'll just be less."

Peyton's eyes widen as she death grips my hand. I stroke the top of her hand with my thumb in reassurance. "It'll be fine. Quit freaking her out, Shell."

"Sorry," she says with a wince.

Inside the house, we follow Shelly toward the kitchen. Hints of garlic and cheese and bread float in the air. Mom asked if Peyton had food allergies, but didn't tell me what was on the menu tonight. By the smell, I'd guess lasagna. Guess we will find out soon enough.

We round the corner and Mom stops whatever conversation she and Dad are having. She looks from me to Peyton, to our hands and back up to me. The warmest, gentlest smile lights her face as she walks toward us.

"Hey, honey. Glad you made it." She gives me a longer than normal hug. "And you must be Peyton," she says. "I'm Nicole. It's wonderful to meet you." Without permission, Mom hugs Peyton.

I stare at the embrace with shock and embarrassment heating my cheeks. Mom *never* hugs strangers. Ever. Peyton and I are in a relationship, but she has never hugged any of my past girlfriends the first time they met.

"Mom, let's not scare her. Okay?"

Mom detaches her octopus tentacles from Peyton and takes a step back. "Oh, I'm sorry, dear. Don't know what came over me."

The oven timer goes off and rescues us from another round of awkwardness. "Be back in a minute," I announce. "I'm going to show Peyton around the house."

"Dinner will be on the table in a couple minutes," Mom replies.

Hand in hand, I lead Peyton through the house and away from my overzealous mother. I point and prattle off each room. "Dining and living room. Mom's home office, formerly Shelly's bedroom. Dad's home office, formerly my bedroom. Bathroom. Parents' bedroom." Then I lead her into the last room on the right and close the door. "Guest room."

The room is minimal, with white walls and smoky blue accents. A queen bed with gray-blue bedding, a white bed frame, and a mountain of throw pillows. A small, four-drawer white dresser and matching bedside table. Gray-blue curtains against white wooden blinds. The white-framed pictures on the wall of blue marine life or beachy images.

Not sure how my mother managed to replicate the same color for the entire room, but she did. On occasion, I wonder if she hired someone and gave them a color swatch. Wouldn't surprise me.

"Doing okay?" I ask as I step into Peyton and hug her close. "Mom has been a little much recently. Not sure what provoked the change, but I hope it fades. Soon."

Light laughter spills from her lips. "It's fine. All mothers probably go through this stage. Wanting to see their children happy as adults." Peyton breaks the hug, walks around the room and stops in front of one of the frames. "I won't try to guess how my mom will be when you meet her. Generally, she's pretty laid back. But I've also seen her at her best and worst."

I step up behind her and wrap my arms around her front. "If she asks weird questions, you don't have to answer. Shell and I are used to deflecting when necessary. You can use a code word, if she makes you uncomfortable." I chuckle but mean every word. Mom isn't *bad*, she just gets intense. Especially if you don't know her.

Peyton rests her hands over mine. "It'll be fine. No matter who we are, parents are always strange to us or people close to us."

"Still think you should have a code word," I mumble into her hair.

"Fine," she says with a laugh. "How about sushi?"

"Sushi?"

"Mmhm."

"How the hell would you work that into conversation?"

She shrugs. "Maybe I won't have to. But if I do, I'll figure it out."

"Alright, sushi. Let's go before they think we're fucking on the bed."

"What?" Peyton's face pales as her eyes go wide.

"Joking, hellcat. C'mon."

We join everyone in the dining room and sit at the table. Each place setting has a small salad and dipping oil for bread. Bread baskets sit at either end of the table—because we love bread. Mom brings out a large casserole dish and sets it at the heart of the table.

"Baked ziti, made with creamy pesto instead of marinara," she announces with a glowing smile.

Peyton shifts in her seat and stares at me with a slack jaw. "Your mom makes dishes like this and all you can cook is breakfast?"

Across from us, Shelly snort-laughs and tries to cover it with a cough.

"Shut it, Shell."

Mom joins in on Shelly's laughter for a second, then stops when she sees my face. "Sorry, Micah. It is funny." Mom shifts her gaze to Peyton. "I've tried to teach Micah for years and it doesn't stick. But I refuse to give up. One day, he'll surprise me, or you, and make something else."

Once all the food is on the table, everyone settles and starts on their salad. Easy conversation flows around the table. Thankfully, Mom hasn't said anything off-putting the entire time.

Every time she glances over to Peyton's and my side of

the table, though, I see the sparkle in her eye. The barely noticeable uptick at the corners of her mouth and eyes. And when Peyton speaks, Mom listens. She lets her say every word, then comments back as if she and Peyton have chatted hundreds of times.

By the end of the evening, we leave with full bellies, a heaping container of leftovers, and warm hugs.

"That wasn't so bad," I say once we are on the road.

"Your mom is nice. She loves you both and just wants the best for you and Shelly."

"Yeah, she does. Glad she didn't make you uncomfortable." I lace my fingers with hers, lift them to my lips, and kiss her knuckles.

A couple songs and commercials on the radio later, I park in the driveway and we walk into the house. I lock the dead bolt and drop her overnight bag to the floor. She opens her mouth to ask something, but I cut her off with my lips to hers.

I frame her face in my hands and kiss the hell out of her. Her hands snake around my waist and fist the back hem of my jeans. We stumble toward the bedroom, our lips never apart. When her legs bump the mattress, I kiss along her jaw, down her neck, along her shoulder.

Grabbing the back collar of my shirt, I yank it off and toss it on the floor. I reach out, trace my fingertips along the dress seam at her breasts. Her eyes drift shut as a shiver rolls through her body.

But I don't want her to shut out the world. Not tonight. Not now.

I trail my fingers up the column of her throat to her chin and tip it up slightly. "Open your eyes, Peyton." Violet irises meet my blues and hum with anticipation. The gray flecks sparkle with delight. I lean in, my lips a whisper over hers as I hold her gaze. "I love you, Peyton."

The sentiment flows with such ease. My whole body comes alive. A blazing buzz spreads like an electrical current, zapping and sparking and jolting anew. Breath fills me with life as my heart learns a new rhythm.

"I love you, too." Peyton closes the space between us and kisses me as if we have found ourselves. Here, in this moment. Together.

We peel away our clothes and rediscover each other. Learn who we are with our proclamations in the open. Make love to each other until we are bone tired and in a pile of tangled limbs. And in the early morning hours, I hug her close to my side and whisper I love you in her ear as we drift off to sleep.

Happy, sated, and head over heels in love.

"Stop!" I shout between giggles.

"Stop what?" Micah digs his fingertips into the side of my rib cage for the umpteenth time.

"Tickling me." I pry at his fingers in the hopes of getting free. But he has a death grip on my waist. "We need…" *Tickle.* "To get ready…" *Tickle.* "For work." *Laugh.* "Oh, god." I clamp my thighs together and clench my internal muscles. "Seriously, Micah. Stop. I'm going to pee."

He digs in harder and laughs. "Liar."

"No, seriously." If I don't make it to the bathroom now, this won't be pretty. I tug him in that direction and hope he picks up on how severe the situation is. "My bladder is about to let go."

He drops his hands. *Thank fuck.* I bolt to the toilet, drop my pants and call it a win that I made it in time.

Micah walks in and winces as I finish up. "Sorry. Didn't mean for that to happen."

"Yeah, yeah. But remember this…" I point a finger at him. "If I say I have to pee, I'm not joking." I stare at his pouty lip while I wash up. For a split second, I consider apologizing. But I let it go.

"Sorry, hellcat." He pulls me in for a hug. I hesitate on returning the hug, wondering if he will tickle me again. When he doesn't, I wrap my arms around his middle and lean into him.

Cool air hits my skin as he brushes hair off my shoulder. Before a shiver passes, warm lips kiss the width of my shoulder, along the curve of my neck and up to that spot beneath my ear. Hands roam the landscape of my body—gentle and rough, caressing and kneading.

One hand slides up my spine, dives into my hair, fists the locks and tugs back. The brightest constellation stares down at me and I lick my lips. Clench my thighs for a different reason.

Micah reads me like an open book. Sees the need in my eyes. Feels my taut nipples on his chest and subtle grind of my hips.

He lowers his lips, stopping a breath above mine. "We don't have time," he says with a smirk on his lips.

"Please," I moan. At this rate, I am willing to be late or speed to work, if necessary. Not like we aren't always early.

Micah tightens his grip on my hair and licks the seam of my lips. "Gonna be quick and dirty. You good with that?"

"You know I am."

Then, he releases my hair, spins me around to face the bed, yanks my pants and underwear down, and forces me to bend at the waist. With a clunk, his pants and briefs hit the floor. He draws circles on my skin just above my ass crack.

As I open my mouth to tell him to quit teasing me, his finger glides between my cheeks. He pauses at the tight hole and presses slightly. "One day, I'll claim this too." The rumble in his tone and the promise in his words make me push into his touch. "Not now, hellcat," he growls out. "But soon."

His finger slips lower, separates my lips and toys with my clit. I fist the comforter and grind against his touch.

"So wet and eager." *Whack.* His free hand slaps my ass. "I love when you're starved for me."

His finger vanishes, but is quickly replaced with the tip of his cock. He rubs the head between my lips—up and down, over and over. Teasing and taunting.

Then he slams forward and fills me. "Jesus fuck," I belt out as I claw the bedding.

"Hold on, hellcat. Quick and dirty time."

Micah slides a hand up my spine, circles around the front of my throat, and tightens his grip. With the other hand on my hip, he holds me in place as his cock pistons between my thighs. Balls slapping my clit. My moans and his bouncing off the walls while pheromones and arousal fog the air.

When the pitch of my cries escalates, he shifts the hand on my hip to my nipple and tweaks the tight bud. His hand around my throat constricts and I go into sensation overload. Heat spirals up my spine, spreads across my chest and up my neck as my walls tighten around his cock. He twists my nipple harder. Slams into me with more aggression. Tips me over the edge and jumps after me.

"God, I love when you come," he growls in my ear and releases my neck. "Fucking spectacular."

"Thanks," I say on a laugh. "I'll take it as a compliment."

～

We walk in the back of Roar—still early—with loony smiles on our faces. Good thing the staff doesn't arrive when we do. It would be ridiculously difficult to hide our euphoria.

Micah and I decide to split tasks to make the evening easier. He will set up for Karaoke Night while I work on scheduling and payroll. Recently, we started dealing with invoices and ordering on Tuesdays and Fridays. Days when we don't work together, but still have another manager on duty. It frees up our joint work nights more and gets us off the floor most of the night when everyone else has it handled.

It isn't long before the staff arrives and Roar opens. The bar lines with patrons ordering drinks. A line forms near the makeshift stage as people add their name to the karaoke roster. Tables fill with people and conversations. And it isn't long before the first singer steps on stage and blesses us with their song selection and voice.

Pouring a beer from the tap, I look up and spot the group walking in. I finish pouring and serve the customer before pressing the button on my headset.

"Starlight."

"Hellcat."

"Everyone's here."

"Be out in a sec." As the walkie cuts out, Micah rounds the corner with bottles from the storage room in his hands.

We both help with drink orders until the line is manageable for Mable and Josiah. Then we exit the bar alley and join our friends at the table.

Great songs spill from the speakers as squawky voices belt out lyrics. Our friends drink beer and discuss which songs they will sing when their turn comes. Micah and I sit back, join in the conversation, laugh and enjoy the evening and our surroundings.

Shelly tugs Cora toward the stage as both my and Micah's walkies crackle in our ears. "Boss man," Ted calls out. "Someone I admitted in asked if you're working tonight."

I meet Micah's gaze with a scrunched brow. He shrugs. "Did you catch their name?"

"No, sorry. But she's wearing a red dress and has brown hair."

Closing my eyes, I take a deep breath and search for my inner zen. Never would I suspect Micah of adultery. So, my mind doesn't go in that direction when I hear a woman is asking for him. Instead, my mind travels to the long list of women he was with over the years and prays another one isn't coming at him with some outlandish accusation.

Micah spins to face me head-on. "Please don't freak out."

"Not the best way to start a conversation," I say.

He nods. "Saturday, I was headed to the office after rounds to catch up on paperwork. Caleb informed me over the walkie that a woman asked for me. By the time he brought it up, she was headed for the exit. I only caught the back of her, but knew who it was."

"Who?"

An angry nest of hornets buzzes in my belly and sends venom through my veins. I am sick and tired of all these women. Do they not understand the concept of one-night stands? From what Micah told me, he made it abundantly clear to all of them.

"Rochelle," he says, loud enough for only me to hear.

Rochelle? As in his ex-girlfriend? As in the woman who fucked another man in his bed and crushed his heart? If Rochelle is here, this isn't some pregnancy situation. This is next level. And I have had it with the bullshit.

I lock eyes with Micah. See fear as his eyes dart between

mine and sweat slicks his brow. Feel anxiety roll off him as he clenches my hands and waits for me to say something. Anything.

"Ted?"

"Yes, Miss Peyton?"

"Please be on standby to escort someone from the premises."

Micah's eyes widen. "What're you doing?"

"Handling this; after we figure out what she wants."

Out of nowhere, Shelly stops singing mid-song. Cora slaps Shelly's arm. "Too drunk to sing already?" Cora teases. But when I look to Shelly, her eyes are laser-focused behind me.

One-way ticket to party town coming up.

"There you are," a brunette says as she stops in front of Micah, in front of us.

Dressed in an overpriced dress and heels, Rochelle has the audacity to rest her hand on Micah's shoulder as she steps into his space. Micah shirks from her touch and inches back.

"First, don't touch me. Second, what are you doing here, Rochelle?"

The woman smiles as if Micah didn't just say to back the fuck up nicely. I ball my fingers into fists and keep them pinned at my sides. I will let Micah be the nice one. But if this bitch doesn't catch on soon...

"Wanted to see you. I miss you."

"Are you fucking kidding me right now?" Micah says louder than before, and eyes dart our way. "You miss me? What, did your fuckboy leave you?"

Rochelle jerks her head back as if slapped. "No need to be ugly. To answer your question, no, he didn't break up with me. I broke it off with him. He was too immature. And like I said, I miss you."

She reaches forward and is inches from touching Micah when I rise from my stool. "Do not touch him."

"Who are you?" she asks with a snarl. "His flavor of the day?"

I step closer, invading her space, and use the few inches I have on her to get in her face. She doesn't back down but looks a little gray in the face. For a moment, I don't say anything. I simply stare down at her. When she swallows, I know I have her.

"Actually, it doesn't matter who I am. What matters is he isn't yours. Hasn't been for quite some time. You don't deserve him. Hell, you don't deserve anyone."

"You don't know me," she bites back. "How dare you—"

"How dare I what? Not be a frigid bitch. Not treat someone like trash." I hold my hands in front of me, palms up, and wave my fingers. "Let's hear it. And it better be good." Rochelle looks past me to Micah. "No." I push her back. "You don't get to look at him."

"I don't know who you think you are, but if you touch me again, I'll call the police."

I tip my head back and laugh. "And I'll laugh as they issue you a trespassing notice because you're harassing an employee." I force her back as I step farther into her. "You can go peacefully or not. The choice is yours."

"You don't know who you're messing with," she bites out. "He's only good for sex. So, you can have him."

A fuse lights in my veins. Burns slow and hot as the flame gets closer to the ticking bomb beneath my rib cage. My breathing kicks up a degree as my cheeks flush. And before I give serious thought to my actions, I take a step back, grab her shoulders, rear back, and drive my knee between her legs. Hard.

Rochelle crumples to the floor and wails in pain as she grabs herself. "Bitch!"

"Right back atcha," I say with a half smile, then press the button on my walkie. "Ted?"

"On my way, Miss Peyton."

No doubt Ted heard and witnessed the entire altercation. And if anyone asked who was in the wrong here, several would say I asked the woman to leave. Did I need to get physical? No, but she wasn't backing down or following Micah's or my request to leave. Her presence was—is—unwanted, and she refused to give in. If I hadn't taken it next level, she would probably continue to harass us.

Ted helps Rochelle off the floor. Soon as she is upright, she goes on a tirade. "You'll be sorry, little girl."

"Actually" —Shelly steps up to Rochelle— "no she won't. Several of us just witnessed the whole thing. You put your hands on the manager without permission. Were asked to leave by another manager and refused. Then you threatened her. She was protecting herself."

Well, damn. Shelly is a viper. Not someone you mess with or want on your bad side. Noted. The fact she stepped up— whether for Micah, me, or us both—has my spine straighter and head higher. No doubt Shelly knows Rochelle and has some inkling of what she did to Micah. She would go to bat for him any day of the week. But for her to reinforce me, that says a lot about us—me and Shelly—and the small bond forming.

Rochelle turns her pathetic eyes in my direction. "You'll get bored of him, just like I did. Then, you'll wish I relieved you of him."

I shake my head. "Love that you're telling me why you fucked around on him, yet here you are." I look her up and down. "Begging for another chance. I feel sorry for you and your pitiful life. He's moved on. Found happiness. Found someone who loves him as much as he loves her. And you lost out. If you step foot on this property or come near me or Micah again, you'll see how much of a bitch I *can* be."

Ted guides Rochelle toward the doors as the crowd claps and cheers. I don't look away until Rochelle is out the door. And for the first time in who knows how long, I breathe.

Until Micah swoops in, cups my cheeks, and kisses the hell out of me in front of everyone. Wolf whistles and hollers to *get a room* come at us from every direction. The kiss is far from innocent as his hands roam my body. To be honest, I don't give a fuck. Because one fact is certain in this moment.

Micah Reed belongs to me. And he sure as hell is letting everyone know I belong to him. Wouldn't want it any other way.

twenty-three

MICAH

Laughter mixes with rock music as Peyton and I sit on a lounger in Jonas and Autumn's backyard. Our typical Sunday get-together underway.

Gavin and Jonas man the grill; flipping burgers, brats, and mojo-marinated chicken quarters while chatting. Autumn, Cora, and Shelly load one of the banquet tables with buns, side salads, fruit, and condiments. Penny and Rex go back and forth over something frivolous—socks in the living room. Reznor and Tatyana watch their son, Ashton, play with Clementine and Spartan. Iliana, Trevor, and Jillian—Jonas's younger sister—sit on the lounger across from us and chat about an upcoming baseball game.

Life feels pretty fucking amazing right now.

A year ago, I would not have pictured my life like this. With Peyton at my side, holding my hand and laughing at jokes told by my closest friends. A year ago, I had no smiles to give. Felt empty inside. Did all I could to fill the void. But nothing worked.

Now, I know the reason.

Fate has never been something I put much thought in.

Especially when my relationship with Rochelle ended how it did. But now I give fate some credit. Give in to the notion that two people are meant to find each other and live their best life together.

Several years ago, fate brought Peyton and I together. I wasn't ready, though. She'd had her eye on me back then, but who is to say where our relationship would have gone had we gotten together.

I look toward the grill, watch how Cora latches on to every word Gavin says with hearts in her eyes. Watch how he kisses her forehead, then whispers something in her ear and causes her cheeks to flush.

Could that have been me and Peyton? There is no definite answer. Although Gavin and Cora are madly in love, shit beyond their control tore them apart early on. Fate found a way to bring them back together. If Peyton and I had been different in high school, would we have drifted apart? Or would we still be together? If our lives were different back then, I don't think we would be who we are now. Nor would we feel the same.

And that is not something I care to dwell on. The what-ifs.

What I *do* know is that I have never been happier. And I owe it all to the hellcat at my side.

I lean in and press my lips to her temple. "I love you."

Peyton stops whatever she was saying to Shelly and faces me. "Love you, too." Then she presses her lips to mine. I break the kiss all too soon, not wanting our friends to give us shit.

Gavin and Jonas announce the meat is off the grill—which is our version of a dinner bell. Everyone evacuates their seats, grabs plates, and piles them high. Minutes later, the only sound outside is the music, occasional crunch of food, and Spartan's whimper for scraps.

Off to the side, Cora asks Shelly about work and I shift my attention.

"Is the shop staying busy? Whenever I ask Mom, she says yes. But she thinks five customers in one day is busy," Cora says with a laugh.

Shelly swallows her bite and takes a sip from her beer. "It's gotten busier in the last few months. Not sure why. We've done a little more marketing, but not much. Whatever the reason, the uptick is great."

"Mom jokingly said maybe she'll retire sooner."

Shelly pales, which I find interesting. It is no secret that Shelly will take over the florist shop when Cora's mom retires. She plans to buy the business over time and make minor changes. But I don't think the plan was for her to own the shop for three to five more years. As a planner, if something changes the overall picture, Shelly freaks out.

Shelly laughs without humor. "Hope she's joking. Not quite ready to fill her shoes yet."

Cora waves her off. "I'm sure she is. Anyway… on to less stressful topics. Have you talked to the hottie painting the shop mural?"

"What *hottie*?" I ask, shooting daggers at my little sister.

She rolls her eyes, then stabs a chunk of potato salad and stuffs it in her mouth. It's an obvious attempt to avoid the subject, so I just sit and wait and stare like the annoying older brother I am. Until she caves. And because I know my sister well, she will cave. Soon.

"Argh!" Like clockwork. "He's just some guy painting a mural on the outside of the shop. No big deal."

"Cora seems to think it's big enough a deal to bring him up," I say.

Shelly narrows her eyes at Cora. "And we will talk about *that* later." She shifts her gaze back to me. "Seriously, though. He's just some artist Elizabeth hired. Nothing else."

I stare at my sister a moment. Try to read between the lines. Zero in on the fine details she leaves out. But for some reason, she has sealed herself off. Has put on her best poker face and enforced the most neutral body language. That alone tells me there is definitely more to this. Tells me she doesn't just look at this guy as *just some artist Elizabeth hired.* She looks at him with newly formed interest.

For now, I won't push her on it. Won't make her uncomfortable and embarrass her in front of friends. But I will get more answers. Soon.

"If you say so. Just don't let Mom find out about said *no big deal* or you'll never hear the end of it."

For a beat, her body sags. The only reason I don't miss it is because I know my sister. Know that finding *the one* is a big deal to her. As an avid romance reader, she is big on the fated-lovers concept. Believes everyone will get their happily ever after.

For years, she harped on most of us about destiny and love written in the stars. Now that someone pops up on her radar, she keeps secrets. Doesn't let anyone pry as she has in the past.

Maybe I need to stop by the floral shop and buy Peyton flowers next week. Find out more about this artist.

The rest of the night flows with great conversation, an intense game of *Never Have I Ever* and belly-aching laughter. Everyone says their goodbyes and goes separate ways until next week.

After the short ride home, I park in the driveway and we walk hand in hand to the door and inside. The door clicks shut and I wrap Peyton in my arms. Kiss her as if I will never get the chance again.

"What was that for?" she asks when we come up for air.

"For everything."

"Everything?"

I nod. "For the longest time, life, and the world, was a restless night. Since you, life is colorful. More brilliant."

"Bright," she adds.

"Bright," I repeat, then kiss her. "And I can't imagine life any better. Or a love any brighter."

epilogue

PEYTON

One year later

Micah steps up behind me and wraps me in his arms. "Almost ready?" His starry-sky irises meet mine in the mirror and, for a moment, we breathe in sync with each other.

Although Micah and I have become practically inseparable the last year, we took things slower than most couples. With our pasts, Micah and I decided there was no need to rush things.

We spent every available minute of the day together and every night in each other's arms. Yet, we waited until two months ago to move in together. The wait had nothing to do with my rent at the apartment or that we wanted occasional solitude. More like we wanted to ease into this step. Ease into sharing space full time with a new person. Ease into cohabitation.

"Yeah. One more minute."

Micah kisses my bare shoulder. "I'll wait in the living room."

He exits and leaves me to finish getting ready. I do one

last once-over to make sure nothing is out of place. After a quick swipe of gloss, I tuck the tube in my purse and join Micah in the living room.

"Ready when you are," I say and offer my elbow to him.

He takes my arm and guides us out the door and to the car. We wind our way out of the neighborhood, then Micah drives us south to an undisclosed location for dinner. He hasn't told me the reason why I needed to dress up, but I suspect it has something to do with us celebrating our "official" one-year anniversary. Yes, we casually dated for weeks leading up to August tenth, but we didn't want to label our relationship.

Then a switch flipped. Since that moment, we let the world know there is an us.

Miles of highway pass before Micah exits and drives along the city streets. I have no clue where he is taking me, but I do know we are in Tampa. Two more right turns, then a left and Micah drives the car into a parking lot. No name appears on the rustic brick building, just a logo of a setting sun.

"What is this place?" I ask, staring out the window.

"You'll see. I only know about it through connections at Roar."

I spin in my seat to face him as we pull up to a valet in a white dress shirt, black slacks, and a black tie. "Micah, this place looks really expensive."

"If it was too much, I wouldn't have brought us." He says that, but I am not buying a word of it.

The valet opens our doors and helps us out. Micah steps around the front of the car, takes my arm, and escorts me inside. The moment we step through the double oak doors, I stop breathing.

This place is expensive. Ridiculously expensive.

My heels clack on antique hardwood as we walk down a long corridor. The interior walls the same brick as the exterior. Soft white light glows from candelabra chandeliers above. Photographs from different eras sit in thick black frames on the left wall—some sepia-toned, others black and white. Tall windows with half-moons on top line the right wall and look out into an enclosed atrium with bonsai, bamboo, stones, and a waterfall pond. From my vantage point, the garden appears to be surrounded by windows, including the rooftop.

We reach a podium where a man and woman wait with warm smiles. "Good evening, sir, miss," the man says. "May I have the name for your reservation?"

"Reed-Alexander," Micah answers.

Why did he put the reservation under both our last names?

There is no time to ponder the answer as the host gathers menus and asks us to follow. He leads us through the restaurant and, as suspected, the entire dining area encompasses the atrium. We are seated at a cloth-covered square table for two. The host lights a single taper candle at the heart of the table, bids us a good evening and steps away.

For a moment, I scan the dining area in slight shock. This place isn't some random place to eat dinner. It is literal fine dining.

Beside the candle is a small vase with a single yellow rose and a sprig of baby's breath. On a spotless white plate in front of me is an intricately folded cloth napkin. More silverware than I use in a day sits on three sides of the plate. A small plate off to the right and two empty wineglasses also fill my place setting.

Not far from where we sit, a wine cellar with a glass front contains several hundred bottles. Chandeliers from the entry —but larger—hang from thick oak beams in the tall ceiling.

"Micah," I whisper across the table. "This place is *too* expensive." I haven't looked at the menu yet, but dinner here feels like hundreds for the two of us.

Micah lays his hand on the table, palm up, and waits for me to take it. Without hesitation, I join our hands. A year has passed and I still feel a jolt when we connect. If anything, the jolt gets stronger with time.

"And as I said before, I wouldn't have brought us if it was too much." He leans in, lifts my hand, and kisses my knuckles in turn. "Let's enjoy the evening. Okay?"

Inhaling a deep breath, I nod. "Yeah. Okay."

Before I pick up the menu, a woman approaches the table in black slacks, a white button-down with a black tie, a black apron tied at the waist that extends below her knees, and a black towel on her forearm.

"Good evening. Welcome to Dusk. Is this your first time dining with us?"

Micah responds with yes and the woman goes into a small story on how the restaurant came to be. Then, she explains the menu. That this is a five-course meal. The menu is a guide for us to choose one of three options for each course. We can choose the same or different. The main course is paired with wine and dessert has beverage options. The dishes are spaced out to give us time to eat and not feel full as each course ends. Once explained, she fills the glasses on the table with water and excuses herself to give us a moment to decide.

I pick up the handheld menu and stare down at the printed card. The options seem simple, but the idea of choosing just one makes me sweat.

"Hey." I peek past the candle to Micah. "It's just dinner." I nod and take a deep breath. "How about we pick different items so we can try more than one."

"Yeah. Sounds good."

When the server returns, we place our full course of options. Micah went with sausage-stuffed roasted cherry tomatoes, spicy tuna tartar, caprese salad, filet mignon, and the chocolate box. I chose the champagne shrimp on endive, caramelized onion and pear tartlets, fig and goat cheese salad, miso-glazed salmon, and berries and cream cake. The server takes our menus and states the hors d'oeuvres will be out shortly before leaving the table.

The moment we are alone, Micah reaches for my hand and I gladly give it.

"This place is more upscale than anywhere else we eat, I know." I lift my brows and pucker my lips, which makes him laugh. "But… today deserves more."

I know what today is, but does he? Not that men should be singled out for forgetting dates, but most men aren't the best at remembering birthdays, anniversaries, or special occasions. At least not the ones from my past.

"It does?" I ask with faux curiosity.

His lips kick up in a half smile. "Don't play the oblivious card with me. You know what today is." My eyes go up and to the right as I shrug. Micah shakes his head and chuckles softly. "As I was saying, today deserves more. Which is why I brought us here." He squeezes my hand. "I never want to take you or our time together for granted. And I plan to celebrate every momentous occasion we share. You're just going to have to deal with it."

I laugh. "Is that an order?"

He tilts his head and half shrugs. "Maybe." He pauses and takes a deep breath. "I love you, Peyton. More than I have loved anyone. And every now and then, I want to spoil you.

Take you to nice places and eat fancy meals together. Hope you're okay with that."

More than okay. The longer our relationship is, the more I know the real Micah. See his sensitive and caring side. His protective and defensive side. The man who will yank my hair and choke me one minute and kiss me tenderly as we make love the next.

I love all the facets of Micah Reed. And I love that there are still more to discover.

"Guess I'm okay with it," I tease.

Our time at Dusk passes with small dishes, sampling each other's food, laughter and our hands connected across the table. After we finish dessert and coffee, Micah pays the bill without giving me the slightest notion of cost. Arm in arm, we casually stroll out of the restaurant, wait for the valet to bring the car up, then hop in and drive home.

"Did you have a nice time?" Micah asks as he lifts my hand to his lips and kisses my fingers.

"Yes. The restaurant was wonderful. Thank you." I lean over the console and kiss his cheek.

"You're welcome. And so you know, the night isn't over."

"Good to know." Anniversary sex sounds like a great way to end the evening.

Before long, Micah parks in the driveway and we stroll up the walkway to the house. Not much has changed with the house since I moved in. A few minor details—more flowers in the yard, additional accent pieces inside, picture frames of us and family and friends. I didn't have much furniture of my own and sold it since the house was furnished.

Micah enters the code to unlock the door and steps inside, me on his heels. On the ride home, when Micah said the night wasn't over, I expected him to tear my clothes off when we got home.

But Micah is full of surprises tonight. And the sight before me is beyond expectation.

The entire open floor plan glows. Lit candles rest on every possible surface. As does a plethora of flowers. Every type of yellow flower sits in vases with greenery and baby's breath. I step farther into the room as my eyes dart from one candle and vase to the next.

"When did you? How?" I spin around to find Micah right behind me.

"Shelly."

I turn back to the room and take it all in. Who knew Micah Reed was such a romantic? Over the last year, he has softened around the edges—only on occasion in the bedroom —and I love seeing this side of him.

"This is…"

I whirl around to tell him how romantic this is, but he is no longer eye level. All the air leaves my lungs as I drop my gaze to meet his. Micah, down on one knee, stares up at me as if I hold all of life's secrets.

A hand flies to my mouth as my vision glazes over. "What are you doing?" I choke out.

His soft chuckle floats through the air. "Being romantic. Now, shh." He presses an index finger to his lips for a beat, then reaches for my free hand. My *left* hand.

"Peyton, it's no secret our relationship didn't start in the best light. In all honesty, I was the biggest asshole." We both laugh. "Through all the banter and harsh words, you still called out to me in a way I couldn't ignore. So, I kept up with my persistence. Once I realized who you were and what I'd done all those years ago, I thought there'd be no chance for me." He rubs circles with his thumb over the top of my hand. "But you gave me a chance. You forgave me."

I blink and the first tear rolls down my cheek. Eyes locked on his, I drop my hand from my mouth and nod.

"Slowly, you went from this woman at work I had the hots for to the woman I don't want to live without." I gasp. "Peyton, I don't picture a single day in my future without you. Nor do I want to." He reaches into the pocket of his slacks and takes out a small black box. He flips the lid open and turns the box in his hand. Nestled in the velvet is a platinum band bridal set—the engagement ring with a yellow cathedral round diamond and the wedding band with small white diamonds that hug the engagement stone.

"Oh my god," I whisper in disbelief.

"Peyton Isabel Alexander, I want to spend every day of forever with you. Will you marry me?"

Tears cascade down my cheeks and blur Micah and the room. But my eyes don't leave his. Not for a second. Not as every ounce of love this man holds spills from his heart through his lips.

Micah just asked me to marry him. Never in my life did I imagine this day, this moment.

"Yes," I whisper. "Yes, I'll marry you."

A new smile lights Micah's expression. A love so bright it blinds me. He plucks the engagement ring from the box, lifts my left hand to his lips, kisses my ring finger, then slides the ring into place. Rising from the floor, he wraps his arms around my waist, lifts me off the floor and kisses the hell out of me.

"Thank you," he says when the kiss breaks.

I scrunch my brow. "For what?"

"For you. For saying yes. And for wanting forever with me."

I plant a chaste kiss on his lips. "I love you, Micah Reed."

"And I love you. Future Mrs. Peyton Reed."

He kisses me slow and soft as he walks us to the bedroom. And then, Micah shows me every way he loves me. Now and forever.

Want more of Micah and Peyton? Get the Insomniac bonus content on my website!

Ready for Shelly's story? The Artist Duet is the last in the series. Buckle up... the last duet is an emotional roller coaster.

Thank you so much for reading the **Insomniac Duet**. If you wouldn't mind taking a moment to leave a review on the retailer site where you made your purchase, Goodreads and/or BookBub, it would mean the world to me.

Reviews help other readers find and enjoy the book as well.

Much love,
     Persephone

The Click Duet

High school sweethearts torn apart. When fate gives them a second chance, one doesn't trust they won't be hurt again. Through the Lens (Click Duet #1) and Time Exposure (Click Duet #2) is an angsty, second chance, friends to lovers romance with all the feels.

The Inked Duet

A man with a broken heart and a woman scared to put herself out there. Love is never easy. Sometimes love rips you apart. Fine Line (Inked Duet #1) and Love Buzz (Inked Duet #2) is a second chance at love, single parent romance with a pinch of angst and dash of suspense.

The Artist Duet

A tortured hero with the biggest heart and a charismatic heroine with the patience of a saint. Previous heartache has him fighting his desire to be more than friends with her. But she is everywhere, and he can't help but give in. The Artist Duet is an angsty, friends to lovers slow burn.

Transcendental

A musician in search of his muse and a woman grieving the loss of her husband. Two weeks at an exclusive retreat and their connection rivals all others. Until she leaves early without notice. But he refuses to give up until he finds her again.

Depths Awakened

A small town romance which captivates you from the start. Two broken souls have sworn off love. Vowed to never lose anyone else. But their undeniable attraction brings them together and refuses to let go.

One Night Forsaken

One night. No names. No romance. Just fun. Nothing more–at least, that's what she tells herself. Until he appears in her coffee shop months later with that addictive smile. She swore off commitment. He vows to never love again. But the more they fight it, the more life brings them together.

Every Thought Taken

As young children, an unshakable friendship brought them together. As teens, they discovered an undeniable love. Then life pulled them in different directions–into darkness and light–and slowly ripped them apart. Years later, he returns home in the hopes of a second chance with his first love and to conquer the demons of his past.

Distorted Devotion

Swept off her feet by love, life takes a dark, unexpected turn. Now the love of her life may be the cause of her death. Check out this gripping, romantic suspense.

Undying Devotion

A long-term couple with a secret life. Their friends envy the bond they share, but remain oblivious to their lifestyle and how deep the bond lies. A turn of events has her wanting to spill every secret.

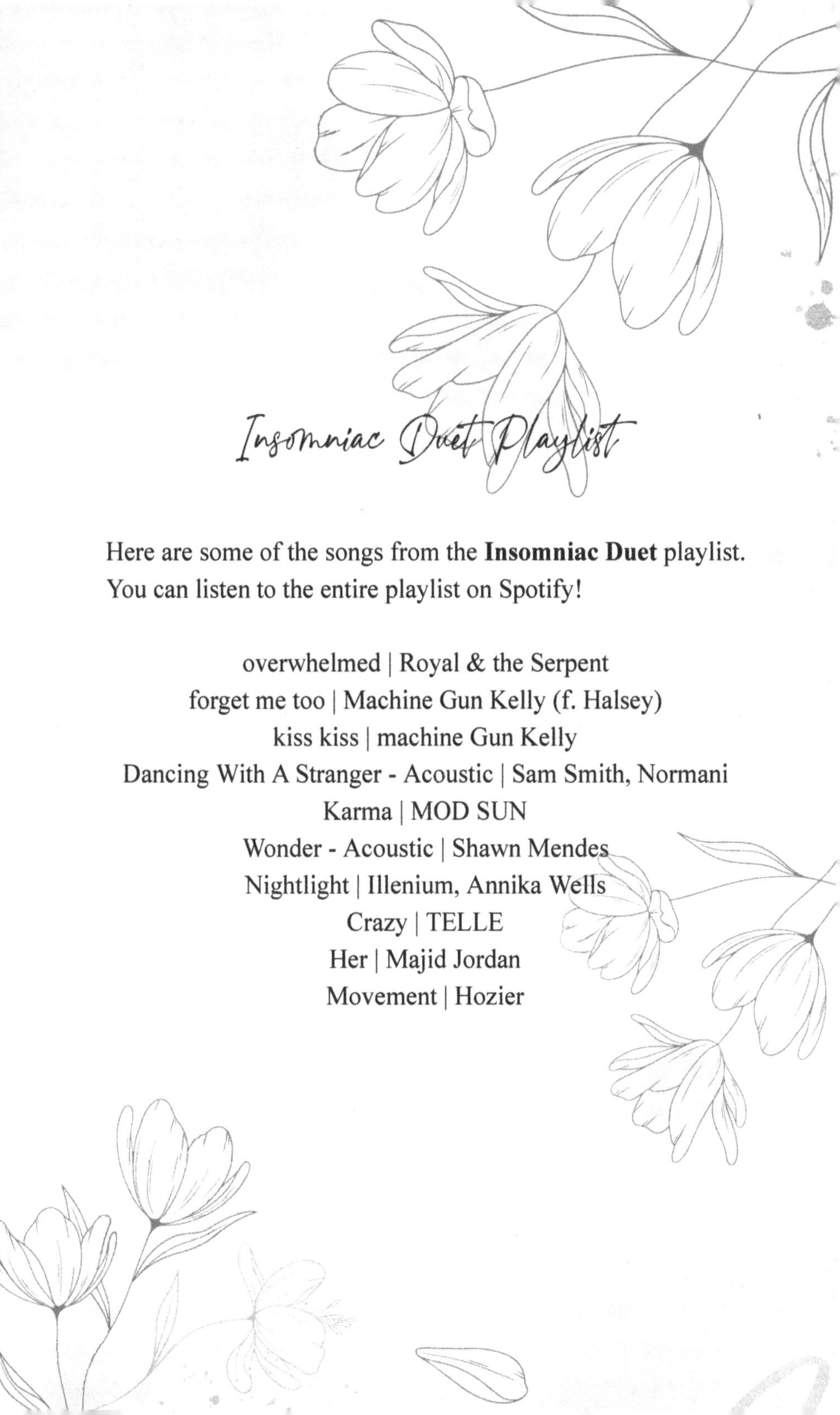

Here are some of the songs from the **Insomniac Duet** playlist. You can listen to the entire playlist on Spotify!

overwhelmed | Royal & the Serpent
forget me too | Machine Gun Kelly (f. Halsey)
kiss kiss | machine Gun Kelly
Dancing With A Stranger - Acoustic | Sam Smith, Normani
Karma | MOD SUN
Wonder - Acoustic | Shawn Mendes
Nightlight | Illenium, Annika Wells
Crazy | TELLE
Her | Majid Jordan
Movement | Hozier

Acknowledgments

So many thank yous, so few pages…

To my family and friends… Thank you for being my favorite cheerleaders. Thank you for pimping my books and telling people I'm an author. And thank you for loving my wild and adventurous brain.

To Ellie McLove and Rosa Sharon… Thank you for your knowledge and brilliance. For all the love notes in the markup area. For your ideas and wise minds when my stories need them most. You ladies make authoring a little less chaotic.

To Kat Savage… Thank you for your cover brilliance and kind heart. Thank you for also being my friend. For listening and talking with me when I needed someone. All the hugs!

To all my author friends… I can't wait to see you all at signing or author conferences and give you a hug. If hugs are cool. Maybe an elbow bump, if that's your thing. I'm just excited to see my peeps again.

To the readers and bloggers who read my words… sending you all virtual hugs. Your reviews and graphics and love give me life. Sharing pieces of yourself with the world is difficult, but your kindness makes it much easier.

And if this is your first Persephone Autumn book… thank you for taking a chance on my words. I hope you loved Micah and Peyton, and the future books to come.

Connect with Persephone

Connect with Persephone

www.persephoneautumn.com

Subscribe to Persephone's Newsletter

www.persephoneautumn.com/newsletter

Join Persephone's Reader Group

Persephone's Playground

Follow Persephone Online

instagram.com/persephoneautumn

facebook.com/persephoneautumnwrites

tiktok.com/@persephoneautumn

goodreads.com/persephoneautumn

bookbub.com/authors/persephone-autumn

amazon.com/author/persephoneautumn

pinterest.com/persephoneautumn

USA Today Bestselling Author Persephone Autumn lives in Florida with her wife and psycho cat. A proud mom with a cuckoo grandpup. An ethnic food enthusiast who has fun discovering ways to vegan-ize her favorite non-vegan foods. Most days, you'll find her with a tea latte or fruity concoction in her hand. If given the opportunity, she would intentionally get lost in nature.

For years, Persephone did some form of writing; mostly journaling or poetry. After pairing her poetry with images and posting them online, she began the journey of writing her first novel.

She mainly writes romance and poetry, but on occasion dips her toes in other works. Look for her non-romance publications under P. Autumn.